TENEBRION

By

James H Longmore

A HellBound Books Publishing LLC Book
Austin TX

A HellBound Books LLC
Publication

Cover and art design by Kevin Enhart for
HellBound Books Publishing LLC

Edition 2

www.hellboundbookspublishing.com

Printed in the United States of America

BY JAMES H LONGMORE

<u>HORROR</u>
Blood & Kisses
'Pede
Flanagan

<u>BIZARRO</u>
The Erotic Odyssey of Colton Forshay
Buds
And Then You Die
Feeder
I Am Joe's Unwanted Penis

TENEBRION

PROLOGUE

**Watsonville Independent Cinema, Watsonville TX.
Friday evening.**

There.

This time she was *positive* she'd seen another one.

It had scurried out from beneath a flip-up velour seat on the back row and now it was skulking amongst the inky shadows at the rear of the theater.

The demons were especially active tonight; in fact, they had become quite the problem this side of town in the weeks following the outbreak – despite the authorities making all the right assurances that the things were being contained at the source. They'd also advised the good people of Watsonville that there really was no need for concern as these were only the lesser demons and therefore more of a nuisance than anything else; ignore them and they'd stick to their shadows.

Nonetheless, it would appear the things *were* in the theater and that was most perturbing.

Melissa Bracken stood in the wings and turned her attention to her boyfriend as he stepped onto the stage. She thought he looked especially tall, handsome and confident in the spotlight – and a particularly striking figure in his rented tux. As Phil made ready to begin his introductions to the eagerly awaiting crowd, Melissa's heart pounded fast and hard in her chest and she began to wish that she'd had the foresight to go pee earlier when she'd had the chance.

Peering out from behind the movie theater's thick, faux-velvet maroon curtains, Melissa could see that they'd packed out the place more than was usual for a *Terrorfest* screening event; there was even a bunch of people standing at the back of the auditorium - which was in violation of pretty much every fire regulation she could think of.

Of course, standing-room would never be allowed at the franchised, out of town multiplex, but the kind folks at the Watsonville Independent Cinema – a one-screen theater older than dirt – were grateful for any patronage they could get; all the more people to spend money on the over-priced soda and mediocre food. There was the old joke in Watsonville – that if you were to call the theater to ask what time a movie started, the answer would always be *what time can you get here?*

Melissa smiled to herself at the joke and then immediately regretted having done so as she spotted that the fat buffoon Jesus Longoria – in his usual front row seat – had mistakenly thought that she was smiling at him. Now the foul man was grinning up at her like he had a good chance of getting into her pants.

Longoria was an opinionated, narcissistic jerk who thought he was a big something in the film community just because he'd won a few local awards and had paid some has-been porn star to appear in one of his independent feature films. Longoria tended to keep schtum that he'd totally lost his ass on the movie that he hadn't a prayer of attracting distribution for – around a hundred thousand dollars of other people's money had been swallowed up making that steaming pile of crap – and yet the man lorded it up like he was a big shot.

Longoria had insisted (Melissa had personally dealt with that particularly unpleasant phone call) that this year that his entire *Terrorfest* team got to sit in the row behind him. And there they were, every last one of them identifiable by their baby pink T-shirts with *TEAM LONGORIA* emblazoned across the chest. It was as if the fat idiot was proclaiming ownership over them whilst at the same time taking the opportunity to belittle the guys on the team by forcing them to wear pink. Longoria most likely thought he was being clever.

"Yeah, I reckon we're gonna do *real* well in the awards this year," Longoria's voice boomed out above the cacophony of chattering voices. Ostensibly, Longoria was talking to a teammate who sat in the seat behind him, but *really* he was addressing the entire theater. As he twisted around to talk, Longoria pulled a disgusted face and wrinkled his nose at the man in the gray hoodie who occupied the seat next to his.

"Our leading lady's slept with at least two of the judges," Longoria proclaimed. "Hell, from what I've heard about that Foxy Malone, she's probably slept with *all* of them!" A blustering guffaw. "*And* at the same time!"

Melissa glowered at Longoria as he paused laughing at his own joke just long enough to stuff his mouth with yet another of the shrimp-stuffed jalapeños he'd ordered from the long-suffering wait staff – stuffed peppers of numerous varieties were apparently something of a speciality at the theater.

The guy in the gray hoodie caught Melissa's attention. He sat stock-still, staring directly ahead at the stage with his hood pulled all the way up to conceal most of his features. Melissa thought she'd caught a fleeting glimpse of his face and that somehow he looked oddly familiar.

But no, she checked herself, it couldn't possibly be. Not after what had happened to the Green Crayon team.

"Good evening, ladies and gentlemen," Phil began his well-rehearsed spiel and the antsy audience quietened down some.

"For those of you who *don't* know me – and I'd guess that's not so many of you by now – I'm Phil Kennedy, your *Terrorfest* organiser. And this is Melissa Bracken, my beautiful partner in crime." Phil held out a welcoming arm towards Melissa's side of the stage and grinned that shit-eating, game show host grin of his.

Well - rehearsed and taking her cue like a seasoned pro, Melissa put on her broadest smile and strode out onto the stage like she loved it.

Every year, Melissa vowed to not let herself be roped into getting involved with Watsonville's amateur film contest, and each year – for twelve years now, five as co-presenter – Phil had somehow managed to talk her into it.

"Thank you, Phil." Melissa flashed her fake, toothy smile out to the audience. "And it's a great-big *thank you* to everyone here tonight for making this year's *Terrorfest* Film Contest the biggest and best in our twelve-year history!"

There was a spontaneous round of rapturous applause from the audience, along with a few whistles and catcalls.

The concept of the annual *Terrorfest Film Contest* had been Phil's idea, albeit not an entirely original one; he'd unashamedly plagiarized it from the countless short film races that occurred on an almost weekly basis the length and breadth of the country. The format was pretty much the same across the board, in which wannabee Nolans, Abrahams, and Taylor-Woods competed against each other to create a seven-minute movie in just one weekend. It really was as simple as that; amateur film makers playing at movie-making for a couple of days in the hope of winning a dated piece of equipment donated by that years' sponsor, a cheap, plastic statuette and perhaps a little recognition.

The majority of the movies submitted to *Terrorfest* were at best awful, at worst execrable and impossible to sit through – even for seven minutes. But every year Phil persisted with his contest even though the entry fees he collected gave him very little income once he'd shelled out for all the expenses. And every year Melissa helped him out with the organizing since that was not Phil's strong point, nor was hosting the screening and awards ceremony at the theater. In the cold light of day, Melissa often wondered just *what* Phil was supposed to be good at and what the hell he'd do without her should she ever grow weary of being his token eye candy.

They all love to see a hot chick at these things, Phil told her year after year.

And she hated that.

Helping Phil to organize the contest was not so bad. It was something that Melissa enjoyed doing and was incredibly good at – were it not for her, *Terrorfest* would have descended into administrative chaos long ago. It was all the being paraded around on stage like a prized heifer that went so totally against Melissa's grain. Phil expected her to strut around on the stage in an uncomfortably short dress like some dumb window dressing – that was what irked Melissa the most.

Melissa glanced down at the tight, red dress that Phil had bought for her to wear for this years' occasion and was dismayed to see far too much of her own tanned thighs than she considered appropriate. She was equally dismayed at the knowledge that everyone in the first two rows would be able to stare directly up the dress and see what color panties she was wearing.

Phil knew this of course and was keen to exploit Melissa's sex appeal to the max in order to build his audience. He'd even gone so far as to suggest that she go commando this year and put an end to speculation amongst *Terrorfest* regulars as to whether Melissa Bracken was a natural blonde or not.

There had been an especially enlightening row following that particular suggestion and Phil hadn't helped his cause any by informing Melissa that she did have *fabulous* legs and ass and she should be *damn well* proud to show them off.

There was that, and that the thought of her *sans* underwear on stage seemed to turn him on to distraction.

So Melissa had gritted her teeth, eschewed panty hose, donned her biggest, thousand-wash-gray pants (the seamless type, she did have *some* self-respect) and figured that it was perhaps time that she re-evaluate her relationship with Phil Kennedy.

"We had fifty-five teams take part this year," Melissa gushed. "All competing for the first prize of a top of the range Sony camera and the once in a lifetime opportunity to work on the next instalment in the *Hellraiser* franchise, *Hell to Pay*," Melissa recited Phil's somewhat labored script. "And of those teams registered, we had a record *fifty-four* movies submitted in time for the judging."

"Fifty-four! A record for us, I think?" Phil picked up the spiel. Once more he treated the audience to that perfected game show host smile of his.

"It is indeed, Phil," Melissa said.

"But if I may be serious for a moment, ladies and gentlemen," Phil switched on both his serious voice and sombre countenance with a professional's ease. "We are all aware of the tragic events that befell Dave Priestley's

Green Crayon team during the filming of their *Terrorfest* movie." He paused for effect and his eyes scanned the audience who sat in hushed reverence. "And I am sure that you will join Melissa and I when we say that our thoughts and prayers go out to the families and friends of everyone in that team."

"Yes, Phil," Melissa chipped in with her scripted interruption, "and having seen the footage shot by Dave and his team, we can honestly say that their movie would have swept the board tonight. It is truly an innovative and unique piece of film making."

"Sadly though, in the light of recent events and as the Green Crayon movie is currently evidence in the on-going police investigation into the – *bizarre* – tragedy; we will not be able to show it to you *in full* this evening," Phil said and muted chatter buzzed amongst the audience.

Wait, what?

Melissa shot Phil a barbed glance.

Was she hearing him right? Surely Phil wouldn't dare go ahead and show ev*en a small part* of the Green Crayon film, especially given what the cops had said when they'd confiscated it as evidence. And especially after all the weird shit that had been going on around town since that night.

Melissa was aware Phil had ripped a copy of the movie to his Mac before the police had called him; he did that with every film entered into the contest so he could add it to the compilation DVD that he'd be selling tonight. Naturally, Phil had neglected to tell this to the pair of surly police officers who'd paid him an unwelcome visit in the small hours almost five weeks ago.

Melissa had only seen half of the movie. She'd not been able to bear sitting through to the end as it had made her feel physically sick. As hardened as she had become to the theatrical blood, home-baked gore and fake terror of the genre, there was just something about the Green Crayon film that had affected her on a deeply profound level. She had also witnessed for herself how come the cops had reason to believe that much of the roughly edited assault on the senses had not been faked.

The auditorium lights went down and the big screen flickered to life. The opening credits rolled with the usual preamble –

This film was shot as part of the
Terrorfest Short Movie Contest:
Team Green Crayon

– followed by the title screen;

The Black Mass

At this, the entire theater fell quiet.

Melissa followed Phil's lead and stepped to the side of the stage, back to the protective folds of the curtain. Luckily for him, they were on opposite sides of the stage, she wanted nothing more right then but to tear her boyfriend a new one. From her sanctuary within the wings, Melissa strained her neck to see the screen and dared herself to watch the movie; she figured she owed Priestley and his crew at least that courtesy. In the periphery of her vision, Melissa saw the guy in the gray hoodie get up from his seat and make his way out of the theater.

A sharp, shrill scream blasted from the theater's ageing sound system and on the screen the movie flickered with rapid, tantalizing snippets of blurry, panicky people and shadowy, stooped figures that shuffled around like Romero extras. There followed lightning flashes of terrified, screaming faces running through darkened, crumbling hallways – all accompanied by a sound track of terrible, haunting cries and screams and tormented voices that seemed to blend in to each other as one continuous and hellish noise.

So far, so much standard horror film fare. Except that to Melissa there was just something about the sounds and the panicked faces that made the whole thing seem so terribly *real*. That and the barely-glimpsed, shadowy thing that slithered out from a viscous, glistening puddle the color of pitch.

The screen flashed with a split second splash of color. Was that an eye? If it was, it looked to be neither fake nor human. If that was the case, then what on earth *was* it? Then came a sudden jump cut and a close up of Dave Priestley's face filled the screen. The assembled theater audience gasped and squirmed in their seats.

Priestley was crying, his face a mask of terror and misery, his pleas thick and choked with tears and phlegm. There were long strings of clear snot swinging down from his nose and his eyes were bloodshot and wild.

"It was just a movie," Priestley snivelled as the camera zoomed in on him. "It was just a *fucking movie!*"

The double doors at the rear of the theater slammed shut and the audience jumped once more. Melissa started herself, but calmed herself with the thought that it was most likely the guy in the hoodie leaving. And it was then that her brain made the impossible connection between the face she'd imagined she'd seen beneath that hoodie and the one magnified a hundredfold up there on the screen.

Mind racing, Melissa peered out across the theater audience and saw them all fidgeting uncomfortably in their seats, some staring down at their feet with puzzled expressions on their faces. Others had stood up to kick out randomly at the darkness that swallowed their feet. Dark, liquid shadows crept along the aisles and oozed like pitch between the seats and within the inky blackness of the murk, Melissa made out the thin shapes of grasping fingers, moist, glistening flesh and the glinting teeth of innumerable slithering, crawling things that glowered out with spiteful eyes.

The screen above Melissa flickered with the dying moments of the movie. The deathly screams and cries for mercy played out amidst the cacophonous ululations of their background as the last of the film's cast ran along darkened hallways illuminated only by a dim, twitching light.

Melissa felt what her fearful mind told her were dank, bone-thin fingers grab at the soft flesh of her bare ankle and the rough scratch of tiny claws scraped at her skin. She chanced a glance down.

And then Melissa Bracken decided that this would be as good a time as any to scream.

CHAPTER ONE

FIVE WEEKS EARLIER
Prince William Pub, Watsonville, TX
Friday night.

"**D**ave, ma' man!" Maurice Labeaux had crept up behind Priestley to give him a hearty slap on the back. "How's it hangin', *bluuuud*?"

"For Christ's sakes, Mo'!" Priestley barked in protest as much of his freshly poured pint of Guinness slopped from its glass and out onto the bar. "Will you quit doing that?!" He dragged a hand through his unruly mop of black hair and turned to face his friend. Priestley's mouth cracked a grin. "Good to see ya, buddy," he laughed and hopped down from the tall bar stool.

"You too, Davy-boy." Labeaux grinned and embraced Priestley with the manliest of back-thumping hugs, his tall, broad frame dwarfing his friend by a clear six inches.

"Sorry about the beer, bud. Let me buy you another," Labeaux dropped his faux-ghetto accent as quickly as he'd put it on. He only used it around Priestley because he knew that it wound the guy up a treat, and playing up his part as the *black guy* of their circle had kind of become

Labeaux's favorite party trick (and always a firm winner with the ladies) even though in real life his diction was more precise, more *white* than most white folk he knew.

Although incredibly proud to be of African descent (*Masai*, if his grandparents were to be believed, although that part of his bloodline had been drastically diluted across the Labeaux generations), Labeaux was the Creole-descended product of middle class, white-collar parents who lived in a respected neighborhood in the more affluent part of town.

At twenty-seven, Labeaux matched Priestly age-wise but was by far the more mature and worldly-wise of the two; just one of the benefits of having actually flown his parents' nest. As handsome as he was tall, Labeaux sported fashionable stubble and buzz-cut hair and was always to be seen in his downbeat uniform of battered sneakers, faded 501's, denim jacket and polo shirt – on this occasion, dark blue and unbranded for just in case he ventured in front of the camera.

The Guinness at the Prince William Pub was tepid, flat as a fart and had all the body of murky pond water. Priestley stared at the remaining half of the lackluster black pint in his glass and contemplated refusing his friend's offer of replacement in favor of something more palatable. Ultimately, he decided against that course of action and drained his pint whilst motioning the girl tending bar for another; although he knew that it would be just another disappointment in a glass.

"Thanks," he said to the back of Labeaux's head.

Labeaux ignored his friend as he was already on the case. He leaned his wide shoulders over the bar to order and couldn't help himself but flirt a little with the pudgy, miserable looking barmaid who had a definite air about her of someone who had pretty much given up on life.

And as disappointing as the beer was for Priestley, it was nothing less than was to be expected; pretend

Guinness in a pretend British pub in the heart of Texas was always going to be somewhat lacking.

Everyone who knew Priestley knew that he'd spent a goodly part of his youth in England – his father had been stationed there with the Air Force – and without exception, they would recommend the local British Pubs to him. *You really* must *try the Red Lion/Golden Goose/Snail and Lettuce, Dave!*

Sadly, pubs in Texas tended to be more the American *perception* of said English hostelries and the corporations that owned them figured putting an *'e'* on the end of the name, sticking a fake English phone box in one corner and putting up framed Manchester United posters would give their strip-mall establishments the authentic feel of *Merrie England.*

They did not.

As for the food, it was wise to not get Priestley started on the fare in such places as these. If he'd been given a dollar for every time someone had recommended a faux-British pub because *'they do real British fish and chips'*, he'd be even more affluent than he was now. Texas fish and chips were as far removed from their British counterparts as President Nixon was from the Queen of England.

And that went without mentioning the total non-availability of Priestley's favorite side to the piscatorial dish; *mushy peas.* Just how to describe that quintessentially Northern English delicacy (and Lord only knows that he'd tried on many an occasion)? Most definitely an acquired taste, they'd take corpulent marrowfat peas and boil the hell out of them until they collapsed into a sort of green slop that more closely resembled something Linda Blair threw up. And although he mourned the peas' presence in the US, it came as little surprise to Priestley that the American palate had not embraced them.

Despite those disappointments, Priestley would still order fish and chips off of the menu in the hope of one day discovering something akin to his erstwhile favorite dish, although thus far, it had only served to give him something to moan about.

It was Sod's Law, then that the *Terrorfest* organizers had chosen to hold their film race kick-off night at the *Ye Olde Prince William Pub*, which was now filling up with the familiar gaggle of amateur filmmakers.

Priestley had arrived early so that he could try out the fish and chips – surprisingly good, as it turned out – and because (unlike most of his fellow movie folk) he didn't have to wait to finish work as he'd not held down a regular job since leaving college. He picked up a little freelance film work here and there, occasional script consulting and movie editing but otherwise he devoted his time to his burgeoning movie career.

Priestley's father had started his own business a decade or so back – something terribly drab in the oil industry – which had bucked the trend and had actually taken off in the post 9/11 recession years. So – because they could afford it and because he was their only child – Mr. And Mrs. Priestley had actively encouraged their son to pursue his lifelong dream of becoming the next J.J. Abrams. Mostly this consisted of providing him an allowance so generous that he had no need to work, even though he'd reached his late twenties with Hollywood nowhere in sight.

The noise level in the pub lifted considerably as Jesus Longoria and his team of shaggy-faced misfits made their entrance. Priestley turned his head and gave the overweight director in the ludicrous pink T-shirt a cursory nod.

"Hey, Priestley!" Longoria boomed across the bar, "have ya made room in your trophy cabinet again this year?" He chortled loudly and his dozen or so teammates joined him in sycophantic unison.

Priestley shot the buffoon a sardonic smile but remained silent. He never had been one for engaging in the bullshit trash-talk that was rife amongst the film community.

"Oh yeah, my bad!" Longoria continued, not one for knowing when to quit, "they don't give out trophies for *second* place!" Again, with the forced – and over-loud – laughter. "There's no shame in being runner up, Priestley, it's still kinda like winning," Longoria just wasn't going to let up. "But then again, that's like saying the English *won* second place in the American War of Independence." The Longoria team erupted into yet more hearty laughter and Priestley noticed that even Labeaux had cracked a smile.

"Asshole," Priestley muttered beneath his breath as he watched Longoria usher his team over to a reserved table at the rear of the pub, their place in the doorway quickly taken by the next wave of eager filmmakers.

Amongst the batch of newcomers, Priestley recognized Foxy Malone. She was the heavily tattooed heroine of many a Longoria production, and most likely this next one. She'd clearly made the wise decision to distance herself from Longoria and not wear the pink team T-shirt and had instead showed up looking as hot as hell in a short, white cotton dress that showed off a fair amount of her alabaster skin and pretty much every tattoo that adorned her perfectly proportioned body.

Foxy shot Longoria a derisive glance of her own and propped herself at the end of the bar next to some nerdy-looking kid who Priestley didn't recognize; he was most likely new to the contest this year. There, Foxy waited patiently for the bar maid to tear her attention away from Labeaux and his dubious charm.

"Don't let him get to you," Labeaux said to Priestley as he plonked two pints of pond-water on the bar in front of them. "He's always been big-fish-little-pond. We'll be looking at that asshole in the rear-view when we're on our way to Hollywood." He flashed a perfect set of teeth.

"Yeah," Priestley agreed with a half-smile, "you're right." He took a slurp of his tepid beer and grimaced at the assault on his palate. People like Longoria really boiled Priestley's piss; they *played* at making movies and their low quality crap shoved the standards of the film community so far down the can that it was laughable. They churned out the same old unmarketable bilge year in year out – all for a pat on the back and a little mutual admiration from their cronies. Priestley knew that Labeaux also saw right through Longoria's type, which is how come he'd gravitated towards the guy in the first place.

The two had hooked up senior year at high school – Priestly had recently returned from England and was struggling through his awkward, sebaceous adolescent phase – and they'd been as thick as thieves from the off. Their mutual love of movies – of the horror genre in particular – had provided the strongest of bonds. Also, the fact that Labeaux owned his own movie camera had been one hell of a catalyst.

They'd spent most of their free time writing and shooting movies that were mostly unwatchable but which had given them the much needed, self-taught lessons on the intricate process of movie-making (even Spielberg had started off in his back yard with a bunch of friends and a Super-8!). They'd remained close throughout their college years, even though Labeaux had gone to New York whilst Priestley studied film at UCLA, and had continued their creative passion upon returning to Texas. Labeaux's degree was in Economics and he worked a day job at a local law firm to fund night classes in film production so he could keep on top of the ever-evolving technology of movie making.

Maurice Labeaux was – in Priestley's opinion at least – the single best camera operator in the state. His eye for those exceptional shots that set *great* movies apart from the mediocre was easily an equal to the best that Tinseltown had to offer. Added to that, he was a director's wet dream to work with; he took direction like a pro and whilst happy to offer an expert's opinion during a shoot, he would do so without trying to take over. In fact, Maurice Labeaux's only flaw was that a considerable amount of his brain functioned exclusively below his belt.

"Thanks for emailing me the script." Labeaux pulled a thin sheaf of paper from the inside pocket of his jacket. "But don't the rules say we're not supposed to start writing until the contest begins?"

"For fuck's sake, Mo'!" Priestley snarled. "Do you *want* to get us disqualified before we even get started?" Priestley looked over his shoulder like some half-assed spy trying his very best to not look suspicious; terrified that Labeaux's indiscretion may have been noted by the contest organizers.

He was lucky. Melissa Bracken was over by the door busily setting up her folding table with registration packs for the contest kick-off. Priestley thought she looked uncharacteristically homely in frayed jeans, blue flip-flops and a particularly unflattering *I Got My Terrorfest On* T-shirt (available for purchase for just $30 – never ones to miss an opportunity, were Phil and Melissa).

Meanwhile, her idle boyfriend was also keeping himself busy. He was leaning on the bar and giving his opinion on *what was wrong with the film industry today* in that loud, self-important voice of his to Foxy Malone and anyone else who cared to listen.

"Oops." Labeaux gave Priestley a deer-in-the-headlights look and stuffed the script back into his pocket. For someone supposedly so smart, thought

Priestley, his friend could be as thick as pig shit sometimes.

Labeaux knew full well that the golden rule of the film contests was strictly *no* creative work on the movies until the start (and that meant filming, prop-making, music and *writing*). The rule was put into place in the competitions to prevent the less scrupulous teams from filming material in advance. Alongside the mandatory elements and themes that were handed out for inclusion in the movies, the strategy served *reasonably* well, although there would always be those who chose to ignore it.

"I thought I'd give us a head start and a better chance than we had last year," whispered Priestley. "And for Christ's sake – don't tell Ashlynn that I've already written the script – you know she hates it when I bend the rules!" Ashlynn was Priestley's long-suffering, straight-laced girlfriend; any whiff of impropriety on his part would be met with instant disapproval and a stern talking-to.

Labeaux raised an eyebrow at this. "*Bend*?" He grinned. "You just fuckin' shat all over rule number one rule, bro'," he slipped back with ease into his ghetto persona, all the best to grate on his friend's nerves. "No shit to me, either way bud," he reassured. "Ya know I'm only in this to get me laid."

"Is that *all* you ever think about?" Priestley rolled his eyes.

Labeaux took a lengthy sup of his lukewarm beer and mused awhile. "Yeah, pretty much." A sage nod. "And speaking of which, here comes the next notch on the Maurice Labeaux bedpost now."

Casting a glance towards the door with that all-too familiar *hello ladies* twinkle in his big brown eyes, Labeaux instructed Priestley from the corner of his mouth, "if you could just say that I've told you *everything* about her, and that you're happy with our arrangement – that'd be great," he said. "I'll fill you in later." Labeaux waved over the heads of the flocking film folk to attract the attention of the voluptuous redhead who'd just walked in.

The girl waved back at Labeaux and fought her way towards him through the growing throng.

"What fucking arrangement, Mo'?" Priestley growled but his friend's attention was all the redhead's.

"Priscilla! I am so pleased you could make it," Labeaux sounded most formal as they hugged. "This is Dave," he made the introduction. "Dave, meet Priscilla, Priscilla, meet the one and only Dave Priestley."

Politely, Priestley shook hands with Priscilla and couldn't help but give her the old up and down. All credit to Labeaux, the gal *was* absolutely stunning. She wore blue cowboy boots – ostrich skin, unless Priestley was very much mistaken – fashionably ripped jeans and an understated, low scooped, white top that clung tight to her voluptuous breasts; all complemented by her beautiful, angled face and cascading mass of wavy, flame-red hair.

"Thank you *so much* for letting me shoot behind the scenes on your movie this weekend," Priscilla gushed at Priestley, "it's going to make for some awesome footage for W-MAS."

"W-MAS?" Priestley was genuinely perplexed.

"Watsonville Music and Art Scene; it's my public access TV show." Priscilla eyed him warily, as if any individual who'd not heard of her artsy show was someone to be mistrusted.

The girl's inclusion on their *Terrorfest* shoot came as news to Priestley, and whilst he'd grown accustomed to Labeaux inviting various attractive young women to their film sets for his own lascivious means, he would have appreciated some advanced warning. Also, did Priscilla *have* to wear a top that was cut so goddamned low? It was hard enough to keep Labeaux's ephemeral mind focussed on a project as it was.

"Of course. It's my *absolute* pleasure," Priestley's tone was exaggerated some. He noted with some satisfaction that Labeaux had begun to shift uncomfortably from foot to foot, a sure sign of nervousness in the presence of a future conquest. "It is *fantastic* to finally meet the face behind the legend. Maurice has told me *so* much about you," Priestley said as he smiled at the girl.

"Has he?" Priscilla picked up on Priestley's sarcasm.

"No." Priestley shook his head – slowly. "No he hasn't."

"Don't mind him, babe," Labeaux interjected and elbowed Priestley in the ribs, "he's only messing with you."

"Yeah, I'm only messing, *babe*." Priestley winked as Priscilla matched his impish smile. "Welcome to Team Green Crayon."

"Great name." Priscilla nodded.

"It's Python," Labeaux told her.

Now it was Priscilla's turn to look puzzled.

"*Monty* Python?" Priestley grinned at seeing the expression on the girl's face.

"The cat licence sketch?" Labeaux explained and there seemed to Priestley to be a tinge of desperation in his friend's voice.

"Not much of a fan," Priscilla told them, "I'm more of an SNL gal myself."

"A guy is at the post office trying to get a licence for his pet cat –" Labeaux clarified.

"Eric," Priestley interrupted.

"Yeah, Eric the Cat," Labeaux continued, "and when the clerk tells him that there's no such thing, he shows the clerk his existing cat licence – "

"*– this is just a dog licence with dog crossed out and cat written on in green crayon*, Priestley delivered the punch line in Michael Palin's exaggerated, clipped British accent and both he and Labeaux laughed.

"Green crayon is our byword for anything dumb and made up," Labeaux added between giggles, "hence the name for our production company."

"Perfect." Priscilla laughed along in the fashion of someone who doesn't quite get the joke and Priestley noticed for the first time that her voice had a light huskiness to it that gave him thoughts that Ashlynn would happily crucify him for.

Priscilla rooted around in her purse and pulled out a small movie camera that fitted neatly in the palm of her hand.

"I was hoping to get some footage of the whole team here at the kick-off point" she said. "And I wanted to film you guys picking out the mandatory elements for your film." She looked around and her silken hair tossed about her shoulders like playful waves. "Where *are* the rest of your team?"

"They're already at the location and setting up the equipment – if Danny's doing his job right," Priestley explained, "I really didn't see the point of dragging everyone *here* just to go back *there*. They should be all good to go by the time we arrive."

Priscilla looked a little disappointed; already the flow of the documentary she'd planned so carefully in her mind had veered off the rails.

"And just wait until you see the location I got for us," Priestley enthused to Priscilla and Labeaux, "you'll shit your pants."

Priscilla pulled a face and Labeaux gave Priestley the *hard look*. This amused Priestley greatly – if the girl's sensibilities were so delicate that she was offended by that tame expression, she wasn't going to fare well on a Green Crayon shoot. It was not uncommon for artistic tempers and the gutter language that went hand-in-hand with them to come blustering to the fore; there had even been fistfights on occasion, but that was the passion that made their movies so damn good.

"So, you'll be writing the script on location?" Priscilla asked and lifted her camera up to Priestley's face to capture his reply. She'd done her homework and knew that it was more often the norm in short film races to write the script on the Friday night and then shoot and edit over the weekend. Clearly these guys had their own ideas.

"Yes Ma'am." Priestley tipped a sly wink at Labeaux. "Although there won't be all that much to write this year," he put on his serious voice for the camera and looked directly into the unblinking glass eye of its lens, "we're going for a found footage style with lots of camera shake and improvised dialogue this year. Think *Cloverfield*, *Blair Witch* and the like," he threw in the references just to sound smart.

"But hasn't the found footage genre been done to death by now?" Priscilla slipped with ease into interviewer mode.

"You try telling that to Oren Peli," Labeaux chipped in and Priscilla swung the camera around to face him, "or the guys behind the *V/H/S* and *Rec'* franchises –"

The piercing, tinny sound of a gong cut Labeaux off mid-flow and all heads in the Prince William turned to face the organizer's table and the inimitable Melissa Bracken. Her antique brass gong may have been tiny – no more than seven inches in diameter, suspended by mismatched string in the center of a skinny, battered mahogany frame – but its metallic resonance never failed to quieten the crowd; perhaps it reminded them of the old Rank gong that signalled the start of so many classic movies?

"If I could have your attention please!" Melissa shouted above the noise of the crowd to make herself heard.

Priestley struggled to hear Melissa's thin voice above the murmur of excited voices – the Prince William had filled up alarmingly in the ten minutes or so he'd been entranced by the deliciously disarming Priscilla.

"Firstly, could any team leader who hasn't already registered please make their way to this table *before* eight PM?" Melissa requested. It was the same speech every year in that same resigned tone and Priestley couldn't help but wonder at what point in her life did Melissa's love for all of this begin to falter? "Everybody *has* to be signed up before the contest officially begins and you only have five minutes left." Melissa smiled her best toothy smile as a handful of last-minuters dug their way through the crowd with panicked expressions on their faces.

Priestley returned attention to his pint which now had an unappetising, beige scum clinging to the insides of the glass like some insipid fungus. Ever prepared, Priestley had registered his team for *Terrorfest* online a couple of months ago to make sure that they didn't miss out on the places that Phil Kennedy had warned were *very* limited and strictly first-come-first-served. Of course, nobody ever actually missed out on said places, Phil only advertised as such to get everyone to sign up and hand over their hard-earned as early as possible.

"For anyone who hasn't taken part in the *Terrorfest* short film competition before and have left things to the last minute, all of the rules can be found on our website," Melissa continued her speech with an icy look at the motley handful who frantically filled in their registration forms on her wobbly desk.

The rules of the contest were simple: kick-off on Friday evening at eight, then write, shoot and edit up your short movie – it *had* to be between four and seven minutes long and *must* include all of the elements that were shortly to be picked out of the hat – and hand it in before midnight on the following Sunday.

It *really was* as simple as that.

"The required elements are the same as last year," Melissa informed her increasingly rowdy audience. She plucked a thin strip of paper out of one of the three brown fedoras in front of her on the table and waved it above her head for emphasis. "There's a character name, a line of dialogue and an object that *has* to be used in a killing," she was forced to raise her voice to full volume above the chatter, "and please remember that to qualify, *all* selected elements have to be used – and absolutely *no* pre-written material, guys!"

At this, Priestley's paranoia tugged at his conscience. Had Melissa looked directly at *him* when she'd made that comment? He exchanged a guilty glance with Labeaux. Had Melissa or Phil seen Labeaux pull the script out of his pocket at the bar? Did they already know the guilty secret of Team Green Crayon?

"Are you okay, Dave?" Priscilla asked, her camera pointed directly at Priestley's face. "You look a little pale."

"Just getting psyched up," Priestley lied "I'm in it to win this year, so it's kind of a big deal."

"One last thing!" Melissa's voice broke into their exchange, "in order to qualify for judging, your movie has to be dropped off here before *midnight* on Sunday. Any handed in after that will still be shown at Watsonville Theater but will *not* be eligible for any awards." She picked up a large manila envelope and held it high. "Your movie must be on DVD in the required format and sealed in the official *Terrorfest* envelope – along with all relevant release forms."

"Is there a nudity waiver form this year?" Longoria bellowed from the back of the room. He laughed loudly at his own questionable wit and tipped a theatrical wink across to Foxy Malone who stared back at him as if she wished him dead. She'd appeared topless in one of

Longoria's feature movies earlier in the year and he'd not let her hear the end of it since.

"Would that be for you, Jesus?" Labeaux shouted over to him and the room erupted with howls of laughter.

"There are copies of *all* of the release forms on our website for you to download," Melissa explained for what must have been the millionth time, "every team leader must ensure that they hand in *all* of the signed releases; cast and crew, location, music and – yes, Jesus – nudity."

Whatever Melissa said next was drowned out by the renewed cacophony of cat-calls, wolf whistles and bawdy laughter and Longoria lapped up the attention like he was a great big somebody.

Big fish, little pond.

Priestley rolled his eyes and gulped down the last of his Guinness. The likes of Jesus Longoria represented everything that was wrong with the amateur film scene, it was crammed to capacity with hobbyists and talentless wannabees who all sat around in their sycophantic little groups to talk loudly about their dreams of Hollywood – a direct contrast to himself and Labeaux who were working damned hard to actually get there. The hobbyists soured the pitch for the serious few, those filmmakers who slogged to carve out a career in the cutthroat industry; it was a category in which Priestley firmly placed himself.

Melissa tapped her gong once more with the small wooden mallet and its sharp note made Priestley jump.

"Okay, people!" Melissa's voice was growing hoarse now but still it managed to rise above the hubbub, "it's time to come pick out your required elements," she announced. "If you could form an orderly line –"

The chaotic dash for the organizer's table more resembled the Pamplona Running of the Bulls than anything orderly, and Priestley couldn't recall ever seeing Labeaux move as quickly as he did at that moment to get to the head of the line. Head and shoulders above most of the others there, Labeaux pushed and squeezed and elbowed his way to the front, eager to garner first choice out of the trio of hats.

"So, you have your own TV show?" Priestley made polite conversation with Priscilla's breasts, unable to tear his eyes away from their mesmerizing cleavage.

"It's just public access," Priscilla said. She was all too conscious of the effect her boobs were having on Priestley and she watched with amusement as he struggled to maintain eye contact. "But I am building up a pretty decent following – I have over four thousand viewers now."

"Impressive," Priestley mumbled as once again his eyes flicked southwards.

"Thank you." Priscilla smiled sweetly and puffed out her chest. "I cover everything and anything involved in the local music and film industry, as well as all other aspects of the art scene."

"Are you and Maurice – err – an item?" Priestley blurted out the question he'd been itching to ask since their introduction. He couldn't really believe he'd given it a voice; was this him hitting on Priscilla? And if it were the case, what about the whole *bros before hoes* ethos that he and Labeaux subscribed to? Did that mean nothing after twelve years of friendship? And then there was the matter of the beautiful and ever-loyal Ashlynn – she'd skin him alive if she knew the lascivious thoughts that were spinning through his mind.

"Good heavens, no." Priscilla smiled and Priestley felt a weird kind of relief. "I know him from media class," she explained, "his camera technique really is quite exceptional."

"It's not his *camera* technique you need to be concerned about." Priestley gave Priscilla a half smile and raised a suggestive eyebrow. He knew Labeaux well enough, and even if he and Priscilla weren't an item as such, he'd already pigeonholed the girl as a future conquest.

"Pardon me?" Priscilla looked baffled.

Labeaux's tall, dark frame reappeared between them before Priestley could offer Priscilla a friendly warning about his friend's ulterior motives. In all honesty, though, Priestly figured that the gal probably had a pretty good idea, and that served only to rankle him some more.

"You're not going to believe what I picked out of the freakin' hats," Labeaux sounded flustered.

Priestley smiled up at him, at the look of concern on his face. The *Terrorfest* people were well renowned for their crazy film elements, some of which made the participants feel handcuffed, creatively speaking. But as much as Priestley hated this aspect of the film competitions, he knew it was a necessary evil and the contests themselves *were* good platforms for gaining recognition (plus, a winner's laurel leaf or two on the resume never did any harm). Besides, whatever Labeaux had picked out couldn't possibly be as bad as last year's allocated murder weapon of dried spaghetti; that one was certain to go down in cinematic history as *the* most bizarre movie death ever.

"We got," Labeaux unfolded the first strip of white paper with trembling fingers, "character; Phil Anderer, a biochemist." He forced a wry smile. "For Christ's sakes, Dave, how are we supposed to make a serious piece of cinema when they give us fucking joke names?" He huffed his displeasure and unfurled the second sliver of paper he'd plucked from Melissa's hat. "Murder weapon – Swiss Army knife. That's not too bad, I suppose."

"In fact, it's no problem at all, Maurice old friend," Priestley smiled, "I *always* carry mine." He patted the black backpack that was slung over the back of his bar stool.

"And our line of dialogue is –" Labeaux paused for dramatic effect like some cheesy beauty pageant host. He shook his head as he read from the third and final strip of crumpled paper. "*I really wish I hadn't eaten that.*"

Priestley gave Labeaux his best serious face, shook his head in despair and peered across at Priscilla. Slowly, he climbed down from his stool, picked up his backpack and made ready to leave. He looked up again at Labeaux who stood stock still in anticipatory silence and Priestley just couldn't keep his face straight any longer.

"Sounds like you after a night out with the ladies," Priestley laughed at his perfectly played gag.

Labeaux joined in with a chuckle of his own; more in relief that it had turned out to be a joke. He'd borne witness to Priestley's serious turns before and they really were no fun at all.

"And by that, I do mean pussy." Oblivious to Priscilla's sensitivities, Priestley carried the gag on and play-thumped his friend's arm. Labeaux thumped him back and they laughed together and all was well with their world.

Priestley ushered Labeaux and Priscilla towards the door. He was eager to be away from the pub and its herd of faux filmmakers and out there making movie history. He had a good feeling about this year's contest, he could feel it in his bones that he had his best chance ever of winning. His planning had been meticulous – even by his own pedantic standards – and he'd pulled together the very best cast and crew that he had been able to lay his hands on. Add to that a head full of killer ideas that were guaranteed to – *finally* – earn him the local recognition he so richly deserved.

Yessir, there was something most definitely in the air on that cold, Friday night and it was shit-or-bust time for one David Priestley Esq. And bust was not even an option.

"So," Priestley addressed Labeaux and their tag-along as he pushed his way through the crowd towards the chilled, dark outside, "did I mention the location I managed to secure for our shoot?"

*

There were miniscule chinks in the suffocating darkness, through which it saw bright, tantalizing glimpses of the world beyond at no more than a hairs-breadth at a time. These, it found to be an unnecessary distraction from its toil so it would use its power to rearrange the darkness in order to fill them in.

Its brethren and kin surrounded it, crawling, slithering, and scurrying about in the pitch black as they went about their own nefarious business. Often, they would peek out through the tiny gaps in the blackness with envious eyes and would on occasion dare to poke through an exploratory finger or two. There were many legends of those who had somehow managed to escape and had ventured out into the beyond, and of the delicious chaos they had wreaked.

It couldn't remember a time when it had not existed. It – and its kind – had always been *– they just* were. *It knew much of the humans' ways, for it had studied mankind for a long, long time. It knew that they would never be able to grasp the fact that its kind had existed for always, what with their finite imaginations that conjured an ever-expanding universe and theories of that single Big Bang.*

It had no idea of what it looked like, nor could it gauge anything from the appearance of its own kind, for in the darkness of the abyss all were rendered blind.

They had no need for gender, for neither sex nor reproduction, as they simply continued their existence as they had since before the dawning of time. Therefore, it had always been an it, *and this was all it had ever known.*

It didn't identify as a demon, a devil, or with of the arbitrary labels with which the humans cared to give it, although it had become familiar with the names that humans had attached to its kind; Abaddon, Melchon, Succorbenoth, Incubus, Antichrist, Yeter'el *and the legion of others – its own being* Tenebrion. *It and its kind had no need for such names, human-given or otherwise; they knew* who *they were,* what *they were. That was just how it was, how it had been from the very beginning in the deepest, darkest recesses of the abyss – the place the humans imagined as Hell.*

What served for its brain was little more than primordial slop yet it worked well to form thoughts and dreams and desires, and it had discovered long ago that it was able to exert its influence upon the feeble will of the creatures that inhabited the light; it could all too easily bend them to its own thoughts and that had proven to be incredibly useful in its machinations.

For, it had important work to do.

It didn't know why, nor did it think to question. It simply knew *what was expected of it, and how it was to go about its tasks, much the same way of an ant whose job it is to nurse the nest's squirming larvae in the dark, dank tunnels of its lair.*

Soon its meticulous preparations would bear fruit and that then its true purpose would become clear.

And so, silently, diligently in the smothering blackness, it went about its labors.

CHAPTER TWO

"You got the school?" Labeaux stared with disbelief from the car window, his mouth open wide, "seriously, dude?"

"Didn't I tell you you'd shit your pants?" Priestley grinned. He swung his Mustang off of the main road and drove slowly down the tree-lined side street that ran alongside and then around to the rear of Watsonville Elementary School.

The school had been left to decay for the better part of nine years, after it was abandoned on the day of the shooting. As a building, it was nothing out of the ordinary as educational establishments go; single storey, constructed of red brick with dull expanses of gray concrete, a smattering of broad, tall windows and topped with the archetypal flat roof.

At the front of the building there stood a hastily erected, flimsy wire fence from which hung a faded, crooked *KEEP OUT* sign along with a sad handful of rotting teddy bears and sparse bunches of long-dead flowers attached by cable-ties. Above the main, double doors the school's name was barely discernible, as most of the letters had fallen off, their places taken by ghost letters on the mildewed flashing.

Surprisingly, the majority of the school's windows remained intact. Only a handful had been broken – most of them on that fateful afternoon – as even the town's vandals had given the place a wide berth over the years. There were the somewhat predictable rumours about the dead building being haunted, and speculation was rife that the place had been built on an ancient Indian burial ground.

It hadn't.

At the school's rear parking lot, Priestley pulled up gently next to a green Escalade and a white U-Haul box van. The back door of the van was open and a pair of thick electrical cables snaked out like spilled guts from the slumbering generator that dwelled within. There were three boxes of camera and lighting equipment in the van, expensive stuff but entirely safe; it was a cold October night and although the school had no perimeter fence at the back, the place attracted so much superstition and appeared so foreboding that no self-respecting thief would be seen dead anywhere near its grounds after dark.

Priestley got out of the car and shouldered his backpack. Labeaux and Priscilla clambered out and the three followed the cables around to the school's front doors. Priscilla lagged a little behind the guys and filmed their every step on her minicam.

They walked on in something akin to revered silence. Each of them in turn peered in to the school's windows, even though there was nothing much to be seen in the dark interior other than the occasional vague shapes and shadows.

A little way ahead, Priestley made out a definite dark outline. It was framed by one of the windows and where he'd imagine the shape's face to be, it was masked by inky-black shadows. He strained against the night to see but whatever it was darted away. Priestley allowed himself a faint smile.

"The crew got here before dark," Priestley broke the silence as they neared the school's entrance, "I figured it best they park the van around the back. We don't want to go upsetting the neighbors now, do we?" He nodded to a white-stucco, single storey house that sat across the street. It was the only one within view of the school that had light glowing from its windows, all of the others along the street stood a silent vigil in their own uninhabited darkness.

"Is *this* is your location release waiver, Dave?" Labeaux picked up a crowbar that lay next to a heaped length of corroded chain and a busted padlock on the cracked paving by the doors. The doors themselves had been left cracked open, and the fat electrical cables had been fed through a small window – clearly broken especially for the purpose – off to the left hand side. "A fucking jemmy?" Labeaux threw the thing into the chains, which jangled their complaint as he snorted his disapproval. "So, we're here without permission. Just how in fuck's name did you intend to get a signed waiver, Dave?"

"Maurice, my old friend," Priestley gave him a condescending smile, "it's not as if we've never forged a document or two to further the cause, is it?"

"Yeah, but this is different." Labeaux stepped away from the doors as if they scared him. "This is the school," his voice was quiet. "*The* school. Kids died here."

Priestley studied his friend's face with concern. Surely the ever-reliable Maurice Labeaux, best buddy, partner in many a filmmaking crime and cinematographer *extraordinaire*, wasn't about to wuss out tonight, of all nights?

"Wow guys!" it was Priscilla who broke the stand off, "I can't believe you are actually going to be filming *here*! This will look so freakin' awesome on my show!" She lowered her camera and stood on her tiptoes to plant a smacker on Labeaux's cheek. Her full lips left a red gloss lip print on his dusky skin. "I owe you big time for this," she gushed.

Labeaux shot Priestley a knowing glance and a hint of a smile that told him that this gross indiscretion was forgiven – at least for now. He shrugged his shoulders in a what-the-hell and pulled open the doors.

CHAPTER THREE

Priestley followed Labeaux into the dark interior of Watsonville Elementary and Priscilla walked close behind him to capture the moment on film. He pulled out a small flashlight from his pocket and illuminated the hallway in front of them.

"You do realize that we're probably the first sane people to have set foot in here for nine years?" Priestley's voice echoed in the frigid hallway.

"Yeah, it still doesn't feel right," Labeaux replied and the unease remained in his voice, "it's like we're disturbing a graveyard or something."

"Quit fretting will ya? The place'll cheer up once Danny gets the generator fired up and the lights plugged in," Priestley tried his level best to lighten Labeaux's mood, damned if he wanted his principal cameraman spooked this early on in the game. "Anyhow, it's not like there's still bodies here, Mo'. *They're* all up at the cemetery," Priestley said with his customary lack of respect. "We're all – *alone,"* he made with his very best spooky voice and was pleased to see that he had elicited some semblance of a smile from Labeaux. *"Hello!"* Priestley shouted into the darkness that skulked beyond his flashlight and faint hellos drifted back from his crew who were ensconced somewhere within the bowels of the decaying school.

They walked on, their progress marked by the tall, skeletal silhouettes of the dormant film lights that Danny and the crew had placed along the hallway.

Priestley played his flashlight beam around as they made their way along and the unrelenting ravages of time and neglect were everywhere he chose to look. There were ragged, gaping holes in the ceilings which dripped dank water that formed slick puddles on the cracked floor tiles, which in turn soaked slowly but surely into the crumbling walls and had them bloom with thick, black mould. The classroom doors – spaced in a seemingly haphazard fashion along the hallway – were all warped out of shape like grotesque, crooked puppets, their wood rotted through and flaking and adorned with residual clumps of peeling paint. The doors clung to their disintegrating frames by rusted hinges and rotted screws, and all seemed so very close to simply collapsing to the sodden floor.

Priestley paused beside a door that stood half open to reveal the classroom within. He shone his light inside and the breath caught in his throat.

The classroom had remained untouched since it had been evacuated on the tragic day that had ripped the heart and soul out of Watsonville. Third grade paraphernalia was displayed on the walls, albeit rotted and peeling away; there were posters that promoted healthy eating, *'A BALANCED DIET IS A GOOD DIET'*, personal hygiene *'ALWAYS WASH YOUR HANDS!'* and the ubiquitous *'SAY NO TO BULLYING!'* – the latter complete with a picture of a miserable looking kid standing friendless in the playground whilst an older, bigger kid taunted him. Children's paintings and drawings adorned every wall, their damp-smeared paint and broad crayon strokes depicted happy, smiling faces, favorite pets and those little square-box houses with a chimney on the roof's apex that billowed out gray smoke (even though Watsonville had been smoke-free for almost twenty-five years).

There were lesson notes – hastily interrupted that day – on the whiteboard at the front of the class. They'd been written in neat print and informed the long-absent pupils about the War of Independence and that how July the Fourth was about so much more than fireworks and barbecues and a day off school. Priestley couldn't help but wonder if the teacher who had written those notes had made it out of the school alive, and just how many of her students now resided in Watsonville Cemetery.

Kid-sized chairs lay scattered around the classroom. Some had been knocked over, whilst others remained neatly and uniformly in their place as if anticipating the return of their occupants to the diminutive tables that were cluttered with sodden schoolbooks, pencils, crayons and educational toys. Dotted atop several of the tables there were the tiny dark cylinders of rat turds and the faint, yet unmistakable odor of the rodents' ammonia hung in the damp air.

"This is awesome," Priestley's voice was quiet, "this has to be the *perfect* location."

"I can't believe that you actually broke in – " Labeaux began.

"– *I* didn't break in to anywhere," Priestley cut him off, "it was Danny who did the breaking in."

"Fucking pedant," Labeaux snarled.

"I think you'll find that it should be *fucking pedantic,* actually," Priestley said and offered Labeaux a grin.

Unamused by this, Labeaux stared his friend down. "Okay, wise-ass. So you had *Danny* break in to one of the most infamous schools in the country. Just so you can shoot a movie?" Labeaux could barely hide his derision; even his original encouragement at Priscilla's delight at being in the school was being eroded by the stark reality of the place.

"What you have to understand, *Maurice*," Priestley put on his serious tone and looked directly into Priscilla's camera, "is that what we are doing this weekend is a far, far bigger thing than *Terrorfest*. We are here to seal our future – not just mine, but that of *everyone* involved. There are greater opportunities waiting just around the corner for Green Crayon Productions, just you hide and watch, buddy."

"Nice speech, Dave," Labeaux said, "but surely we could shoot our movie anywhere." He peered once more around the classroom and his huge frame shuddered like a goose just marched – jackboots and all – across his grave.

"We *could*, Mo'," Priestley replied, "but I feel that it is important that we have a genuine, creepy location that will look absolutely phenomenal up on the big screen. And you have to admit - you really couldn't recreate this atmosphere anywhere but here. The icing on our cake is that Watsonville Elementary has a terrifying back story that people will connect with." Priestley paused for effect and smiled into Priscilla's minicam. "What we have here is a location that oozes an *evil* that will seep out of our movie and chill the very souls of our audience." Priestley's flair for the over dramatic was legendary.

"So you picked the scene of a mass shooting?" Priscilla's comment was more for the benefit of her TV show audience than any indignation she may have shared with Labeaux, "I have to say, Dave, you've sure as hell gone straight to number one with this location."

"Fifty-six little kids and nine teachers all shot up in one afternoon," Labeaux said quietly as he gazed around at the array of smudged artwork.

"Fifty-seven." Priscilla lowered her camera. She switched it off. "It was fifty-seven kids. My youngest brother was only six years old when that sick bitch pointed her gun at him." Tears formed in Priscilla's wide, green eyes. "They told Mom to be thankful that at least Petey died instantly," she wiped at her eyes with the back of a trembling hand, "some fucking comfort that was."

At least two thirds of Watsonville had been directly affected in one way or another on that terrible July 2nd. Most people knew someone, or knew someone who knew someone who had lost a child in the tragedy. Almost a decade on and the events of that day remained indelibly ingrained in Watsonville's history and no matter what the town may go on to achieve in its future, it would always be the place where one Mrs. Rachel Villanueva went batshit crazy with a twelve-gauge in the elementary school.

No one knew what on earth had possessed the supposedly happy and mentally stable Mrs. Villanueva – mother of three and member of the Watsonville Elementary PTA – to do what she did. She'd lived up until then what had appeared to be a perfectly average, if somewhat uneventful life in the town that she'd called home for every one of her thirty-four years. She was married to a successful corporate attorney and lived in a four-thousand square feet, two-story house on an extensive corner plot which housed its own heated pool; she also drove a brand new Lexus SUV and had no money or health issues.

Absolutely nothing had come to light in the aftermath of her actions and the endless round of enquiries and attempts at psychoanalysis. There hadn't been any affairs – either on her part or that of Mr. Villanueva – no history of mental illness in her or her family (and they'd dug back four generations), absolutely nothing at all.

And unfortunately, Mrs. Villanueva had not been in a position to shed any light on her behaviour that day, either. Despite having murdered a large proportion of the school's population – including one of her own children – all she'd been able to offer when caught was that the voice inside her head had told her to do it. That much she'd told to her arresting police officer and had not repeated it nor spoken a single word since, even during the trial at which she was declared not guilty of murder on the grounds of insanity.

Indeed, Mrs. Villanueva was still maintaining that infuriating silence through her indefinite incarceration at the Gateway Mental Health Facility over in Dallas.

"I'm sorry," Labeaux said to Priscilla. "I didn't know."

"Of course you didn't." She braved a smile. "It's not the kind of thing that one goes around telling everyone is it?"

"I guess not," Labeaux agreed. His family had moved to Watsonville a couple of years after the fact and whilst he had gotten to know plenty of people who had been touched by the tragedy, Priscilla was the first he'd met who'd actually spoken to him about losing a sibling.

"Everyone says that you learn how to live with something like that, given time," she said, anticipating the question that formed in Labeaux's mind, "but my Mom never did."

A sudden movement ahead startled them and broke the sombre moment. Priestley spun his flashlight's milky beam away from the classroom and out into the hallway, but he was too late to catch more than a fleeting glimpse of a large, dark shape that darted into the inky black of a classroom farther down along the hallway. There came the unmistakable clatter of something heavy being knocked over, followed by the scraping of tiny chair legs.

"What the fuck was that?" Labeaux spoke for all of them, trying his damndest to retain his composure and appear cool. It had been less than ten minutes in this place and he could feel his nerves already starting to fray.

"Search me," Priestley replied with a wry smile, "it can't be Danny or any of the others; they'll all be in the gym setting everything up." He walked with brisk strides towards the classroom that had swallowed the mysterious figure and pointed his flashlight inside.

Priscilla pointed her minicam at Priestley.

As with the first classroom they'd inspected, this one – room 4b – was filled with third grade accoutrements. There was the artwork and informational posters on the wall, the diminutive tables filled with dank, decaying books and paper all waiting for the kids to return from their deadly recess. Tables and chairs lay scattered in a haphazard manner, many of them upended and it looked like someone had deliberately kicked a pathway through them. At the far end of the room, Priestley's flashlight beam picked out a child's ride-on toy, which lay on its side with its wheels spinning.

"Oh, well done guys!" Priscilla laughed and play-slapped Priestley's arm, "you almost got me there! I damn near peed in my panties, too." She laughed out loud and her voice resounded along the hallway like something that didn't belong. "That's an amateurish effect, Dave – considering what I've heard about you." She pointed her camera back at Priestley's face. "Fishing wire on a timer?"

"Yeah, something like that," Priestley said, but his forced smile failed to conceal a look in his eyes that sent a shiver down Priscilla's spine.

Priscilla twisted her head around to follow his gaze and saw on the wall above her head, the words *GET OUT!* Scrawled in thick, ragged cursive and dark against Priestley's flashlight beam, the words stunk like stale shit.

"We need to go find the others," Priestley said and neither Priscilla nor Labeaux argued with that.

Priestley made his way away from the classroom and continued on. As he walked, he danced the flashlight beam to and fro across the dilapidated hallway and followed the trail of thick electrical cables, which led the way to where he knew he would find his crew.

"I figured that somebody really ought to take advantage of the place before they demolish it," Priestley spoke more to break the eerie silence than for the need to explain himself (that was something Dave Priestley *never* did).

"And it may as well be us. It's too good an opportunity to miss, don't you think?"

"You do know that they'll never *actually* tear this place down, don't you?" Labeaux interjected, "the town council have been talking demolition for nine years and they've still not gotten around to it. Christ only knows why, if ever there was a place begging to be reduced to rubble and stuffed in a landfill, it's this one."

The decision not to reopen Watsonville Elementary post-Villanueva had been made in part because of the heinous event itself, but in the main because not enough children had survived to make the place fiscally viable. The school district had begun bussing the surviving kids to a school in a neighboring town, it was supposed to have been a temporary solution but it had just kind of stuck. Fast forward nine years, and Watsonville's elementary level kids still got their education at Clarksville Park.

"They still can't agree on what to do with the land after demolition," Priscilla told them, "the original plan had been to build a memorial on the site. Then it was gonna be a park, *then* some real estate company offered millions of dollars to build a housing estate but everyone was horrified at that. So the town council just keep on talking about it."

"You know a lot about this," Priestley was impressed, "is it because of your brother?"

"No. I did an expose on it for my TV show last year after they found the Cuckold Killer had been hiding out here," Priscilla replied. "My angle was that if they'd pulled the school down when they were supposed to have, the killer would have had nowhere to take his victims. Or at the very least he'd have taken them to some other town and left Watsonville the fuck alone."

Labeaux shook his head. He'd all but forgotten about the serial killer that had made Watsonville his home a year or so back. Hell, someone had even made a deplorable straight-to-DVD movie about it, and still the massacre had managed to overshadow even everything that sick bastard had done.

It may also have had something to do with the fact the Cuckold Killer had been pretty dull by serial killer standards. Even his real name had been unremarkable – Gregory Harris. He'd popped up as if from nowhere (actually he'd been living an uneventful, single life in San Antonio) with no previous history of violence or criminal record. There'd been none of the tell-tale signs of childhood abuse, compulsion to torture animals or unstable family background – he was just a regular *Joe Schmo* who'd apparently never harboured a violent thought in his life.

Until that one day when he'd woken up with a deep-rooted, sinister compulsion to punish adulterers. After capture, when they'd questioned Harris about his chosen victim demographic, he'd replied that he had to pick *something* to justify murder, and choosing the perpetrators of unfaithful couplings had been more of an *excuse* than his actual reason to kill.

"Talk about negative energy," Priestley enthused, "not only do we have a mass killing, but we have a serial killer to boot."

There was a salaciousness in Priestley's voice that Labeaux didn't much care for; this wasn't a side of his friend he admired all that much.

"His victims were all couples who were having affairs," Priestley continued, "and he brought them here to torture and kill them. I guess he figured he'd be left in peace since no one dares go near the place." He smiled at himself with just a hint of pride. "Did you know that his favorite thing was to strip the woman naked and tie her to a chair with a light bulb in her pussy? He'd switch it on and once the bulb heated up enough –" Priestley's voice hung stagnant in the cold, damp air.

"*POP!*" he shouted.

"Sweet Jesus, Dave!" Labeaux jumped and Priestley's voice was swallowed up by the darkness.

Priestley laughed at his friend, and was pleased to see that Priscilla had joined in with a strained laugh of her own. Perhaps Labeaux's high expectations regarding the gal were not quite the sealed deal he imagined them to be.

"He'd make the guy watch while he mutilated the woman," Priscilla added to the gruesome tale, "then he'd kill him and let the woman go. Most died not long after but one of them actually survived."

"Yeah?" Priestley's ears pricked up, "I didn't know that. Perhaps we could track her down and use her in a movie sometime?"

"They kept quiet about it – for her sake and for that of her family," Priscilla told him. "She lives down the road from my Mom and rarely leaves her house," she added with a sombre tone. "Then again, I guess I wouldn't go out much if I'd had most of my face and both of my breasts cut off."

Labeaux shook his head to dislodge the horrific images that Priscilla and Priestley had planted in there. "Shit, man. That's a crap-load of bad stuff to happen in one place," he said.

"They say that Harris got off on killing his victims at the scene of so much death and that was what attracted him to the school in the first place," Priestley told him, "or perhaps – as some great philosopher once said – it was simply a case of *evil attracts evil*."

"It was Stephen King," Priscilla chipped in.

"Eh?"

"It wasn't a philosopher who said that," Priscilla corrected, "it was Stephen King. *Salem's Lot*."

"Case, rested," Priestley said with a smug look on his face.

Labeaux turned to Priscilla. He placed a comforting hand on her shoulder and for a fleeting second or two he was genuinely *not* thinking about boning the girl. "If this is going to be difficult for you – being here, I mean – I can take you home before it gets too late."

"Heck, no," Priscilla barked, "there's no way I'm missing out on this." She perked up some. "And if your movie gets me some good exposure, then I'll fuck the both of you." She winked at Labeaux and Priestley who in turn looked at each other, nonplussed.

"That was never – " Labeaux began.

"Oh, come now, Maurice," Priscilla laughed, "did you *really* think I didn't know?"

Before either could either reply or attempt a protest, there was a loud *thrum* and a blinding blaze of light as the generator in the U-Haul kicked in and the arc lights in the hallway burst into life.

"Shit," Labeaux exclaimed and staggered back a step or two as he shielded his eyes from the harsh glare. And then he began to laugh that nervous laugh of his.

Priestley smiled. He clicked off his flashlight and looked down along the hallway. Danny and the crew had placed the lights – each one atop a seven-foot tripod and covered by a silver cloth shade that made them look like oversized, metal tulips – at thirty feet intervals along the hallway to provide essential light to the school. And now, somehow the school didn't seem quite so sinister, even though the walls still crumbled with fat chunks of flaking plaster, soggy posters continued their slow extrication from the walls like rotted, blistered skin and the classrooms looked for all the world as if the kids would be coming back any minute soon.

"Looks like it's all systems go," Priestley announced and strode with purpose in the direction of the school gymnasium, "let's go make this goddamned movie."

*

Its moment crept ever closer.

Working tirelessly and with obsessive diligence in the cold and lightless world, it mentally checked off each completed task against its convoluted plans whilst ignoring the others of its ilk that crowded around it.

Their frustration was fierce, knowing that they would not immediately be able to follow it into the world of light once it embarked upon that final stage of its journey – no matter how hard they pressed themselves against its skin. It jostled them out of the way.

Their time would come too, but they grew ever impatient with their pioneer as it worked industriously at its preparations as it had done across the eons.

Soon, the meticulous plans would begin their alignment

CHAPTER FOUR

Priestley gave the double doors a hearty shove and they flung wide open. He stepped over the electric cables that meandered through a freshly kicked hole in the rotting wood at the bottom of one of the doors and wound their way into the brightly lit cavern that had been made of the school's gymnasium. Priscilla – still filming – and Labeaux followed him in.

"Hey, folks!" Priestley announced their arrival and not one of the four people in the gym offered up more than a cursory wave of a hand, all completely immersed in their preparations.

Priestley's crew had taken over a wide area of the gymnasium's center. Equipment boxes, lights, camera parts, props – all the usual movie making paraphernalia – were scattered between the faded lines of what had once served as a basketball court. To the untrained eye it would appear as utter disarray, but to Priestley things looked just as they should; he was more than confident in his team's own, specialized brand of organised chaos.

The section of the gym they'd occupied was lit by a quartet of portable arc lights that were perched high on ten-foot poles, the splayed feet of which made them appear to be somewhat alien in nature. They spewed a harsh, white light in to the gloomy room to give everything an over-bright, ethereal glow.

Alongside the equipment there stood three fold-out tables, two of which were laden with cameras, lenses, fat rectangular batteries, sound equipment and a pair of state-of-the-art laptops crammed with the very latest movie editing software; as always, their plan was to edit on the go to save precious time. The third table was stacked with *Taco Cabana* takeout bags and surrounded by a half dozen camouflage patterned, canvas camping chairs.

As for the gym itself, it was in much the same condition as the other parts of Watsonville Elementary Priestley had viewed thus far. A large chunk of the ceiling was missing, the walls ran with damp and were festooned with the ubiquitous black mould, the denser patches of which sprouted small, chubby gray mushrooms that looked like tiny dicks. The once highly polished, wooden floors were tarnished beyond redemption, split and peeling, the climbing ropes were furred with a gray-green moss and the wall bars had thick tendrils of some creeping green weed growing down them. At the far side of the gym, the bleachers lurked in the semi-darkness of the shadows created by the lights, the wooden supports beneath the rotted seats horribly warped and disintegrating.

Labeaux– shadowed by Priscilla – made the somewhat predictable beeline for the gorgeous, honey-skinned girl who was struggling to see to apply her makeup by means of a small mirror perched precariously atop a stack of equipment crates. Labeaux fixed a warm smile on his face as he switched on his indubitable charm and strode over to say *hi*.

Priestley made his own way towards the trio of tables. He was keen to get to Ashlynn (who was busy screwing an impressively sized lens onto a Canon C500) and to get his hungry hands on the Tacos before they were all gone, although not necessarily in that order. On his way there, he walked past Danny and slapped the older man lightly on the top of his cue-ball head, Benny Hill style.

"Good work on the lights, Danny-Boy," he said.

Danny George turned around and pointed at the cell phone he had pressed tight against his ear, but gave Priestley a smile and a thumbs-up nonetheless. Priestley mouthed *sorry*, raised his hands in apology and took a few steps to the side to afford the man his privacy. Priestley studied Danny intently and couldn't help but think that his usually pudgy body had lost more than a little weight since they'd last been together, and that his complexion had more of that peculiar, grayish tinge than usual; although the latter could simply have been a trick of the rather unforgiving light.

"Daddy just wanted to say goodnight to his little princess before bedtime," Danny said into the phone, "you know I have to work late tonight." He smiled as if his smile would be transmitted by some magical means across the airwaves to his daughter. "Hey, don't be sad, baby girl, Daddy'll be there when you wake up in the morning – and if you're a good girl for Mommy, I'll bring breakfast bagels."

Danny listened intently as the five-year-old apple of his eye took her turn to speak, the smile wilting on his lips.

Apparently, Mommy had gone out for the evening with *'Uncle Russ'* again and had left Addison with Andrea, the sitter she'd found online who Danny was convinced was borderline special needs. It seemed to Danny that this was becoming more of a regular occurrence; every time he was away from the house for an evening, Shannon would be out and about with Russell Hedges, who she maintained was *just a friend.* Hedges was, in fact the new guy at Shannon's office who just so happened to be going through a particularly brutal divorce and also *just happened* to share her interest in Salsa dancing.

Coincidence to be sure, since Salsa was an interest of Shannon's that had developed around the same time Danny had been diagnosed stage four.

"Okay, time for bedtimes, Princess," Danny struggled to hide the hurt in his voice, "I love you." He listened, tears welling at the *I love you too, Daddy* that came back. He swallowed hard as he hung up the phone and then strode over to Priestley, hand extended and his very best and brightest grin on his lips.

"Hey, Dave!" Danny grabbed Priestley's hand and shook it hard, "what a fuckin' *inspired* location!" He slapped Priestley hard on the back. "This year's *Terrorfest* is as good as in the fuckin' bag! How can we possibly fail with Watsonville Elementary as our setting?"

"Thanks, man," Priestley looked into Danny's yellow-tinged eyes, "you sure you're up to an all-nighter?"

"Couldn't be more ready if I tried," Danny assured him and went about with his sound recorder, "we'll be good to go in no more than a half hour." He looked at Priestley with an expression that craved affirmation.

Priestley had never been one to pick up on such signals, being far too self-absorbed for life's subtleties. Nonetheless, the limp smile he gave Danny seemed to do the trick and the bald man seemed to perk up a little.

Priestley noted with some displeasure that Danny had brought along a boom mic in addition to the directional mic that plugged into the sound recorder. Between the latter, the above-par microphone on Labeaux's camera and the exceptional acoustics in the school, Priestley knew from the off that they wouldn't need the boom (he'd even allowed time in their weekend's schedule to ADR dialogue should they need to). It was just one more thing for them to lug back to the van when they finished filming. He peered down at the boom mic and thought it looked like a stumpy, furry Jim Henson creation with an extendible twelve-foot aluminium pole stuck up its ass – stick a pair of googly-eyes on the thing and it could well qualify for its own pre-schooler TV show.

"That's awesome, Danny," Priestley said absently as he began to drift off in Ashlynn's direction.

"Any time, boss," Danny called after him and went back to going through the motions of checking the sound equipment – although none of it really needed checking a fourth time.

Priestley sidled up to Ashlynn and gave her trim waist a playful squeeze. She looked especially good in her tight, ass-hugging jeans shorts over red hose and her canvas shoes (red – Ashlynn had her own *chic* style that was classy and alluring without seeming provocative). Even the chunky, pale blue sweater she wore did little to dampen her man's ardour, as it enhanced her curves to perfection.

Ashlynn was attractive without being a classic beauty. Just two years Priestley's junior, she was tall – around five-seven – with a near-perfect hourglass figure and piercing sapphire eyes that complemented her shoulder-length, mousey brown hair and twinkled wickedly when she smiled.

"Hey there, lover," she turned around to plant a light kiss on his lips, "you took your own sweet time getting here. I hope you had a Guinness for all of us." Ashlynn's laugh let Priestley know that she was just a tiny bit pissed at him. "Oh yeah," she added, "before you do anything else, could you and Maurice and that tragically ginger hanger-on you brought along please fill out your release forms? Everyone else has done theirs already."

"Will do," Priestley said as he returned the kiss.

"So, who is she?" Ashlynn hissed with a nod in Priscilla's direction. Ashlynn was a fairly easy going kind of gal, but not so good at hiding her insecurities when it came to other women; Priestley had learned from bitter experience that his girlfriend's bitch-level increased proportionately according to the attractiveness of the female in question.

"She's a friend of Mo's from his film class, her name's Priscilla something or other," Priestley told her, "and I think she's actually more redhead than ginger."

"Could she have worn *anything* more low-cut?" Ashlynn ignored him and cut right to the chase. "Now we all have to spend the next twenty-four hours being faced with those tits," she growled. "Does she not know what Maurice is like?"

"Quite possibly," Priestley offered, "perhaps that's why she wore the shirt."

"Hmm," Ashlynn grumbled her displeasure and shot Priscilla and her overflowing chest a withering glance.

If looks could kill, Priestley thought to himself, *we'd be burying Maurice's new friend in the sports field out back.*

Ashlynn held up the Sony camera she'd just finished assembling and looked over at Labeaux. The camera was a hefty piece of equipment, an old-school style that perched on the shoulder and recorded to incredibly expensive magnetic tapes. Labeaux preferred the bulky cameras to the smaller digital ones, he claimed that the images they produced were more *film-like* – much in the same way that music purists will swear blind that vinyl records make their precious tunes sound more *honest.*

"Your camera awaits, Mr. DeMille!" she called over to Labeaux.

Labeaux waved a hand at Ashlynn as a thank-you and tore himself away from the olive-skinned beauty and her makeshift make-up table to wander across with the ever present, ever filming Priscilla in tow.

The whole DeMille thing was his and Ashlynn's personal in-joke; she'd called him it the first time Priestley had introduced them because at the time, she hadn't known that the renowned Cecil B. DeMille had been a director and not a cameraman. And once an incredibly amused Labeaux had explained Ashlynn's mistake, the joke that Ashlynn then couldn't actually think of any famous cameramen had stuck.

As Labeaux and Priscilla sauntered over, Priestley decided that now would be as good a time as any to stamp his authority as director and begin the often-painful task of getting his team to focus on the job at hand. This, he would begin by making the necessary introductions even though most of those he'd assembled knew everyone else. They were all to be bedfellows – metaphorically speaking – for the weekend and a formal introduction was kind of expected.

"Hey, people!" Priestley shouted and everyone turned to face him, "if I could I have your undivided for a few?"

The handful of souls in the gym gave their attention and gravitated towards Priestley as he spoke.

"Okay, everyone, so this is Priscilla," Priestley pointed over to Priscilla who lowered her camera long enough to smile and say hi, "Priscilla has her own show on Channel 99 and she's filming a documentary of us tonight as we create our masterpiece. And, she has also promised to make us a behind the scenes piece for our website."

Everyone murmured their gratitude at Priscilla, not knowing that she hadn't promised anything of the sort.

"And this is Ashlynn, our supporting actress, general dogsbody, love of my life and muse," Priestley continued; Ashlynn had been his thespian muse since the first time he'd laid eyes on her – her predecessor in his affections having been an over-acting Estonian actress whose thick accent had made her *the* go-to gal for anyone with an Eastern European character in their script, even though her acting was somewhat wooden.

Ashlynn smiled, although she knew everybody already and resented being called a dogsbody. She'd have much preferred the term *multitalented.*

"The odd looking guy over there is Chris Sherwood. He's one of the finest actors in the state and we've known each other since Middle School." Priestley waved a hand in the direction of the tall, broad-shouldered guy with chiselled film-star features and muscular body that bulged in every one of the right places.

Chris Sherwood was thirty next birthday and was one of the few local actors who were genuinely on the up. He had a *bona fide* agent (who was not entirely happy with him taking on non-paid, non-union work but what the hell – he and Priestley went *way* back) and had had a speaking part in *Dallas* in the bag before they'd cancelled the show after Larry Hagman's untimely demise. At the end of the year, Chris was moving to L.A., and the fact that he was more than just another handsome, square-jawed type who felt he owed it to the world to be in front of the camera – he *really* could act – would take him to the top of the A-List and away from waiting tables, pumping gas or gay porn. Yes sir, Chris Sherwood was one of the good guys, even though he did have the predisposition to play the diva when the mood struck him.

Chris flashed a coy smile and hiked up his fashionably frayed jeans. "Howdy," he said.

"Over there is our leading lady, Carolyn Nguyen." Priestley pointed towards the impossibly attractive, half-Asian girl whom Labeaux had been fawning over. She worked *understated stunning* in her flimsy dress – virginal white with huge red poppies – which appeared more suited to high summer than this time of the year, and black, strappy sandals (the type Ashlynn more often than not referred to as *fuck-me shoes*) that showed off perfect feet and delicate, immaculately manicured toes.

"Say hi, Carolyn," Priestly prompted her.

"Hi," Carolyn replied with a dismissive wave of a hand and wandered back over to her chair to work on her makeup.

Carolyn was the relative newcomer to Green Crayon, having been cast in only three of Priestley's short movies to date. She'd been around the movie scene her entire life as her folks hailed from Santa Monica – her mother was a script writer for a laundry list of day time TV shows and a handful of lesser known features, mostly sequels, reboots and remakes. They'd moved here a couple of years ago to get away from the Tinseltown fakery and BS and from the first time she'd set foot in Watsonville, Carolyn had been fighting to get back to the bright lights of Hollywood.

"I think that everyone – apart from Priscilla – knows Danny." Priestley gesticulated towards the oldest one amongst them with an open palm and cheesy grin. "Danny is our technical wizard and Green Crayon Production's father-figure."

"Good to meet you, Danny." Priscilla held out a hand for the shaking.

"Cancer," Danny said as they shook.

"Err – Scorpio." Priscilla gave him an amused look.

"Rectal," Danny explained with a serious countenance, "I have stage four rectal cancer."

"Oh, I am so sorry –"

"And it's an absolute *pain in the ass*!" Danny's face cracked and he burst out laughing. "Gets 'em every time!" He glanced around at the gathered few, once more craving affirmation.

"Pardon me?" Priscilla looked across at Labeaux and Priestley, noticeably uncomfortable at being the unwitting stooge to Danny's gallows humor.

"You mustn't mind Danny," Priestley interjected with a chuckle; he'd heard all of Danny's cancer gags before, of course – many times. "He was diagnosed a year ago and he's been making lame jokes about it ever since – that right Danny?"

"Damn right," Danny growled. "It's the first time in forty-eight years I've had something interesting to talk about!" He laughed again but this time just a little too hard. For all of his false bravado, Danny George fooled no one, especially himself.

It had begun as a dull throb in the small of his back that Danny had written off as backache caused by nothing more than the rapid onset of middle age. It hadn't been until he'd begun pooping stale, rust-colored blood that he'd begun to take the whole thing seriously, and by then the cancer had taken a firm hold.

Danny was *by far* the elder statesman of the group and was easily the best crew person in town. Capable of turning his hand to practically everything and anything on a film set – from rigging lights to fixing broken cameras to recording and mixing sound and organizing food – Danny was indispensable, despite his bad taste humor. Everyone knew about his cancer and the brutal treatments that he was being put through (he certainly wasn't backward at broadcasting *that* at every possible occasion, either), including the chemotherapy that had murdered his hair follicles and made him feel permanently nauseous, and the radiotherapy that scorched red marks on his skin and left him kitten-weak for days at a time.

Nonetheless, Danny was confident that he would beat the errant cells in his lower gut that were on their single-minded mission to kill him, or at the very least be the cause of the removal of his lower intestine. Indeed, his check-up earlier that day had shown that the tumor in his bowel had notably *not grown* since the last time the oncologist had stuck a camera up Danny's ass and whilst the cancer hadn't actually shrunk, it hadn't grown any and that was a good thing, right?

Danny had always been a fighter – his first two wives would testify to that; a little too free with his fists in his younger days, was Mr. George – and now he was in the fight of his life, *for* his life and for the privilege of watching his daughter grow up.

As a stay-at-home-Dad, Danny had raised Addison whilst Shannon brought home the lucrative bacon from her Management Consulting career; there were times that Danny thought his wife preferred her job and associated social life to her family and that would hurt him more than the dull pain that gnawed away at his insides and the thought of crapping in a plastic bag for the rest of his life.

Priestley smiled at Danny and couldn't help but think that as nice a guy as Danny was, he did carry the stink of death about him these days. It was as if the rot in his bowels permeated his pores and no amount of *Axe* deodorant could hope to mask it.

"Aren't you going to introduce yourself, Dave?" Chris chimed in and broke both Priestley's reverie and the awkward atmosphere between Priscilla and Danny, "what is it that *you* do again? Ya know – when the rest of us are working our butts off to make your shitty scripts look good?" he laughed.

"Oh very droll, Chris," Priestley went along with the deprecating humor. "If only you were as funny *on camera* as you are off it." The comeback elicited a good-natured titter from the crew and the tension was duly dissipated.

Priestley turned to face Priscilla and her ever-inquisitive camera and spoke clearly, "for the benefit of the great viewing public, my name is David Priestley. I am the writer, director, editor – basically the entire creative heart of the whole Green Crayon operation." He grinned as he revelled in his faux big-shot routine. "In fact, the only thing that I *don't do* is act," he added with a smirk, "although, in common with the late, great Alfred Hitchcock, I do like to have a small part in every movie that I make –"

"– yeah, Ashlynn's told us all about your *small part*," Chris threw in and everyone belly-laughed – including Ashlynn (who even blushed a tad). Priestley joined in with the merriment; he knew that if they laughed together – they'd make movie magic together too.

Carolyn walked back over from her make up and stepped forward as the laughter died down. "While we're making announcements –" her voice was quiet, yet firm, and all eyes were now upon her. She took another couple of steps towards Priestley (although *sashayed* was perhaps a more descriptive term of how the girl walked) Carolyn even *moved* as hot as she looked.

"I finally heard from the production company in L.A.," she said, "the one I've been talking to, like forever." She paused for effect, clearly relishing the attention. "And it looks like we have a green light!" She clapped her hands with delight and was met by a stunned silence. "Which *means* that there is a big, fat Hollywood contract waiting in Lala Land for Green Crayon Productions," she added for just in case the others were going to be slow at catching on.

This was something they'd all been working towards and dreaming of for more years than any of them cared to admit and as collectively the realization sank in, there were cheers and high-fives all round. Carolyn flung her arms around Priestley's neck and took the opportunity to plant a wet, smacking kiss full on his smiling lips, much to Ashlynn's chagrin.

"Now that's what I'm talking about!" Priestley voiced his excitement as he extricated himself from Carolyn with a guilty glance towards Ashlynn, "we're moving to L.A.!" Once more there was rejoicing, although Priestley did note that Ashlynn's cheer was a little more restrained than the others'.

Troubled by this, Priestley watched as his girlfriend turned away to wander back towards the collapsible tables and there she resumed her fiddling with the camera equipment. Much to Priestley's consternation, Ashlynn had quite the unreadable expression on her face.

With the introductions and Carolyn's Big Announcement done, everyone save Ashlynn made their way to the food table, each of them abuzz with excited chatter. Priestley muscled his way to the front and proceeded to stuff his face with the single biggest burrito he could find.

"See, I told you that these film competitions were more than just some piss-pot waste of time," Priestley said to Labeaux as he swilled down a mouthful of cold burrito with tepid Diet Pepsi, "as much as a pain in the balls these competitions have been, didn't I tell you that they'd be our ticket to the big time?" He draped an arm around his friend's shoulder the best he could, given the height difference.

"That's really cool, man," Labeaux grinned, "there *are* hot chicks in Hollywood, right?"

"More than even you could eat, buddy," Priestley replied with a hearty backslap. He finished up his burrito and slurped the last of his flat Pepsi.

"Thought as much," Labeaux said and he looked like the cat that had just caught the mouse.

"Okay, people," Priestley once more addressed his cast and crew, this time with his very best *motivational* voice, "it's almost time to make *The Black Mass* the very best seven-minutes of celluloid ever!" Everyone murmured their excitement through mouthfuls of food as Priestley left the table and walked over to Ashlynn who was still busy finding things to do with the boom mic.

"I know we really film in digital, but that doesn't sound quite as cool as *celluloid,*" Priestley whispered to Ashlynn and studied her eyes for a smile that failed to materialise. "Are you okay, baby?" Priestley slipped an arm around his girl's waist and was surprised to feel her tense up. "You're not upset about that thing with Carolyn just now, are you?" he asked, "she kisses *everyone*, you know it's just how she is."

"I know *exactly* how she is, Dave." Ashlynn looked him directly in the eyes. "And no, I'm not upset about that."

"Carolyn's news annoyed you?" Priestley's heart sank. "You know it's the news we've been waiting for. I thought you'd be happy for us."

"I am happy," Ashlynn sighed, "I'm happy for *you*, Dave. But you could have discussed it with me before blurting it out to everyone like that."

Priestley took the microphone out of Ashlynn's hands and gently laid it on the table. He took each of Ashlynn's hands in his and gave her his puppy-dog eyes. "Hey, come on, babe. I only found out just now, how could I have discussed it with you first?" He gave her hands a loving squeeze. "You know that Carolyn's been working on her contacts for months, you can't really expect her to keep quiet about getting a result like that." Priestley thought that he sounded reasonable, although that wasn't always a given when Ashlynn was in one of her moods. "And, you have to admit, it's great to start this shoot on a high."

She forced a weak smile. "And we have. I'm really pleased for you – honestly."

Ashlynn was worrying about her father; Priestley could see it written all over her face. Lewis Jones Senior had been a constant niggle throughout his and Ashlynn's five-year relationship, so much so that Priestley secretly referred to the old boy as *The Albatross*.

Ashlynn's Dad had already been in his mid forties when she was born, and her Mom had walked out the week before Ashlynn's tenth birthday and left Dad and Daughter to care for each other – not the most auspicious start to a young life. And despite Mr. Jones' advanced age, all had gone well until he'd experienced his breakdown – he'd been found hunkered in a foxhole he'd dug out behind Costco, play-sniping at the customers with a stick that he'd fashioned into a pretend gun with some twine and a crumpled up soda can.

It transpired that Ashlynn's father had been suffering early-onset Alzheimer's, compounded by residual PTSD from his days in Vietnam. One of the very few stories he'd relate about that time was that he'd once been given orders to return a prisoner to the prison compound and be back in five minutes or face discipline. The compound had been five minutes away even at a run, so the task was impossible and the inference had therefore been unambiguous. The second Lewis Jones had put a bullet in the back of the Viet Cong's brain; something had begun to unravel in his.

The Alzheimer's had taken a rapid, firm hold following the Costco incident and as a result, most of Lewis Jones' short term memory evaporated and his prosopagnosia was so bad that most days he failed to recognise his own daughter during her twice-weekly visits to the Silverado Springs Memory Care Center. Unhappily though, his recollection of the time he served in 'nam was so vivid that in his own mind, the war raged on.

Of course, there was absolutely no question of the old man ever recovering; he was destined to remain institutionalized for the remainder of his days. Especially so after they discovered that he'd yanked out his teeth with a pair of old pliers to raise money from the tooth fairy for the grandkids he didn't have. And when he'd run out of his own to pull, Jones Snr. had moved on to those of the other Silverado Springs residents.

Deep in his heart, Priestley knew that Ashlynn would never move any farther away than her current two miles from her father, and she flatly refused to discuss relocating him. Thus the Alzheimic old man was in real danger of holding her (and by default) Priestley back.

"I'm sure they'll have fantastic places for your Dad in L.A.," Priestley tried to reassure, "and with the money that

Carolyn's people are talking about, we'll easily be able afford the very best for him."

Ashlynn kissed Priestley gently on the lips, her mouth dry and warm. "I know, sweetheart," she said. "I'm sure we'll figure something out. It was just a shock finding out like that, and you know I always need time to process." She took a deep breath and in that instant donned the mantle of *supportive girlfriend*. "I *really am* thrilled for you and the guys; you've all worked so damned hard for this and you deserve your big break." Ashlynn pressed her body into Priestley's and the firmness of her breasts dug into his ribs. "If you'd care to, we could slip off to the kindergarten restrooms for some celebration sex?" Ashlynn was the grand master bar none at deflection.

Priestley wrinkled his nose at the suggestion. "Thanks, Hun, but you know I don't like it when it's your time –"

"– you *sure* you don't fancy stirring the paint a little?" Ashlynn gave him her naughty laugh and accompanying lascivious smile.

"Eww, you really can be disgusting sometimes, Ashlynn Jones," Priestley laughed off his discomfort.

Ashlynn pushed him away with a playful shove. "And don't you just love it!?" she giggled and gave her lips an exaggerated, porn-film lick.

"I hate to interrupt the foreplay here, Dave," Chris's voice broke the moment, "but we'd all *really* love to know what you and Maurice picked out of the hat for us at the kick-off." He winked at Ashlynn who blushed just a little. "If it's not too much trouble, that is."

"Yeah, sorry, dude," Priestley apologized and turned away from Ashlynn. He was troubled by her reaction to Carolyn's news – there were no doubt more discussions to be had on the subject of her father – and Priestley couldn't help but wonder what implications the old man would have on their future together. "Hey, Mo'!" Priestley's voice echoed high amongst the rafters of the gym, "would you be so kind as to let everyone know what *you* picked out of the *Terrorfest* hat?"

Labeaux nodded and fished the crumpled strips of paper out of his pocket. He shot Priscilla a raise of his eyebrows, happy to be the focus of *her* attention once more; the sooner he got this show on the road and impressed her with his prowess behind a camera, the sooner she'd be melting into his arms.

And so, having garnered everyone's attention, Labeaux unfurled the first piece of paper and read it out.

CHAPTER FIVE

"You have *got* to be fucking joking, Maurice!" Chris was particularly vocal in his displeasure, determined to let everybody know about just how pissed he was. As he spoke, his bottom lip actually stuck out in a petulant pout and his handsome features turned ugly pretty damn quick.

"That's exactly what *I* said," Labeaux attempted some humor. "Don't shoot the messenger, man."

"No way on God's green earth am I going to be *Phil –* fucking *– Anderer,"* Chris spat. "Who's going to take that shit seriously?"

Priscilla pointed her tiny camera at him, and then panned around the collection of concerned faces.

"It's the name we picked out, Chris," Labeaux told him, "and the rules state that we *have* to use it, so it may as well be you, dude." Labeaux held firm. Unlike Priestley, he'd never been one for pandering to the flaky egos of the acting fraternity. Also the truth was that Labeaux didn't care all that much for Chris Sherwood, and thus relished the opportunity to put the over-inflated asshole in his place.

Priestley stepped forward, his every move recorded for posterity by Priscilla. "Look, Chris," he put out his hands in a would-I-let-you-down gesture, "I *promise* that we will have the name said early on in the script so that it's out of the way." He gave Chris an earnest nod. "By the time our film gets to the good stuff, the audience will have forgotten the joke name."

"That's if the audience picks up on it being a joke name in the first place," Carolyn threw in, "you know how dumb they can be." She gave Chris a sly wink and a purse of the lips that had more of a placating effect than any number of Priestley's assurances.

"You'd fucking better, *Priestley*," Chris huffed and then mumbled something inaudible beneath his breath.

"So, Mr. Bigshot writer-person," Carolyn persisted with her diversion of attention away from Chris's diva strop, "what *is* our movie gonna be about this year? I do hope it's not werewolves again." At this, she laughed and puffed out her impressive chest.

"Not after last year," Danny chimed in with a wry smile, "he wouldn't dare."

Priestley gave an inward shudder at the returning thoughts of the previous year's debacle. Yes, it had been werewolves and yes it had come in second in the *Terrorfest* line-up; but he knew in his gut that the movie would be a source of embarrassment throughout his future career. It was just the kind of crap they dig up for those *'Before They Were Famous'* filler shows the networks put out on late night TV.

Things had begun to go wrong the minute Priestley had pulled *'Werewolf'* out of Melissa Bracken's hat. That particular year (and for reasons known only to themselves), Melissa and Phil had decided to dictate what horror genre each team would shoot and because Priestley had made preparations to shoot a poignant zombie romance (*Zombie*

Hooker: A Love Story), werewolves had been totally the wrong species of monster for him to have to deal with.

And so, with help from practically everyone on the team – another dire mistake, since script writing by committee rarely turns out well – the Green Crayon team had cobbled together a screenplay on the fly, one that was far too long and threw in pretty much every werewolf movie cliché that they could think up.

The story itself had been half decent, adapted in haste from a short story Priestley had been working on. It concerned a popular high school jock, who was deliberately turned into a werewolf by a town's elders in order to represent the town in the annual werewolf fighting tournament. Priestley had paid a professional stuntman and a special effects company to create the gore and practical effects, and those had looked awesome, but despite all of the hard work and hard cash Priestley had thrown at it, *The Five Towns Pageant* had fallen woefully short of perfect.

Editing the movie had also been by the whole team, yet another in the catalogue of disastrous decisions. At fifteen minutes long the film had looked good, but by the time they'd cut it down to the required seven minutes it had resembled an over-long trailer for a low-budget, 1970's Hammer Horror. Indeed, all it lacked was Christopher Lee in a black satin cape and Ingrid Pitt with her tits out – although Carolyn had actually put in an admirable performance on the latter front.

Priestley – ever the perfectionist – had been bitterly disappointed with the movie and had even refused to put it up on *YouTube* or on his own website in his attempt to wipe it from existence.

"I think we all learned our lesson with that one." Ashlynn looked over at Priestley whose stony-faced silence said it all. "Putting an *e* at the end of werewolf doesn't make it original."

Everyone laughed, and even Priestley himself managed to crack a smile.

"So what's it gonna be this year, Davy-boy?" Danny asked, "zombie ninjas – but spelled with an 'X'?"

Again, everyone broke into laughter – even Chris, his diva moment all but forgotten.

Priestley reassured them that no, there were definitely no werewolves, zombies, vampires or any other horror cliché, especially since Phil and Melissa had forgone the genre-enforcement this year.

"Although I do like your zombie ninja idea, Danny." Priestley laughed. "Maybe next year."

"I'll make a note," Danny replied and made a big show of keying the reminder into his phone.

"As tempting as Danny's zombie ninjas sounds, I promised you originality this year, and originality is what you're going to get." It gratified Priestley to see the nods of approval and a few smiles. It was also a relief to see his team getting on board; they really were going to have to be for this one. "And I promise not to write too much this year."

"Thank the good Lord for that!" Labeaux raised his eyes to the heavens in mock praise.

"Amen, *sista*!" Chris added and grinned as Priscilla pointed her camera at him. "Last year's movie could have been award-winning if we'd been allowed a forty-minute run time," he said to the camera. "But after we'd butchered it down in post-production to get it to seven, it was –"

A door slammed somewhere in the dark recesses of the school. The hollow sound resonated like distant thunder along the abandoned hallways and into the gymnasium.

"Shit!" Labeaux jumped.

"A little harsh, Maurice, the movie wasn't all that bad," Chris joked in his attempt to cover for the fact that he was well and truly spooked. There were nervous laughs all around.

"Come on, Dave," Ashlynn spoke up, "don't keep us all in suspense, what *have* you got for us?"

Priestley cleared his throat. "Well," he said. "I thought that this year, we'd go for *realism* and ride the found-footage-bandwagon." He studied the faces surrounding him, most of which expressed cynicism. "That way, we can let our fantastic location tell the story for us." This was met with approval; there could be no denying that he had chosen one hell of a location. Priestley paused a beat or two to allow his words to sink in. "So, I planned to scribble a couple of pages of direction tonight, and improv' the rest."

This resulted in disconcerted chatter.

"You want us to *improvise*?" Carolyn spat the last word as if it were a dirty one. "You always said that improv' was just a fancy way of saying *can't be assed to write a proper script*, Dave," she said with air-quotes for emphasis.

"Did I say that?"

"Yep," Labeaux replied, and everyone murmured their agreement.

"Well in this case, nothing could be further from the truth, Carolyn," Priestley placated. "After last year's scripted mess, I aim to get a *real* flow going and let your natural acting talent take over," he emphasized *real* with the exaggerated air-quotes that from him, served only to irritate.

"And the story?" Labeaux prompted.

"I'm keeping it simple," Priestley told them, "nothing too difficult for you simple folk." He laughed alone at that one. "Okay, here's how it's going to go down," he continued, "a bunch of people break into an abandoned school –"

"– go fucking figure," Chris growled and Priestley noticed that his leading man was once again pouting.

"You really don't have to explain *every* detail to us, Dave," Ashlynn ran interference. She could see that Priestley was beginning to lose his people, explaining his ideas verbally had never really been a strongpoint.

"Yeah, we don't look half as dumb as we actually are, Dave," Labeaux attempted to lighten the mood.

"Okay, okay. With my humblest apologies to *everyone's* fucking sensibilities, could I please finish?" Priestley's impatience shone through and threatened to morph into the famous David Priestley temper.

"Yeah, you carry on, Mr. Cronenberg," Danny joined in, ever keen to curry acceptance.

"Now, where the hell was I?" Priestley stumbled.

"You were talking to us like we were special needs kids who've tied our own shoes for the first time." Danny was on a roll. He looked around for approval and was met by stifled chuckles.

"That's very funny – *for you*, Danny," Priestley was a little more acerbic than intended, "is your *Interferon* kicking in again?" Once more, Priestley's tone came out as more cutting than humorous and Carolyn actually gasped.

"The school has a malevolent history; it's where a brutal serial killer brought his victims to horrifically torture and murder them," Priestley made with the spiel.

Carolyn was first off the bat with the sarcasm. "And what inspired such a unique and off the wall story line?" she asked.

"I thought that by sticking close to the truth, Carolyn, our movie will be all the more authentic," Priestley explained himself calmly, "and why make shit up when the story practically tells itself?" There could be no argument with that one at all; Watsonville Elementary was steeped in a history far more grotesque than even Priestley's dark and fertile imagination could have dreamt up. Carolyn and the others seemed pleased with his explanation and there were even a few sage nods.

"Our story involves an intrepid group of documentary film-makers who decide to perform a satanic ritual in order to communicate with the spirit of a serial killer that haunts the school," Priestley explained, "of course, everything goes horrifically wrong when one of them is possessed by the evil spirit of the killer." He clapped his hands and the sharp sound in the cavernous gymnasium startled them all – himself included. "And then, said evil spirit hunts everyone down until they're all dead." There, Priestley paused, painfully aware that the whole scenario played out much better in his head. "That's pretty much it. The end."

He was met with stunned silence and incredulous looks. Even Danny and Chris shook their heads.

"That's it?" Carolyn broke the quiet, "that's fucking *it*?" She put her hands up to her head and sighed heavily. "You know how important this is to our Hollywood deal, Dave. And you come up with that bullshit?" Carolyn stared hard at him, her angry eyes committed to film by the ever-watchful Priscilla.

Danny and Chris stared at Ashlynn as if this was all somehow her fault. Ashlynn simply shrugged her reply; she was not her boyfriend's keeper; it really was as simple as that.

"Gotcha!" Priestley erupted with a fit of laughter. He pulled a bunch of scripts from his backpack as a magician would colored handkerchiefs from a voluminous sleeve. "You really didn't think I'd let you guys down, did you?" He smiled and was happy to hear a murmur of relieved giggles from everyone in the room. For a moment there, he'd thought things were going to turn unpleasant thanks to Carolyn and her dumb intensity; as fuckable as she was, there was a broad who really needed to learn how to take a joke.

"Davy?" Ashlynn shot him sternest look. "You didn't cheat and write the script already did you?" Her lips turned down at the corners and she placed her hands on her hips as if further illustration of disapproval was in the least bit necessary.

"Err, kind of," Priestley blanched, "but only because I wanted to make this movie perfect. And this really is some of the best material I've written so far." He held up the scripts as if Ashlynn would be able to *feel* just how well written they were from twenty feet away.

Chris, Danny, Labeaux and Carolyn all nodded in silent approval and gave Ashlynn a look to let her know that she was in the minority here.

"Can you edit that bit out?" Priestley asked Priscilla. He'd lapsed, forgotten that she was filming and was suddenly aware that he had just confessed to committing an almighty sin directly into her minicam.

"Sure thing, *Davy*," Priscilla giggled and everyone chuckled along.

"Joking aside, guys," Priestley pulled his people back in. "We *will* be filming an actual, real and one-hundred per cent authentic Black Mass for the movie," he informed them, "and I've brought along everything we're likely to need." He patted his bulging backpack and the collection of things within shifted and crackled together as if they were alive. "And I wouldn't be me unless I'd done my homework and I can assure you that *authenticity* is most definitely the operative word tonight." He smiled as he saw everyone roll their eyes; they all knew just how pedantic he could be when it came to his films – there were times that Priestley could make Kubrick seem lackadaisical.

Priestley handed out the scripts, one by one.

"I'll be taking the minor role of the expert in satanic rituals who has been brought in by your character, Chris," Priestley thrust a script into Chris's hand, "to perform the titular ritual." Ashlynn snatched the penultimate copy from Priestley's hand with a disapproving look and began to leaf through the crisp, white pages. "As for the rest of the plot," Priestley realized that he had in an instant lost the attention of each and every one of his team as they immersed themselves in his written words, "I think you'll all agree that it's the best demonic possession script that you've ever read." Downcast, Priestley mumbled this latter part upon realizing that no one was actually listening to him.

Priscilla thrust her camera towards his face.

"Of course, it wouldn't be a Green Crayon Productions production if I didn't have a few surprises up my sleeve," Priestley said into the camera. Then in his best Vincent Price voice he added, "tonight, we're going to make *The Exorcist* look like *Frozen*." He added the sinister Price laugh at the end – an impersonation he was particularly good at – and the sound echoed through the gymnasium and lingered a fraction longer than perhaps it ought to have.

"I'm looking forward to it," Priscilla said with a wink to Priestley that may have hinted at the promise of a little more than a fellow artist's admiration. It was fortunate for her that Ashlynn missed that one.

"Oh yeah," Priestley raised his voice and waved the final script – his *director's* copy – above his head, "does anyone know if Corinne's coming tonight?" He was met by shrugs.

"No idea, buddy," Labeaux said, "I guess that's what you get for picking unknowns off of Facebook. She's probably another timewaster."

"I was hoping not," Dave replied, "her email was really enthusiastic and she's had tons of experience."

Ashlynn grunted and turned away from this exchange. Priestley had a history of booking attractive young actresses to his shoots and as far as the elusive Corinne's application email was concerned, it was more likely that the girl had big tits than a wealth of experience. Ashlynn allowed herself a little gloat; it served her jerk boyfriend right that she hadn't shown up.

"She did say in her last email that she'd be here." Priestley was once more met with blank looks. "Still, no worries. We can easily work around her part." Priestley returned his attention to Priscilla and her camera. "Don't let the others hear me saying this, but that's the problem with young acting types. They're all too goddamned flaky and unreliable at the best of times," he confided with a wry smile to the camera.

CHAPTER SIX

anny busied himself by repositioning one of the lanky film lights that gave their welcome illumination to the center of the gymnasium. Beyond the white glare of the lights, murky shadows lurked around the periphery of the room like a pack of ravenous yet timid animals plucking up enough courage to make their move.

Danny glanced over to where Ashlynn, Chris and Carolyn had retreated to the canvas chairs to pour over Priestley's scripts. Each one of them was totally absorbed in blocking out their individual lines with the bright yellow highlighter pens Priestley had instructed him to pick up from the stationery store on the way in. Priestley himself was busy being interviewed by the delightful Priscilla, as if they had all the time in the motherfucking world to make this movie.

Danny jumped when Labeaux approached him. He felt a little foolish but really couldn't help it; the school had him spooked and his mind had been dwelling on his wife and Addison and *Uncle Russ* – he'd simply not heard the cameraman's soft shoes as they'd squeaked quietly towards him on the damp floor.

"I figured I'd take a mosey around to pick out some scene locations," Labeaux said, "I could do with my wing man on sound." In anticipation he held out one of the audio recorders to Danny; a four-track portable, and despite the fact that it more resembled a nineteen-seventies' cassette tape recorder, one of the best in the business. "And since Dave is preoccupied with playing Captain Hollywood for the Priscilla Big Boobs Show; I thought I'd ask you." Labeaux smiled at Danny who mirrored him with a twinkle in his eye.

"Why, Mr. Labeaux, if I didn't know any better, I'd say you were displaying all of the more obvious signs of the green-eyed giant," Danny mocked.

"Me? Jealous of that conceited runt?" Labeaux grimaced and glanced over at Priestley making cosy with the woman he'd brought along for himself to impress. "Give me a fucking break, Danny-boy." The two shared a laugh and Danny took the recorder from Labeaux's hands.

"Whatever you say, boss," Danny said as one hand absently twiddled with the silver microphone that plugged into the recorder's base. "Go get your camera and we'll go take a look-see."

"Thanks, Danny."

Danny caught a glimpse of what looked to be relief on the big guy's face as he turned to walk away; surely the Great and Fearless Maurice Labeaux wasn't scared of being by himself in a little kid's school?

*

Priestley stuffed the remnants of yet another burrito into his mouth. He chased it down with a loud slurp of his soda and shuffled nervously in the canvas chair.

"If you could just talk naturally into the camera, as if we were having a casual chat," Priscilla coached him from the chair opposite. "Do you think you can you do that?"

Priestley chewed slowly to make time in which to compose himself. If there was one thing that made him uncomfortable, it was being in front of the camera without a script or a character to hide behind. Still, he told himself, as the big time beckons, this was something he'd have to get used to. "I'll give it my best shot," he told Priscilla with a nod. "Just say when."

"Okay." She switched on her camera and lifted it to Priestley's eye level. "Three, two, one, go."

"I am – first and foremost – a writer," Priestley spoke with his *earnest* voice, "but, as a writer with ambition to write for the movies, the first thing I learned was that one has to get involved in *making* movies. And remember, every great movie starts with a script." He smiled. "And that is why I have spent the past few years getting involved in local film projects – it's the best way to get oneself noticed by Hollywood's movers and shakers."

"Hey, Dave," Labeaux interrupted and his tone left no uncertainty that he now considered Priestley a pretentious dick, "me and Danny were thinking –"

"– really, Mo'?" Priestley whined "We're in the middle of a take here. I'm trying to get this interview down while everyone learns their lines."

"Yeah, sorry about that, dude," Labeaux said, although he really didn't sound all that sorry. He tipped a raised eyebrow to Priscilla. "I just wanted to let you know that me and Danny are going to take a look around the school and scout a few locations. I didn't want you worrying where we'd got to." Again, a wink in Priscilla's direction. "You can do that take again, right?" Labeaux treated himself to a lingering glance down the front of Priscilla's shirt before he turned away.

"We're good, Maurice." Priscilla fidgeted with her neckline and gazed up at Labeaux's handsome face.

"Catch ya later, Davy-boy," Labeaux said and walked off to collect his camera.

"Yeah, later, *Maurice*." Priestley shot his friend a look to let him know that belittling him in front of Priscilla to play the big man was definitely not cool. This was neither the time nor the place for a pissing contest, and Priestley found it astounding that Labeaux thought he'd even consider making a move on Priscilla with Ashlynn in the same room.

Although, if Ashlynn *hadn't* been in the room, or would never stand a chance of finding out – it wasn't as if Labeaux had staked a claim on the gal, was it? *And* since she'd given them *both* that loud and clear vibe earlier on, perhaps all bets were actually off?

...then I'll fuck the both of you.

It really doesn't get much clearer than that.

"Let's pick up from movers and shakers," Priscilla instructed and Priestley's oh so pleasant daydreams of her shattered.

"Err – oh yeah," Priestley stammered and worried for a split second that she may have been reading his mind. He forced his eyes away from the deep, dark, tempting crack of her cleavage and focussed on the camera.

"They like to have something visual, you see," Priestley continued, "the days of throwing scripts at producers are long gone; you need to have something to *show* them what you can do." Priestley paused to catch his thoughts. Oddly enough, he'd never originally set out to be a director, or an editor or actor – or anything other than a writer for that matter. But, as the man said, needs must when the Devil drives.

"So the more short film productions you make and get out there, the greater the chances are of being discovered."

Priestley smiled. "And as we found out this evening, that strategy has finally paid off."

"I see," Priscilla prompted.

Paused.

"So, tell me how you got involved in the Watsonville movie scene."

Priestley nestled back in his chair and the canvas yielded a little before it took his weight. Perhaps the more appropriate question here would have been *how were you damn near put off the whole film thing before you'd even got started?*

With the distance of hindsight, it was quite the funny story.

Priestley had been invited by a guy who knew a guy to join his team as one of four writers for a national short film competition. The guy had introduced himself as Darren DeNeche (although Priestley discovered later that his given name was the more mundane Stanley Wheat), a man who'd had the definite air of knowing what he was talking about. Of course, Priestley had jumped at the chance; this being seven years ago when he'd started out along the arduous path of finding his place as a writer, and as such he'd been ill-prepared to sift out the bullshitters from the good guys.

As it worked out, DeNeche had been nothing more than a talentless hack that fancied himself as a moviemaker. He did have all of the expensive camera equipment though, which had looked impressive to the incredibly wet-behind-the-ears new writer in town. But when it came to writing time, Priestley and his fellow scribes had found themselves *sans* the enigmatic Mr. DeNeche – he'd chosen to remain in another room to play the hotshot with the impossibly good-looking cast he'd assembled.

Although Priestley and his compadres had the script completed in just four hours, it had been an absolute doozy; action-packed, thought-provoking and incredibly funny to boot. DeNeche, however, had failed to see its quality and the second his writers had gone home he'd trashed it (*literally*) and written his own tawdry piece of crap.

"It was fucking frustrating, I can tell you," Priestley told the camera, "oops, sorry." His face reddened as he realized his *faux pas*. "Can we do that again?"

"Please," Priscilla said.

"It was *incredibly* frustrating to be treated that way, especially so when we all finally saw the abortion of a film that DeNeche had finished up making."

As it had worked out, DeNeche had eventually run out of time to complete his own script, which meant that much of the film had to be improvised by a bunch of actors who were spectacularly inept at improvisation. Somewhat flatteringly, one of them had called Priestley up during filming the next day to ask if he would write them a few lines to say, a request that he'd had no qualms about turning down flat.

Thus the movie was never finished in time to be entered into the contest and thankfully had never seen the light of day.

Priestley had thought at the time – indeed he still did to this day – that the conclusion to the sorry saga was a mercy for both his career and the viewing public, even if it had meant the entire rigmarole had been one tremendous waste of everyone's time.

"There's an old adage in the film world," Priestley informed Priscilla's camera, "that making a movie is much like having a baby; once all the pain and mess is over and you have a shiny, pink newborn in your arms, you quickly forget just how bad it all was, and you *really* want to make another."

In the true spirit of that sentiment, and less than a year after the fact, Priestly had shot and produced the script he and the other two writers had written (thus giving rise to

Green Crayon Productions) – and it had gone on to win a whole bunch of awards.

"And you know." Priestley leaned forward to give Priscilla a beguiling smile. He inhaled her heady scent deep into his chest and his eyes wandered the hills and valleys of her mouth-watering body. "Looking back, I really should have known how things were going to go after setting off on the wrong foot with DeNeche."

Priscilla returned the smile and raised a quizzical eyebrow.

"You see, Darren DeNeche's house was immaculately decorated and had the most beautifully coordinated soft furnishings, a Wizard of Oz poster on the lounge wall, Lady Gaga on the iPod – *and* he had a cat called Alejandro." Priestley patted Priscilla's knee and his heart skipped when it didn't jerk away. "I guess everything began to head south when I asked the man if he had a wife and kids." Priestley laughed out loud at the anecdote and once more squeezed the knee he'd laid claim to. "I guess my gaydar must have malfunctioned that night!"

A cacophonous clatter jolted Priestley and Priscilla from their cosy *ménage a deux*. They both jumped, eyes wide with fear and just a soupcon of guilt.

"For Christ's sakes!" Priestley shouted as he and Priscilla twisted around in unison in the direction of the harsh sound.

"Sorry, Davy!" Ashlynn called over as she picked up the toppled light stand she'd just tripped over, "my bad."

CHAPTER SEVEN

*I*n the smothering darkness it sensed that they were close; it could, smell them, taste them, hear them – although their words were little more than meaningless sounds that served only to irritate. As its mind crept with ever pervasive and dark, malevolent tendrils into theirs, it knew their thoughts and sought out their fears and it knew that as with all of the others, they would easily succumb to its will.

But, trapped as it was in the dismal, frigid lightlessness of its own realm, it understood that they whilst they were close, their corporeal entities remained an entire existence away.

It went about its work, tirelessly bringing together the elements it had assembled and making ready to reap its rewards.

*

"So, if one of the special needs kids are late for class – "Danny's voice cut through the dark as he followed Labeaux along the hallway, "is it still politically correct to refer to them as *tardy*?" He laughed at his own joke and Labeaux chuckled along.

"That's a bad one, Danny," Labeaux said, "even for you." He was grateful for the sound of their voices in the dark, ominous hallway; the place was giving him the creeps so bad that his balls clung tight to his body, begging to be let in.

From the moment he and Danny had turned the corner from the main hallway – gaily illuminated as it was by the dazzling film lights – they had been plunged into the damp, gloomy murk of the much shorter hallway that lay beyond.

Labeaux glanced over his shoulder at Danny who followed close behind and played his fat flashlight beam around the hall. The yellowed light created countless eerie shadows that cavorted like living, frolicking things as the darkness closed in behind them. In addition to the flashlight that he gripped so tightly that his knuckles had turned white, Danny lugged a sound recorder strung around his neck with a broad canvas strap and he kind of resembled a fifties cigarette girl. The recorder bounced against Danny's pudgy belly as he walked, keeping time with his nervous footsteps, whilst in his left hand Danny carried its microphone. This he held out a little way in front of himself as he took great care not to get its delicate wire tangled up with the recorder's beige strap. Labeaux returned his attention to the gloom that awaited them both, hitched his camera to a more comfortable position and took a deep, shaky breath to steady his nerves.

They paused awhile by one of the handful of classroom doors that populated the hallway. Danny shone his flashlight over the rotting wood and picked out a small brass plaque, which was tarnished to a dull, lifeless green and had *4b* etched into it. Labeaux switched on his camera and peered through the viewfinder. He had to bend slightly at the knees in order to focus through the door's rectangular, reinforced glass window to catch a glimpse into the classroom.

Of course there was nothing to see – the room beyond the grimy, cracked glass was as black as ink.

"Coming, ready or not," Labeaux spoke loudly and his voice boomed into the classroom. He wanted to fool Danny into thinking that the school wasn't *really* getting to him and he hoped that his powerful voice would scare away the various undesirable things that his overactive imagination had conjured up to torment him with.

Labeaux pushed at the door with his foot. Both the door and its frame had swollen with the years of damp and they clung to each other like doomed lovers who refused to be parted. Labeaux pushed again – harder this time – and the door gave a little. Encouraged by this, he gave another push, accompanied by a hefty kick and the door juddered its complaint and crashed open.

As he stepped forward into the classroom, Labeaux hit the switch for his camera's built-in light and its white brilliance lit up the place. He heard a faint scurrying sound and saw what he assumed to be a handful of rats scuttle away. They squeaked their high-pitched annoyance at him as they jostled away – hadn't he read somewhere that rats use *sonar* to see in the dark the same way as bats and dolphins? – and Labeaux could have sworn that the vermin were *cussing* him. Gone in the blink of an eye, all the rodents left behind were scattered droppings and their unmistakeable, earthy piss smell.

Oblivious to the rats that Labeaux's light had dispersed, Danny followed on into the classroom with his trusty flashlight and between that and Labeaux's camera, light was introduced to most of the room.

"This looks perfect for scene five," Danny's voice was subdued and seemed oddly out of place in a room more accustomed to the raucous noise of small children, "I'd like to get an ambient sound reading while we're here," he said, "if that's okay with you."

"Sure thing, boss – knock yourself out." Labeaux flashed a nervous smile and crept slowly across the room, shoes *squish-squish-squishing* on the sodden laminate floor as he panned his camera across the walls and up onto the ruined ceiling.

They discovered that 4b's classroom had fared little better against the ravages of time and moisture than the hallways, the gym and the few other rooms they'd peeked into so far. Its walls dripped with a reeking damp that stained the paint and had turned the drywall into something that reminded Labeaux of those provincial, crumbly French cheeses that stank like feet. Above them, the thin, Styrofoam tiles sagged and bulged downwards as if the false ceiling were some grotesque, pregnant thing about to give birth to something slippery and disgusting. A cluster of the tiles had fallen away in one corner to expose the roof's support beams, wrinkled, silver air conditioning ducts and the tangles of faded, multi colored wire that ran through the ceiling proper. The dank, black mould – omnipresent in its determination to take over the entire school – crept down along the walls and bloomed rich and dark and wet in the four corners of the classroom.

Stepping with great care around the diminutive tables and chairs, Labeaux swept his camera to and fro so best to capture the haphazard disarray of the furniture. The chairs, barely knee-height, had been scattered about the room and many of them were upended and lay like the skeletons of long dead, beached sea creatures. The small tables, askew from their once-uniform rows, were festooned with rotted picture books and crayons and glue pots and paints and curling paper that was adorned with the uncontrolled scrawl of second-graders' handwriting.

Labeaux turned his camera's attentive eye to the walls, keen to distract it – and himself – from the sight of furniture that had been upturned in a frenzy of blind panic.

The sight made him feel uneasy and, if he were to be truthful, just a little nauseated.

Like the walls of school rooms the world over, 4b's were decorated with a multitude of drawings and paintings and macaroni art (although the pasta itself was absent, no doubt food for the vermin that skulked *within* the walls. And, although the pigments in paint and crayon alike had run and smeared and seeped into one another across the years, Labeaux could see in his mind the once vibrant colors that had so vividly illustrated the children's imaginations; pictures of gangly stick people – on their own or grouped into little stick-families – dogs, cats, turtles and barely discernible, box-square houses sketched with wobbly walls and surrounded by erstwhile verdant lawns from which sprouted uniform trees and ginormous, people-high daisies; all under the watchful gaze of happy, smiling suns.

Behind Labeaux, Danny stood unmoving, mute with his microphone in hand and bulky headphones covering his ears. His face was a picture of strained concentration. He was recording the deathly silence in the classroom that would give them a base level from which they could measure dialogue and other sounds once filming started. It would also serve in post-production to cover over the unavoidable audio anomalies that befell any film shoots that weren't done with the benefit of a sound stage.

Happy with his recording of the *nothing* next to the whiteboard, Danny turned his attention to the silence in the corner opposite to where Labeaux was busy filming the sodden artwork that clung to the wall. As Danny spun around, his flashlight lit up something large that loomed from the shadows in the corner, something with a dozen long, broad arms and wicked, curled claws that reached for him from the dark.

"Shit!" Danny gasped and backed away.

Danny's startled inhalation caught Labeaux's attention and he turned on his heels. The light from his camera illuminated the paper silhouette of a multi-branched oak tree that was pinned to the classroom wall and stood floor-to-ceiling. The tree had a fat, wide trunk and arm-thick branches, some of which had peeled away from the decayed wall and reached out into the room like grasping fingers. The leaves of the tree were made up of the outlines of tiny hands that had been cut from thick green paper and upon each one there was a scrawled name. Labeaux remembered the hand-trees of his own school days, and just how proud he had been to have his name – and the outline of his hand – pinned up there for an entire academic year.

Danny let out the breath he'd been holding, along with a nervous chuckle. He was amazed at how much the school's ominous atmosphere had affected him, as normally he prided himself on being virtually unflappable.

Labeaux's camera light flittered from the tree and to an adjacent wall where it chased away the shadows from a collection of pictures that nestled there. "Sweet mother of God," he mumbled and lowered the camera from his shoulder to concentrate its light upon the artwork, "take a look at this, Danny."

Danny trudged over, microphone in hand. His knee knocked against one of the tiny chairs and it clattered against its neighbor with a sharp, metallic rattle.

Labeaux pointed to a picture in the center of the group, his hand trembling with more than the chill air. Pictured in crayon before them was a building that was undoubtedly Watsonville Elementary. Although the letter-sized sheet of paper that contained it had yellowed with age and curled with mildew, and the patches of thick crayon had soaked through the paper and bled into each other, the colors of the drawing somehow seemed ever so slightly *fresher* than those on the works elsewhere in room.

In front of the building there were the depictions of dozens of tiny stick-figure students and there amongst them, a long-haired figure toting a large gun that had been drawn to be almost the same size as its holder. From the muzzle of the gun was colored a flash of bright orange crayon. The children on the picture were running every which way with their little mouths fixed wide open and they held their skinny stick-arms aloft as they stepped over and upon their fallen classmates who lay on the schoolyard with puddles of red crayon spreading out from beneath their slender frames.

"Oh my –" Danny echoed Labeaux's dismay.

"Doesn't make sense," Labeaux said.

"The kid drew what he saw." Danny's attention was entirely absorbed by the picture. "None of it ever made sense."

"I get that, Danny," Labeaux looked at him. "But the school was evacuated *during* the shooting and the kids never came back." He screwed up his eyes and squinted closer at the picture.

There, framed in one of the school's windows was a little red face with tiny black horns and wicked, yellow eyes that peered out at the carnage.

The face was smiling.

"So who the fuck drew this?" Labeaux said.

A sound of scraping chairs and quickening footsteps came from the hallway outside the classroom and made them both start. Labeaux's breath snagged in his throat and he almost dropped his camera as he twisted his neck to see through the crooked doorway and into the darkness beyond. The unmistakable chirp of a child's laughter rang out through the dark and spread icy shivers down along his spine.

"What was that?" Danny whispered.

"No idea," Labeaux replied, "most likely somebody fucking with us." He shrugged and offered up what he hoped to be a reassuring smile. "Hello?" he called out and his voice boomed around and beyond the empty classroom. "Is that you, Dave?"

Silence.

"Did you pick anything up on that?" Labeaux nodded down to Danny's sound recorder.

Danny slipped the headphones down around his neck and unplugged the jack from the recorder. He rewound the tape and listened intently as tiny cogs whirred around within the machine with a sound reminiscent of bothersome gnats on a warm summer evening. Danny hit the play button once the tape had jarred back to its beginning.

"You sure you had it switched on?" Labeaux asked as they stood there in the gloom and listened to a whole lot of nothing.

"Positive," Danny checked and rechecked the settings on the recorder. He knew the equipment like he knew the back of his hand and he'd stake his life – and more importantly, his *reputation* – on the thing being set up correctly. "It's analogue, it should have picked up something," he informed Labeaux, "even ghosts."

"Ghosts?" Labeaux couldn't help but let out a nervous laugh. "Did you just say *ghosts*, Danny?"

"You never watched *Ghost Hunters*?" Danny's face was solemn. "They use analogue all the time to capture voices from the netherworld."

"And *that's* your point of reference?" Labeaux all but sneered in Danny's face. "A whole bunch of Z-list nobodies running around in supposedly haunted houses with their night-vision cameras and screaming every time their crew slams a door?" He smiled at Danny's serious countenance; the guy obviously took the show as gospel. "*Ooh*, I felt a cold presence there. Oh my God! The door closed all by itself!" Labeaux gave a fairly accurate emulation of the show's vacuous presenters. "Insert fake scream here," he giggled.

"Mock all you want, Maurice, but don't forget that they're paid stupid amounts of money *and* were just commissioned a sixth season on prime network TV for their trouble," Danny countered with a well aimed and barbed dig at Labeaux's lack of commissioned work.

Labeaux was forced to concede that one, Danny made a good point (sore though it was); as long as there were gullible folk like Danny George out there in their millions amongst the viewing public, shows like *Ghost Hunters* and its myriad copycats (a fourth season of *Bigfoot Hunters*, anyone?!) would continue to flourish.

"I wouldn't worry too much, it'll be Dave messing with us – he'll think he's being fucking funny," Labeaux growled.

"But if the recorder didn't pick anything up – and there's nothing wrong with the equipment, I can assure you – does that mean we *imagined* the noise?" Danny pressed, "you heard it too, right?"

"Yep," Labeaux nodded his head, "at least I *think* I heard something. Maybe this place has us more freaked out than we realize and we're experiencing mass hysteria or something."

"There are only two of us, Mo'," Danny said and smiled up at Labeaux with a faint quiver on his lips. "How can it be *mass* anything?"

Labeaux shrugged his shoulders once more and fiddled nervously with his camera. Damned if he knew what it was they'd heard if it *hadn't* been Priestley fucking with them, especially if Danny's ever-reliable equipment hadn't picked it up – although for all he knew, Danny was in on the gag too. All Labeaux wanted to do right now was to get the hell out of that classroom and back into some proper light, but his ego wouldn't allow him to show Danny just how edgy he'd become; the picture of the school with that smug, devilish, face staring out from the window had really thrown him a curve ball.

"Let's try it again." Danny clicked on the recorder and held the mic up to the center of the classroom. "Hello?" and *now* he sounded very much like a hokey boardwalk medium, his voice adopting the subdued tone that people deem essential when conversing with the dead. "Is there anybody there?"

At this, Labeaux tried to stifle a giggle. It shot out through his nose like a strained sneeze and Danny shot him a withering glance.

"Speak to me, oh restless spirits," Danny implored the cold air and then paused as if expecting a reply. "Okay, let's see if we got anything," he said and the suddenness of his voice in the silence startled Labeaux.

Danny thumbed the stop button, rewound the tape once more and hit play.

Again, nothing.

"Are you *sure* that thing's not broken?" Labeaux asked. "It didn't even pick up *your* voice."

"I tested it earlier in the gym," Danny's impatience crept through. "There's nothing wrong with the recorder, Maurice."

They listened a little longer as silence played from the machine until finally Danny switched the confounded thing off.

A shrill, blood-curdling scream pierced the darkened hallways.

Labeaux jumped back and thumped against the damp wall and Danny let out an audible *squeak* and dropped his microphone. They both stood there, immovable in fear as if waiting for something – *anything* – to happen next, for some hideous, unspeakable *thing* to slither out from the shadows and devour them.

Of course, that particular fear failed to materialize and before long they both felt a little stupid.

The scream remained singular and nothing emerged from the inky shadows to consume either their flesh or their mortal souls and Labeaux made a mental vow of retaliation for Dave Priestley's asinine pranks – his friend was pushing him just a little too far this time.

But as convinced as he was that Priestley was pranking him, Maurice Labeaux experienced a deep down unease that crept slowly around to the back of his mind that was something entirely unfamiliar.

"I think we have enough shots now," Labeaux broke the thick silence with a rumble in his deep voice that was menacing.

Danny said nothing and followed Labeaux from 4b with gratitude in his every step.

Out in the hallway Labeaux caught a fleeting movement in his peripheral vision. He spun his camera around in the hope of its light catching whatever – *whoever*, he checked himself – it was but he wasn't quick enough, the shape was all too quickly embraced by the murky shadows.

Somewhere in the darkness ahead of them, a lavatory flushed.

"What the hell was *that*?" Labeaux's patience had worn dangerously thin.

"You don't have flushing toilets at your house?" Danny's attempted humor fell somewhat flat.

"Fucking Dave fucking Priestley," Labeaux growled and strode with purpose in the direction of the sound, "I'm going to fucking *kill* him." He ground his teeth as he walked and was barely aware of Danny following close on his heels like a faithful, lolloping puppy dog. Labeaux was well and truly pissed that Priestley was trying (*trying?!*) to spook him, but was even more pissed that his friend was actually succeeding.

"I'll scare *his* sorry ass for this," Labeaux grumbled as he placed the camera on the floor outside the restroom door. Without so much of a *please* or a *thank you*, Labeaux snatched the flashlight from Danny's hand. "I'll be back in a minute," he said and pushed open the door with a clenched fist.

The sound of the lavatory cistern refilling reverberated around the tiny restroom, the *drip-drip-drip* of water on water pinging off of the three stalls, which served well to magnify it. The air in the restroom was cold and damp and tainted with the faintest hint of urine and disinfectant, the darkness heavy and oppressive.

Labeaux pulled open the first of the stall doors and shone the flashlight in with an aggressive thrust. Nothing lay within save a perfectly small toilet with its seat up and it looked like a bizarre deep-sea dweller waiting – mouth agape – for an unsuspecting fish to happen by. The cistern behind it had finished its filling and there was now only the irregular sound that the final drops of water made as they fell from the pipes.

Yanking open the door to the middle stall, Labeaux's light illuminated nothing out of the ordinary; another small toilet bowl (seat down this time) and an empty cardboard tube on a toilet roll holder. He gulped down a deep breath and began to wonder if perhaps what he'd seen out in the hallway had been little more than a conspiracy between the shadows and his own jangled nerves. Perhaps the toilet had flushed simply because the lavatories at Watsonville Elementary were of the self-flushing variety and not because of the mischievous deed of some evil toilet-spirit? As he pulled open the final door to yet another empty stall, Labeaux's mind took him back to his sister's son who was terrified of self-flushing toilets, ever since he'd sat on one at the age of three and it had flushed beneath him. The poor kid was eight now and would still rather pee his pants than go into a public restroom.

Labeaux sighed heavily and closed the cubicle door, at the same time chastising himself for being so goddamned gullible. He hoped he could rely on Danny to keep schtum about all of this; he'd hate it to get back to Priestley that for once he'd managed to put the willies up the supposedly imperturbable Maurice Labeaux.

Labeaux made the decision to *most definitely not* give Priestley the unknowing satisfaction of having him look in that third stall and he turned to go.

Caught in the harsh beam of Labeaux's flashlight, there was a face.

Sharp, angular and disembodied, the heinous visage floated at eye level and Labeaux saw rough skin that appeared like burned red parchment, a grinning, toothy maw, twin, black horns and piercing, golden eyes.

Labeaux uttered a low, strangled scream and stumbled backwards into the restroom's single tiny washbasin. Panic swept over him in a nauseous sheet and he grabbed at the basin with his free hand in order to steady himself. Beneath him, his feet scudded wildly, unable to find purchase on the wet floor, and his body slid to one side and he almost toppled into the grotesque face that mocked him with its rictus grin.

The flashlight tumbled from Labeaux's hand as he lost the struggle to maintain his balance and it smashed on the slippery tiles, the light snuffed out in an instant and the restroom was smothered with the oppressive darkness.

CHAPTER EIGHT

Priestley was busy putting the finishing touches to the black Duck-Tape pentagram he'd created in the dead center of the gymnasium when Labeaux and Danny returned. He gave them both a perfunctory glance and thought to himself that they both looked more than a little dishevelled.

"Hey, guys!" he called over. "I hope you found us some cool locations." With meticulous care, he cut off a twelve-inch strip from the stocky roll of tape with a pair of black handled scissors, making sure that the severed end was neatly squared off.

"Yeah, Dave," Danny replied with a strained tone to his voice, "like you wouldn't fuckin' believe." He cracked a crooked smile as he made his way past Priestley and his neat pentagram.

The flashlight that Labeaux had dropped and broken dangled loosely from Danny's fingertips as he walked, as if it were a filthy thing that disgusted him. He'd retrieved it from the restroom floor when he'd gone in to help Labeaux following the ruckus; he'd burst in to find the big guy slumped against the wall adjacent to the wash basin, his pants soaking up the wet from the slick floor as he groped around in the dark to retrieve the busted flashlight. Labeaux had explained to Danny that he'd lost his footing on the slippery tiles but the scream Danny had heard – along with the haunted look in the cameraman's eyes – had told a much different story.

"We picked out a few possibles," Labeaux's voice was quiet, "depends on just how dark and scary you want to get with this thing." Already Labeaux was well on the way to convincing himself that what he'd seen – *thought* he'd seen – in the restroom had been either his mind playing tricks on him, or another one of his friend's poor-taste jokes at his expense. He'd sworn Danny to absolute secrecy – *'I don't want the motherfucker to know he got one over on me'* – as he'd so eloquently put it.

Labeaux looked around in the comfort of the glaring lights that created semi-daylight in the gymnasium. He saw Ashlynn, Chris and Carolyn in their canvas chairs reading scripts, Priscilla prowling around Priestley with her enquiring minicam, and he told himself that yes, he may well have imagined the entire incident after all.

"As dark and scary as we *can* get, Mo'," Priestley said as he smoothed down an errant piece of black tape that had curled up on one of the points of his pentagram, "I want the audience to piss in their popcorn when they watch our movie."

"Then I think you'll be more than delighted," Labeaux was deadpan, not really in much of a mood to engage in banal banter.

Labeaux stepped around Priestley and followed Danny over to the mound of equipment on the table where he was busy picking out a fresh flashlight – luckily Danny had had the foresight to bring along plenty of spares – and hoped that Danny would have the good sense to double check his equipment before they started shooting for real; he'd much rather avoid any potential issues with substandard sound, along with Priestley's inevitable tantrums should that dare to occur.

Priestley smoothed down that final strip of tape and stood back to admire his handiwork. The pentagram was of precisely measured proportions and sat in an exact circle of precisely six feet, six and six tenths inches, created by a multitude of small lengths of tape so that its outline appeared even and smooth. The lines of the pentagram within the circle, Priestley had constructed from single strips of black tape, each one neatly sliced at its ends and pressed firmly down on to the clammy floor. In the center of the pentagram, Priestley had positioned a Ouija board that looked fresh out of the box, a brace of black candles and a pewter chalice, the latter's metal sides dented and dulled with age.

Delighted with his handiwork, Priestley rummaged around in his backpack and pulled out a large, oval something wrapped tight in a faded front sheet of *USA Today* dominated by a large color picture of Sarah Palin. With the greatest of care, Priestley peeled away the newspaper to expose the human skull that nestled within. He stepped cautiously into the circle, avoiding the Duck-Tape lines as a superstitious kid would avoid cracks in the sidewalk (*step on a crack, break your mother's back!*) and he placed the skull between the black candles. Shaking his head, Priestley then moved the skull a fraction of an inch to the left. The chalice, he placed in front of the skull and a tad closer to the north point of the pentagram. He then shifted the Ouija board an almost imperceptible distance closer to the chalice and finally, Priestley appeared satisfied that all was as it should be.

With a conceited smile, Priestley stepped out of the circle, once again each step carefully placed so as to avoid the black tape. He picked up the retractable tape measure that lay un-retracted alongside the five-pointed star and flicked the switch on its side. The tape rattled back into its metal casing like a skittish metal snake and the harsh rasping sound it made drew everyone's attention.

"Okay, people," Priestley announced – he really did have no concept of just how much his overuse of that particular phrase irritated everyone – "it's time to get this show on the road!"

All eyes upon him, Priestley resumed his role of ringmaster, "if we could all gather 'round, I'd like to get started," he adopted his *professional voice;* the one he always used when sharing his single-minded vision with cast and crew.

Clutching their scripts like security blankies, Ashlynn, Chris and Carolyn left the relative comfort of their canvas chairs – shadowed by Priscilla with her increasingly intrusive camera – and sauntered over to where Priestley stood by the pentagram. They too made sure not to step onto the circle and each one of them stared with unease at the hollow-eyed skull – and it seemed to be staring right back at them. Taking Priestley's not so subtle direction, Danny and Labeaux tore themselves away from Equipment Mountain and joined the cosy gathering.

"Before you get started, Dave," Carolyn half-raised her arm like a school kid needing the bathroom. "I have a question."

"Can we save questions until the end, please?" Priestley deflected, "I don't want to lose my thread here." This was bullcrap of course, what he *really* didn't want were the inevitable dumb questions to which his answer would invariably be *because I said so*. He smiled at Carolyn and she lowered her arm. Priestley took in a breath and continued, "now that you guys are familiar with the script, you can see where I – err – *we* intend to go with this one."

The thespian contingents nodded in unison and exchanged glances. Chris was the one to speak up, with a tone to his voice that was bordering upon confrontational. "*So*, if I'm reading this right, we're just a bunch of people who break into an abandoned school to film ourselves bringing a serial killer back from the dead." He fluttered his script towards Priestley, just in case anyone thought he might have been referring to something else.

Priestley gritted his teeth to fight back the exasperation that bubbled up inside of him like painful gas. "That's a question, Chris," he did his level best to keep the annoyance out of his voice; it would be bad form to stir up bad feelings this early on in the proceedings, "cleverly disguised as a statement – I'll grant you – but a question nonetheless. And what did I just say about questions?" There was a faint waft of laughter and a couple of smiles from the team. Priestley congratulated himself having diffused Chris's insubordination with a little of the old Dave Priestley charm.

"To clarify, our characters are merely attempting to *communicate* with the killer's spirit," Priestley explained for everyone's benefit, "nowhere in the script is *anyone* brought back from the dead." Once more, Priestley found himself fighting to maintain what little patience he possessed, *had these people not read the fucking script?* "And because Carolyn's character's Mom was one of the killer's victims and her body was never found, her *motive* is to ask his spirit where he hid it," Priestley paused to let that information sink in; he'd worked with enough acting-types over the years to know that they could be a difficult – and sometimes downright stupid – lot.

"Got that?" Priestley gave Chris his warmest smile.

Chris nodded and leafed through his script with a self-conscious blush on his cheeks. Yet another one of the cast put back in their box, metaphorically speaking.

"And *your* character kills himself when the killer's spirit possesses him, because he knows that he will be a danger to the others," Priestley told Chris, just in case the dimwit had missed *that* point in the script as well. Priestley fished around in his backpack and pulled out his Swiss

Army knife – shiny red casing with a neat little white cross on it – "You'll need this to slit your own throat with later – catch." He tossed the knife to Chris who snatched it one-handed from the air with the ease of a seasoned ballplayer.

Chris turned the knife over in his palm and immediately began pulling out its multitude of blades. "Thanks," he mumbled as he pried out the odd looking attachment that was apparently designed for gouging stones out from horses' hooves.

"But… if our characters are trying to communicate with the killer's ghost, why all the Black Mass and devil stuff?" Carolyn asked the question she'd raised her arm for only minutes before, obviously forgetting Priestley's previous request to the contrary.

"Because the killer is in Hell, I thought that I'd made *that* quite clear in the script," now Priestley's frustration shone through loud and clear. He knew that his script was a good one, a piece of work that was way above the exacting standards that had previously won him awards and a little paid work, so why were these nimrods finding it so difficult to comprehend? It had all made perfect sense to *him* when he'd written it; the satanic stuff was to entice the killer's spirit back from the fiery pits of hell, the real human skull was in lieu of a sacrifice and the Black Mass they were going to perform was to draw the killer's soul back into their world – they could all read, did he really have to *explain* it to them as well?

The whole thing was all there in black and white, twelve-point Courier, in front of their dumb-ass noses, just how fucking difficult could it be?

"But surely the Black Mass is a *satanic* ritual, Dave," Ashlynn threw in her two cent's worth Priestley could have done well without, "what you have detailed here is essentially just a séance"

"No, it is *not* a séance," Priestley growled at his girlfriend, "our characters will be performing the Black Mass because the killer is now a *demon* who's been banished to the darkest bowels of Hades."

"Can't be, dude," Labeaux added in *his* two cents, "demons are denizens of hell who have never been human. They're a different species altogether, Dave." Of everyone in the room, Labeaux was the one Priestley had thought could be relied upon for unconditional support. What was this, National Deride Dave Priestley Day or something?

"Give me fucking strength!" Priestley's eruption was met with startled, if somewhat amused stares. He took one more calming gulp of air and worked hard to contain his temper. "Look, guys – I have gone to a great deal of trouble to be as authentic as I can with this," he said, "the chalice for the Host was stolen from a Catholic church, the candles have been blessed by a *genuine* black magician and the pentagram is laid out precisely as instructed by Ravenscroft." He fixed Labeaux with a stare. "Even the fucking skull is real." Priestley forced a strained smile. "So can you *please* grant me just a *little* creative licence?" Priestley looked around at the lowered faces; he'd done what he did best and bullied them all into submission – the artistic temperament outbursts usually did the trick.

And now Priestley was back to happy again.

Despite the slight deviation from fact, Priestley knew that performing an actual Black Mass inside Watsonville Elementary would look far better on film than some clichéd, round the table séance with all of your *'knock once for yes and twice for no'* bullshit.

Unsurprisingly, it was Carolyn who jumped to Priestley's defence, albeit a little late in the day, "Dave's got a good point, guys." She elicited a bitchy sideways glance from Ashlynn for her trouble. "We all want this movie to look good, right?" Everyone had little choice but to agree with the rhetorical question. "So perhaps we should put our confidence in Dave and that he knows how to shoot a damned good film.”

“Thank you, Carolyn,” Priestley was grateful for her support; he hadn’t anticipated any form of reluctance from his team so he was grateful for *any* support he could garner, even if it had earned him a dirty look or two from Ashlynn. He scanned his team’s faces and saw the comforting, familiar look of compliance as it crept amongst them.

“Okay, people, we should all know the script by heart now, and I’ll assume that everyone is deliriously happy with their characters.” Priestley was keen to close down the meeting before anyone else came up with a stupid question that would serve only to waste more of his precious time. “Then I think we should get started on scene one at the school’s entrance.”

Eager to get moving, Priestley’s plan was to have the initial scenes and the Black Mass ritual in the can that first night and then have all of Saturday to shoot the remainder of the script – none of which would happen if his cast insisted on dissecting its every word.

“Okay, let’s make a movie, people!” Priestley gave them his signature rallying cry in the jolliest voice he could muster. This was met with the prerequisite *whoops* and cheers as the group disbanded to prepare for filming.

Relieved to have that necessary evil over and done with – Priestley always hated the pep-talk part of any shoot, he often wished he could just transmit his ideas telepathically – he picked up his backpack and shoved the tape measurer into one of the side pockets. He took great care to zip up the pocket, he’d borrowed the measurer from his father without asking and the old man would be furious if it went missing because, apparently it had some kind of sentimental value. A strange guy was David Priestley Snr.

“It *looks* real.” Danny sidled up to Priestley.

“Eh?”

"That." Danny pointed at the grinning skull that sat in the center of the pentagram.

"I wasn't joking when I *said* it was real, Danny."

"Where on earth did you get a real human skull from? I thought it was illegal to buy human parts in Texas." Although perturbed, Danny seemed suitably impressed.

"It is illegal. So let's keep it between these four walls, Danny," Priestley lowered his voice, "I found a guy through the Onion who sells all kind of weird shit," he explained; Priestley's love of the Dark Web was certainly no secret amongst his inner circle, "even the illegal stuff."

"So you just placed an order on the Internet and now you own somebody's head?" Danny appeared to be dumbfounded by the very concept.

Nope, Priestley had driven all the way to fucking New Orleans for that particular privilege.

*

It was kind of cool how he'd become the proud owner of another man's head bones.

After seemingly endless to-ing and fro-ing via clandestine phone calls and cryptic messages through a ridiculous number of dummy e-mail accounts, Priestley had finally made his trip over to Louisiana. There, he'd been surprised to find that after his nine-hour drive, the store had been nothing like he'd expected.

To judge the place by the grainy picture on the front of the poorly photocopied stock list he'd been emailed by the proprietor, Priestley had expected to find some archetypal, dingy little voodoo store in the back streets of the French Quarter; one of those with dusty velvet curtains draped across the doorway and heaps of fading voodoo paraphernalia in the window display – a facsimile of Marie Laveaux's store he'd seen in countless advertisements for the seamier side of the Big Easy.

Instead, he'd found the store a little way off of Bourbon Street and Lafayette and it was a clean, modern looking business with a legitimate shop front adorned with a neat display of specimen jars of varying sizes and shapes that contained an array of pickled animals from frogs to snakes to piglets, all destined to float forever in their sealed, formaldehyde tombs.

The store had no name above the door. Instead, there stretched a banner across the window that read *'human material for medical and educational use only'*. After the innumerable correspondences he'd enjoyed with the store's owner, Priestley understood that this notification was for the benefit of the general public and any government agencies that may deem it necessary to take an inquisitive sniff around; for in this emporium one could buy practically *anything*, providing one knew the right questions to ask.

Upon entering the store and introducing himself to the smartly-suited assistant who in turn introduced him to the owner – a swarthy looking individual with distinctly Eastern European features – Priestley had signed something to the effect that declared himself to be Dean of Biology at some small, obscure Texas college, handed over his eighteen hundred bucks in cash (naturally) and the skull was his.

The store's owner had taken the time to explain that the skull was Chinese in origin, that it was around two hundred years old and was an especially prized specimen as it contained its full compliment of teeth (which certainly begged a question or two regarding dental care in nineteenth century China). Priestley had been eager to learn more about his acquisition but there had been something in the proprietor's countenance that had warned him that it was probably best not to ask.

Once the transaction had been completed and Priestley was complicit with the more nefarious aspects of the store's business, he was led over to a narrow, unassuming door that stood at the rear of the showroom. The owner punched in a five-digit code on the pad and swung open the door.

Immediately Priestley was transported into a hellish world of elaborately fashioned artefacts, statuettes of gnarled, inhuman looking things, leather-bound books – ancient and new – by the shelf-load, of intricately carved knives with wicked, curved blades, shrivelled, withered things, strange looking potions in tiny glass bottles and myriad human body parts – both pickled and mummified. And whereas the front part of the store had been spotless and had the clean, clinical smell of preservative, this back room – although scrupulously clean – invaded Priestley's nose with the earthy undertones of damp soil, decay and sewers.

"Wow," was all he'd been able to say.

"You will find what you are looking for in here," the proprietor had advised him with that clipped voice of his, "we have *everything*."

Awestruck, Priestley wandered about the strange room that to him more resembled the showroom of some *Avant-garde* jewellery store than a purveyor of the occult. And as he walked around like a little kid lost in a toy store, the owner (who, Priestley realized later during his long drive home, had not once offered his name) had explained that this part of the enterprise was his main interest, and that the educational supply business was *quite literally* a front for this less than legitimate trade (he'd chuckled lightly at the pun), as more and more of his clientele were interested in body parts, books and all the paraphernalia necessary for dabbling in what he'd referred to as the Dark Arts. He was a man most knowledgeable in the subject and had patiently answered Priestley's questions for well over an hour before suggesting a number of choice items for purchase.

"I would very much recommend this particular volume, Sir," he'd placed an especially antiquated book into Priestley's hands with all of the care one would exercise in handing over a newborn baby, "it makes the perfect compliment to the *Satanic Bible*."

Priestley had picked the latter volume from the shelf himself, along with a couple of books that dealt with the more practical aspects of the satanic rituals. The *Bible* – in contrast to the ancient book the owner had offered – was black and shiny and smelled new, and when Priestley had checked the price on the musty old book he'd almost choked.

"The price reflects the efficacy of the book, Sir," the proprietor had assured him, "trust me when I say that you will not be disappointed." And for the first time during Priestley's visit (and the penultimate, as it transpired) the proprietor had smiled.

Priestley had bought the book – how could he have not? – on the *Amex* card his father had given him for emergencies. And along with it, he'd procured the other books, the pewter chalice, a handful of other accoutrements that the proprietor insisted he would require, and something that wouldn't have looked out of place in a BDSM store but was of an altogether more practical use.

"Many of our more *serious* collectors favor this particular item, Sir," the proprietor had told Priestley as he'd jangled the weird looking thing in front of his face, "it has become quite our best seller." Then came that final smile and without hesitation, Priestley had paid for everything the man had suggested.

*

"So I picked up a few extra books and things while I was there for the skull," Priestley told Danny. He pulled a trio of books out from his backpack and Danny thought he heard something jangle in there. The books were modern day versions of the *Satanic Bible, Satanic Rituals: The Black Mass & Others* (Danny was quite disappointed, he'd imagined that *all* occult books had to be variations on Lovecraft's ancient and gnarled *Necronomicon*) and an older, leather bound book the size of a pocket Bible that Danny couldn't quite make out the title of.

"Must have cost you a small fortune," Danny observed, "especially that old one."

"Don't ask," Priestley said with a grimace, "my Dad's gonna have apoplexy when he gets his *Amex* statement – I just hope this is all worth it." As Priestley pushed the books back into his backpack Danny noted that he handled the antique volume as if he really didn't want to – as if the touch of its rough, crumbling cover was repulsive to him. He also appeared to be going to great lengths to conceal something that was secreted in the backpack – the jangling thing perhaps?

"Still, eighteen hundred bucks is a shit load of cash for a skull," Danny said, more to break the silence between them than anything else, "couldn't you have just bought a plastic one?"

"It's like I've always said, Danny-Boy," Priestley grinned as he shouldered the backpack and made his way towards the gymnasium door, "with me, everything has to be one-hundred per cent, no-shit authentic."

CHAPTER NINE

It was dark outside the school, and more than a little chilly in the tight wind that buffeted in from the North. Of the group, Carolyn looked especially icy in her flimsy cotton dress, every inch of her bare arms and legs was covered in angry gooseflesh, and her teeth were starting to chatter.

Priestley looked around, nervous. He was painfully aware of how exposed they all were standing as they were outside of Watsonville Elementary (*the* Watsonville Elementary!), and his paranoia taunted that people from miles around would be able to see exactly what they were up to. Although he'd made the decision to film the opening scenes using only the built in lights of the camera – the free standing lights would illuminate most of the immediate neighborhood and definitely draw unwelcome attention – should anyone happen by whilst they were shooting, you could bet your bottom dollar that the cops would be along in the time it took to make a busybody cell-phone call; no one in Watsonville liked people messing with their school.

"Can we hurry it up, please?" Priestley urged, "all we have to do is make the establishing shots and intro' the characters, it really shouldn't be taking us this long to set up." There was a hint of desperation in Priestley's voice, which he hoped, hadn't been picked up by the others; he couldn't afford to show any sign of weakness – film crews, like angry dogs, could smell fear a mile away.

Priestley knew from experience that the first scene of a movie – any movie – *always* took the longest to shoot. There were cameras to fiddle with, lighting to get just so, sound levels to tweak, a crew to get to know each other's working style and nervous actors to remember their goddamned lines; there was that inevitability about the whole long-winded process. One of the first movies Priestley had made had an opening scene – less than a minute long – outdoors and it had taken a full four hours to get it in the can. In that time the pleasantly warming morning sun had transformed itself into a brutal heat that had burnt the back of Priestley's neck so badly he'd wound up in A&E the following day.

"Ready when you are, boss," Labeaux said and turned his camera around to shine its light square in Priestley's face.

Priestley winced and covered his eyes with his script. It never ceased to astound him the sheer amount of wattage a camera-mounted light could blaze out. And it also never ceased to amaze just how much of a dick Maurice Labeaux could be when he had a lady to impress.

Moving away from the harsh stare of Labeaux's camera, Priestley tucked his script into his back pocket and positioned Chris, Ashlynn, Carolyn and Danny on their marks a little way down along the school's walkway. He'd gauged the distance to be far enough to give them a reasonable walk up to the school but not too close to the road to risk being seen should anyone drive by.

Meanwhile, Labeaux busied himself with filming a wide, sweeping shot of the school's facade, even though most of it was stifled by the night.

"Do we all have our lines down?" Priestley asked his cast. This was greeted with a half-assed nod from each one of them and he knew at that point that this was unlikely to be a one-take scene.

"Camera, ready!" Priestley raised his voice and Labeaux swung around to focus on him and the other actors. Priscilla, for her part, kept her camera fixed firmly on Priestley.

"*The Black Mass* – scene one, take one," Priestley announced and clapped his hands together to emulate the clapboard that Danny had forgotten to pack. "And – *action*!"

Danny clicked on his flashlight and the five began their slow walk towards the school, every step followed by Labeaux's camera.

"Jeez, Mr. Anderer, it's *really* good of you to help me find my Mom's body," Carolyn delivered her line with professional aplomb.

"It's my pleasure, young lady" Chris replied, a little wooden on the delivery but at least it was word-perfect. "And please, call me Phil."

It was Danny who laughed first and sadly, this was somewhat foreseeable. Priestley rolled his eyes as he called *cut*.

"Sorry, man," Danny snickered. "I just got that. The joke name, it really is quite funny." Danny's laugh was contagious and soon everyone giggled along, even Chris who was still smarting from being lumbered with the idiotic name in the first place.

And thus the tension, and along with it *The Curse of the First Scene* was lifted. Priestley felt everyone relax as they repositioned on their respective spots along the path, even Ashlynn who was always as nervous as hell in front of the camera. And there was a warm feeling in Priestley's gut that told him that this was all going to turn out just dandy.

"Let's go again," Priestley reined them in once the giggling fits had subsided. "Once more from the top. *The Black Mass*. Scene One, take two. *Action*!"

Once again, they walked towards the school and the cold, white glare of Labeaux's camera light lit up the ghostly plumes of their breath in the chilled air.

"Jeez, Mr. Anderer," Carolyn said. "It's really good of you to help me find my Mom's body."

Perfect.

"My pleasure, young lady," Chris's line was delivered with a tad more credibility than before as he settled into character. "And please, do call me Phil." There was the slightest of pauses as everyone anticipated Danny's giggle fit. However, much to everyone's surprise, he managed to retain his composure and the laughter failed to materialise. Priestley was especially relieved by this; he'd be able to edit out the minor pause in postproduction.

"Okay, Phil it is," Carolyn smiled and pushed out her chest. "And thank you again for buying us dinner, I *love* tacos."

"Yeah, thanks, Phil," Ashlynn added with just the right amount of sarcasm in her voice. "Although I do think that the cheese and egg with salsa has given me heartburn." She made with an exaggerated rub of her chest. "I really wish I hadn't eaten that," Ashlynn delivered the contest-required line unerringly and Priestley allowed himself an inward sigh of relief now that it was safely out of the way; two of the mandatory elements were thusly checked off.

They covered the short distance to the school's main doors in a dozen or so steps. Labeaux had manoeuvered himself to the side of the group as they walked, to frame them all in shot, himself circled by Priscilla and her minicam.

"Well, here we are at the school," Danny said as he tried his best not to look directly into the camera, or at

Carolyn's nipples that had reacted most aggressively to the cold air. "It sure does look creepy." He placed his hand on the left-hand door and paused.

"Are you scared, buddy?" Priestley then made with the chicken clucking sounds he'd written into the script and which he performed remarkably well. "It's just an old school."

"It's the school where the Watsonville Hacker killed eight people, including my Mom," Carolyn said her lines with conviction; Priestley could even hear the quiver in her voice (although that may actually have been more due to the cold than good acting).

"They say that because the cops killed him here, his spirit haunts the building to this very day," Chris's woodenness had completely vanished and one could just about believe that he *was* the ridiculously named Phil Anderer.

"Say, Mr. Anderer, you do seem to know an awful lot about the serial killer for a biochemist," Ashlynn delivered her line right on cue.

Ah, clumsy exposition, thought Priestley. That most ubiquitous friend of screenwriters and last bastion of the director – where would they all be without it?

"I guess I do," Chris said with a subtle hint of mystery in his voice, "shall we go in?" He reached over Danny and pushed open both of the school's main doors with a dramatic flourish.

Chris strode into the school's dark interior, followed closely by the others who maintained the formation. Labeaux remained outside and filmed as the actors were swallowed one by one by the shadowy gloom within the school and the double doors eased shut with a rusty squeak and a low, ominous *clang* behind them.

"Cut!" Priestley shouted from inside. "Can you put the lights back on now, Danny?" he asked.

As Danny fiddled with some switch or other he'd rigged up to operate the film lights in the hallway, Priestley allowed himself to relax a little; relieved to be in from the biting cold and the ever present risk of discovery. That relief became complete when the lights sprang to life with an electrical *thud* and once more brightness reclaimed a small part of Watsonville Elementary.

"How did that look?" Priestley asked Labeaux as the cameraman made his way in through the doors.

"Pretty good," Labeaux replied as he strode into the hallway with Priscilla close behind. The main doors closed behind them both and narrowly missed thumping Priscilla on her shapely ass. Labeaux gave Priestley a thumbs-up and a grin. "Could have done with a little more light though," he said.

"I was thinking it would be more atmospheric if we just used the camera light," Priestley told him, "is the footage usable?"

"If it's dark and creepy you're going for, then yep, I'd say it was usable."

"Perfect." Priestley beamed and everyone let out an audible sigh – they wouldn't have to do the first scene a third time. Dave Priestley was well known for his perfectionism and had not garnered the moniker Twelve-Take Priestley for nothing.

"Now, if we can just shoot some footage of everyone walking around." Priestley plucked the script from his pocket and raised it above his head for emphasis. "Right up to when we hear the noise."

"Do we have a cue for the noise?" Ashlynn asked, "I'm assuming that you'll add it in post - production."

"That's the plan, my lover." Priestley snaked an arm around Ashlynn's waist and gave her a squeeze. He felt her body stiffen and he removed his arm pronto; not entirely sure if she'd just invoked the *'no PDA while we're working'* clause in their relationship or whether she was still pissed at him over Carolyn's L.A. thing. "You think you could you give us a noise to react to at the appropriate moment, Mo'?" he asked Labeaux.

"I think I can just about manage that, Dave," his friend's reply was sardonic. Labeaux tipped a wink at Priscilla and she smiled.

Priestley called *action!* once more and he and his fellow actors made their way along the hallway whilst Labeaux filmed and made sure to commit to film every peeling poster, rotted curl of paint and smudge of mould that clung to the crumbling walls like some virulent disease. Priestley, Danny, Ashlynn and Carolyn made like they were studying the decay for the very first time as they followed Chris past the main office and into the bathrooms.

Chris pushed open the door to the boy's bathroom with hesitance, as if the touch of the warped wood offended him. The door – bowed into a gentle bow from years of damp – groaned open and light from the hallway crept in.

They followed Chris into the bathroom, in turn trailed by Labeaux and the welcome glow from his camera's light. The door closed and they stood in silence as Labeaux filmed the child-height washbasins, and then the diminutive toilets that crouched in each one of the three stalls.

Labeaux glanced around with some trepidation, the memory of his encounter in the restroom all too fresh. His sneakers squelched softly in the puddles of water on the tiled floor as he stalked around the restroom to capture the *Please Wash Your Hands* poster, half-empty paper towel holder and the rotted toilet rolls that held quiet vigil on the plastic spindles adjacent to each of the lavatories.

"I can't believe that I'm actually in the place where Mom died – it's like I can feel her presence," Carolyn's voice was dulled by the confined space.

"She could still be here," Danny spoke up, "I heard that the killer buried some of his victims around the school."

He injected just a *soupcon* too much Peter Cushing for Priestley's liking, although that would be easily sorted in editing.

"He's right," Chris delivered, he always came into his own playing that guy in every movie that elucidates the various plot nuances and generally keeps things moving along for the benefit of the audience, "perhaps her soul still walks these very corridors looking for release. If so, I hope that we can help your Mom to find her peace tonight."

Labeaux blew a loud raspberry and on cue all of the actors jumped as if startled.

Carolyn grabbed Priestley's arm and pressed herself into his side. "Did you hear that?" she asked with a tremble in her voice.

"It sounded like – like someone laughing," Ashlynn replied. Her face portrayed fear although she struggled not to laugh.

Labeaux blew another raspberry that sounded far too real and everyone cracked up. Priestley tried to be annoyed at the interruption and break of character, but farts had always amused him and he simply couldn't help himself but join in with the belly laughs.

Something small and dark scurried between them and out through the door.

"What the hell was that?" Carolyn jumped for real as the small shape hauled ass across the hallway and sped off into the office opposite.

As if in reply, they heard a faint mewl from across the hallway.

"Aww, it sounds like a kitty cat," Ashlynn said and before anyone could say a thing, she'd snatched Danny's flashlight and was on her way out of the restroom and across the hallway.

Priestley rolled his eyes,—it was a good job Ashlynn wasn't there to see him do that, it was one habit of his that she *truly* hated.—He had yet to fathom how come his girlfriend could be such a ball-busting bitch, yet would consistently crumble into a gooey mess at the sight of a small, furry animal with take-me-home eyes and a wet nose? If it hadn't been for her allergies, Priestley was positive that Ashlynn would have filled her home with countless wayward puppies and kittens by now, and be well on her way towards being one of those crazy ladies on *Animal Hoarders*.

"Really?" Danny sighed loudly for effect, pleased that for once he wasn't the one to be holding things up.

Ashlynn ignored him and made her way into the administration office, playing the flashlight beam to and fro to banish shadows from some of its darkened corners only to create them in others.

"Here kitty, kitty, kitty," Ashlynn called out in her sweetest tone as she stepped cautiously across the room. Her light picked out the peeling veneer of the laminate counter top that once had been the barrier between grown-up staff and the marauding hordes of little people; it sported a long-dead, bonsai ficus and was scattered with sodden tardy slips, which had spilled onto the floor like a pale yellow waterfall. On the desk behind the counter sat an ancient IMB computer – its bulky, cathode ray monitor had been old hat even back in its day – and next to that, an age-yellowed telephone that had rung off the hook on July the second, nine years ago.

The phone had remained silent ever since.

Ashlynn turned around and the edge of her light's beam caught the amber reflection of wide, feline eyes and she froze. The eyes shone huge and unblinking in the dark, and hovered twelve inches or so above her head – way too high for any kitten she'd expected to find.

Breathing hard, Ashlynn stepped backwards towards the counter and with one hand she groped around for the lift up section that would get her to the other side. She flicked her flashlight beam away from the golden sparkle of the eyes, not daring to confront what may have lurked behind them, yet too damned stubborn to run or cry out for help.

Ashlynn's hand located the gap in the counter and she ducked behind it with all the grace of a seasoned hunter. There she crouched and listened to her own laboured breathing and racing heartbeat. Ashlynn reproached herself, she knew she was acting stupid; the school had her freaked out and she was imagining things - that was all.

But she hadn't *imagined* those terrible, staring orbs. They were the fixed, intense eyes of horrendous creatures that prowled around in the shadows and called the darkest of nights home; the slobbering, rabid and insane things of nightmares.

"What the fuck are you?" Ashlynn muttered to herself and it was a comfort to hear a voice, albeit her own.

Ashlynn took in a deep breath to steady her nerves and quieten her pounding heart. Gingerly, she forced herself to peek around the sanctuary of the counter and she trained Danny's flashlight once more upon those hellish eyes.

The flashlight's shaky beam darted about the office and alighted upon the ugly, snarling face that was home to those golden eyes, its mouth gurning wide open and ragged, and curled lips revealed vicious, curved fangs in a red, glistening maw.

"You bastard," Ashlynn grunted as she studied the bobcat that she had pinned by her light. It was perched up on the wall in a glass case with its fat paws secured to the fake grass glued to its base.

Ashlynn let out a thin, strained laugh and suddenly felt rather foolish – boy was she glad now that she'd not shouted for help! The long-abandoned Watsonville Elementary School mascot (*Go Bobcats!*) stared down at Ashlynn with its cold, glass eyes. And looking at it now, with its mouth fixed in a permanent snarl like that,

Ashlynn thought that the wild cat actually appeared more pissed off than ferocious. She felt a pang of sympathy for the thing, frozen in its prime by a hunter's bullet, stuffed with sawdust and mounted in a hermetically sealed case – although on the plus side, it *was* perpetually immune to the death and decay that was going on around it.

If only that immunity had been afforded the students; the stray thought flashed into Ashlynn's mind and the sudden sting of tears blurred her vision.

She heard the mewling sound again. This time it came from beneath the roller-chair that had once supported the school secretary's formidable backside as she'd *tap-tap-tapped* away at the IBM.

"There you are." Ashlynn walked towards the sound and the tiny shape that trembled beneath the chair. "How would you like to come home with Ash –"

The kitten darted out from beneath the chair with a terrified squeak and scampered off towards the rear of the office. Ashlynn tried to follow it with her flashlight but it was far too quick for her and instantly vanished within the dark room. Then the faint keening started up again from somewhere in the vicinity of the beige bulk of the photocopier; the kitten sounded truly scared and Ashlynn felt bad at having given the poor thing such a fright.

"I'm sorry, kitty," Ashlynn cooed, "I'm only trying to help you." She took short, quiet steps towards the photocopier, her ears tuned in to the kitten's cries. Being Ashlynn, she'd given little thought as to what to do with the cat once she'd caught it, what with a movie to shoot and her being allergic to practically anything with fur. However, such practicalities were not about to come between Ashlynn Jones and a cute, fluffy kitten that needed her help.

Abruptly, the mewling ceased and the office fell back into silence.

Ashlynn crept forwards.

"There you are." Ashlynn picked up a movement in the dark and shone her light between the copier and an overflowing wastebasket.

A huge, bristling rat stared back at her. Frozen by the sudden appearance of light, it perched atop the mangled remains of a small, tabby kitten. The rat glowered at Ashlynn, its nose still buried deep in the kitten's body, its fur matted wet with blood.

Ashlynn shrieked and staggered back as the rodent burst to life and scurried between her legs, its naked tail snaking behind it, and Ashlynn felt the coarseness of its fur scrape her calves.

In the tight gap between the copier and waste basket the rat had left behind the bloodied remains of the butchered kitten; the tiny corpse a mess of blood, tattered fur and spilled viscera, its head laying a few inches away in a dark, spreading puddle as its paws twitched with their final reflexes, pinprick claws curling in and out.

Ashlynn gagged and turned her flashlight away and towards the door to illuminate her escape.

The rat – the biggest Ashlynn had ever seen in her life at almost half the size of the Watsonville Bobcat – stood by the door with its snout twitching and dripping with gore and its eyes reflecting dark red in the light. It chattered its curved, yellow incisors in admonishment before turning tail to scamper off into the hallway with a lazy, bounding gait.

And Ashlynn would swear later that she'd been able to hear the rat's monstrous feet slip-slapping on the tiles long after she'd no longer been able to see it.

*

It smelled the sudden and sharp tang of fear, the sour stink of adrenalin and panic sweat.

Sweeping aside the darkness that it had summoned, it peeked through the hair-thin cracks in the darkness with burning, inquisitive eyes. It saw them, although they remained nothing more than fragmented, tantalising glimpses within the realm that lay beyond, of prizes it worked so diligently towards. Fondly, it touched the fractures and the lightless, icy facade that harbored them. It knew that more would be required to widen the fractures, to tear open the once immovable barrier that had separated the two dominions since before time began.

Content in its understanding, and its part in the great and wondrous scheme, it quietly and steadfastly went about its business.

*

Back in the restroom with the others, Ashlynn was still visibly shaken following her encounter with the rat. Despite comforting hugs from both Priestley and Danny, and the substantial nips of cheap, throat-scorching brandy from Danny's silver plated hip flask, Ashlynn's hands were still trembling when Priestley asked everyone to assume their positions for the next take.

"We'll take it from the noise," Priestley informed them. "It was a keeper up to that point." He gave Danny a hard stare, as if daring him to screw up yet *another* take. Danny returned a half-smile, cleared his throat and readied himself.

"*The Black Mass*, Scene two, take two." Priestley paused for quiet to descend, counted to two in his head. "And – *action!*"

"It sounded like someone laughing," Ashlynn said and the quaver in her voice most definitely added something to her performance – now she sounded genuinely scared.

"You heard it too?" Danny delivered his line deadpan.

Good man, Priestley mentally praised the asshole.

"Perhaps it was the tormented soul of the serial killer," Priestley gave his line.

"Please don't say that," Carolyn played the weak heroine to a tee. "I'm spooked enough as it is. It was probably just a door creaking or something."

Priestley made with his scared-but-hiding-it-with-sarcasm voice, "yeah, a door creaking. That's what that was."

"And how exactly is all this going to help find her Mom again?" Ashlynn directed her line at Chris and Priestley winced at the clumsy exposition he'd written. It was a little clunky, even for him. Still, needs must and all that.

"We will be performing the Black Mass in the school tonight." good ol' reliable Chris was, as always word perfect. "Because the killer's soul is condemned to the deepest, darkest recesses of the afterlife." He paused for two beats (for dramatic effect). "And that way we're going to drag that sonofabitch's sorry ass out of hell and make him tell us where he hid this poor girl's Mother."

"And – cut," Labeaux's voice rumbled.

"Hey! I'm the one who calls cut!" Priestley complained; he hated it when Labeaux undermined his authority like that, especially when he knew it to be deliberate.

"Sorry, boss." Labeaux flashed a laconic smile.

"I guess that's a wrap on scene two, guys," Priestley added. He made the snap decision to let Labeaux's indiscretion go – just this once – there'd be no benefit in making himself appear childish by taking Labeaux's bait. Best friend or no, Maurice Labeaux *really* could be a complete dick when he wanted to be. "If we can quickly move on to the gym and get ready for the next one."

"Well done, people," Danny chipped in and slapped backs and dealt high-fives as if he was running the whole fucking show, and at that precise moment Dave Priestley could have gladly murdered the sad old bastard.

CHAPTER TEN

"I can't believe I let you talk me into this," Ashlynn voiced her protest by means of a loud moan from her canvas chair. "And how come I'm the only one wearing a ridiculous outfit anyway?" she complained again – in the whiny voice that was guaranteed to grate on Priestley's nerves – just on the off chance that someone may have been unfortunate enough to have missed it the first three times.

"Because *somebody* has to wear it, and that somebody happens to be your character, Ash'," Priestley explained to her for the umpteenth time yet somehow managed to remain remarkably civil. "It's one of the key requirements for a Black Mass." He lifted up the book in his left hand – *Satanic Rituals: The Black Mass & Others* – for all to see by means of justification. "This book is quite clear on that point; one of the congregation must be a nun, or at the very least, someone wearing a *nun's habit*."

Labeaux threw in a sly grin. "And you guys just happened to have one lying around in your role play cupboard?" he laughed. "I'm surprised you didn't have one in latex."

Ashlynn chose not to grace Labeaux's comment with a reply and instead flipped him off. She felt dumb wearing the brown, floor-length habit – a real one, thanks to her ever pedantic boyfriend – and the coarse material of the wimple itched the sides of her face like a bastard and made everything sound a bit muffled. The habit was warm, though as it was made from a thick wool/cotton blend and for that she was grateful, although equally grateful that she'd had the foresight to remove her sweater and shorts – she was positive she'd have roasted half to death otherwise before the night was done. Ashlynn snorted her displeasure once more for good luck and clambered from her seat.

"Shit!" Ashlynn snapped as the chair listed beneath her. One of its rear legs had sunk into the floor, puncturing through the rotted boards like a hot stiletto through ice. As the chair toppled backwards, Ashlynn went with it and plopped ass-first back into the canvas, fortunate that the crumbly hole in the gym floor held on to the chair leg, and that the thing hadn't completely collapsed – the only thing hurt was her pride.

"Are you okay, babe?" Priestley dashed to her side and offered a hand to help her out of the chair.

"I'm fine," she huffed, her face crimson with embarrassment.

Although Ashlynn looked immensely comical sitting askew in the semi-toppled camouflage chair in full nun's regalia, Priestley knew better than to laugh. Even so much as a smile in such circumstances could ignite his girlfriend's wrath.

With some reluctance, Ashlynn allowed Priestley to heave her out of the chair. She straightened her habit, composed herself and sauntered across to join Danny and the others and pretended like her near-disaster didn't just happen.

"I'd give this spot a wide berth, everyone," Priestley said as he struggled to extricate the chair from the gymnasium floor whilst trying his very best not to giggle.

Still grumping about her enforced attire, Ashlynn joined the rest of the cast and crew who stood solemnly around Priestley's pentagram as if expecting something magic and otherworldly to happen. Labeaux was busy pretending to fiddle with the wide-angle lens on his camera whilst Priscilla filmed both him and Chris. Carolyn and Danny simply stared down at the thick black lines that nestled within the perfect black circle, their faces blank.

"Okay," Priestley demanded everyone's attention, "this is the *pivotal* scene for our movie." He paced behind them all, hands clasped behind his back like an expectant father; stick a big, fuck-off cigar in his mouth and the illusion would be complete. "We get this one right and the rest of the movie will fall neatly into place."

Priestley paused behind Chris, placed his hands on the guy's shoulders and couldn't help but marvel at just how rock-solid the rippling muscles beneath that white shirt actually were. "I need you here." Priestley manoeuvered Chris to the west point of the pentagram, "Ash', if you could go there," he pointed towards the north-eastern point. "Looking good in the outfit, by the way." He gave her one of the special smiles he held in reserve for such placatory occasions and was relieved to see that she had appeared to have thawed a little.

He placed Danny at the northwest point, and then sidled up to Carolyn. He'd reserved the South point – the most powerful according to the book – for himself whilst Carolyn as the human altar would take her place in the center of the pentagram alongside the chalice, skull and candles, her feet by his knees and head farthest away.

"Dammit," Priestley spat.

"Something wrong?" Labeaux lowered his camera with a look of dread on his face.

"I just realized that we're a body short," Priestley told him. "It looks like Corinne's a definite no-show and we need a person at each one of the five points. If Carolyn's in the center, we still need a sixth person."

"What about her?" Danny pointed over to Priscilla who scowled at him.

"Would you mind?" Priestley's eyes lit up. "Just for the ceremony? We'll kill you off quickly after that and you can go back to your filming." He made with the puppy-dog eyes that few could resist and let the awkward silence do the rest.

Priscilla sighed. This was not what she'd signed up for but what the hell? "I guess I could, if it helps you guys out," she said. "But I am *not* getting naked."

"Nothing to panic about, Priscilla, nobody's getting naked," Priestley assured. "Unless they really *want* to, that is." Ashlynn slapped his arm and shot him a dirty look that could have felled a bull elephant at fifty paces. Danny and the others made with the suggestive chortles like a bunch of creepy old men at a strip joint.

"And how exactly do you intend to explain her sudden appearance?" Labeaux asked.

"Yeah, it's going to look a bit odd that she wasn't in the hallway scenes and then suddenly here she is around the circle," Chris added with a frown, all too aware that he may just have talked them all into re-shooting the first scene after all.

"Don't worry about it," Priestley told them, "we can shoot an extra scene after we finish this one – we can have Priscilla dash in and say *'sorry I'm late'* or something." He looked rather pleased with himself at that; thinking on the fly was definitely one of Priestley's strong points. However, it was a comfort that he could pretty much rely upon Labeaux to bring a female tagalong to their shoots. "That ought to do the job," he concluded.

"That'll work," Danny gave his endorsement, as if Priestley ever needed it.

"Okay, people," Priestley reined his people back in, "if we could all take our places please."

Everyone sat down at his or her designated points of the pentagram, and like obedient kindergarten kids at story time they sat cross-legged and eager-eyed. Carolyn positioned herself dead center of the pentagram and lay on her back with her head cradled in her hands. She'd kicked off her shoes and her feet were deliciously bare.

Priestley pulled a blue Bic disposable from the backpack he'd set behind his place and lit the black candles before taking his position at the pentagram. The candles sputtered reluctantly to life and flickered their sickly yellow glow onto the skull to paint sinister eyes of dark in its hollow sockets.

Priscilla – clearly uncomfortable at being in front of the camera – had placed her minicam with great care upon one of the canvas chairs she'd dragged to the periphery of the group. She'd positioned the camera to capture the entire cast in order to get at least *some* half-decent footage whilst she took part in the film, albeit without her favored moving camera style.

Labeaux stalked around the circle with the angular bulk of his camera perched on his shoulder, its record light a solid red. He focussed in with a lingering shot of Carolyn's reclining body framed by the five pointed star and was delighted to see that the combination of her thin dress and the xenon lights had given her a dream-like quality that one could never hope to recreate with any amount of special effects or foils.

"*The Black Mass*. Scene three, take one," Priestley said. "And – *action*."

Chris mentally counted the required two beats and then delivered his lines with conviction, "we will now to prepare the unholy Host." He gestured towards Priestley who acknowledged him with a solemn nod. "And it is imperative that *all* of the unsacred ingredients are included.”

Priestley dug out a fistful of Ziploc baggies from his backpack, along with a small egg whisk. He placed the baggies on the floor between his knees and began to open them, one by one.

“Blood.” He popped open the first baggie and poured the contents into the chalice.

“Urine.” Pouring the yellow liquid into the chalice, he used the whisk to blend the mix.

“Semen.”

“Pus.” The thick, yellow fluid oozed into the chalice with a *plop*.

“Feces.” When Priestley opened the fifth baggie and the unmistakable aroma of fresh shit wafted around the circle it was Ashlynn who broke the silence. “Oh my God, Dave!” she exclaimed with absolute disgust in her voice, her nose wrinkled up like a pug’s.

“Cut!” Priestley called it. Now, *that* was aggravating, if she’d not used his name that would have made for one hell of a reaction shot.

“You used real stuff, man?” Danny added. “I thought it would be all fake.”

“Of course it’s not fake,” Priestley was nonplussed. Actually, he was *offended*; they all knew him much better than that – the very thought that he’d ever fake anything! “I did tell you all that I was going for one-hundred per cent authenticity.” He flashed a reassuring smile. “And as the man said, the Devil’s in the detail.” As if that went anyway towards defending his use of actual bodily fluids.

As he spoke, Priestley whisked the foul recipe into a sickly brown sludge that clung to the sides of the chalice. “Do you think you could make that reaction again?” he asked Ashlynn.

“You filled those bags with bodily fluids?” Ashlynn ignored Priestley’s idiotic question, completely aghast.

This was a departure, even for him, and she noted with distaste that he'd actually gone to the trouble of neatly labelling each one of the baggies in blue Sharpie (as if the contents could ever be mistaken). "I'm *assuming* they're all yours, Dave?" The thought that the guy with whom she shared a bed could possibly have gathered such substances from other people lurched through her mind with an unwelcome clarity.

"Of course they're mine." Priestley was genuinely appalled at such a notion. "Just what kind of sick person do you take me for?" There was a slight upturn to the corners of his mouth. "You really have no idea what I had to go through to get these."

"I think we all have a fairly good idea, Dave," Labeaux chipped in and laughed that deep, booming laugh of his.

"This isn't in the script," Chris spoke up. "I can't see this anywhere in the *script*." There was panic in his voice as he flipped through the crumpled, highlighted pages he had before him with a dramatic flourish to accentuate his point that it *just wasn't in the script*. If there was something not in a script, it had the tendency to unbalance Chris Sherwood's entire universe.

Priestley rolled his eyes and bit his tongue – literally, people *do* actually do that – and counted to ten (that too). He knew full well what was – and wasn't – in the script since he'd written the damned thing. And no, he'd not detailed the exact elements of the ritual itself. He was the director and the visionary here, and *he* knew what was going on and that was the important thing, he'd typed into the script *'a black mass is performed'* and that was good enough for him. It also allowed for a little improvisation to keep the action flowing as natural as was possible.

"It won't hurt us to go off script a little," Priestley explained once he'd counted to that magic ten in his head, "that way we will get some *real* reactions from you guys. I think we've got some great dynamic going so why don't we improvise some of this and see where it takes us?"

There was some disconcerted chatter between Danny, Chris and Ashlynn. Not one of them was all that comfortable with straying too far from the security blanket of a script, they were weak at ad-libbing and it did seem to scare them.

Carolyn sat up. Like a true pro' she'd remained motionless in the center of the pentagram and had kept herself well out of the argument, despite the nausea that had risen in her throat at the stink of Priestley's unholy concoction. "I hate to say it, guys, but I think Dave's right," she said, "I think we would all agree that some of the dialogue has been a little – *stilted* – so far? No offence." She tipped Priestley a wink to diffuse said offence.

"None taken," once more Priestley bit his tongue, this time until it hurt.

One, two, three…

"Look, if we're going to stand a chance of winning this competition *and* use the movie to impress L.A. when we get there, we have to pull out our A-game." Carolyn ran a hand through her hair and it fanned out across her shoulders. She sighed. "And I really don't think that this is it. Again, no offence Dave."

This time, Priestley simply shrugged.

"I say we let Dave go right ahead with his excretions and we improvise the fuck out of this scene." Carolyn paused for breath. She appeared every inch the inspirational speaker, despite the flimsy floral dress and the fact that she was sitting barefoot in the middle of a giant satanic symbol in a school gymnasium.

"I couldn't have put it better myself," Labeaux endorsed.

"Yeah, let's do this!" Danny added with his usual enthusiasm.

"Ash'?" Priestley coaxed Ashlynn. Her part in the movie may have been a small one but her acquiescence (or lack thereof) could mean life or death to the project.

"How could I not?" she told him, "I wasn't going to say anything about the script, but even you have to admit that it's not one of your best, my love." She offered Priestley a peace offering smile to smooth over his delicate ego and he appeared to take it with some good grace.

"Then it's agreed," Priestley spoke quietly. He didn't want to appear too delighted at his team's compliance, it was important at this stage that they considered the ideas to be their own. He tossed aside his script to show solidarity with his team's exceptional thinking and the others followed suit.

Everyone was happy again, the unpleasantness of the unholy host all but forgotten.

"Oh yeah, sweetheart, there *was* just one more thing," Priestley said as he reached for Ashlynn's hand.

"What *one more thing*, Dave?" she groaned. He only ever called her sweetheart when he wanted something he knew she wasn't going to like – the first time had been on the subject of that weird foot thing he'd asked her to do, the second when he'd suggested putting her old man in the home; and Ashlynn hadn't much cared for either. "Go on," there was dread in her voice.

Priestley read from his book, choosing to hide behind its words rather than face his girl directly, "there *is* one more ingredient required in order to complete the Black Host." He traced a studious index finger across one of the thin pages, "ah, here it is." He stabbed at the page with his finger. "Menstrual blood," he announced, "I'm afraid it's the one thing I couldn't donate myself, but –"

"For fuck's sake, Dave," Ashlynn snarled. This one surpassed the foot thing by a mile and a half. "Surely you don't mean –?"

"In order to maintain the authenticity of the Black Mass, and our movie," Priestley spoke with the most serious voice he could muster. "I'd *really* appreciate it if you could donate some of your –"

"– okay, you don't have to spell it out," Ashlynn growled at him; she had no more desire to hear Priestley say the words *menstrual blood* a second time than she wanted to have an all-out row with him in front of the cast and crew. "You knew it was my time of month days ago, but you wait until *now* to say something?" she spat. "You really are unbelievable sometimes, Dave."

"I could do it," there was eagerness to please in Carolyn's voice, which seemed somehow inappropriate under the circumstances. "I just got my period this morning," Carolyn sounded quite proud of the fact. Truth was she'd only just begun spotting but she was more than happy to squeeze out a little to get into Priestley's good books; surely he wouldn't need all that much anyway? She stood up and her naked toes knocked against the skull and skewed its jawbone into a twisted, maniacal grin. She smiled at Priestley and he smiled right back.

"Oh, for God's sake." Ashlynn scrambled to her feet with an irrepressible territorial feeling and jealousy that rose up inside of her like steam in a teakettle. "You stay where you are, *hun*, I've got this." She gave Carolyn a firm stare that froze the poor girl to the spot; *don't mess with a woman's boyfriend, bitch* – especially *a woman who's in the middle of her monthly – there'd only ever be the one winner.*

Ashlynn picked up the chalice as carefully as she could, the last thing she wanted to do was spill its vile contents down her habit. She elected to breathe solely through her mouth and so to avoid the rancid stink *(just how long ago had he collected these samples?)* that wafted up from the ungodly mix.

"Just so it's perfectly clear," Ashlynn grumbled, with her nose blocked she sounded sinusy like she had a bad case of the flu. "I'm only doing this for the good of the film, and so nobody can say that I would ever let the team down." She acknowledged the nods of gratitude – admiration from Chris – and turned to Priestley. "But, by Christ on a goddamn bike, you owe me big time."

Ashlynn walked from the circle, plucked her purse from the equipment table and made her way towards the unlit exit sign. Labeaux shuffled along behind her, filming as they went.

"Really?" Ashlynn rounded on the cameraman.

"But Dave said –" he protested.

"There is no way *he* is filming me changing the mouse, Dave, authenticity or not!" Ashlynn shouted across the gym at her boyfriend. It always made Priestley uncomfortable when Ashlynn talked crude in company – *trailer trash talk,* he called it – hence her unnecessarily raised voice. At times such as this she loved to see him squirm.

"But it would make a great scene, babe." Priestley blanched; he'd not anticipated any sort of protest. "Think of the movie."

"If you think I'm going to let this *oaf* point his camera at my pussy, you're sadly mistaken, David Priestley!" Ashlynn derived yet more satisfaction from the mortified look on Priestley's face.

Priscilla got to her feet and placed herself directly between Priestley and Ashlynn's lines of sight. "It's okay, I'll go with her." She grabbed her minicam from its perch. "We can film discretely, won't show a thing – I promise," she reassured Ashlynn, "and the hand-held footage will look good on my documentary."

"Are you okay with that?" Priestley asked Ashlynn.

"It's the lesser of the two evils I suppose." Ashlynn shook her head at him and the wimple slipped forward a smidgen. Ignoring the rough edge of the material that poked at the rim of her eye, Ashlynn recommenced her walk towards the gymnasium exit and as she made her way across the uneven floor, she kept her hands steady and eyes unfalteringly focussed on the chalice.

"But there'll be no fucking hamburger shots!" she shouted back at Priestley and just *knew* that he'd blushed bright puce.

CHAPTER ELEVEN

The tiny lavatory seat was cold and far too small for Ashlynn's adult-sized backside. She perched precariously on the black plastic ring and used a hand against the cubicle wall to steady herself. And as she sat there with the heavy cloth of the habit bunched up around her waist, Ashlynn was beginning to regret the decision to go pee whilst paying her visit.

Priscilla stood at the open cubicle door and looked down at her subject. She held a bright flashlight in one hand, her minicam in the other. "I really can't believe that you're doing this for him," she said, aiming the camera squarely at Ashlynn's handsome face and taking great pains to film her only from the chest upwards for the sake of the gal's modesty.

"This is not for Dave's benefit." Ashlynn shook her head. "It's for mine. Am I the only one who sees the way *she* looks at him?"

"Carolyn?"

Of course, Carolyn – the honey-toned sex goddess with the over-demonstrative hands, blowjob lips and three-cock mouth. "She has every male she meets falling at her goddamned feet." Ashlynn winced at the word; what was it about *feet* that had so prickled her mind tonight? "And yet she just can't wait to get her slutty hands all over Dave," Ashlynn growled. "She knows she has him hooked with all of her '*I know people who know people in Hollywood*' bullshit," Ashlynn's impersonation of Carolyn was actually quite uncanny; she captured not only the girl's tone but also the nuances of her faint Asian accent too, "I have to watch him like a fucking hawk every second she's around."

"You don't trust him?"

"He has a Y-chromosome. Would you?"

"I guess not." Priscilla smiled. "But then again, he's not my boyfriend." She winked at Ashlynn.

"Which is precisely how come I'm squatting on a miniature toilet in a freakin' nun's outfit making ready to donate my tampon to the cause." Ashlynn allowed herself a chuckle at the absurdity of it all. "And all because I didn't want *her* to be the one to do it," she spat the word *her* with resentment. "Marking my territory like a dog peeing up a tree stump, I guess."

They both peered into the squat chalice that sat between Ashlynn's feet, and at the thick glop of human waste soup that slopped within.

"Oddly enough, this is not the sickest thing Dave's ever asked me to do on film," Ashlynn paused, preferring to remain cryptic rather than to enter into detail; it never failed to make her shudder at how her toes had felt all *squooshy* after that particular incident.

"I'm guessing there's a whole other movie right there?" Priscilla said.

"Like you wouldn't believe."

"Well, I say good for you for standing up to Carolyn," Priscilla said.

"Thank you," Ashlynn was genuine. "Although, what *must* I look like?" She laughed loudly and her voice was gobbled up by the gloom.

Priscilla laughed along, so hard that her camera wobbled. Then her flashlight chose that moment to cut out and the two of them were plunged into pitch black. Ashlynn let out a choked scream and Priscilla let out a stream of expletives that were most unladylike.

Ashlynn had to force herself to stay seated and fight the overwhelming urge to panic and run. To do so would mean stumbling around in the dark and was therefore not the most sensible course of action; especially with Priestley's precious chalice somewhere close by her feet and just begging to be kicked over. She heard Priscilla call the flashlight a *fucking thing* and *bastard crap* and heard it slap against the palm of the girl's hand. Heaven only knew why that action was thought to bring dead batteries back to life – but nine times out of ten it actually worked.

"You okay, Priscilla?" Ashlynn asked.

"I will be when I get this fucking light back on," Priscilla's voice was disembodied and floated out through the dark.

A noise.

Ashlynn froze and Priscilla's flashlight slapping ceased.

Something akin to minute footsteps from somewhere above them, as if someone – *something* – with the tiniest of feet was walking on the ceiling directly above their heads.

Ashlynn reassured herself that this was simply her brain playing tricks again; thoughts of the rat she'd encountered earlier were still etched fresh and bloody on her mind.

Or there could really *be something scurrying around on the ceiling?*

Did rats bear grudges? The creature had looked especially pissed at Ashlynn for disturbing its kitten dinner; perhaps the oversized rodent had been following her, biding its time for an opportunity to even things up a little?

"Are you out there, Dave?" Ashlynn called out and hoped that her voice would carry through the closed bathroom door, "a little help in here!" Panic raised her voice an octave or so as she fought to steady her breathing, she really couldn't afford a full-blown panic attack right now.

The footsteps stopped. The sound of low, rhythmic breathing and the *drip-drop* of moisture on cold tiles filled the chilled air. And then there came a faint whispering and a barely perceptible giggle that shot a shiver through Ashlynn's body and made the hair on her nape stand to attention.

There was a resounding, hefty slap of hard plastic against skin and Priscilla's flashlight beam blasted Ashlynn directly in the face. Ashlynn screwed up her eyes and shielded them with a hand. "Ouch!"

"Sorry." Priscilla tipped the light upwards and away from Ashlynn's face. The beam faded slightly and there was a heart-sinking moment when it threatened to cut out again, but then it regained full strength and illuminated the cubicle.

From her toilet, Ashlynn looked up at Priscilla and didn't have to ask if she'd also heard the footsteps and the impish giggle. Priscilla's face said it all.

Priscilla raised her minicam to focus on a spot above Ashlynn's head. She spoke quietly, with a slow and deliberate voice, "I didn't notice that when we came in."

To twist around, Ashlynn had to push with both hands against the lavatory stall for balance to facilitate a squint over her shoulder.

There on the wall above the cistern, written in childish scrawl

LEAVE US ALONE

The words stood out stark and raw like a new wound, the lettering fresh. It was impossible to make out the precise hue of the words because the intense flashlight washed out the color to make some indeterminate shade of brown but Ashlynn made an educated guess that the message was written in Priestley's very best fake-kid handwriting and would be in *Cliché Red* to give the appearance of blood.

It was also safe to assume that since this had been the first and only graffiti they had encountered in the school so far, that it was meant for her.

"It'll be Dave horsing around," Ashlynn theorized out loud. Voicing the idea made it sound plausible but she couldn't quite figure out how her boyfriend could have possibly made the footsteps on the ceiling sound so damned real. "So let's get this over with and get back before he thinks he's scared us."

Priscilla nodded her agreement. She was beginning to wish she'd never set foot in the school. She'd felt an unease the moment she'd arrived with Priestley and Labeaux and now it had crawled to the back of her mind and festered there like some malign, slimy parasite; a sick feeling that had nothing to do with practical jokes.

"If you could point the camera thataway," Ashlynn requested with a forced smile. "She's coming out."

Priscilla handed the flashlight over to Ashlynn and pointed the minicam out of the stall and into a corner of the bathroom. Something small and crouched shifted in the inky shadow beneath the washbasin, as if taking great trouble to be away from her camera's stare. Priscilla blinked hard to shift the image from her sight and when she looked back, whatever it had been had gone.

From the cubicle in the dark, Priscilla heard a faint *plop*.

"All done," Ashlynn's voice was so close to her ear that it made Priscilla jump. She hadn't heard Ashlynn finish up her ablutions, nor reassemble her habit and struggle to stand up in the cramped confines of the toilet cubicle. Yet there stood Ashlynn, looking incredibly pleased with herself and holding the pewter chalice – complete with its newest addition – in her hands.

Priscilla looked at Ashlynn. "Good, can we go now?" she said.

*

It sensed that they were close. It smelled the heady, metallic scent of stale blood and tasted their fear and knew that its influence over their minds grew ever stronger.

Within the claustrophobic confines of the dark place of its realm, the soft warm bodies of its compatriots jostled and nudged in their excitement, as if they knew that their own destiny rested firmly on its success – or lack thereof.

It had laid down its plans with great care and had taken every step possible to ensure that success was assured.

Almost there now, and anticipating the rush of victory, it focussed on the final steps towards that goal.

CHAPTER TWELVE

"Fuck me, girl, you actually did it!" Carolyn clapped her hands and giggled like a big kid as Ashlynn and Priscilla returned triumphant. She raced up to Ashlynn and gave her a solid hug, although being careful not to jostle the chalice and its precious cargo. Then she peered in at the bloodied tampon that floated within and crinkled her nose.

Ashlynn had to admit that it felt awesome to have made a stand against Carolyn – who was now looking at her with an admiration she'd never experienced before (from *anyone*!) – and her boyfriend who regarded her with pride although Ashlynn knew that he was totally grossed out by what she'd just done.

It also felt good to have done something so completely out of character for once. The last time Ashlynn could recall having allowed herself to bow to spontaneity had been with her previous boyfriend and two of his friends from the soccer team. Yes, indeed, it was gratifying to be able to send out the message to Priestley that Ashlynn Jones wasn't always the stoic one in their relationship, and that she too could be impetuous and silly.

Ashlynn placed the chalice back into its place in the center of the pentagram. She stepped back with hands on hips and a chest-swelling sense of pride and gave a sardonic smile as everyone peered down at the battered grey cup with its murky, rank contents that were now resplendent with her blood stained tampon bobbing around on its surface.

How do ya like your authenticity now, Davy-boy?

"This movie had better win something after what I just went through for you guys," Ashlynn smirked, "even if it's *'best use of a female sanitary product'*."

Everyone laughed at this – even Priestley, although he was looking slightly green about the gills – and they arranged themselves back in their respective places around the pentagram.

Priscilla skirted around the circle and placed her minicam back on the canvas chair, positioning it once again to point towards the pentagram. Then she sat down.

"Thank you for your – err – *contribution*, Ash'," Priestley sounded genuinely *genuine* for once, "it really is much appreciated." His sentiment was echoed by the others, which made Ashlynn feel warm and weird all at the same time. It seemed strange to her that she'd gained so much kudos for doing what was perhaps one of the grossest things she'd ever done in her life.

This and Dave's foot-thing, her brain prompted. Ashlynn shuddered.

Priestley slipped with ease back into *director-of-this-goddamned-movie* mode and announced in that self-important voice of his. "Okay, so we're going to perform the actual Black Mass ritual for this next part of the scene," he said as Chris flicked through his script for verification. "And I want to get the whole thing in one take so we don't break the momentum. Is that okay with you, Maurice?"

"S'okay with me, dude," Labeaux was laconic as usual, "you just do your thing and I'll film the shit out of it."

"Perfect." Priestley looked at each one of the people around the pentagram. "With that in mind, I would appreciate it if we could all remember not to break character – no matter what," he gave them his *serious* tone to drive home just how important this point really was. "I have a couple of surprises in store and want to catch your natural first reactions as and when they happen." He ignored the looks of concern that passed between his cast; they knew Priestley and his surprises all too well.

"Dave?" Carolyn sat up in the center of the pentagram and hugged her knees close to her chest.

"Carolyn?"

"I was thinking that perhaps this scene would play better if I were naked."

What?!

Ashlynn did a double take, had she been a kid's cartoon character, her head would have shaken side to side to side accompanied by that *wibble-wobble-wibble* sound. Just how Carolyn had managed to keep her face straight at such an audacious suggestion was beyond Ashlynn's comprehension; trust the exhibitionist bitch to try to go one better than a freshly donated tampon.

"You know I'm okay with doing nude scenes." Carolyn glanced down along her body and pushed out her chest. "As long as they're essential to the plot, of course."

Ashlynn hit Carolyn with the stink-eye and fumed inwardly. It was hard for her to admit it but if her body was every inch as perfect as Carolyn's, she'd probably want to show it off at every possible opportunity, too. Ashlynn bit her lip to maintain composure and shot Carolyn another evil look to let the dumb girl know that this really was a bad idea. The look was caught by Carolyn, duly noted and ignored.

"If we are trying to be truly authentic with this movie then I guess it couldn't hurt," Priestley said with a tremble in his voice and a nervous glance at his girlfriend, "the altar should ideally be nude, according to my research."

Ashlynn rolled her eyes. The man was a fool, but he was *her* fool, and she figured that the saddest thing in all of this was that Priestley's only thought would be for the good of the movie. Bless him, he was so completely oblivious to Carolyn's blatant attempts to curry favor by use of that magnificent body that he couldn't see that she was desperate enough to do anything to jump his bones.

And this latest stunt pretty much constituted the true meaning of *anything* in Ashlynn's book.

"Yeah, we gotta stay with the *authenticism*," Danny chimed in with typical lascivious over-enthusiasm. "Waddya say, guys?"

Labeaux and Chris nodded their approval while Priestley tactfully abstained under Ashlynn's icy glare.

"I say we go for it, why the hell not?" it was Ashlynn who spoke up, surprising not only Priestley, Labeaux and the others, but herself as well, "if you *insist*, Carolyn." The emphasis she placed on *insist* spoke volumes; *go ahead, flash your goodies all you want, you cheap slut, you still won't stand a snowball's chance in hell with my man.*

"Okay, nobody look," Carolyn giggled and pulled her dress up over her head. She threw it in the general direction of the canvas chairs. Next she unhooked her nude-colored bra and tossed it aside with all the finesse of a seasoned stripper. The cool air in the gym perked up her nipples in an instant and they stiffened to angry, jutting points. With all eyes on her, Carolyn wriggled out of the silk high-leg panties that matched the discarded bra, revealing a small *Hello Kitty* tattoo at the crease at the top of her thigh. Playfully, she threw her warm panties at Chris who caught them with both hands. Finally, she kicked off the shoes she'd put back on to keep her feet warm during the impromptu break and wiggled her liberated, scarlet-tipped toes. Done, and quite resplendently naked, Carolyn lay back on the cool floor and assumed her role as the most exquisite human altar.

"You could do with a trim of the old George W., Carolyn," Ashlynn couldn't resist the dig at the girl's hirsute crotch.

"Tell me about it," Carolyn retorted without embarrassment, "if I'd known I was going to be getting naked for the camera, I'd have had a Brazilian." Absently, she stroked her dark thatch of pubic hair and gently parted her labia as she did so, giving Priestley a cheeky flash of the warm, pink moistness that nestled within. She lifted her head and gave him a lascivious wink.

Priestley couldn't help but stare down at Carolyn, his mouth dry and with an awkward stirring in his loins. He cleared his throat and leaned in towards her. "Er, if you could hold a candle in each hand – that would be just perfect," his voice was strained.

"Anything you say, Dave," Carolyn purred and much to Priestley's relief she moved her hands away from her vagina and spread them, Christ-like, at her sides.

Priestley placed the black candles in Carolyn's hands, taking special care not to let the molten wax drip onto her skin. Thus posed, Carolyn looked mouth-watering; her smooth, dusky skin shimmered in the light of the candles, breasts topped with cherry nipples lay full and pert against the faint outline of her ribs and long, lithe legs stretched out towards Priestley with shapely thighs slightly parted to tease with the delights that dwelled between.

Fighting to stay focused, Priestley addressed the group whilst at the same time doing his level best to avert his eyes from Carolyn's body, "now that the Unholy Host has been created, it is up to me – my *character* that is – to perform the ceremony." He coughed once more to clear the croak from his voice. "I will be reciting the incantations, calling on the denizens of hell, generally building up the tension – etcetera, etcetera," as he spoke,

Priestley flicked through the well-thumbed pages of his ever-present *Satanic Rituals* to pick out the passages he'd highlighted in yellow.

There had been a plethora of satanic mumbo-jumbo from which to choose, and true to form Priestley had gone to great pains to pick out the most relevant verses and readings – all with that famous Dave Priestley eye on authenticity. If his assembled cast could manage to do what they were supposed to do (and when they were supposed to do it), then the ritual would be a resounding success.

"Are we ad-libbing this part?" It was somehow inevitable that Chris the Pedant would ask that question.

"No, Chris," Priestley held his patience, "it's all here for you on the Post-It notes." Taking this as his cue, Priestley passed around a bunch of neon pink squares he'd prepared earlier – one for each of them. "I will begin the ritual by passing the prepared Unholy Host around. Take it, and then pass it on to your left – that detail is particularly important, it *has* to be to the left," he paused for effect, "once it's been all the way around the circle, I'll call cut before we move on to the second stage of the ceremony," Priestley said. "Now, nobody has to actually *drink* from the chalice, but if any of you had the desire to keep it real –"

"Fuck off, Dave," Chris growled, his sentiment seconded by all. Everyone shook their heads and made with a universal look of disgust in the direction of Priestley and his chalice.

Priestley couldn't manage to hide all of his disappointment. It was one of his personal failings that he would all too readily attribute his own dedication to the art to others. "Yeah, that probably is asking too much," he said in the passive-aggressive voice that he had down to perfection, "but if you could put it to your lips and *pretend* to take a sip, we can work with that in post-production."

"We need to get a move on," Labeaux interrupted with an exaggerated glance at his watch, "it's gone ten already."

As if doubting his friend, Priestley checked his watch and found to his astonishment that Labeaux was correct. If they failed to pick up the pace they were in danger of running out of time.

"Okay, let's do this thing." Priestley clapped his hands. "*The Black Mass*, scene three, take two."

An expectant silence filled the room, a silence that *echoed* about the darkened corners of the abandoned gymnasium and ruffled the shadows that lurked there.

"And – *action*."

Priestley bowed his head to read from the book that lay open on the cold floor between his knees.

"*In nomine Magni Nostri Satanas. Introibo ad altare Domini Inferni*," he chanted.

"*Ad eum qui laefificat meum,*" on cue Danny, Chris, Priscilla and Ashlynn intoned from their notes. They were pretty much in harmony and certainly close enough for Priestley to be happy with their performance.

A distant cry pierced the night. It had the lonely resonance of a seagull on a cliff top; it faded away and was replaced by the faint sounds of children's laughter.

Only Ashlynn looked up. She'd heard that noise before.

"Oh great Lord Satan, Prince of Lies, Lord of the Darkness," Priestley spoke with unyielding conviction and picked up the chalice. He held the vile thing aloft as he'd seen done in countless late night movies. "*Qui regit terram*. Ruler of the damned, God of Evil. We offer you this Unholy Host as a sacrifice and in return we ask that you send us the soul of Richard Carroway that you torment in the fire-pits of your domain."

Priestley passed the chalice over to Chris who took it from his hands as if it was about to gnaw on his fingers. Chris held his breath and clamped his eyes tight shut as he lifted the Host to his lips. He tilted the chalice slightly to give the appearance of sipping at the revolting beverage but made dammed sure none of the stuff touched his lips. Danny and Ashlynn grimaced at each other solemnly as Chris passed the chalice. (Flows better)

Labeaux stepped in as close as he dared to Danny without casting a shadow across the shot. He zoomed in on old man's face to catch him raising the chalice to his lips. Danny feigned a sip with a look of sheer abhorrence as Ashlynn's tampon bobbed over to the side of the chalice as if to greet him. Then, happy to be rid of the thing, Danny passed the Host along to Priscilla and only then did he let out the stale breath he'd been holding on to. It rushed from his lungs with an audible *whoosh*.

Priscilla lifted the chalice to her mouth, play-acted taking a sip of the unholy Host and passed it over to Ashlynn.

"*Et beneficium tuum da nobis*," Priestley half-chanted as Ashlynn pretended to drink from the Host, "we shall all drink of this most unholy of unholy Hosts in that you will grant our desire."

He widened his eyes to prompt the others.

"*Dominus Inferus vobiscum*," the cast joined in as Ashlynn handed the chalice back to Priestley, visibly relieved to be rid of the revolting thing.

Priestley's raised voice had a surreal timbre in the stillness of the gymnasium; it sounded *hollow*. "Come, O Mighty Lord of Darkness, and look favorably on this sacrifice which we have prepared in thy name," he said without the slightest hint of irony, as lost as he was in both his character and the moment.

"*Dignum et justum est,*" his congregation said, all in perfect time.

What Priestley did next really shouldn't have come as a big surprise to those who knew him well. However, that didn't lessen the revulsion that his actions invoked amongst his cast and crew.

He lifted the tarnished chalice to his lips, and without a moment's hesitation he drank its contents – all but the tampon which tapped teasingly against his lips – down in three voracious gulps.

Ashlynn gagged. She raised a hand to her mouth and willed her stomach's contents back down. Chris, Danny and Priscilla stared open-mouthed at Priestley as if he'd just sprouted a second head whilst behind them Labeaux noticeably retched and had a look of sheer disbelief on his face that mirrored the others'.

Priestley placed the chalice back down next to Carolyn's feet – she was mercifully unaware of what Priestley had just done as she'd chosen to keep her eyes closed throughout – and stifled a small but foul belch as he wiped his mouth with the back of his hand.

"Therefore, O mighty and terrible Lord of Darkness, we entreat *You* that You receive and accept this sacrifice, which we –" Priestley stumbled over his words as his stomach lurched and the acrid, acidic tang of bile crawled up his throat. "We offer to *You* on behalf of this assembled company –" Priestley's stomach cramped up again, and this time it squirted a gobbet of its vile, scorching contents up into his mouth. He swallowed hard and fought against the nausea, determined to get to the end of the scene. "– upon whom You have set Your mark, that You may grant us the request of communion with the eternally damned soul which we seek –"

Labeaux kept his camera firmly focussed on Priestley as he scrambled to his feet, his face *literally* a queer shade of green. Resolutely, the cameraman raced after his subject as Priestley dashed to the corner of the gymnasium with one hand clamped tight over his mouth. And there, Labeaux relished the opportunity to capture for posterity his friend as he vacated the contents of his stomach through his fingers with great, heaving retches. With the eye of a seasoned cinematographer, Labeaux expertly framed Priestley's face *and* the floor in order to record the full effects of the vomit forcibly rejected in thick, stinking globs that looked like lumpy molasses; the unholy Host, soda, burritos, tiny shreds of salad, salsa chunks and all.

Priestley threw up in the corner of the gymnasium until there was nothing more than dry, unproductive heaves that hurt his gut muscles like hell. The stink of his wastes buffeted back up at him from the floor and made him heave even more until he turned his head away.

And when Priestley had finished, he called *cut*.

"What happened?" Carolyn opened her eyes as from a deep sleep. She sat up and eyed Priestley propped up in the corner of the gym, his hands resting against the soggy walls.

"It must have been something he ate," Danny – forever the joker in the pack – smirked, much to everyone's amusement.

And for the second time that night, Priestley wished the old fucker dead.

*

The slits in the darkness widened and the light ventured in to taint the blackest of the shadows, cautious yet ever eager to explore.

It eased itself ever closer towards the cracks; senses alight with seductive promises of the dominion that it had anticipated for an eternity.

It was time.

CHAPTER THIRTEEN

"The price of realism, eh?" Priestley offered up a weak smile as he wiped a smear of dark brown vomit from the corner of his mouth. He creased his nose with distaste; some of the stuff had shot out of his nostrils before he'd reached the corner and he knew he'd be smelling puke for the next couple of days. "The things we do for this business."

Labeaux threw him a fluffy white hand towel from the knee-high stack that was piled next to Carolyn's make up boxes. Priestley wiped his mouth, then blew his nose on the thing and threw it away into the shadows.

"Are you okay, Dave?" Carolyn voiced her concern from the center of the circle where she sat cross-legged despite the floor being hellishly cold on her bare buttocks, arms wrapped about her chest. There was an oily sheen to Priestley's pallid skin and he looked more than a little green about the gills, but no one but Carolyn – Ashlynn included – showed any concern, the collective thought being that it served him right for trying to be *too* damn clever.

"Yeah, thanks," Priestley replied and took his place back at the circle as Labeaux circled him like some huge, predatory bird, "I guess I should have expected that something like that might happen." He cracked a self-deprecating smile and sat himself down.

"That's *Taco Cabana* for ya," Danny made with the funny and for once Priestley was genuinely grateful for the deflection.

"You ready to pick it up, Dave?" Labeaux asked with yet another surreptitious glance at his wristwatch.

"Yeah, sure thing, Mo'," Priestley replied, "although there *was* one other thing." He looked around the circle.

"Go on," Chris groaned.

Priestley made eye contact with each of the four seated around the pentagram. "In the interests of realism –" he plucked a dog-eared copy of *The Satanic Bible* and flicked to somewhere near its center, "– the book does recommend one more thing." Priestley seemed a little sheepish, which was most unusual for him.

"Nice segue, dude," Labeaux said, his brow furrowed.

Priestley ignored his cameraman and continued, "this next scene – and no, Chris it isn't in the script – would *really* benefit from a release of sacrificial energy." His eyes made another round of the concerned faces around the circle. "It states here," he read from the book by finger-tracing the words like a first grader's first attempt at *Pete the Cat*. *"The release of energy during the human orgasm is considered to be as strong as that as during a ritualistic killing."*

"You have to be fucking kidding," Ashlynn voiced her displeasure and loudly. "We are *not* having a fucking orgy! I did tell you *never again*, Dave." She folded her arms across her breasts and looked comically stern as she scowled at her boyfriend from beneath the brown wimple.

Eyebrows were raised from every point of the pentagram and Carolyn raised her head to give Ashlynn one of those knowing looks. "Oh, I don't know, Ashlynn," she chuckled as she sat up with her hands planted on the floor to support her body, breasts uncovered, high and firm, "I think it sounds fun." She let out a dirty giggle and tipped Priestley a comely wink.

Chris was less than impressed. "You're joking, right?" he growled, "you're going to turn this whole thing into a porn film?" He stared long and hard at Priestley. "Because if that was your intention, you could at least have had the balls to let us know from the off."

"No, no, no," Priestley's exasperation spilled over. "If you'd all just let me finish up what I was going to say." He waved the black book in Chris's general direction, but equally for everyone's benefit. He'd read through the *Satanic Bible* several times during his preparations and a large proportion of it seemed to relate to sexual energy in some form or another. "Look, as far as I can see, a whole lot of Satanism is just thinly-veiled, ritualized justification for getting old men laid."

"Just the same as Catholicism, then?" Danny chimed in and proceeded to laugh along to his own joke. He raised a hand over his head to have it high-fived by Labeaux.

"To answer your question, Ash' we are *not* going to have an orgy." Priestley gave his girl a placatory grin.

"Boo," Carolyn said and gave Ashlynn a filthy look, deriving great pleasure from the uncomfortable squirm it provoked.

Priestley paused and attempted to read the faces around him; he was about to hit them with the biggest ask ever, one which could go one of two ways by his reckoning. "However," he took a heavy breath, "what we *do* need is a volunteer to – err – *expel some sexual energy*," he read this last part from the book in part to substantiate his request and in part to mask his own embarrassment.

"You mean jerk off, don't you?" Chris sputtered. "He does, he wants one of us to *jerk off* for the fucking movie!" Chris looked around at the others for back up. "For Christ's sakes, Dave – this is going too far, even for you!"

"Calm down, Chris." Priestley raised an arm, hand palm down to mollify his lead actor. In his other hand, he held up the *Satanic Bible* as if it were a shield. "I suppose you could put it *that* way, if you really wanted to be blunt about it," Priestley played his humor card with a cheeky smirk.

"What other way is there to put it?" Chris was petulant.

Priestley glanced at Ashlynn, whose eyes were disapproving in advance of *anything* he was about to say. "In the interests of authenticity, I'd appreciate your consideration on this, Chris," he said. "Unless someone would like to volunteer to be *actually* sacrificed?" Priestley looked around the room and noted that from their expressions, at least two of his team thought he was only half-joking.

Silence.

Priestley simply couldn't abide silence. "C'mon guys, you've all worked with me enough to know how anal I am about keeping shit real," he said.

Labeaux snorted at Priestley's appalling attempt to sound *ghetto*.

"I–I guess so," Chris began crack, all thanks to his actor's ego; *never say never* and all that. "Even so –"

"Chris!" Ashlynn interrupted, "tell me you're not *really* considering this?" she spat. "I really didn't think you were this much of a pervert, Dave." Ashlynn rounded on Priestley with a viciousness she'd not felt in a long time.

"I'll do it."

All eyes settled on Carolyn who now hugged her knees primly, her tits mostly hidden from view.

"*Pardon me?*" was all Ashlynn could manage to get out of her mouth.

"I said I'll do it," Carolyn repeated. Her voice was soft, calm, "I'll jerk off for the film."

If looks were bullets, Carolyn would have been dead right then and there, but nonetheless she truly relished

Ashlynn's displeasure. "It wouldn't be the first time I've flicked the peanut on camera." Carolyn smiled at fond memories of an older guy she'd dated three or four years ago who'd had a penchant for filming their sexual encounters. His particular favorites had been those of her solo performances, some of which he'd posted up on a pay-per-view site on the internet. That had excited Carolyn to the extreme; knowing that random guys the world over were beating off to her as she masturbated.

"I thought you said you had your period?" Ashlynn *really* wasn't happy about this.

"Yeah, but what's a little menstrual blood between friends?" Carolyn nodded at the chalice and its bloodied content. "What do *you* think, Dave?" there was a suggestive tone in her voice that served to further aggravate Ashlynn.

Priestley pulled a face and both Carolyn and Ashlynn took delight in his discomfort at the subject.

"I guess there'd be no harm in Carolyn faking it for the camera, Ashlynn," Priscilla attempted to break the tension before all out war broke out, "it may even add something to the film."

"Oh, I wasn't planning on faking," Carolyn made deliberate eye contact with Ashlynn, "all in the interests of authenticity, of course."

"Oh, for fuck's sake," Ashlynn groaned.

"Thank you, Carolyn." Priestley was grateful to the girl although he knew for certain that he'd pay for this later with Ashlynn. All that mattered right now was getting the damned film made, and made well. "Thank you for your infallible commitment to our art," he said to Carolyn and they shared a smug glance that made Ashlynn look sick to her stomach.

"I do have one rider, though." Carolyn let go of her knees and stretched out her long legs, one crossed demurely over the other. She was lapping up the attention now and enjoyed how the balance of power had tipped her way and how everyone was hanging on her every word. "If I'm going to do this, I want *someone* to do it with me," she said and stared directly at Priestley, "I mean, at the same time. No touching."

"The script only requires one –" Priestley stumbled.

"This part is not in the script, remember?" Chris threw in. "At least, not in the one *you* gave us." He flipped roughly through the pages of his script to make the point.

"I knew this thing would turn into a porno-fest the minute you said *Black Mass,*" Ashlynn spat, "this whole fucking thing is about sex, isn't it, Dave?"

"What do you say, *Dave*?" Carolyn slid a hand along her silk-smooth thigh and caressed its baby-soft skin. Breathy, she sighed, "care to join me?"

Priestley swallowed hard. There was a fat, dry lump in his throat and his heart thumped quick and loud and painful in his chest. His mounting excitement at this peculiar turn of events – he'd really not expected anyone to agree to this, although he had figured that if anyone did, it would have been Carolyn – he'd certainly never anticipated having to join in. Ashlynn was going to skin him alive, but what else could he do?

"As director, I guess I shouldn't ask my cast to do anything that I wasn't prepared to do myself," Priestley said with an apologetic shrug to Ashlynn. "I'm sorry, Ashlynn, but you have to understand just how important this film is to me – to *us*. And if it takes me –"

"I got this," Chris butted in, fiddling with the buttons on his 501's as he spoke.

Danny could barely contain his excitement at the promise of a free smut show. "Yay! Go Chris!" he blurted out and clapped his hands together, sounding like a nine-year old girl at cheer class, "I'd have volunteered, but the chemo' killed my wood stone cold. I've not had a proper hard-on since Nancy Reagan died." He forced out an empty laugh that contradicted the hurt in his eyes.

Carolyn looked as decidedly disappointed as Ashlynn appeared relieved; she'd been looking forward to getting down and dirty with Dave Priestley for a long time – on film or off of it. "Yay," Her voice was flat, "okay, let's do this, Chris."

"Yes Ma'am."

Carolyn lay back down in place with a dramatic arch of her back. She snaked a hand down between her legs, which she parted slightly to allow her fingers unhindered access.

Chris shuffled his jeans down his muscular thighs. He reached inside his boxers and took hold of his growing erection, making sure to keep it hidden from sight. He peeled back the foreskin – his parents were strict non-conformists and had spared his twenty thousand nerve endings from unnecessary circumcision, for which he'd be eternally grateful – and made ready to choke the chicken on camera for the first time in his life. He saw Ashlynn staring at him across the circle and looked up to meet her gaze; she smiled and mouthed him *thank you*.

Priestley made an exaggerated clearing of his throat to garner attention. He tore his eyes away from the reclining, mouth-wateringly naked Carolyn whose fingers were already burrowed and busy in the dark tangle of her pubic hair, and he addressed the team.

"In this scene, Carolyn and Chris will do their thing while I call out blasphemous words against the Virgin Mary, Jesus and anyone else holy I can think of," Priestley explained in order to pre-empt any possible shock or offence at what he had in mind; he wanted to avoid any of his cast either taking the moral high ground or getting all religious on him.

"Ashlynn, Danny and Priscilla, if you guys would just keep your heads bowed, eyes closed and do your best to look – well – *satanic*." He expected a wry smile from the trio, but was met with stony faces. "And you guys," to Carolyn and Chris, "if you're ready?"

"Good to go, man," Chris said and gave his penis a squeeze.

"I already started," Carolyn's dirty laugh said it all.

"Okay, good," Priestley said as he composed himself, "*The Black Mass*, scene *four*, take one. Camera." The ubiquitous pause. "And – *action*."

Priestley closed his eyes and dropped his chin to his chest. Priscilla, Ashlynn and Danny followed suit and Labeaux circled around to capture each one of them in turn on film.

Meanwhile, Carolyn and Chris made busy with their hands; and whilst Chris seemed to be in a hurry to get the whole thing over and done with, Carolyn was taking her own sweet time, relishing the unashamed exhibitionism along with the cool, moist air that prickled her exposed skin.

Priestley counted four silent beats before beginning his chant, *"incensium istud ascendat ad te, Domine Infernus, et descendat super nos beneficium tuum,"* his voice was clear and resonant, his pronunciation clear and precise. "Oh Great Lord Leviathan," he increased in volume and his booming tones cavorted around the gymnasium, "in your name, we ravish the Virgin Mary; we sodomize her and defile her flesh."

Priestley paused to allow for yet more dramatic effect and Labeaux zoomed in on his intense expression.

"Feel our human spirits soar as we penetrate her hallowed cunt and become one with her earthly vessel."

Danny and Ashlynn both stifled giggles at this and even Labeaux allowed himself an amused smirk. Acting or not, Priestley was sounding more like a pretentious prick the further he went on.

Chris let out an involuntary grunt and his hand quickened its pace as his dick strained to burst out from the plaid material of his underwear. Carolyn moaned her own ecstasy and arched her back as the fingers of one hand buried deep in the soft folds of her vulva, while those of her other worked diligently at her clitoris.

Priestley opened his eyes to check the scene. So far, so good; everyone was doing as directed and he was as happy as he could be with that. Over Ashlynn's shoulder, however, in the corner in which he'd deposited his dinner and from which wafted the cloying stink of puke and excrement, Priestley caught a slight movement in the thick shadows and he smiled.

"*Gratias agamus Domino Inferno Deo Nostro,*" Priestley recommenced his chant with an increased enthusiasm, "God of the Underworld, hear us as we force our pleasure in the rape of the physical flesh of the mother of *He Who Banished You.*"

Carolyn groaned and chewed down on her lower lip, her fingers thrusting deep inside her vagina in rhythm to Chris's pounding at his cock, her hips bucking to meet her hand.

"Hear how the virgin whore delights in such carnal pleasures; listen to the obscenities that she cries out in your name!" Priestley's voice filled the gym.

Over in the corner, something began to take shape, metamorphosing from liquid to something altogether more solid. It rose up from the midst of the thick, rank puddle and in the ink black of the shadows its surface oozed and shifted as if fighting to adopt some tangible shape. Priestley strained his eyes. He was desperate to see more, but could only make out a vague, amorphous outline topped by a misshapen lump that may have been a head or possibly something altogether different. As the liquid form skulked back into the protective darkness of the smothering shadows, Priestley closed his eyes.

"Cunt!" Priestley shouted so loud that he made everyone jump, himself included, "Cock! Tits! Fuck! Ass fuck Jesus Christ! Fuck the virgin's mouth *and* her foul cunt! Let her swallow the come of a thousand horses! Sodomize the Christ Child and cast him to the flames of the eternal pit!"

As the obscenities spilled from Priestley's mouth, Chris uttered a stifled grunt and his hips moved with the involuntary twitch that signalled ejaculation. On cue, Carolyn screamed out her own, over-dramatic orgasm and her body tensed, taut and sweat-slicked, and then shuddered with release.

"Fuck! Fuck! Fuck!" Carolyn screamed at the very top of her lungs.

No one comes *that* hard, Priestley couldn't help but think to himself.

Do they?

"Cut!" Priestley called and when he opened his eyes, the shape in the corner was gone.

"Damn, that was fucking hot," Labeaux hissed through clenched teeth. He held out a hand for Carolyn to low five.

Carolyn sat up. Her skin was flushed face to feet and she had a delicate sheen of sweat that covered her body. She pulled her hand away from her vagina with a moist *slurp* and held it up to show Labeaux her glistening, red-tinged fingers.

Immediately, Labeaux retracted the low-five offer.

"Why, thank you, Maurice," Chris made with the funny, "I can only hope that it was as *amazing* for you as it was for me." He wiped his slimed hand on the outside of his boxers, never one to be squeamish about a little ejaculate.

"I was talking to Carolyn, you asshole," Labeaux kind of missed the joke. He strode over to the equipment table to retrieve a fresh battery for his camera, astounded that he'd eaten through a whole battery's worth of juice already.

"I know," Carolyn said with no false modesty. "I had this boyfriend once who used to film me for a porn site," she bragged. "I paid my way through college with these guys." She wiggled her bloodied fingers for all to see.

"I wish I'd been paid for jerking off," Danny quipped. "A dollar a time and I'd have been a millionaire by the time I was nineteen!" Danny's gag was well received and everyone laughed, the oppressive post-orgasm mood lifted somewhat. "Okay, *fourteen*," he milked his audience one more time and they laughed together as the tension of the scene evaporated.

"That really was pretty intense, guys," Priscilla said as she crawled on all fours over to the chair to check on her camera.

"I hate to admit it, Carolyn, but that *was* one heck of a performance," Ashlynn told her in a tone that could have been either genuine praise or Total Bitch. "Good for you for maintaining the *authenticity*."

And there it was; *Total Bitch*.

"Thank you, Ashlynn," Carolyn was unphased by Ashlynn's jibe; "It's what *anyone* would have done for our movie." She cracked a wicked smile and ran her fingers through the sweat that had gathered between her breasts. "I'm sure even *you* would have stepped up, had you not been – err – *indisposed*."

Ashlynn pulled a face that illustrated *touché* to perfection. Although she'd never admit it to anyone – *especially* Carolyn – she was actually beginning to feel a modicum of admiration for the girl, in spite of everything.

"Can we take a short break?" Chris asked, "I could do with tidying up a little and somebody really ought to clean up Dave's puke sometime soon." He wafted a hand in front of his nose to highlight his point. "The *stank* is making me feel quite nauseous," he added in his very best campy voice.

"He's right, Dave," Labeaux threw in, "it is getting pretty funky in here.

Funky was putting it nicely. The gymnasium stank of bile, part-digested Mexican food and shit.

"The same goes for your mouth, Dave," Ashlynn half-teased, "I'll not be Frenching you until you've brushed, rinsed *and* flossed."

"Is that because he just ate shit?" Carolyn's bitchy streak just couldn't resist such an easy feed line, "– or is it because you're out of bounds Ashl–?"

Carolyn froze.

Her eyes widened and the blood drained from her face as she stared at the hellish apparition that had appeared over Ashlynn's shoulder.

The mottled gray color of dead flesh, it best resembled some hideously distorted skull over which the moist leather of skin had been stretched; it bulged and undulated and shifted as if the bones that lurked beneath were liquid and undecided as to what shape they should take. There sat a ragged, inverted valentine-heart hole at the skull's center – where a nose should have been – a wet, black crevasse that exposed behind it a glistening pink, bloody and pulsing brain. The thing sported an ugly, vicious mouth that yawned impossibly wide and was filled with long, crooked and wickedly sharp teeth that curved inwards to prevent the jaw from closing.

The thing's body was a bloated, bulging abomination coated with viscous, black slime that glistened like spilled oil. As with the skull, the body also shifted and rippled as if still undecided as to its final form and the gray skin that stretched taut over its corpulent form was slick, smooth, *amphibious* and oozed putrescent mucus that stank of death and putrefaction.

As Carolyn stared, she could only make out three of the thing's legs – along with a vulgar, jutting bulge that dangled between two of them – but she was certain it possessed more. Each emaciated leg was a bony spindle with three or four sharply angled joints that served to give them an insect-like appearance, and they were mimicked by a pair of gangly arms that sprouted from the thing's bulbous torso. Fleshless, dripping with disgusting shit-tainted slime, the arms ended with abnormally elongated hands and long skeletal impossibly dextrous fingers.

The demon glowered intently at Carolyn and her mind tumbled down into its terrible eyes; ethereal, intense they nestled deep in their sunken sockets, a glacial, piercing blue that blazed bright from that hellish face with unfathomable curiosity and a deeply intelligent malevolence.

Carolyn opened her mouth to scream but nothing came out save a strangled gasp of air. In her panic she scrambled backwards in the pentagram, bare feet gaining little purchase on the smooth, damp floor, her naked breasts jiggling around like angry Jell-O. Her flailing arms knocked the skull scudding out of the circle with its jaw lolling at a crazy angle, and tipped over one of the candles, which spilled hot wax on her hand as its yellow flame snuffed out with a puff of black smoke.

Perplexed by Carolyn's reaction, Ashlynn twisted her head to take a peek over her own shoulder.

And then she screamed long and loud.

CHAPTER FOURTEEN

inally, its first taste of freedom.

At first flush, it had found the new realm to be a strange, hostile and thoroughly alien place. Even though it had previously experienced glimpses through the cracks, little could have prepared it for the overwhelming onslaught of extraordinary smells and sounds that pressed in on its senses, and the vicious light that assaulted its light-starved eyes; almost unbearable following a perpetual existence in the void.

It studied briefly the things that had until now been nothing more than fragments of psyche and dim light and voices and had found them to be both intriguing yet as expected. Their weak minds had been undemanding to manipulate and it could see for itself that their delicate bodies would take little effort to collect.

It also heard the begging, pleading cries of the kin it had left behind, their voices faint but growing as their numbers swelled in its wake, their desperate anticipation bolstered by its success.

It paid them no heed – their time would come soon enough.

Ripping apart the weakened membrane that had for so long been an impenetrable barrier between the worlds, and the seemingly endless crawl through the cloying, sucking slime of putrefaction had left it thoroughly exhausted. It summoned around it the comforting darkness and welcomed the protection of the shadows in which it would regain strength, for as meticulous as its machinations had been thus far, its work was far from complete.

CHAPTER FIFTEEN

Labeaux fumbled with trembling, panicked hands to click the fresh battery in to the camera but his attention was distracted by the commotion going on behind him. He saw that there was *something* behind Ashlynn and judging by her shrill scream and the way she skittered across the floor on her ass to get away from it, Labeaux knew that whatever the dark shape was, it wasn't a good something.

Likewise, Priestley, Carolyn, Chris, Danny and Priscilla scrambled away from the pentagram like their backsides were on fire but from where stood, Labeaux could only make out a black, nebulous silhouette that was mostly obscured by one hysterically screaming Ashlynn.

By the time Labeaux had clicked the fat battery into place the thing was gone, its squat, crooked lump of a body carried away by an array of scuttling legs – five, *six*? – he really couldn't be sure – as the thing high-tailed it out through the gymnasium door.

"Shit," Labeaux growled, annoyed at having missed the action. "What the fuck, guys?" he shouted over as he hoisted the bulky camera to his shoulder. "Nobody called action –"

Labeaux's complaint was interrupted by a piercing, blood-curdling scream from beyond the door; a high, ululation that ached with terrible, unspeakable torments and resounded with a haunting, otherworldly tone that was altogether *inhuman*.

And then silence settled.

"What the fuck *was* that?" Carolyn, subdued, spoke more to break the deafening silence and kill the echo of the scream that bounced around in her head than with desire to hear the answer. She sat down in her canvas chair with her knees tucked tight to her bare chest and she hugged on them for comfort.

Chris and Priscilla stared at each other, unsure of exactly what they had just witnessed, Priestley appeared unnaturally calm (although he too had not been able to get away from the pentagram quickly enough), and Danny was bursting like a kid who'd forgotten to take his *Ritalin*.

"Did you see it?" Danny enthused. "Did you see *that*?"

"Did you get it, Maurice?" Ashlynn broke her silence. She looked pale, drawn and her voice was croaky from screaming. "Did you film that thing?"

Labeaux shook his head. "Sorry, no," he said. "I couldn't get the battery changed in time."

"Oh for fuck's sake, Mo'," Priestley admonished.

"And fuck you too, Dave." Labeaux was in no mood for Priestley's bullshit. He ambled over to the pentagram with his camera up on his shoulder and doing its thing. "If I'd had more fucking warning that you planned to unleash one of your practical effects –"

"Warning?" Priestley scolded, "you're the fucking cameraman, you shouldn't *need* any warning," he fumed. "And *that* – that wasn't an effect."

"Yeah, right," Labeaux rumbled.

"I think I got it," Priscilla butted in. She plucked her minicam off of the chair with great reluctance, as if whatever it had captured on its memory card could possibly be lurking inside. "My camera was on the whole time. Give me a minute," she said with a nervous laugh and rewound the footage to where she figured the action to be.

Everyone gathered around Priscilla – even Carolyn eschewed the comfort of her chair – and with shaking fingers she thumbed the minicam's play button and the playback commenced.

Carolyn flashed up on the camera's tiny viewing screen, her striking face screwed up into a snarl as she delivered her bitchy comeback to Ashlynn; *'– or is it because you're out of bounds Ashl –?',* her voice pitchy and *miniature* coming from the camera's tiny speaker. Then came the seemingly endless split-second of Carolyn's silence, followed by Ashlynn's shrill scream. Priscilla allowed the movie to run for a second or two more before she hit *pause.*

"What the fuck is that thing?" Labeaux had positioned his camera over Priscilla's shoulder and zoomed in on the small, blurry figure on the diminutive screen.

"Is it really – *real*?" Carolyn stared at the fuzzy image that glowered out from the LCD display with piercing blue eyes. "It *looked* real."

"Do you know what this is, Dave?" Chris asked, "tell us you know what that fucking thing is?"

Priestley shrugged and gave them his best *search-me* smile. "No idea, guys, I'm just as surprised by that thing as the rest of you," he said.

Ashlynn slapped Priestley's arm and gave him her sternest look. "You're a lying sonofabitch, Davy," she said. "you totally set that up –"

"It came from over there," Labeaux broke in, he hated it when Ashlynn got on his friend's case, it made him want to beat some respect into the domineering bitch, "if you follow the trail it left, you can see that it came from where Dave threw up." He panned his camera to pick up the dark, glistening streak that ran from the corner of the gym to the pentagram, and then off towards the double doors.

Labeaux crouched down and dipped a finger in the slime trail where it ran uncomfortably close to his feet. "What is this stuff?" Labeaux drew the finger to his nose. "It smells like –" He gagged and pulled a disgusted face. "Oh sweet Jesus," he grimaced, "it *is* shit!" Labeaux wiped his finger on the floor, desperate to remove the offending substance from his skin. "This stuff stinks worse than your puke, Dave – and that's *really* starting to churn my guts right now." Labeaux was right; the rank stench from Dave's throw-up had permeated the cool gymnasium air like some noxious wartime gas. He looked up at Priestley like this was all his fault but held his thoughts, struggled upright and carried on filming.

"You're not telling us the truth, are you?" Ashlynn looked straight into her boyfriend's eyes, convinced that she could read him far better than she actually could. "That thing scared the living shit out of us." She prodded Priestley in the chest with one expensively manicured fingernail. "You've frightened us all and you've got your scene – so come on, spill." She studied her boyfriend's face for any one of the multitude of visible tells that she knew all too well.

"Spill what?" Priestley returned her eye contact, cucumber-cool.

"How you did it. How you made the monster."

"Yeah, awesome effects, dude," Labeaux joined in, some relief in his voice, "that has to be some of your best work to date." He gave his friend an admiring glance. He'd seen practical effects nowhere near as good on professional film sets, Priestley really had outdone himself this time.

"Got to hand it to you, Dave, you've done us all proud again," Chris smiled, "so come on – who's in the creature suit?"

"Is it Corinne?" Carolyn offered.

"Yeah, it has to be Corinne," Danny said, "is that how come she hasn't been around for shooting any of the scenes, Dave?"

Priestley kept his face straight and stepped away from the group a little to reinstate his position as head honcho. "Okay, people, you got me." He raised his arms, palms up and cracked a smile as he spoke directly into Labeaux's camera lens, "I guess it's time for me to 'fess up."

Priscilla manoeuvered around Labeaux's back to give herself a good shot of Priestley's grinning face and the rapt expressions on everyone else's.

"What we performed tonight was not *strictly* a Black Mass." Priestley glanced at everyone in turn and appeared amused at the look of relief on each face. "What I mean to say is that it *was* a Black Mass, only I kind of threw in an invocation." He took a deep breath – tasted the cloying shit-stink at the back of his throat – and continued, "I thought it only appropriate since our characters are supposed to be *invoking* the serial killer's evil spirit."

"Going for the *authentic* again?" Ashlynn mumbled. If she heard the A-word in reference to Dave Priestley once more, she swore she'd snap his motherfucking dick off.

"Exactly," Priestley confirmed her suspicions and gave her his *serious* face. "Only, I think that in this instance we may have been a little *too* authentic." He paused there to let the chilled silence say the rest.

Chris gave a sideways glance at Carolyn who was busy chewing on the inside of her cheek; a sure sign of nerves and it kind of tarnished the unquestionable allure of her brazen nudity for him. "You do realize that this is just a movie we're talking about, right Dave?" he said.

"Yeah, it's supposed to be *just a movie*," Priestley

air-quoted, "but I'm afraid that it just turned in to a heck of a lot more, Chris." Priestley was sounding serious, but then again, fake sincerity was something he was incredibly good at. "I think we may have accidentally invoked one of hell's denizens." He offered them all a weak smile and ran nervous hands through his hair.

Ashlynn ground her teeth so loudly that Priscilla heard it and looked over to see what the noise was.

"And that's what we saw just now." There was a definite tremble to Priestley's voice, which could either have been nervousness or exhilaration. "We summoned it, and now it's free and running around the school." He lowered his voice to a barely audible whisper, "and God only knows what it's planning to do to us." He paused once more with yet another trademarked Dave Priestley poignant silence.

Labeaux made with a slow handclap.

He had his camera gripped firmly between his elbow and midriff and stood grinning ear to ear like the dog with two dicks. "Oh yeah," he boomed, "*that* really is some awesome shit, dude. With acting talent like that, you really should spend more time in front of the fucking camera." Labeaux looked around at the others, amused by their solemn faces and embarrassed by his own initial fear. "And look, he's still keeping up with the pretense to keep us all spooked," he addressed them all. "You really *are* some kind of fucking genius, Dave, I'll give you that!"

Labeaux had worked with Priestley for most of his film career – had known the man for even longer than that – and he'd seen this tactic before. There'd been the time that Priestley had organized a police raid of a shoot location (*real* cops, no less!) and had kept the cameras rolling to catch the very real and horrified reactions from his cast as they were all arrested for trespassing on top secret government property. Even as they were carted off in police vans to be processed and released 'on bail',

Priestley had had the *chutzpah* to carry on the pretence right up until the wrap party.

That particular cast and crew had almost lynched Priestley for that particular stunt but the scenes had looked fantastic in the completed movie.

To this day, Labeaux had no idea how his friend had managed to pull that one off, and equally he couldn't wait to find out the secrets behind Priestley's brilliantly realistic demon/monster/creature thing.

"Yeah, nice one, Dave," the relief in Chris's voice was practically palpable," you *actually* had me scared. Well done, Sir"

"You sly old coot," Danny chipped in, "ya' even got *me* believing your parlour tricks. Just for a minute or two, mind you – and *I'm* the cynical old bastard," he laughed. Priscilla, Chris and Carolyn joined in with the uneasy mirth and everyone relaxed a little. Even Ashlynn allowed herself a gentle, snorting chortle and Priestley winked at her with the wryest of smiles dancing on his lips.

"So, come on, Davy," Carolyn teased, "w*ho* did you get to dress up in the bug suit and smear themselves in shit?"

A shriek cut through the air.

Painfully loud, high pitched and shredded by terror, the scream filled the gymnasium and clawed at the souls within.

The doors flew open and a flopping, dark shape crashed through. With macabre grace, the shape spun end over end in the air like a pinwheel, covering half the length of the gym until it hit the floor with a sickening, wet smack. From there it slid across the ground and left behind it a slick, dark trail before crashing against the wall with a *splat* and a halo of dark fluid that sprayed up and out and high.

Carolyn screamed and hid her face with her hands whilst the others stared, open-mouthed in disbelief at the crumpled heap that lay half in-half out of the murky shadows created by Danny's arc lights.

"What the fuck, Dave?" Labeaux voiced what he guessed everyone was thinking. "More special effects?" And this time, he was pleased to have caught most of Priestley's display on camera.

Slowly, Priscilla made her way across the gymnasium, filming her own progress as she went. She gagged at the violent stink that wafted across from the motionless thing that lay against the wall and she fished out a handkerchief from her pocket to hold over her nose. She leaned over the crumpled shape.

"Oh," Priscilla's simple statement – muffled by the 'kerchief – belied her shock, horror and disgust at the sight before her.

It was unmistakably a body.

A very *human* body.

Priscilla had been expecting to see some special effect-laden dummy; this being Priestley's dramatic reveal of a monster lovingly crafted in modelling latex and awash with fake blood. But no, this all looked far too real.

Chris, Ashlynn and the others had followed Priscilla across the room, and Labeaux had filmed them as they made their way in single-file silence. They gathered in an uneven semi circle and stared down at the body, each one with a hand to their nose to guard against the stink that reached up from it.

The body was that of a girl, no more than in her early twenties; its frame bulged with curvaceous hips and ample buttocks and although it lay on its front, evidence of the body's generous bosom lay in the way in which its – *her* – chest was raised from the floor. The girl's head had been twisted around in a near perfect one-eighty on her snapped neck and so she faced her onlookers over the ugly bulge below her jaw, the cruel knot of shattered vertebrae.

The girl was clad in a black latex body suit that covered her body from head to toe, except for where there were fat, ragged rips in the polished rubber through which glistened flashes of raw, red flesh. Her legs were broken, bent at impossible angles and upon her feet she wore black ballet shoes, the satin ribbon of one had undone and lay soaking up a puddle of blood. The girl's hair was tucked in neatly beneath the suit's shiny latex hood and her face was covered by a red Halloween mask that clung to her head with broad, black elastic.

Labeaux leaned in for a closer look and he recognized the mask with its stubby black horns and demonic, yellow eyes from his less than elegant encounter in the restroom. "What the fuck happened to her?" his voice was thick, phlegmy, as if he were about to throw up.

"Why is she covered in shit, Dave?" Carolyn gawked at the girl's corpse, at the thick clots of brown slime that clung to the latex, the viscera and congealing blood that oozed out from the frayed rips in the costume, and the spreading pool of blood from beneath the girl's smashed skull that looked black in the dim light.

"Where's her skin?" Chris asked as if he were merely asking the time of day.

It was evident that the girl had been flayed, as where the body suit had torn, glistening muscle and innards showed through. And, judging by the few shreds of remaining, lacerated skin that pouted outwards through the rubber, it seemed unlikely she had been skinned and *then* dressed.

"It looks like something clawed its way out of her," Ashlynn articulated what they were all thinking, "she's been skinned from the fucking *inside*," there was more than just a tinge of hysteria in her voice.

Ignoring his girlfriend's distress, Priestley stepped forward. He leaned over and pulled the devil mask from the dead girl's face – at least she had been spared her skin there – and studied with intent her bloodied features. Even in death she was beautiful, although her face was slack, lifeless, her eyes half closed, glazed and accusing.

This is all your fault, Davy-boy.

"Shit," Priestley muttered, "shit, shit, shit."

"What's going on, Dave?" Labeaux demanded. "Do you know who this is?"

"Corinne." Priestley's voice was barely there, "*this* is Corinne."

CHAPTER SIXTEEN

"I thought you said Corinne wasn't coming," Danny's voice shook. He had also recognized the corpse's mask, but from the drawing he and Labeaux had come across in the classroom and it made him feel sick to the pit of his stomach.

"I know what I *said*, Danny," Priestley snapped, and was that panic in his tone? "That was all part of the ruse. I told you all she was a no-show but I'd had her follow you guys in here," the quiver in his voice was gaining ground. "She was supposed to sneak around, make scary noises, slam a few doors and all that other clichéd crap." He let out a heavy sigh as he stared down at the ruined body by his feet. "And she was supposed to jump out and scare the bejesus out of us for the finale."

"So it was Corinne making all those noises and moving stuff around?" Chris stated the obvious.

"She even brought the goddamned cat in," Priestley said.

"*She* was your monster?" Ashlynn scoffed, "sex store Catwoman outfit and a crappy Halloween mask? *Really*?" She gave Priestley *that look* and wrinkled her nose. "You go to all this trouble to be authentic and then you create the world's least convincing monster?" She pointed at

180

Corinne with her foot and eyed the polished latex that covered some of the girl's body.

Ashlynn still couldn't be sure that what she was seeing was *not* one of Priestley's movie effects; it certainly looked nothing like the thing that had crept up on her by the pentagram. Sure, the ruined corpse of the girl he was claiming to be Corinne (Ashlynn did note with some satisfaction that she'd been right about him picking the girl for her boob size) looked – and *smelled* – real enough and this was a far cry from Priestley's usual chicken giblets viscera and theatrical blood-soaked paper towels for intestines, but she knew that her boyfriend was capable of amazing things when it came to special effects. And, rather selfishly, it ate away at Ashlynn that Priestley had evidently spared little expense when it came to Corinne's costume; couture, fitted latex of this quality didn't come cheap.

And if this was real, the *wunderkind* movie-man David Priestley really had gone too far, and someone had finally gotten hurt.

"I was going to show her in small glimpses," Priestley said by means of an explanation. "Like Ridley Scott did with his alien – in – er – *Alien*." He shrugged his shoulders, his face pale. His plan had been to build up a suspenseful atmosphere based on what the audience *didn't* see rather than relying on jump-scares and in-your-face horror; mostly to keep costs down, much like his thrifty hero Scott. "I didn't tell you guys about Corinne being our fake demon so that I could get your genuine reactions to all the creepy stuff." He glanced down at the body again. "I guess that's kind of sorted itself out now."

"Not funny, Dave," Ashlynn gave him a hard slap on the arm and walked away, no longer able to bear being near him.

"So what happened to her, Dave?" Chris demanded, "and how come she looks nothing like the other thing we saw?"

"I don't know," Priestley said quietly.

"I don't buy that, man," Labeaux lowered his camera; he'd filmed quite enough of Corinne's mutilated corpse. "This chick is dead. *Real* dead, not special effects dead," he couldn't help his aggressive tone. Seeing dead bodies up close and shredded will have that effect on a person, although there remained a (*very*) small part of Labeaux that thought this may still be part of Priestley's ruse – wishful thinking perhaps?

"Do you think I don't know that, Maurice?" Priestley defended.

"Dave," Labeaux squared up to his old friend, "did you do this?"

*

Its first physical encounter with a human being had been one filled with wonder and a delightfully inquisitive naiveté. Although, the frailty of the body had come as an unpleasant surprise, just how easily and quickly it had broken and how little strength it had taken to snap even the heavy bones that ran through the legs.

With all of the enquiring eagerness of a child who pulls the legs and wings off of a squirming bug, it had torn away the human's outer covering to take a peek at what marvels lay beneath, and the mechanics that made its strange body work. And very quickly it had learned that a human's head was not designed to rotate completely around.

And then it had experienced its first disappointment, as the being *had evaporated from the human, the bleeding had ceased and it had become no more than a simple, lifeless vessel. The petulant tantrum had followed soon after and it had thrown the thing away as if it were a broken toy.*

As much as the human had caused displeasure, it would have to be reclaimed – reanimated as necessary – for it constituted the cornerstone of the nefarious construction. No matter, there were others with which it could sate its boundless curiosity.

CHAPTER SEVENTEEN

"You actually think *I* killed her?" Priestley sputtered at Labeaux's accusation, "for fuck's sake, Mo'." He was genuinely shocked – or at least he provided an incredibly good appearance of such.

"You can't blame him for asking," Chris had a smug look on his face, "authenticity and all that."

Carolyn chewed on her cheek as she cogitated, seemingly unaware – or unconcerned – that she was still naked. She stepped forward. "Just how many more people *do* you have sneaking around in here, Dave?" she asked and the inference was loud and clear.

Did you put other people up to this?

Ashlynn sprang to Priestley's defence. As scared and angry as she was right now, and as uncomfortable as she felt in the habit, she didn't much care for the direction in which the conversation was heading, especially as it was being fronted by a most conspicuously nude Carolyn. "Just listen to what you're saying, for Christ's sakes," Ashlynn took a deep, calming breath and stalked back across the gym, "Dave may be more focussed on his movies than is probably healthy – he may even qualify as *sociopathic*."

Her attempt at a wry smile fell somewhat short. "And I'll be the first one to admit that this whole *authenticity* thing makes him a complete asshole to work with – but I know Dave better than any of you and I can tell you for damned certain that he wouldn't kill someone just for some stupid fucking movie."

Priestley looked at his girlfriend with a hurt expression in his eyes; the *asshole* jibe had hurt.

"Would you?" she asked.

Priestley shook his head and tried not to look too offended that Ashlynn had seen fit to ask him the question. And whilst her tone had been a little too accusatory for his liking, Priestley was grateful that she had leapt to his defence. Labeaux's and Carolyn's allegations had left him feeling vulnerable and although they had backed off at Ashlynn's intervention, he knew that they still suspected that he had something to do with Corinne's unfortunate demise.

In truth, Priestley was just as scared as everyone else, if not more so. This had never been a part of his plan; all Corinne was tasked with was slinking around to make with the spooky stuff, not get herself ripped to shreds and killed. This turn of events was an absolute disaster, perhaps even a portent of things to come, and Priestley was beginning to wonder just what he had gotten them all in to.

Priestley turned and walked away from Corinne's body and back towards the pentagram, the others following yet keeping their distance. His mind churned; there were things that he still needed to complete – for the movie and otherwise – so he knew that he had to think quick and smart in order to salvage the projects. And, his selfishness consoled him; perhaps Corinne's death didn't have to be the fuck-up that it appeared to be.

"We could work with this," Priestley said quietly.

"Pardon me?" Ashlynn queried.

"I said, I think we can work with this. Work *around* it if we have to – but we can still get the movie finished."

"You're *suggesting* we carry on like this didn't just happen?" Chris pointed over to Corinne's bloodied (Once a heartbeat stops, the body stops bleeding) body, thoroughly convinced that Priestley had finally turned the last corner to crazy.

"Seriously?" Danny was shocked, "what we need to do is call 911, pack up our shit and get the hell out of here," and for once, Danny was completely devoid of humor; sharing an elementary school with a fresh corpse was certainly no time for gags – he prided himself with having more respect than that.

Danny knew with mounting dread that along with the inevitable explaining to the relevant authorities how they (*he!*) had broken into the school, there would be expected to be a plausible explanation for the decidedly dead Catwoman. Shannon was going to have a goddamned field day with all of this, as if she would need yet another reason to berate him, it may even cost him Addison. "We really need to cut our losses and go," Danny told the others. "And just hope that we can talk our way out of this clusterfuck," he reiterated and was greeted with nodded agreement from everyone.

Everyone except Priestley.

Danny pulled his cell phone from his pocket, pressed the nine and then followed it by the first of the ones.

"Guys, guys!" Priestley's voice, loud in the stunned silence, made them all flinch. He sounded manic, on the verge of hysteria and that made everyone feel uncomfortable. "Before we do anything rash," this was directed at Danny who paused with his thumb over the *1* button on his phone, "just hear me out. Please," Priestley implored.

All eyes fell on Priestley and his face reddened as he prepared for his shit-or-bust speech. "I know you're all going to think that I'm a gigantic asshat for saying so, but this could actually be beneficial to our film," his voice was passive, almost timid.

"Are you fucking serious?" Ashlynn gasped. She'd never been more appalled at her boyfriend. "Corinne's fucking dead, Dave! *Dead*!" she raised her voice to near-screech and pointed an accusatory finger towards the corpse, as if she really needed to.

"I wasn't referring to Corinne," Priestley explained, "and you have to believe me when I say how truly sorry I am for whatever happened to her." He was going to add even *though I had absolutely nothing to do with it in any way* but figured that since he wasn't going to convince any of them otherwise, why bother?

"What I *mean* is that if what has happened here tonight is what I *think* has happened, then that would make us the first people to have filmed a demon. *Ever*," Priestley paused to give time for his point to sink in.

"Why can't you just leave it alone?" Chris growled. "Don't you think it's time to drop the play-acting, Dave? Somebody just died here and you're still trying to sucker us in with your dumb games."

"Think about it," Priestley ignored Chris, voice rising as his excitement refused to be contained. "Green Crayon's *Terrorfest* film could have a genuine, *bona fide*, one-hundred per cent demon as its star." He smiled at the incredulous faces that gawped at him and in his fervour he genuinely failed to see why they weren't sharing his enthusiasm. "And after *Terrorfest*, who knows where this could take us? *The Black Mass* could be the next *Blair Witch*, people."

Ashlynn shook her head and dropped her eyes. She was embarrassed by – and *for* – her boyfriend. It was at times such as this that she really didn't think she knew him at all.

"And what if –" Priestley said with an air of mystery, "– what if this *is* all part of my master plan and Corinne is *simply* an incredibly good effect?" Thus were sown the seeds of doubt; Priestley knew that they all knew modern movie prosthetics and creature effects could be so lifelike as to pass for the real thing – so long as they weren't required to move or interact in any way. And besides, how many of them had ever seen a real dead, mutilated body? "So what say we finish up filming and if Corinne's still dead tomorrow, we call it in then?"

"That's crass, even for you, Dave," Labeaux grumbled. He was beyond disgusted with his best friend right now, and that wasn't earned easy – they'd even shared hookers in their murky, distant past, for heaven's sake. "Why don't you just say that it's *what Corinne would have wanted* and have done with it?" Labeaux turned away and made for the equipment table. Danny was right, it was time to pack up and leave.

It was Carolyn – somewhat predictably – who spoke up in defence of Priestley's suggestion. She folded her arms over her bare breasts and spoke slowly as if she were addressing a half-wit rally, "Dave may have a point." *That* guaranteed everyone's attention. "We *all* have a real opportunity here, if what Dave says is true about his demon," as the words tumbled from her mouth, Carolyn had an inkling of just how certifiable she must be sounding right now. But if Priestley *was* being truthful about there being a demon loose in the school, then this really was the chance of a lifetime.

And, of course there was always the strong chance that Priestley was playing each and every one of them and that this was just part of his master plan to shoot a convincing movie; the demon-thing being little more than smoke and mirrors and Dead Corinne not all she seemed to be. Carolyn had worked on enough professional horror shoots to know just how convincing practical effects could be. "And if it's not, then what do we have to worry about?" Carolyn said firmly, "I say we carry on."

Ashlynn looked at Carolyn like she was dirt, turned her back and slunk back towards the equipment tables.

"Carolyn's right, guys." Priestley spread his arms like a snake-oil salesman pushing his dubious wares on simple townsfolk. "This could be the *fuck-you moment* we've all been waiting for, and I really think we'd be foolish to waste it."

There was something they *all* understood. The Holy Grail *fuck-you moment* is that moment which filmmakers, writers, actors, musicians – artists of *all* persuasions – dream of reaching in their career. It is that one glorious instant when having 'made it' they get to flip the big old bird to everyone who'd ever ignored them as they'd struggled to hone their craft; unreturned calls, bounced emails, scripts returned unopened or the myriad, despicable purveyors of false hopes who preyed upon the dreamers with grandiose promises of fame and fortune.

"I can't believe I'm hearing this," Chris broke the moment. "Corinne is dead. Someone – or some*thing*, if you want to believe *him* –" he addressed Carolyn whilst pointing at Priestley, "– did that to her body and threw her across the room like she was fucking inflatable!" Chris's face was flushed, his eyes brimmed with panic. "We are all in so much deep shit over this, and you're saying we should make a fucking movie?"

Priestley faced Chris square on. Chris rarely swore, and when he did, Priestley knew that the guy was close to caving. "Yes," Priestley spoke with deliberation, "that's exactly what we're saying, Chris." He looked around at the others to size up his support, and figured that he was fairly close to hitting home with most of the others; only Ashlynn had her back to him. He knew she was listening though, even though she pretended to be doing something with one of Labeaux's spare cameras.

"I propose that we do a quick rethink of our script – rewrite a little where necessary – and make the movie about us catching the demon that we just summoned," Priestley said, as if what he was suggesting was the most natural and reasonable suggestion in the world.

Labeaux gave Priestley a derisive snort. "And just *supposing* that we buy into your idea that this thing is for real, and conveniently forget the fact for now that Corinne has joined the ranks of the recently deceased – do you actually expect us to chase after that thing?" He gave another snort to hide the unease at the back of his mind, that Corinne's 'corpse' could well be nothing more than a brilliant fake. Labeaux had considered going back to examine the body a little closer but didn't want to risk destroying the fragile illusion he had built up in his mind, nor did he relish the thought of putting his DNA all over it; there remained the possibility that it *was* the mysterious – and quite dead – Corinne.

"You must be putting your therapist's kids through college, buddy," Labeaux said by means of reproach, although he knew deep in his guts that Priestley was going to get his way.

He always fucking did.

Priestley pushed his crew harder. He sensed that he was getting through to Labeaux and Danny and he knew he definitely had Carolyn on board. Priscilla didn't really count either way and Priestley knew that Chris would go along with the majority, despite his protestations. And that left Ashlynn to serve as the potential sticking point. If they all had this figured for some elaborate hoax, Priestley could be confident of their buy-in. "You can believe whatever you want to believe," he continued, "but if the demon *is* for real – and I know you may be sceptical on that one – then this is *our* fault for summoning it." Another one of those dramatic pauses. He scanned the faces around him, watched as his words sank in. "In which case, it's *our* responsibility to send it back to wherever it came from," Priestley hit them with his final shot – if all else fails, simply appeal to their sense of humanity – and hoped that he had planted sufficient uncertainty in their minds.

"I say we track the demon down, catch it and perform a revocation," Priestley concluded, "and film every damn thing we do."

Labeaux approached Priestley, placed a firm hand on his friend's shoulder and looked down at him. "I've seen you do some crazy shit, dude," there was sad resignation in the big man's voice. "But *this* – this is one step too far. Fuck, it's a million steps too far, Dave." He shook his head. "But you are right on one thing – I don't believe your demon bullshit for one minute," Labeaux's voice lowered to a resounding baritone. "But I do believe that *something* happened here tonight, even if your Corinne is a fake." He smiled at Dave; it was not a friendly smile.

Carolyn stepped up. "So what say we go along with Dave's story – for the sake of our movie?" She touched Priestley's arm in a gesture that was a tad more than a show of solidarity. She looked up at Labeaux. "I get that you don't believe that we've actually invoked the Devil – I think all of us are probably sceptical on that one – but you have to admit that what we *do have* is the opportunity to shoot an amazing piece of film." She touched Priestley's arm again, this time attracting Ashlynn's attention. "If nothing else, we owe it to Corinne."

Yep, she went there.

Ashlynn made her way back over from the equipment table with a broad fisheye lens clutched in her fist like it was a weapon. "Nice speech, Carolyn," Ashlynn snarled, "but since when were you Dave's official spokesperson?"

"I was just trying to help – "

"Well don't," Ashlynn growled and her eyes blazed with fury. "And will you *please* put some fucking clothes on?"

Defeated, Carolyn lowered her eyes and shuffled around the pentagram to retrieve her dress; well and truly put back in her place, she looked much like Eve after the apple incident.

"I need everyone to buy in to this, guys," Priestley told them, "*everyone*." He glanced across at Ashlynn who looked daggers back at him. As always, without her on board with this, nothing was going to happen.

The silence that greeted Priestley told him all he needed to know and he smiled with relief. "Whatever you believe, *I* think that the universe is giving us the chance to do something truly extraordinary," he concluded, "just imagine how good it will look on film when we corner a *real* demon and send it back to hell."

Labeaux let out a long sigh. This was going to happen – like it or lump it – so he figured he might as well play along. Still, he struggled to believe that Priestley was expecting them all to carry on as if there wasn't a corpse in the room. Experience had taught Labeaux that his friend had a wily aptitude for drawing people into his crazy schemes and – hoax or not – he did make a valid point; it *would* look fantastic on film.

Labeaux looked Priestley square in the eyes and asked, "and just how are we supposed to do that, Father fucking Karras?"

CHAPTER EIGHTEEN

Priestley had covered Corinne up with a blue tarp he'd found in the equipment cupboard and everyone seemed relieved that the body – real or otherwise – was out of sight and, had it not been for the God-awful stink of death it had brought to the gymnasium, all but out of mind.

Back at the equipment table and surrounded by his cast and crew, Priestley rummaged through his backpack and its contents jingle-jangled like so much loose change. Eventually his hand grasped what he was searching for and he pulled out a yellow, padded *Jiffy* envelope.

He opened it.

In the envelope there were eight miniature glass phials, each no more than an inch and a half long and a little less than the width of his pinkie finger. They were stoppered with a tiny cork bung and contained a crystal clear liquid. The phials were threaded onto a length of leather cord, which made them into functional – if not terribly fashionable – necklaces. They were purported to be powerful amulets; part of Priestley's numerous purchases from the medical supply store, bought on the solemn insistence of the manager.

"I need each one of you to take one of these," Priestley instructed his team with a morbid air of gravitas. Everyone stepped forward and took a phial from his outstretched hand and draped it around their neck – all except Ashlynn who lingered at the back of the group, reluctant to be part of any more of her boyfriend's shenanigans; she had changed out of the habit and was once more in the comfort of her sweater and shorts, although missing the habit's warmth. However, after Corinne's appearance, she had felt understandably out of place and uncomfortable in the thing.

"There's one for you, too," Priestley told Priscilla; it was to have been Corinne's, and perhaps in hindsight he should have given it to her when they'd had their clandestine meeting the week before to hand over the latex catsuit and go through a final briefing.

Too late now.

All things considered, it was fortuitous that Labeaux had the habit of inviting some female or other along to their shoots, and that Priscilla had filled in admirably – Priestley couldn't quite shake the feeling that so far as replacing Corinne went, somehow he had *known*.

"Thank you." Priscilla took the phial from him and slipped it around her neck.

"It's holy water with a fragment of blessed communion wafer," Priestley explained as he held up the last remaining amulet to Ashlynn. "It will offer protection from the demon."

Ashlynn snatched the thing from Priestley's hand, grasping it by the cord as if the flawless glass would strike her down stone cold dead should she touch it.

"I have the revocation written down on Post-Its," Priestley told them – ever the King of the Post-It, was Dave Priestley. "There's one copy for each of us to read out loud, once we catch up with the demon." He pointed to the neat array of pink neon squares he'd laid out on the table.

"And you think that it's just going to sit there like a good little puppy while we do this?" Danny plucked a note from the table; his eyes twitched side to side as he read through it. "We all saw what that thing did to Corinne and you expect a smidgen of Latin and some water is going to put it in its place?" Danny gave a nervous laugh that failed miserably to hide his fear.

"This all seems to be very well prepared, *babe*, even for you," Ashlynn said. "You either planned this, or you *knew* this was going to happen, didn't you?" her accusation drew everyone's eyes to Priestley as they awaited his answer.

"I'll admit that I knew that there was always the possibility that it *might* happen," Priestley edged around Ashlynn's accusation like an evasive politician, "there is always the chance that you can invoke *something* when you mess around with this shit, everybody knows that, Ash'." He made eye contact with each one of his team in turn. "But I *honestly* didn't expect anything like this; which is why I organized Corinne to play our demon in the first place," as he spoke, Priestley saw that Priscilla had zoomed in on his face – nice and close – to capture his response.

"That doesn't answer my question," Ashlynn stood firm.

"Hey, don't look at me like that, guys," Priestley attempted to garner everyone's sympathy at Ashlynn's bullying. "Believe it or not, I took great care to ensure that the ritual was safe. I specifically left out one of the key elements." He picked up his copy of *Satanic Rituals* and leafed through the rumpled pages to get to the appropriate passage. "You can read it here for yourselves – *a nun or someone dressed as a nun is required,*" he read it out for their benefit, "*black candles, a skull or other major bones, human altar* – ah, here it is – *a gong to signal the commencement of the ritual*." Priestley smiled at his doubters. "There you go. I didn't bring the gong, and it specifically states here that there *has* to be a gong."

"If I could have your attention, people!"

"Well ain't that a goddamn comfort?" Labeaux muttered. He cast a glance over at the heaped blue tarp and then down at the shit-trail the demon had left behind. Either it was his imagination or the air in the gymnasium had become a little colder, and the feculent stink had grown somewhat thicker whilst they'd been standing around debating Priestley's bullshit.

As they walked across the slick, rotting floor of the gym, Danny, Chris, Carolyn and Ashlynn twiddled nervously with their amulets. None of them were what you would call true believers in any form of God – fair-weather believers at best – but Priestley's little glass phials went some way towards providing a modicum of comfort as they each contemplated the foreboding shadows that skulked beyond the gymnasium doors. Slowly, reluctantly everyone followed Priestley towards the doors as Labeaux filmed their progress and Priscilla filmed Labeaux filming them.

"It is imperative that we all stick together with our story," Priestley spoke up as he paused by the door. Even as leader of the group and chief instigator, he was stalling the inevitable. "I give you all my word that I'll call 911 first thing tomorrow and take the fall for everything," his accompanying smile was weak, "so, all I ask is that you guys trust me, no matter what." He turned on Labeaux, "especially if you happen to think that this is all some clever set-up." He stared into the dispassionate lens of Labeaux's camera. "Please?"

"Damn right I think it's one of your set-ups," Labeaux growled, "and I'll deal with that later, Dave. Meantime, I promise I'll keep it zipped and just point my goddamned camera."

"I've come this far, Dave, so I may as well see it through for the good of our film," Carolyn reassured.

Chris nodded his own hesitant concurrence, "I guess I'm in too, then. But can we set up base camp in another room? It smells *really* gross in here." He held a hand to his nose to block out the cloying stench that really was getting worse by the minute.

"Sure thing, Chris," Priestley agreed. "Guys?" he addressed the conspicuously silent Danny and Ashlynn, both of whom gave him the faintest of nods.

Ashlynn's face reddened. "Am I the only one who's not forgotten that there's a *dead girl* over there?" as she spoke she gave each and every one of them a withering look of contempt. "She's fucking *dead*, Dave!" her raised voice compressed Priestley's eardrums and made him wince.

"It's totally down to you, babe," Priestley told her, "do you want to leave?"

"Yes," Ashlynn replied, "that's *exactly* what I want to do." She looked around at the trepidatious faces that surrounded her. "But I guess I'm fucking-well outvoted, aren't I?"

"Okay. Then we're all good." Priestley let out the breath he'd been holding. Slowly, calmly, he eased open the gymnasium door and lead them all out into the hallway.

*

The fetid reek of shit, vomit and something altogether less corporeal wasn't all that much better out in the hallway. There it seemed to ooze from every damp pore of rotting plaster, shred of peeled paper and dripping hole; it had a substantial, *sticky* reek to it - the dank aroma of decay and corruption, of diseased, suppurating flesh and the foulest excrement.

And it *was* getting worse.

The smell served to churn Priestley's belly over again; a constant reminder of the abhorrent cocktail he'd thrown up in the gym along with his soda and burritos. And yet – somewhat surprisingly – the thought of the latter was making him feel hungry.

Priestley had split the team up into three groups, and that had made him feel a little like he was stuck in some macabre, real-life *Scooby-Doo* adventure. He'd chosen Carolyn (much to Ashlynn's chagrin – but he'd really needed some time away from that constant look of condemnation on his girlfriend's face) and Priscilla for his group, as he'd also hoped to find somewhere to film an introduction for his hastily-revised movie; Danny and Labeaux had gone on to investigate the classrooms whilst Ashlynn and Chris had been tasked with moving essential equipment into the Principal's office, even though that had meant them venturing back into the gymnasium.

Priestley had decided upon the Principal's office to decamp, and hoped that the smell that emanated from Puke Corner wouldn't be quite so bad in there, although it did seem to have percolated through the rest of the school at an alarming rate.

Playing his flashlight beam along the hallway, Priestley danced the stark light in amongst the shadows that prowled between the arc lights and around the uneven floor as he followed the slime trail that practically effervesced with the unearthly smell. Carolyn – fully dressed once more – followed close behind, the fingertips of one hand touching the glass amulet that bounced against her bountiful chest; she walked so close behind him that Priestley could feel the warmth of her sweet breath on his nape.

Priscilla walked alongside them, the tiny, red LED on her camera blinking incessantly as she captured their progress on film. In her free hand, Priscilla clutched her Post-It in a grip so tight that her French-manicured nails had stabbed clean through the paper.

The hallway made a ninety-degree turn at its end and the hallway beyond was out of the sight of the gymnasium. At the junction, Priestley halted before of a pair of rotting posters that had been peeled from the wall by time and moisture; one was anti-bullying, the other featured an odd looking animal that may have been either a beaver or a groundhog (or some perverted hybrid of both) that advised *'just say no to drugs'* – as if that were the easiest thing in the world to do.

"This looks like a good place," Priestley said. He ushered Carolyn to an arbitrary spot in front of the posters, her back to the wall. "Are you ready for your piece to camera?"

"Yes, sir," Carolyn replied with a half-smile. This whole thing had her scared witless and she was starting to wonder if her hopeless crush on Dave Priestley really was worth the effort. "Err, what am I supposed to be saying exactly?"

Priestley stroked a strand of hair from Carolyn's face. She looked a little rough around the edges and he wished now that he'd booked a make up artist for the shoot. No worries, Carolyn was a natural beauty and perhaps the slightly bedraggled look would add yet more of that wonderful authenticity to the movie.

"Just improvise," Priestley told her, "we're hunting an escaped demon in a creepy, abandoned school with a tragic history – just let your imagination run wild, babe." Priestley gave an inward cringe; if Ashlynn ever heard him call Carolyn – or any other female for that matter (but *especially* Carolyn) – *babe,* she'd have his balls for bookends. It was an irrational worry, he knew, because Ashlynn was safely occupied somewhere between the gym and the Principal's office. Nonetheless, Priestley found himself glancing over his shoulder all the same.

"Do you want me to look *into* the camera, or slightly off to the side?" as with most acting school graduates, Carolyn was nervous about breaking that fourth wall – very much the greatest of all thespian taboos – even though Priestley had already explained the scenario at least twice.

"Imagine that you are recording a video for the people who will find your body, should you not survive this terrifying ordeal," Priestley told her once more and tried to ignore the look of horror in the girl's eyes, "we'll cut this footage in with Maurice's shots; trust me, it's going to look *awesome*."

Carolyn composed herself, smoothed her dress down over the bulge that her well-rounded thighs made under the material and tapped a nervous finger on the glass phial that snuggled in the deep, dark slit of her cleavage. She didn't care much for Priestley's analogy for her motivation, but he *had* called her *babe* and that almost made up for the unease she felt as she shivered in a decomposing school with just a flashlight between herself and total darkness.

A deep breath.

"It's ten minutes to midnight, and this old, haunted school is deathly quiet," Carolyn said with her best anchorwoman voice, "and we haven't seen anything or even heard so much as a sound since – *um* – since we last saw the demon," she paused to peer into the gloomy silence. "Our search for the demon – or whatever the thing turns out to be – continues." She plucked the amulet from between her breasts and lifted it up to the camera. "We can only hope that these talismans will protect us as and when we find it and send it back to whatever dark, disgusting place it crawled out from."

"Cut!" Priestley called, "that was perfect, babe –" *shit!* he really was going to have to watch that when they got back to Ashlynn. "– You made the hairs stand up on the back of my neck." He contemplated hugging Carolyn. She sure looked like she needed it, but Priestley thought that would be a step in the wrong – and a particularly slippery – direction. "Okay, if you would walk slowly over to the classrooms over there," he directed, "and we'll follow as you investigate." He glanced at Priscilla to ensure that she was still filming. "And don't forget to act scared."

"*Act*?" Carolyn laughed nervously.

From a dark-clad classroom a little further along the hallway they heard the sound of chairs scraping along the floor and a low, guttural growl. Priestley figured that there would be the perfect place to film their next scene.

*

At the same time as Carolyn was doing her piece to camera, Maurice Labeaux was walking through a classroom at the opposite end of Watsonville Elementary. Illuminated by the light from his camera, he worked diligently to capture footage of the yawning gaps in the black-speckled, Styrofoam ceiling tiles that looked like some monstrous mollusc had gnawed away. The holes were gaping, festering wounds that exposed the school's fleshless bones and from within, sickly colored water drip-drip-dripped from water pipes that rotted quietly away in the crawl space, to pool on the warped floor beneath Labeaux's footsteps.

Labeaux panned the camera from the ceiling and down along the walls to take in the damp-smudged artwork and an educational poster that portrayed the life cycle of the ubiquitous Monarch – complete with an intimate photograph of an adult butterfly emerging from its chrysalis. Labeaux zoomed in on that and thought it made for a particularly poignant juxtaposition – the birth of the new amidst the decay of the old.

Danny, headphones clamped over his ears, followed Labeaux around with a flashlight in one hand and his microphone held out at arm's length in the other, much like a fencer's sword. He lagged behind a little to avoid picking up any unwanted sounds of Labeaux's clumsy stumbles around the classroom, careful not to disturb any of the tables and chairs, as much in reverence of the room's erstwhile occupants as to not creating unnecessary noise. Danny glanced downwards as he stepped between two small, hexagonal tables and discovered to his irritation that the headphones' wire that draped around his had become entangled with the thin leather strap of the phial Priestley had issued. With a grunt, Danny pulled the 'phones down from his ears and began to untangle them.

Of course he considered it nothing less than pure hokum that Priestley had insisted they wear the dumb amulets and nothing so far had helped change that opinion. Danny thought they looked amateurish and he *knew* they'd look as crappy as hell on film – Addison could have done a better job of making the dammed things.

"You don't believe any of this, do you?" Danny's voice sounded hollow in the gloom.

"What gave me away?" Labeaux chuckled, "the fact that I called bullshit on the Priestley Puke Monster?" Again, with a conspiratorial snigger. "I've seen Dave pull some crazy stunts over the years, Danny, but this has to be his best one yet." He turned to face Danny. The harsh light from his camera lit up the old guy's face and served well to highlight the gray pallor of his sickly looking skin. "It is going to make one hell of a good movie, though."

"But if all this *is* a hoax, how do you explain the dead girl?" Danny asked.

"Corinne?" Labeaux furrowed his brow. "To be perfectly honest with you, Danny, I'm not *entirely* sure how Dave managed to pull that one off."

"Do you think he killed her?" Danny asked.

"Hell no," Labeaux laughed loudly and his booming voice seemed to *shift* the silence. "Our Davy-boy may be a borderline lunatic, but he's not quite homicidal – at least not yet, anyway," Labeaux said and just a tiny part of him doubted that particular statement. "My guess is that either he spent a shit-load of Daddy's money on an uber-convincing dummy or he found someone who's the world's best at playing dead and splashed some cash on the gore make-up," Labeaux clung to his denial. Corinne couldn't *really* be dead.

Could she?

"Corinne's probably sitting outside, smoking a fat one and laughing her ass off at us jackasses in here chasing someone else in a monster outfit." Labeaux laughed at his own comment and was gratified by just how well the hypothesis sat with him.

A child's cry crept into the classroom. A shrill, tormented wail that faded hastily away into the silence.

Labeaux and Danny stared at each other, eyes wide, adrenaline pumping.

"Did you hear that?" Labeaux asked and once more his denial mechanism kicked in; yet another sound effect? *This is getting old now, Davy-boy.*

Danny slipped the headphones back over his ears and hit the rewind button on his recorder. He stopped it dead where he figured the cry had come in and hit the play button.

Nothing.

"Fuck," Danny growled and rewound the tape once again and wished that he'd brought the back-up recorder; Labeaux was not going to be happy that the equipment had failed them yet again. He played the tape a second time.

Silence.

"Say something," Danny pointed the mic at Labeaux's face.

"Like what?"

"I don't know," Danny barely hid his frustration. "How's about *is there any fucker there*?"

"We did this before, remember?" Labeaux grumbled.

"Humor me," Danny said and with the headphones bulging out over his ears, he looked like a squat, shiny-headed bug.

Labeaux *harrumphed* like a petulant teenager and kept his camera focussed on Danny. "Okay, is there anybody there *now*?" he asked the shadows. "Any ghosts, killer devils from outer space or friends of Dave Priestley who are being paid in two dollar bills or weed of questionable quality to put the scares on us?"

Danny lifted a finger to quieten him and they both stood in silence whilst Danny ran the recorder for another thirty seconds or so. Then he rewound the tape and listened intently through his headphones.

"Nothing's coming through on the cans." He lifted the headphones from his ears and placed them back around his neck. "Let's see what happens when we do this –" he pulled the headphone jack out of the recorder, rewound once more and hit play.

"*– or weed of questionable quality to put the scares on us?*" Labeaux's baritone resonated from the built-in speaker and was followed by a deafening cacophony of discordant sounds that surged out as if carried by an ethereal wind. It was a maddening dissonance of screams and cries and low, grumbling moans as if myriad unearthly souls had been rudely disturbed from their eternal torments. Woven tight like a nefarious thread, voices upon voices clamoured to be heard: (Flows Better) trapped amidst the hellish din were the agonized shrieks of what sounded like children's voices – heart-rending cries that swept out from amongst the howling wails like lost souls in the unspeakable throes of agony.

"Jesus Christ, Danny – *what's going on?!*" Labeaux had to shout to make himself heard above the nefarious hubbub, in between which he discerned cracked cackles of laughter – the maniacal chuckling of something most terribly and darkly inhuman.

Taken aback by the suddenness and the intensity of the terrifying sounds, all Danny wanted to do was press his palms hard on to his ears and block the noise completely from his head. He fought hard against that instinct and forced himself to fumble with the buttons on the recorder until finally, a trembling finger located the stop button and he stabbed at it.

The noise continued.

"This is not on the tape," Danny replied to the quizzical look on Labeaux's face. "*I said – I didn't record this!*" he yelled and this time he was certain that Labeaux had understood him. "We are hearing this in real time!" Danny yelled as the noise abated as unexpectedly as it had arrived, and he found himself shouting into the quiet as the hideous noise faded to an annoying background buzz.

"It must be the Tannoy speakers – every school has them," Labeaux said. He was visibly shaken; he'd heard things slithering about in the noise that had triggered appalling images inside his head that were refusing to dissipate. It put him in mind of the recording a bunch of Russian geologists claimed to have made at the bottom of the world's deepest borehole. The inference was that they'd drilled so deep that they'd pierced one of hell's antechambers; the resulting screams of the supposed damned had gone viral across the internet in a matter of hours. Although the sounds that had just assaulted his ears were subtly different to the Russians' – Labeaux was positive he'd heard *words* in amongst the screaming – he guessed that it was feasible that Priestley had simply plagiarized it to broadcast around the school.

"I suppose that after the stunt Dave pulled with Corinne, a few sound effects wouldn't really be too much of a challenge," Labeaux shared his rationalization with

Danny.

Danny was sceptical. Had Priestley set this up, Danny would have been the person he'd have asked to do it. And he hadn't. And even if he had, Danny would never have been able to create such a horrifying mix of sounds – as if the wailing hadn't been disturbing enough, he'd heard *something* struggling out from amidst the torments, something that had clawed at his soul with a malicious hunger.

"I don't think it's sound effects, Maurice," Danny's voice was flat. He shook his head again, unsure as to whether the barely perceptible noise he was hearing now was for real or simply echoes of before lodged inside his head. He prodded at the play button on the recorder, his finger slick with nervous sweat.

He and Labeaux listened awhile to the silence that the recorder played back.

"And?" Labeaux furrowed his brow.

"I was recording through most of that." Danny glared at the recorder, as if the thing had purposefully let him down.

"You should have brought your backup equipment," Labeaux chastised.

Danny shrugged his shoulders as if the world's weight rested there. "You're probably right," he said, "we should go back." He turned on his heels and walked back towards the classroom door.

*

Ashlynn and Chris were lugging the last of the smaller ATA cases out of the gymnasium when the noise began. It raced towards them in a monstrous, tidal *whoosh* that crashed into their senses with a brutal assault of screams and shrieks of pain and distress. Ashlynn dropped the box she was carrying and clamped her hands tight to her ears, but still she heard the terrible sounds that forced their way inside her head to whirl and buzz and feast upon her sanity. Beside her, Chris froze to the spot and looked frantically around for the source of the dreadful sounds, his face a mask of confusion and terror.

In synch, Ashlynn and Chris cast a terrified glance across at Corinne, expecting her corpse to be the cause of the otherworldly sounds; perhaps resurrected as an evil, undead thing sent to exact revenge upon those who had been instrumental in her death.

But Corinne was gone.

The blue tarp that Priestley had so thoughtfully tossed over her mutilated corpse lay flat and lifeless against the warped floor.

And as they stared at the limp blue shroud in stunned disbelief the noise faded away until it became a low, annoying ambience.

With reluctance, Ashlynn took her hands down from her ears, her heart pounding hard and heavy in her chest. She could still hear the hellish noise, could even make out the occasional word or two amongst the now quietened jumble of broken, homogenised muttering and heart-wrenching cries. Ashlynn cocked her head to one side – dog-like – and sadness brimmed in her eyes as she spoke quietly to her companion, "just what the hell *is* that?"

Chris shook his head and peered around the gym, as if searching for answers amongst the shadows.

"It could be Dave up to his old tricks again," Ashlynn offered, although she didn't totally believe the words that tumbled from her mouth; there was just something about the noise, something *inside* of it that made it seem far too real to be anything but. "I'll bet he had Danny rig up the speaker system to give us some *atmosphere,*" as she spoke she made air quotes with crooked fingers that mocked her boyfriend.

At this Chris relaxed a little and a degree of relief crept across his face. "You're probably right, Ash'," Chris's tongue clicked as he spoke – his mouth was desert-dry, "I'd have preferred some Gaga, though."

They laughed together with an anaemic, nervous laugh that didn't quite manage to drown out the hellish noise that circled high up amongst the rafters and the ragged tear in the roof.

Neither one of them dared ask where Corinne may have gone.

Quickly, quietly, Ashlynn and Chris folded the remaining canvas chairs, picked up the last of the cases, and struggled with their loads towards the door. It was a task that really ought to have taken two trips, but neither of them relished a return trip to the gym and the dreadful sounds that crawled around its disintegrating walls.

Chris looked back as they neared the door. He'd figured they'd get the lights come morning since there were plenty others in the hallway, and he knew Danny would throw a fit if a couple of amateurs attempted to take down his precious rigs. As Chris scanned the room for anything they couldn't live without, Priestley's pentagram caught his attention. It sat there in the center of the gym, a huge, hateful eye, its extinguished candles and the chalice kicked over and beside it, the skull that grinned back at him with its lopsided jaw.

"I'd best get the skull, Dave'll go nuts if we leave it," Chris said, "can you manage the boxes if I carry all of the chairs?"

"Sure thing," Ashlynn would have agreed to pretty much anything to be away from that dreadful place. Between the appalling noise and the gut-wrenching stink, she couldn't get to the Principal's office quick enough (although the foul odor had made its way to the office, it was nowhere near as strong as in the gym). "But don't be too long," she told Chris as he stacked his ATA case on top of hers.

"You can count on it," Chris said with something akin to a smirk.

Ashlynn turned, pushed open the door with her butt and then she was gone.

Chris lay down the chairs and walked over to the skull, which smiled up at him like it was party to some wicked but inherently private joke at his expense. Chris picked the thing up and looked around for something to carry it in. Much to his chagrin, he realized that he and Ashlynn had relocated everything suitable for that purpose to the Principal's office and he'd be stuck carrying the skull by hand. He shuddered as the cold, chalky touch of the dead bones made his skin crawl.

Back at the gym door, Chris scooped up the canvas chairs with his free hand and made his way out, relieved that Danny's lights illuminated the hallway outside; it meant he wouldn't have to juggle a flashlight on top of the chairs as well as manhandle the creepy skull. Although, he knew he would have to make the most of the artificial light whilst he could; once he rounded the corner at the end of this hallway, the remainder of the journey to the Principal's (Need to be consistent with the capital P) office was unlit and cloaked by the damp night.

In the hallway the noise was fainter than it had been in the gym, but that did little to prevent its insidious rumble from eating into Chris's mind. He had to remind himself that Ashlynn's hypothesis was a sound one – that this was simply Dave messing with them – and that actually made him feel a tad better. Chris braved a low whistle as he walked, partly to cancel out the noise and because everybody knows that whistling is *the* sure-fire means of keeping at bay the odious creatures that loiter within the darkest shadows. The thin tune wheezed out between his parched lips flat and unrecognizable but served its purpose by drowning out the worst of the faint sounds that infected the school's hallways.

Something off to the right caught Chris's eye.

There it was again, the sudden movement of a door just a few steps ahead. Chris watched the door gently close as if in the wake of someone who'd just a moment ago made their way through it.

"Is that you, Ash'?" the hallway swallowed Chris's words. He put the chairs down, placed the skull neatly on top of them and fished out the flashlight that nestled in his back pocket.

Slowly, his breath no more than shallow gasps and his pulse pounding in his ears, Chris made his way over to the door. As he drew close, he espied the fading plastic sign that declared the room to be Watsonville Elementary's kitchen; in its day the bustling scene of mass crimes against cuisine, now it stood abandoned, dark and quiet.

Chris pushed open the door, clicked on his flashlight to penetrate the darkness with its beam.

"Are you in there?" his voice quivered, "Ashlynn?"

The yellow, stippled light picked out the ghostly outlines of the giant cooking pots that sat motionless on commercial sized stoves, and of others that dangled in their dozens from ceiling racks and looked like execution victims. Many of the storage cupboards were opened, their shelves crammed with rotted catering-sized condiment packets, flour bags and boxes of things with labels that had peeled away or faded to dirty white over the years and were therefore unidentifiable.

Chris's foot knocked against something hard and he yelped out loud as it jarred his toes. The thing spun across the floor with a piercing, metallic clatter and the breath caught in Chris's chest. He calmed himself down with a deep breath or two and aimed his light at the offending item, which turned out to be nothing more than a large, metal serving spoon – indeed the kitchen floor was littered with stainless steel ladles, spatulas, culinary knives and sundry cutlery, all scattered in that blind panic nine years ago.

The faintest of sounds rose above the whispering background noise.

Footsteps?

Chris interrogated the kitchen with his flashlight. "Hello?" he ventured, "who's there?" Doing his level best to mask the fear that made his voice shake, he said with as much courage as he could muster, "if you're another one of Priestley's phoney monsters, I'm afraid the game's up, buddy. We're on to you." A weak laugh.

"*Ego sum quis vos votum*," a deep, rasping baritone cut through the dark.

Startled, Chris spun his light around to where he guessed the owner of the voice to be.

And saw nothing at all.

A shape took form from within the impenetrable shadows behind Chris. In a thick, swirling, black fog the shadows congealed and moulded themselves into something altogether more solid. The shape they formed moved towards him.

When Chris turned back around, he saw the girl. She was completely naked – beautifully so – and Chris guessed her age to be no more than eighteen or nineteen. The girl had shimmering, raven-black hair with bouncing, natural curls that cascaded down the sensual curve of her back to the top of the delicate cleft between her pear-shaped buttocks and eyes that were the darkest brown, so deeply dark as to appear black in the poor light. She gave Chris the slightest of smiles as she approached and her glistening, scarlet lips parted to display perfect teeth.

Chris gawped at the vision before him like a love-stuck teenager. With the adrenaline awash in his veins, and the aching arousal that stirred his loins, Chris went into sensory overload, his body unable to move. Sure, he'd enjoyed the view and close proximity of Carolyn's nudity earlier on – she was a hot gal, what red-blooded guy wouldn't? – but in comparison to the girl who now stood less than an arm's length away, naked Carolyn had been nothing.

This was quite simply the most exquisite example of *female* that Chris Sherwood had ever had the delight of casting his eyes upon.

A step closer and Chris saw that the girl's body was adorned by a spider's web of delicate gold chains, a deliciously exotic and sensual contrast against silken skin that was so pale as to be almost translucent.

The fine chains clung by tiny golden hooks to the girl's stiff cherry-red nipples that perched atop her full voluptuous breasts. The chains snaked over and around the hourglass of her body, between her fingers and toes and were fastened by a triumvirate of barbed hooks that pierced her pouting, denuded labia. As the girl moved, Chris noticed the chains pulling gently at her delicate and beautiful flesh between her thighs. It teased him with a hint to open. (Suggested)

"Thank *you*, Mr. Priestley," Chris muttered to himself as the girl smiled a suggestive, wanton smile. He glanced around the kitchen for the tell-tale red light of hidden cameras – but he simply couldn't bear to have his eyes away from the girl for more than a moment. "Shouldn't we wait to get this on camera?" he asked, "or has Dave rigged up remotes in here?" His voice quivered, "I'm Chris, by the way." He offered his hand. "But I guess you'll know that already." Chris felt incredibly nervous – he always did around beautiful women – and knew for a fact that his face would have flushed that crimson color he'd been teased mercilessly about since puberty had hit him head-on.

The girl ignored the suggestion of a handshake greeting and instead held out her arms to beckon Chris to her embrace.

No further prompts required, Chris pulled his shirt off over his head and stepped towards the girl and into the warmth of her welcoming arms. Her lithe limbs folded around him and pressed him tightly against the heat of her naked skin as she moulded her body to his.

Then she kissed him full on the mouth. It was a deep, sensual kiss filled with the flavours of promise and delights beyond imagination, her tongue snaking long and languorous between Chris's lips in its fervent search for his. Eager hands trailed down along Chris's flanks and pulled at his belt and his jeans and before he'd fully registered what was happening, Chris felt the cool night air caress his thighs and freshly liberated penis.

And there Chris stood in their lover's embrace with his pants and shorts puddled at his ankles and his dick pressed hard and ardent into the mystery girl's thigh.

"Rehearsal?" Chris mumbled between kisses and still the girl held her silence. He stroked her skin with an anxious fervor he'd not experienced since his first time with Debbie Mellor back in eighth grade, his fingers caressing the long, smooth arc of the girl's back, the gentle rise of her buttocks, and up along the sides of her ribs that moved with the steady rhythm of her breathing. Chris lingered along the nape of her slender, graceful neck to delight in the downy skin that nestled there, before burying his fingers deep into the girl's long, luxurious hair that smelled of musk and humid summer nights.

Chris gasped – and in the midst of their kiss he stole a little of the girl's breath from her mouth – as slender fingers curled around his erection to guide it between the tantalizing chains that dangled from the wet, swollen lips of her pudendum. The girl rose up on her slender, bare toes to meet Chris's sex with hers and he felt the chill of the delicate chains against his penis as her hot flesh drew him inside.

CHAPTER NINETEEN

Out in the hallway, Ashlynn was looking for Chris.

She'd lugged the last of the ATA boxes over to the Principal's office, done some sorting out in there to make the room a little more accessible, and still there was no sign of Chris. Just how long did it take to pick up a damned skull? Truth was, she was getting worried about him *and* she hated being alone, especially with her boyfriend's whatever-it-was-supposed-to-be running around unchecked. Elaborate hoax or not, Ashlynn had learned the hard way that on occasion, Priestley's movie tricks could – and did – end with somebody getting hurt; look no further than Corinne as a prime example of that one.

Or the Deakins kid last year.

That one had been a grace of God escape for Priestley, as his father had been able to buy the kid's parents off with a six-figure lump sum and a week at Universal Studios while their house was made wheelchair-ready. It was an offer the Deakins simply couldn't refuse; Priestley's father was a ruthless negotiator and had made it perfectly clear that either the kid's folks agreed the settlement or by the time the whole sorry incident had been dragged through the courts, little Jimmy Deakins would be in his forties before they saw one red cent. And besides which – Priestley Snr. had solidified the case – what thirteen-year old in his right mind would climb up on a two-storey roof without some kind of safety harness?

Ahead, Ashlynn espied the haphazard heap of canvas chairs that she'd last seen in Chris's custody. Her flashlight glinted on the cold, white gleam of the skull that perched on top of the chairs, the creepy noseless hole in its center pointing towards the kitchen door.

"For fuck's sake, Chris," Ashlynn grumbled as she walked down along the hallway, not entirely relishing yet another darkened room.

Suddenly, the floor gave way beneath Ashlynn's left foot and she lost her balance. "*Shit*!" she yelped as she jolted forwards. Instinctively, she threw out her hands to break her fall and landed hard on her palms and knees, rump in the air like some sexual subservient. Ashlynn's flashlight flew from her hand and clattered away, but mercifully it stayed on.

"*Sonofabitch,*" Ashlynn growled as she yanked her foot free from the rotting floor – *what* was *it with her and the floors in this God-forsaken place?* She reclaimed the flashlight and sat awhile to rub her sore knees and check the soft flesh of her palms for splinters. Remarkably she found herself to be unscathed, save reddened hands and a dull ache in the shoulder that had taken most of her weight as she'd hit the deck.

Ashlynn shone the light down into the hole she'd made in the floor and saw that the wood was rotted through and looked soft and flaky. The supporting joists beneath the floorboards that had splintered beneath her weight ran through the hole like shattered bones in an open sore; their surface powdery and pockmarked by years of unchecked termite activity. At this, Ashlynn shuddered at the thought of being in close proximity to the repulsive creatures, but upon further inspection it appeared the termites had moved on to pastures new a long time ago.

Ashlynn struggled back to her feet and pointed her light at the kitchen door.

Pushed it open.

"Are you in there, Chris?" she called out as the door swung open with a loud, belligerent squeak, "you were supposed to be back at the Principal's office by now." She paused in the doorway and listened for the reply that meant she wouldn't be forced to venture inside. She heard nothing above the infuriating whisper – was it her imagination, or was the noise actually *louder* here in the kitchen?

With a hearty sigh, Ashlynn stepped inside and allowed the door to click shut behind her. She used her flashlight the best she could to displace the darkness that dwelled within the spacious room and its glow twinkled back at her from the abandoned pots and pans. As she made her way ever so slowly along, Ashlynn's feet nudged against the spilled utensils and they jangled and clattered as if chattering their annoyance at having been disturbed after so many years of peaceful solitude.

A movement in the shadows snagged Ashlynn's peripheral vision and she swung her flashlight around.

"Chris?"

There he stood, in front of one of the industrial-sized refrigerators. He had his back to Ashlynn and his flashlight lay on the floor by his feet, illuminating a narrow strip of beige-tiled kitchen floor and the rusted leg of one of the stoves. Chris's pants and underwear were crumpled around his feet and his bare, broad shoulders moved with a rhythm that Ashlynn found all too familiar.

"Really, Chris?" Ashlynn walked towards him, thinking herself worldly-wise enough to not be the embarrassed one in the room, "we have all this bullshit going on and you come in here to jerk off?"

The demon sat at Chris's feet and out of the way of the cold beam that spilled from his discarded flashlight. As Ashlynn approached, it scurried away on impossibly thin, twisted legs and scrabbled up the wall like some bulbous, oversized crustacean. It squatted upside down in the corner and glared at Ashlynn from the shadows with hate in its eyes and a thick, vicious fluid dripping from the hole in the center of its face.

Ashlynn shrieked out loud and fought every urge in her body that screamed at her to run. She ground her teeth together and gripped the flashlight so tight that her fingers cramped.

"Chris?" her voice trembled.

Slowly, Chris turned to face her.

There was a peculiar expression on Chris's face that looked to Ashlynn as if she'd caught him in the throes of an intense orgasm. Then her flashlight caught a metallic glint of the Swiss Army knife that Chris held in his left hand and which she recognized as Priestley's – a gift for their very first Christmas together – with which he hacked at the soft flesh of his belly. In his other hand, Chris had a hold of a slippery pink coil of his intestine, pulling it to one side as if it had been getting in the way of his work. The ecstatic look on Chris's face remained fixed as he butchered his innards – he seemed quite oblivious to the bloodied mess he was making of his body.

Ashlynn screamed and her stomach heaved up acid that scalded the rear of her throat. She staggered away until her back hit the cold steel of a gigantic oven and its handle dug hard into her spine and she could move no more; and then all she could do was stand rooted to the spot and watch the horror unfold.

Chris cast a serene smile in Ashlynn's direction and drew the knife's honed blade in one swift, upwards motion until the ragged slit in his abdomen ran from the tuft of dark hair atop his pubic bone to his sternum. Viscous blood of the darkest crimson cascaded out to soak Chris's legs and pool at his feet.

"My heart belongs to you, Ashlynn," Chris's voice was distant, dreamy, like it wasn't really him speaking, "it always has." He slid the hand that held the knife up into the slit in his belly. His arm vanished up to the elbow and displaced more of his viscera, which bulged out of the gash he'd made. "And I would like you to have it." Chris groped and sliced around inside his body and thick dark slime oozed out from the gaping wound as his ruptured organs added their spoiled stench to the shit-stink that corrupted the cool air.

"Chris, no," Ashlynn's voice was not much more than a desperate whisper, soaked up by the quietly ravenous noise that filled the room.

"*Goddammit,*" Chris spat his annoyance, "it's in here somewhere." He rummaged around in his chest and the outline of his hand bulged its flesh outwards. Then the tip of the knife poked out through the taut skin between his ribs and a thin trickle of scarlet dribbled down Chris's chest like some gore-soaked serpent.

Ashlynn slid her back against the chilled steel of the oven and sidestepped away from Chris and the horror that he had become, at the same time trying to fool herself that her eyes were deceiving her.

"Hey, don't go," Chris frowned, "there's no need to be such an ungrateful bitch." And with that, Chris wrenched out his heart and threw the bloodied mess at Ashlynn.

Ashlynn's reaction was too slow to dodge the gruesome missile, Chris's aim too accurate, and the hard, rubbery flesh hit her square on the chest with a sodden thump. Chris's quivering heart left a large, bloodied splat across Ashlynn's breasts before it slopped to the floor with a sickening, sopping *squelch.*

Ashlynn screamed so hard that she tasted blood in her throat. Mercifully, this broke the spell and she found her feet and ran away with the discordant noise pounding in her ears.

There was something akin to amusement in the demon's eyes as it watched Ashlynn flee the school's kitchen to the sound of Chris's angry cries for her to *please come back, bitch!* as he went to work on his genitals with the Swiss Army knife.

*

The undertaking had been a simple one – to manipulate the darkness that resided within the human's soul as surely as it manipulated that which lurked in the deepest corners of hell – a trick it had performed for innumerable years in order to have the feeble-minded creatures do its bidding in their own domain.

It had tapped into the human's psyche and rooted out his innermost desires and had made itself appear as something altogether more human and alluring; something so desirable that the human hadn't been able to resist penetrating.

To have part of another being's corporeal self enter its body had been a unique and altogether fascinating experience, one that its own emerging desires were eager to explore further; the very basic of curiosities to be sated.

It worked feverishly at the human's ruined corpse, oblivious to the greasy blood that made the hairless skin slick and slippery beneath its busy fingers. It bent each limb this way and that until their brittle structure snapped and the bones beneath the flaccid flesh grated shattered ends together. And when that task was complete and the human lay twisted and contorted almost beyond recognition, it filled the lifeless body with darkness. At this the human's eyes snapped open and he gasped at the agony that greeted his resurrection, mouth agape in a long, silent scream.

*

It was Priestley who heard Ashlynn's scream first.

He cocked his head in its direction, although it was difficult to be precise through the tormented cries that had once again increased to an almost deafening volume. He'd assured Carolyn and Priscilla that they could ignore the noise, told them that it was probably just Danny playing tricks with his sound system. However, Priestley knew for certain that this was no hoax.

"Ashlynn?" Priscilla mouthed at him.

"For Christ's sakes!" Priestley exploded and both Priscilla and Carolyn heard *that* loud and clear. "She's probably seen another fucking mouse or something," Priestley spat, his compassion running on fumes.

"Shouldn't we go back and see what's going on?" Carolyn suggested. It really was the last thing she wanted to do but there was something about the scream that had resonated with her, set her adrenaline flowing.

Priestley lip-read the gist of Carolyn's suggestion and as much as he resented the thought of dropping everything to go running for yet more of Ashlynn's histrionics, he knew damn well that if he didn't, he'd never hear the end of it. He gave Carolyn a pained smile that Priscilla recorded for posterity and the three of them headed back along the hallway.

"I'd never treat you the way *she* does, Davy," Carolyn purred as they walked briskly amongst the gloom, so close that her breath was warm and moist on his ear, "I respect you far too much for that." She stroked Priestley's arm with her fingertips and brushed her lips lightly against his earlobe. She couldn't be entirely sure if he'd heard her over the haunting cacophony but Carolyn was pretty sure he'd got the gist.

*

"Danny?" Labeaux lowered his camera and strained to hear against the intrusive noise that crammed the classroom.

Danny shrugged his response. His mic had *definitely* picked up the scream, but he wasn't entirely sure if it had been a component of the maddening background sounds or something altogether more – *real*.

Labeaux peered around the classroom as if hoping to find the answer amongst the ruined artwork and scattered furniture. He'd already decided to call it and go back, since there was clearly nothing doing in the classrooms this side of the school – definitely no sign whatsoever of the demon (or whoever Priestley had *paid* to play said demon – Yessir, Labeaux remained ever the cynic).

"We need to get Dave to turn these fucking sound effects off," Labeaux growled, not really caring if Danny heard him or not. "All this bullshit is getting on my fucking nerves," So saying, Labeaux turned on his heels and marched out of the room with Danny in hot pursuit.

CHAPTER TWENTY

In her blind panic to be away from the kitchen and the horrors it harboured, Ashlynn ran through the dark hallways. She didn't really register – or care much – where she was going, as long as it was away from that sickening spectacle of Chris's self mutilation and the leering demon. Ashlynn ran with the dirty beam from her flashlight bouncing in crazy patterns ahead of her, her legs aching with exertion – too much time away from the gym – and her lungs stabbing with each ragged breath as if fit to burst. The noise in the hallway was deafeningly loud – enough to drown out the pounding of her heart that hammered its relentless pulse inside her head – as the voices and screams and wails ebbed and flowed like waves on hell's distant shore.

Turning a sharp corner, relief washed over Ashlynn as she caught sight of the tall arc lights that stood sentry along the hallway that lead the way to the school's main doors. The lights were out, cold and lifeless but for Ashlynn they pointed towards escape from the madness that bore down on her like some great, dead weight.

Slowing to a quick walk that reminded her of those ridiculous speed-walking pensioners she'd see at the mall, Ashlynn fumbled her cell phone from her pocket. She had half expected not to see any signal bars on its tiny, glowing display, but to her relief there were three tiny black LCD rectangles in the top left of her screen.

"Fuck you, Dave – and fuck your fucking movie," she rambled, painfully aware as to just how close to full-on hysteria she was inching. Images of Chris swirled around and around in her mind; his ruined body, the impossible amount of blood that cascaded down his belly and legs, how he'd ripped his heart right out from his insides, the inane grin as he'd thrown it at her.

Ashlynn jabbed a thumb at the virtual buttons on her phone's touch screen. The numbers looked blurred and danced wildly through the tears that sprang up in her eyes. The call went through and she lifted the cell to her ear.

"Hello? 911?" Ashlynn's voice croaked in her parched, aching throat, "please help me. I want to report a –"

•*tormentisunbearablewewantyoutojoinuswewanttoenjoy youhelpusfreeus* –

She heard *words* amidst the hellish cacophony, actual words that were roughly discernible although they overlapped and entwined and ran into each other within the maniacal babble of the multitude. Ashlynn froze as the voices reached out from her phone to burrow into her brain and they brought with them such a feeling of absolute and utter despair. She sobbed loudly and an uncontrollable surge of scorching tears coursed down her cheeks.

"Fuck you!" Ashlynn screamed so loud that her raw throat clenched up and forced her words out as a shrill squeak. She wrenched the phone from her ear and hurled the infernal thing away with every ounce of strength she could muster. The phone flew from her hand and smashed against a rusting fire extinguisher that clung to the wall opposite and rained spilled, plastic innards across the floor.

Gripping her flashlight and determined to get herself as far away from Watsonville Elementary as was humanly possible, Ashlynn crashed through the double doors and out into the cold, dark night beyond.

Ashlynn ran a yard or two before she stopped dead in her tracks.

She'd heard the doors groan shut behind her, they had sounded quite disappointed at her departure, but then the silence outside had hit her like a brick wall.

It was a relief in the first instance to have found freedom from the haunting voices – even if the inside of her ears still buzzed with their residual, tinnitus whine – and to be away from the horrific images they conjured in her mind, but now all she heard was the harsh sounds of her own breathing.

It occurred to Ashlynn just how dark it was outside. That she was entirely enveloped by a black void that carried within it the sour stink of death and rot. She could see no winking stars, nor any sign of the half-moon she'd seen glowing in the clear sky through the hole in the gymnasium roof. Nor were there any glowing lights from neighboring houses or the cheerless sodium-yellow glow that seeped out of the streetlights – there was not even that ever-present, electric light haze that hung over the town. Quite unlike the night, this was a complete and total *absence* of light – as if every single, solitary photon had been hunted down and devoured by the cruel blackness.

Everything out there beyond the school seemed to be all so impossibly *dark.*

Ashlynn's mind raced with a sick, mounting terror as panic sent long, clammy fingers to grip her stomach and run riot inside her imagination. She waved her flashlight's beam to and fro and strained to see something, *anything* – yet at the same time she was terrified of what that might be.

What (Suggested) she saw was the profuse, impenetrable blackness that sucked the light from the flashlight's bulb to be consumed before it could reach beyond the glass lens. Ashlynn lifted up her free hand and wiggled her fingers directly in front of her face – a cliché, she knew but what else *could* she do? – and was damned if she couldn't see them at all. Even as she touched the end of her nose with her fingertips, all Ashlynn could make out was the clinging, inky-black darkness and she wondered if she'd gone blind.

At this thought, Ashlynn sobbed a little and the darkness smothered her face like a killer's pillow; cloying, pressing hard, it wound thick, damp tendrils down into her chest to steal her breath.

Disoriented and hysterical, Ashlynn found that her legs simply refused to move no matter how hard she willed them. And even had she managed to overcome that, Ashlynn had no idea which way she should run; farther out into the soul-sucking blackness and the terrors she imagined lurked within, or back to the school and the *very real* horrors she had witnessed there? That said, although Ashlynn remained *fairly* sure of the school's direction, she could no longer be certain that it would actually still be there.

A sound – imagined or real?

A *sense* she was no longer alone.

Ashlynn strained her eyes to see who – *what* – could possibly be lurking in the dark.

"Hello?" her voice was dampened by the lightlessness and Ashlynn wondered if it had carried much beyond the glow from her flashlight, "my friend is hurt, please can you help me?"

The stifling blackness kept its silence.

Then a scream punctured the dark. Unmistakably a child's scream, it jolted Ashlynn's body from its torpor and the flashlight fell from her hand and rolled away into the black.

Another scream split the darkness, shrill like that of a small girl's and it was followed by the resounding crack of gunfire and a dazzling flash of light. A fine, warm rain speckled Ashlynn's cheek and she followed the next scream with her own.

Another sharp report – closer this time – and in the powder flash that accompanied it, Ashlynn saw the figure of a squat, middle-aged woman clad in a gray business suit and three-inch heels. The woman cradled a double-barrelled shotgun in her arms as if it was a favored pet, and she grinned maniacally as she fired off shot after indiscriminate shot into the dark. Intense flashes of blinding light ripped the blackness apart and elicited terrified screams from victims unseen. The woman was nearer to Ashlynn now, and her menacing frame inched ever closer with each shot as if she were being viewed through a surreal strobe effect. Yet more shots and screams filled the void.

"Stop it! Please stop it!" Ashlynn implored but the woman simply smiled within each brief burst of light and moved closer until she was near enough for Ashlynn to reach out and touch her.

And then Ashlynn was *the woman.*

She looked out from the woman's eyes and perceived the darkened world with an all-consuming insanity. Glancing down, she saw the grey pant suit she now wore, along with the tan hose and the patent kittens with sensible heels – and the gun that felt so unnaturally heavy in her hand, its smooth, wooden stock clammy from her sweat. She felt upset that several of her fingernails had snapped off, their raw ends split from gripping the gun so goddamned tight and she was pulling on the trigger again and again and she couldn't stop.

Through the swirling mist of madness, she knew that she was Rachel Villanueva – Mrs. – and her head was crammed to bursting with an inexplicable rage that had built up to a boiling point inside her head and spilled out into her guts, every muscle, square inch of skin and single, solitary nerve ending. Something drove her actions – not exactly a voice – it was something rooted so very deep inside that urged her ever onward towards that red-clouded madness and over-rode every shred of humanity she'd ever possessed.

The only way to give relief to the fury was by doing what she had done that day and whilst each pull of the trigger had quelled her wrath, it only did so momentarily; it would all too quickly rise up again like the heads of a rage-filled hydra.

And Rachel would only stop when she ran out of shells – even the one she'd promised to save for herself – and she felt in her blackened heart that had she had seven billion rounds she'd not only rip the heart and soul out of Watsonville but would wipe out every man, woman and child on the planet.

As the next shot rang out and the shotgun flashed bright and jerked once more in the aching arms that weren't hers, Ashlynn saw in the transitory light the untidy litter of small bodies spread out in front of her. And making her way slowly between the tiny, devastated corpses – bare feet bright scarlet and sopping wet from the blood that had puddled on the schoolyard's asphalt – was a young woman in a filthy, tattered dress, her torso caked in old, dried blood and half of her face missing. She tiptoed between the dead children and Ashlynn saw the electrical flex that dangled loosely from between her blood-smeared legs.

Ashlynn fired the gun again and in the flash her eyes traced the flex across to a tall, ashen-faced man with black straggles of grease-sopped hair that fell about his narrowed, soulless eyes. In his hand he held the plug at the end of the flex – up high as a magician would demonstrate his newest trick – before inserting it into a disembodied socket that floated knee-high in the darkness.

The woman screamed in pain and fell writhing to the ground. An eerie pink light shone bright from beneath her dress and wisps of gray smoke plumed from between her thighs.

Another blast from the gun and Ashlynn saw that behind the tortured woman, crawling over the bloodied corpses scattered about the yard was the demon. Scrambling towards Ashlynn on its repugnant, bony legs it fixed her with an iniquitous, penetrating stare that stayed burned in her mind even as the cloying dark closed in on her.

"No no no no!" Ashlynn cried out and put a hand over her eyes and prayed for all of this to end; she had seen far more than she could bear, even through the eyes of madness.

"Mommy?" a small voice shone through the blackness and immediately Ashlynn knew that the crazy woman recognized it.

Ashlynn lowered her hand and looked down and somehow she could see – or imagined *that she could see – the little boy who stood at her feet with his little hands clasped at his belly, his upturned face the picture of innocence.*

She didn't register her finger squeezing the trigger. A deafening roar, a burst of light, the sickeningly familiar mule-kick of the gun in her hand and the child was gone.

Ashlynn cried out as she experienced the pain of Rachel Villanueva's anguish flooding through her shocked mind and she dropped the gun. Distraught beyond all comprehension, Ashlynn buried her face in her hands and screamed into the blackness like she'd never be able to stop.

CHAPTER TWENTY-ONE

Priscilla's minicam caught the movement ahead of them first. She studied the camera's tiny foldout screen as she followed close behind Priestley and Carolyn as they all made their way along the hallway. They'd headed in what Priestley had hoped was the direction of Ashlynn's scream, although they had heard nothing more from her above the tormented sounds that cavorted around the darkened building.

"Ashlynn?" Priestley's flashlight picked out the familiar shape framed in the black that lay beyond the school's main doors. "Are you okay, babe?" He ran to her as she stumbled back into the school with her shoulder pressed hard against the wall for support, head bowed and sweat-slicked hair flopping over her face.

"Oh, *fuck*!" Carolyn cried out and stopped dead in her tracks.

Startled by Carolyn's outburst, Priestley slowed up a handful of paces away from Ashlynn and he stifled a cry at the sight that greeted him.

Ashlynn's sweater was soaked through with blood that shimmered in the cold beam of his flashlight. Her face was a wet mask of dark red, which glued matted hair to her empty eye sockets. And in her right hand, she swung her eyeballs in a nonchalant, almost jaunty manner as she walked, dangling them by their optic nerves and extraocular muscles as one would a favorite purse.

"It won't make me see now," Ashlynn giggled as Priestley reached out to her. "It fucking *can't*." And with that Ashlynn collapsed into his arms.

At that moment Labeaux and Danny rounded the corner, their arrival heralded by the bouncing light from Labeaux's camera. They came to a sudden stop beside Carolyn and Priscilla and could do little more than stare, dumbfounded.

"Oh, dear lord," Danny groaned and fought the nausea that raced up from the pit of his stomach.

Labeaux fumbled his cell phone from his ass pocket and with shaking hands stabbed out 911. No sooner was the phone's glowing screen to his ear than dropped it and hopped away as if it had burned him. *"What the fuck?!"* he yelped as the phone skittered away and came to rest amidst the shattered remnants of Ashlynn's cell.

Priscilla and Danny pulled out their phones too – Carolyn couldn't, no pockets in the flimsy dress – and even before they'd dialled all they could hear were jumbled words and nefarious screams.

"What have you done, Ash'?" Priestley held his girlfriend tight and her blood soaked into his shirt.

"It's all good, my sweet lover," Ashlynn's laugh was charmingly blasé. "You're so much better off without these – *out there*," she whispered conspiratorially and waved her bobbling eyes in the general direction of the school's doors. She turned her face to Priestley's as if she was looking directly into his eyes, but of course she wasn't.

Priestley couldn't help but stare into his girlfriend's gaping eye sockets, which brimmed with thick, coagulating blood that slopped down Ashlynn's front with each movement of her head. And as if that weren't enough of a torment for Priestley, Ashlynn's loose eyelids twitched nervously above the empty holes in her skull and it looked for all the world like she was trying to wink at him.

Labeaux and Danny ran over to the double doors. Behind them ran Carolyn and the ever-filming Priscilla. Labeaux hoofed the right-hand door hard and it flung wide open on screeching hinges.

The foul, pervading blackness and its uncanny silence greeted each of them as it voraciously gobbled up every drop of light from Labeaux's camera.

Carolyn stuck her arm out of the doorway and was most alarmed to see it swallowed by the darkness, so definitively do that it appeared amputated and ending abruptly at the elbow. "Are you seeing this?" she asked the others as she doubted her own eyes. Anxiously, she pulled back her arm and was somewhat relieved to find that her hand was still attached.

CHAPTER TWENTY-TWO

Ashlynn sat still and quiet on the floor in the corner of the Principal's office. Priestley crouched by her side and held a towel pressed tight to her face. He'd only just applied the towel but already it had soaked through, and soon it would join the others that were discarded crimson and sodden with Ashlynn's blood in the trashcan. She'd remained silent all the way back to the office – not a single word, cry or even a giggle – and that worried Priestley even more than the reluctance she'd shown to part with her eyeballs; Ashlynn clung onto them by their ragged optic nerves like they were a pair of rare and exotic orchids.

The office was a small one, made all the more cramped by the piles of film equipment that Ashlynn and Chris had piled up in there before – *before whatever had happened to Ashlynn*. There was a large, pale oak desk upon which perched Labeaux, Priscilla and Carolyn, and behind it a high-backed, black leather chair on castors which Danny had made home. Behind the desk and against the wall stretched a tall bookcase in matching wood which was crammed to bursting with damp, decaying volumes on teaching; the psychology of teaching and novels about teachers – talk about being single minded! The only other piece of furniture the office had room for was a sparsely populated trophy cabinet screwed to the wall to the left of the desk. The cabinet contained but a sad half dozen gold painted, plastic figures behind its age-grimed glass.

On the wall beside the cabinet, proudly displayed in a guilt-edged frame, was the Principal's Certificate of Education from Columbia University. As with everything else in the school, moisture had made its way beneath the glass and had caused the ink to run and obscure the Principal's name, almost as if to erase it from existence. To no avail, *everyone* knew the name Principal Gregory Pruitt, the same way everybody on the planet knew exactly who Mayor Rudy Giuliani was after 9/11; not the most salubrious way for history to remember a man – as being the one on whose watch that an insurmountable tragedy occurred.

Rumor had it that Principal Pruitt had finished up managing a general store somewhere in the frozen wastes of Alaska. Although unfounded – nobody actually knew *where* he'd vanished to following the inquest – he'd made little secret of his desire to be as far away from Watsonville Elementary and teaching as he could physically get, and that he favored Alaska because the government would actually pay him to live there.

To counteract the claustrophobic feel of Pruitt's office, Danny had it lit up with a duo of film lights and now it resembled the *Close Encounters* closing scenes. The garish light offered some small comfort to the people within, although it did mean that they couldn't easily ignore Ashlynn's self-inflicted wounds.

Thankfully, the rotten stench that had followed Priestley and the others from the gym and down the hallways didn't seem quite so bad in the office and the hellish noises had subsided once more to that infuriating murmur that nibbled at the brain and picked at the loose threads of sanity.

Priscilla panned the minicam around the sorry faces around her. She lingered a beat or two longer upon Ashlynn and her blood soaked clothing before zooming in on Labeaux's phial that hung limply around his neck. Labeaux sat in quiet contemplation beside her on the desk – camera perched across his knees as if for protection – and stared unblinking into the middle distance with a slack, vacant look on his face.

"The bleeding won't stop," Priestley was the first to speak in what had felt like an eternity. "We have to get her out of here, she needs medical attention," his voice adopted the wobbly edged panic of a man who is infinitely way out of his depth. Everything had gotten *really* badly out of hand since the demon had made its appearance and Priestley now feared that everything was spiralling completely out of control.

"And just how the fuck do you expect us to do that, Dave?" Labeaux snarled, clearly in no mood to be civil.

"Maurice has a point," Carolyn joined in, "you saw what's outside. How in God's name are we supposed to get any of us through *that*?"

"Practicalities notwithstanding, that's probably the best idea you've had all night, Davy-boy. We really *do* need to get out of here." Danny leaned his chair back and it teetered precariously on its rotted hinge; sometimes it could be difficult to ascertain if the man was being facetious or not. "But don't you think we ought to find Chris first?"

Shit, Priestley had forgotten all about Chris – most likely they all had up until Danny's mentioning him. Who wouldn't have though, faced with the mess that Ashlynn had made of herself? Danny was right of course, they couldn't leave Chris behind, or leave the school without finding out if he was alive.

Or otherwise.

Priestley cringed at that thought. All too quickly, death had become a plausible conclusion to jump to, although it was kind of understandable following Corinne – and now Ashlynn. He most certainly hadn't planned for any of this to happen, although he had come along *prepared* for it. And although Priestley hated himself for thinking it at such a time, he hoped to hell that Ashlynn had remembered to retrieve his backpack from the gymnasium before she'd ripped her eyes out.

"Baby?" Priestley stroked Ashlynn's hair, "do you have any idea where Chris is?" he coaxed.

"He gave me his heart," Ashlynn's voice was a low, flat monotone that sounded so unlike Ashlynn Jones that Priestley had to check to see if her mouth was moving. "I think he thought he was being romantic when he threw it at me," she continued. "And you know what they say? It's the thought that counts." She laughed and it was the abrupt, insane laugh of the borderline insane.

"What did you do to him, you crazy bitch?" Carolyn slid her ass off of the desk and stood over Ashlynn with her fists balled. "Did you pull his fucking eyes out as well?"

"Leave her alone!" Priestley shouted. "You can see she's in shock, Carolyn." He was desperate to diffuse the girl's anger. "She hasn't done anything to anyone, just *look* at her."

"You won't get out of here," Ashlynn cackled, "none of us will." She shook her head and smiled. "*It* doesn't want us to leave," Her voice cracked, "and there's no way out through the darkness. It's all too – *black*." There was not a trace of humor in her ominous words, but Ashlynn laughed anyway.

Labeaux glowered at Ashlynn, his sympathy evaporating and patience wafer-thin. His mood had crashed to rock bottom when he'd seen the impenetrable dark that hung around the school doors. Discovering that all he – *any of them* – could get on his phone was the screams and ululating wails he'd first heard on Danny's recording equipment a fucking lifetime ago hadn't helped much either. He'd planned to confront Priestley about the noise but that seemed moot point now; it was obvious that it had nothing to do with him – not after all of this – although that relevance eluded him right now. Hell, he was even beginning to consider Corinne's corpse and Priestley's devil may actually have been the real deal after all.

"If we can't call for help, then we have to at least *try* to get out of the school." Labeaux fidgeted uneasily on the desk, the hard wood was making his butt ache something chronic. "*And* we do have to look for Chris."

"Sounds like a plan, Stan," Danny chirped, "but what if Ashlynn is right and there *is* no way out? And what if that – *that thing* – is out there just waiting for us to make a move?" he voiced everyone's fear; no one had mentioned the demon since they'd discovered Ashlynn and were forced to deal with that very *real* and tangible horror.

"Perhaps someone should at least take a look around for him," Priscilla added.

Labeaux climbed from the desk and laid his camera gently down on the warm spot his backside had made. "Priscilla's right," he said, although the shake in his voice made him sound unsure. "Anything has to be better than sitting here in the stink and waiting for Dave's fucking monster to come back." Labeaux had never been one much for sitting on his hands waiting for shit to happen, and the sewer-smell really was offending his nose big time; he'd hoped to have gotten used to it by now, but no – if anything it was getting worse. His grandmother (on his father's side) had always told him that the human nose got used to smells after a while and would then ignore them;

otherwise everyone would think the whole world smelled of snot.

Priestley opened his mouth to protest – it wasn't *his*, nor was it a *monster* – but there was a look in Labeaux's eyes that advised him that silence was probably the best policy right now.

"So, who's with me?" Labeaux asked.

"I'll go," Danny stepped up, "you're right, Mo', *anything* has to be better than doing *nothing*."

Carolyn raised her hand like she was about to ask if she might be excused to the restroom. "I need to get out of here, away from –" She checked herself, but her eyes flicked towards Ashlynn and gave her thoughts away.

"I'll stay here with Dave and Ashlynn," Priscilla said. "If – *when* Chris comes back, he may need someone who's holding things together a little better." She smiled an apology at Priestley who didn't even notice. In reality, Priscilla just didn't want to leave the relative sanctuary of the Principal's office.

"Okay then," Labeaux made his way to the door, "let's do this." Danny and Carolyn stepped over and around the clutter to join him.

"Mo'?" Priestley looked up at him.

"Yeah, dude?"

"Take the camera, film as much as you can."

Labeaux grunted his disgust. "You really are un-fucking-believable, Dave – do you know that?" he growled. Even so, Labeaux plucked the camera from the desk, checked that the fat battery had plenty juice and hoisted it up on his shoulder like a pro.

"Give us twenty minutes," Labeaux said to Priestley, "if we're not back by then, I guess you guys should start thinking about making your own way out." There was a worry in Labeaux's eyes that Priestley had never seen before, as if perhaps he really believed that not returning was now a distinct possibility. Although, Priestley couldn't help but wonder that if Labeaux was to find a way out of the school, would he just run and keep on running?

"Sure thing," Priestley replied.

"What time have you got?" Labeaux asked Priscilla and checked his own watch.

"Eleven-fifty."

"That can't be right," Priestley mumbled as he peered at the Brietling he always wore wrist-side in. "It was eleven-fifty when we filmed in the hallway."

"She's right; it *is* ten minutes to midnight." Danny's face looked sickly in the torpid glow from his cell phone.

"What the fuck?" Priestley was rattled.

"I've been hoping that you could tell us that." Labeaux studied Priestley who cut a sad sight huddled up to his gore soaked girlfriend. "You're supposed to be the fucking expert," Labeaux snarled and shrugged as he pulled open the office door. He was convinced that they were all beginning to lose their collective grip on reality at an alarming rate of knots; all the more reason to get the fuck out of Dodge.

The ever-conscientious Priscilla watched – and filmed – Labeaux, Danny and Carolyn as they vacated the office. And as the door closed ever so slowly behind them on its rotting dampener, she couldn't help but wonder if she'd see any of them again.

Priestley gritted his teeth and teased the towel back from Ashlynn's swollen face. The flow of blood from her eye sockets did seem to be easing up some – although she was very much in need of a fresh towel – but that offered him little reassurance.

Ashlynn appeared to have fallen asleep. It was difficult to be entirely sure what with her lack of eyes to close, but her chest rose and fell with an even, rasping rhythm as if she was in a deep sleep. Looking at his girlfriend, Priestley began to fear that it may not be so much sleep as unconsciousness due to shock and blood loss.

Quietly, Priestley closed his eyes and offered up a prayer to a god that he desperately needed to believe in that Labeaux would find them a way out.

CHAPTER TWENTY-THREE

inding himself once more at the main entrance, Labeaux dreaded the thought of facing the lightless void that he knew lurked beyond like some ravenous and efficiently lethal predator. He played his camera's light around the vestibule, on the lookout for Priestley's *thing* lest it sneak up on him. The harsh beam picked out Carolyn's and Danny's pale, nervous faces and the wet, vivid stripes of Ashlynn's blood smeared across the floor.

"I *thought* we were supposed to be looking for Chris?" Carolyn broke the silence that had settled between them.

"We were – I mean, we *are,*" Labeaux told her. "But I figured our priority should be to make sure we can get the fuck out of this place before we do," he sounded nervy. "Otherwise what would be the point?"

"He may have found his own way out, anyways." Danny chipped in, "I wouldn't put it past Chris to run off and leave us to it. It certainly wouldn't be the first time he's disappeared mid-shoot."

Danny made a valid point; Chris had gone AWOL from a Green Crayon shoot a year or so ago following a dumb row about who was supposed to be lead actor. Therefore, the idea of him having left the school once the weird shit started up was not too much of a stretch of the imagination. "So, I guess we should do this," Danny said, his fake bravado fooling neither of his companions.

Carolyn rested a hand on Danny's shoulder to offer comfort and found herself to be shaking more than he was.

"Here goes nothing," Labeaux muttered to himself, aimed his camera forwards and pushed open the doors.

If the soundless absence of light could ever be described as *deafening*, then what confronted Labeaux was it. He strained his eyes 'till they ached in order to see *something* in the smothering blackness and envisaged that this was how the darkest depths of the starless corners of deep space would appear. The darkness absorbed his camera's light abruptly at the school's threshold; the bright, white bridged the six or so inches between Labeaux and the doorway but stopped immediately upon touching the gloom that lay beyond.

"Maybe there's a power-out," as ever, Danny tried to be helpful, even in the face of the glaringly obvious.

"Even in a power-out, there's always *some* light," Labeaux growled and only just stopped himself short of calling the old man a *fuckwit,* "it's never *completely* dark."

This spun Labeaux's memory back to the Great Watsonville blackout of '95, when a municipal garbage truck had hit the power company's sub-station. The subsequent inquest had found that the driver had been so completely wasted on high-grade skunk that it had been a miracle he'd ever managed to find the steering wheel, let alone his way out of the depot. There'd not been that much left of the poor sap after he'd been fried by the town's entire electricity supply - barely just enough to run the tox' tests. And in the three days it had taken to fix up the sub-station, the only people to have had juice were those with paranoid foresight enough to possess home generators.

At the time, Labeaux had considered *that* to be dark; there had been no light from homes, businesses or the regimented rows of street lamps that had been rendered impotent – pretty much all the town had for three nights was the silver glow of a waning moon, the peppering of distant stars and the fuzzy haze from Clarksville.

Yet, as eerily dark as it had been back then, it paled beyond comparison against the darkness he faced now and Labeaux just knew in his bones there was something terribly unnatural, just plain *wrong* going on; something very much *eleven out of ten* on the weirdshitometer wrong.

Driven by grim determination – Labeaux had never been one to not face his fears – he cast a glance back at Danny and Carolyn and even forced a smile.

And then Maurice Labeaux stepped out into the blackness.

*

Three, no more than four steps away from the school and Labeaux chanced another backwards look and immediately wished he'd resisted the temptation.

Watsonville Elementary was no longer to be seen.

The blackness had wrapped around Labeaux in its soundless, inky embrace and had rendered the building quite simply *not there*. Labeaux was also in no doubt that he would be equally invisible to Danny and Carolyn who he could only assume awaited his return at the school's door.

There was, however, the one saving grace in that the haunting sounds hadn't followed Labeaux out into the dark, nor had the stomach-churning stink; and for that he was grateful, even though his was now a world of utter and absolute *nothing*.

Labeaux wanted nothing more than to gulp down great gasps of the air to rid his lungs of the putrid stench that had huddled inside his chest, but he didn't dare; it worried him that the air outside was neither hot nor cold, nor felt – or smelled – of *anything*. It was as if the blackness had absorbed the very *character* from the air as easily as it had consumed light and Labeaux feared that the void would soak up his body and render him *neutral* should he breathe in too much of it.

Labeaux took a single, tentative step forward. He tapped the ground with his foot before planting it down to assure himself that the cracked pavers were still there. Ever the consummate pro', Labeaux filmed his progress, although he knew that footage of nothing but total darkness would neither add much to the movie nor help explain just what the fuck was going on.

A movement.

Labeaux swung his camera around, although he had more *sensed* the movement as opposed to having actually seen anything definite. Neither Labeaux, nor his trusty camera caught sight of anything.

Although he couldn't see it, the comforting hardness of the ground beneath his feet filled Labeaux with some hope; if the ground was still there, then it stood to reason that the school would be too – and so would the street, the road and the whole crappy little town of Watsonville. There *was* a way out of this sorry mess, there just *had* to be.

Thus buoyed up, Labeaux ventured ever forward into the darkness that was all but palpable against his face. And with each wary step he swept the camera in a one-eighty arc, in the hope of capturing something or that the powerful light would manage to pierce the gloom and highlight a potential escape route.

"*Please, no,*" a man's voice, strained and desperate.

Labeaux jerked his head around so hard that he heard the bones in his neck pop; the noise was quickly gobbled up by the darkness. It was impossible to tell from which direction the voice had come so he twirled around in a full circle and hoped for the best. "Who's there?" he said and the noise that came from his mouth didn't sound like his at all, the words flat and lifeless as if whispered in a vacuum.

Upon completing an incredibly agile three-sixty, Labeaux realized that his body and mind were no longer his own. Weirdly, he felt *shorter* and the weight of the camera was missing from his shoulder. His thoughts sputtered in a jumbled, alien concoction of confusion, terror and an all-consuming, burning hatred the likes of which he had never felt before – he could all but *taste* it.

He looked down at a young woman he'd tied to the rickety wooden chair. She wore a white, blood-soaked silk dress and half of her face had been meticulously carved away; the skin and flesh stripped to expose gleaming skull bones and furnish her with a toothy, half-rictus grin. The woman was alive – very much so – and although her head lolled at some impossible, crazy angle, she struggled against the rough hemp ties that held her fast with expert knots. He was delectably aroused to see the woman's dress hoisted up her smooth thighs almost to her pussy. And from there snaked a white electrical cord.

Opposite the woman sat a man of approximately the same age – mid to late twenties – whose pitiful pleas echoed in the dark. He had been tied to a matching chair and wore a gold wedding ring with an engraving upon it, most likely the date of his nuptials. By contrast the woman's wedding band was plain and smooth and it was thus glaringly obvious that although the pair were married, it was most certainly not to each other. The rings that symbolised the eternal circle of love and faithfulness had been their downfall.

Labeaux tried to turn away from the gore-soaked mess of the woman's face; it reminded him too much what Ashlynn had made of hers. Is this what she had seen out here in the stifling blackness? Could that be why she'd done what she'd done, so she'd not have to look any more?

But the raging insanity of the mind that ensnared Labeaux's wouldn't allow him to turn away; it was far too busy enjoying the couple's torment and so very badly wanted to do it all over again.

And again.

He looked down at his hands and they were red and sticky with fresh blood. In one he gripped a yellow handled box cutter that dripped with blood and had raggedy shreds of flesh stuck to its blade.

And then the box cutter was a three-pronged electrical plug and the flex that dangled from his fingers and away into the blackness had its other end inserted deep into the woman.

He bent down a tad to plug in the flex. There was the briefest flash of light from between his victim's legs before he heard the muffled popping sound the bulb inside her vagina made as it imploded. Crimson blood ran freely down the woman's inner thighs and she screamed shrill and loud and oh, how he loved that scream, how it sated the hate that was consuming him and it made him feel powerful and virile and – complete.

The woman's illicit lover sobbed and called out her name and that enraged him further because the man's thoughts should have been with his own wife. There was no doubting that he knew that he would shortly be meeting death at the hands of the lunatic, but before that his mind would crack and render him little more than a snivelling wreck.

And then he would be granted the mercy that dying would bring.

Then, somehow the woman had freed herself of her tethers and was upright and she staggered towards him like some undead creature in a bad B-movie. Behind her trailed the electrical flex and thick globs of blood slopped down from her ruined sex. She reached out for him with clawed hands and he saw agony blazing in the one hazel eye that remained within the face he had destroyed.

And then there was nothing.

The darkness repressed the horrific apparition and crawled deep into Labeaux's screaming throat.

He ran.

Labeaux's mind was once more his own and the reassuring weight of the camera was back on his shoulder. Blindly, he staggered around in the dark, his free arm outstretched like a kid playing blind-man's-bluff in the vain hope of connecting with something – *anything* – that would lead him back to the school. And as he ran round in desperate, ever-widening circles, Labeaux's breathing grew ever more labored as the air jabbed at his lungs and he felt the tight clench of panic deep down in his gut.

Aimlessly, Labeaux lurched forward. Direction no longer meant anything to his light deprived eyes – the best he could do was to hope that the escalating terror that gripped him wouldn't lead farther away from the school and into –

•*what?*

Just then, Labeaux's groping fingers barked against cold, moist wood so hard that they bent back and he let out a resounding yelp.

*

"It really wouldn't surprise me if Dave *was* behind all of this," Danny was trying to appear brave to Carolyn, "I'd even make an educated guess that Ashlynn's eye thing is faked too; you saw what Dave did with the gouged eye effects when we shot *Blood and Kisses*."

Carolyn stared blankly at Danny and chewed off another fat chunk of skin from the inside of her cheek. She savored the sharp tang of blood in her dry mouth and the taste of dirty pennies made her salivate. "If you're right, then how is he doing *this*?" Carolyn pointed towards the rich darkness that brooded beyond the doors, "there's no light at all, Danny – nothing."

A tall, looming figure appeared, as if the blackness had just coughed it up. "Oh, hi, Mo', you forget something?" Carolyn asked Labeaux.

Labeaux staggered through the doorway and into the vestibule, gasping for air. He groped his way along the wall like a blind man, eyes wide, empty and scared; Labeaux's face glistened with bulbous beads of sweat that stood out on his dark skin like honeydew on a spring leaf, his sweat-sodden shirt was plastered to his torso.

"Eh?" He grunted.

"Did you forget something?" Carolyn repeated. "Or did you want us to come with you after all?"

"I'm *really* not getting you," Labeaux mumbled, genuinely confused and disoriented. His eyes struggled to focus on Carolyn; after the void, the light from the camera hurt his eyes like a bastard.

"Are you okay, buddy?" Danny relieved Labeaux of the camera and Labeaux dropped to the floor, sliding down with his back against the wall.

"Yeah, I'm just glad I made it back. I thought I'd never get out of there."

"Er – you stepped out and pretty much stepped right back in again, Maurice," Carolyn said. "You were only gone a few seconds." She crouched down by his side.

Labeaux drew a trembling hand down his face and grimaced as he wiped stinging sweat into his eyes. "I was in there for ages," he said. "I couldn't find my way back, everything is so motherfucking dark in there – it's like everything has been sucked out of *everything*."

"Carolyn's right, Mo' – you'd barely gone before you came back." Danny remembered watching how the darkness had folded around Labeaux like groping, sinister arms. "Look, it's only –" Danny thrust his watch towards Labeaux and Carolyn and then choked on his words.

Three a.m.

"What?" Carolyn stepped back from Danny's watch as if it had suddenly sprouted teeth and would bite given the chance. "That's *impossible*. This is not a good time to fuck with us, Danny," Carolyn tried her best to rationalise the sudden disappearance of three hours – three *fucking* hours – and once more she dug her teeth deep into the inside of her cheek and gnawed on the soft flesh there.

"I am *not* fucking with you," Danny's voice was steady and there was something dark and terrified in his eyes that told Carolyn he was telling her the truth; and at that moment Danny looked like a small and very scared child.

Labeaux struggled to his feet and was forced to accept Danny's outstretched arm to help him accomplish the feat due to the wobble in his legs. With some relief, his breathing and vision had returned to somewhere near normal and the sour stink of fear-sweat was drying out of his shirt. But for as hard as he tried, Labeaux couldn't shake the images of the mutilated woman and the feeling of just how thrilling it had been to have spent even a fraction of time inside the lunatic's mind.

"I really don't know what's going on here, guys," Labeaux grunted through the exertion of standing, "but I really don't see us getting out of this fucking place anytime soon." He stilled the panic in his voice. "There's definitely no way out that way," he said with a nod towards the doors. "I say we go back and see what Dave has to say for himself; if he got us into this goddamned mess, then he can get us out of it," there was anger in his tone now, rising up to replace the terror that had jarred his senses. One way or another, Priestley was at the bottom of all of this shit – either he was fucking with them *or* he had invoked something heinous – and Labeaux was going to make the bastard fix it, and with violence if necessary.

Carolyn and Danny followed on in silence as Labeaux made his way back down the hallway, his camera light illuminating the walls as he took meticulous care to search each corner and every shadow.

"Wait!" Carolyn's voice was unexpectedly loud and brimming with excitement. It made Labeaux and Danny jump, although that was not a difficult task given the jangled state of their nerves. "Look! People!" she pointed with a quivering finger at the only window the hallway possessed.

Labeaux peered outside and sure enough, there was a middle-aged couple out walking a small dog on the sidewalk directly in front of the school, their shadows squat and fuzzy beneath a flickering, yellow streetlight.

He could see the street!

Heart racing, Labeaux banged a balled fist on the window. "HEY!" he yelled.

"IN HERE!" Carolyn added her own fist to the racket, pounding on the glass fit to break it; and then Danny's voice joined in with both of them,

"*HELP!*"

*

George Alcorn tugged on the thin leather leash to encourage his wife's dumb little dog to get a move on. As per usual, it was taking its own sweet time about deciding where to drop its diminutive load and had thus far paused to sniff at what seemed to George to have been every single lamp post, hydrant and blade of goddamned grass.

Tyson was his wife, Liz's Chihuahua/Mastiff mix – the very logistics of such a coupling had never ceased to confound George – and to say that he hated the dog would certainly be the understatement of the year. It was no exaggeration to say that George wholeheartedly resented the crappy little dog's very existence on the planet; he particularly hated the way it would insinuate itself on his wife's lap every evening, baring its teeth should George dare sit next to her, how it trotted around with that permanently *worried* expression on its stupid, pointy face and its skinny, piggy-tail stuck up in the air (and usually with a phallic-looking chew toy in its mouth like it was some miniature boxing mogul chomping on a fat cigar) *and* the way it considered every stick of (not inexpensive) antique furniture in their house to be its own personal toilet. And now, as if deliberately going deliberately out of its way to make George's life even more miserable, the pointless little animal was dragging back on its leash like it didn't want to go by the school – which meant that it was now inevitable that George was going to miss the opener of the CSI re-run that kicked off at eleven.

"I'll be glad when they pull that place down," George said as he and Liz ambled along arm-in-arm by Watsonville Elementary, "I must have walked past it four times a day for ten years now and it still gives me the creeps." He felt his wife's grip on his arm as if she, in empathy with her useless dog, really didn't want to walk past the place.

George's vehement dislike of the school was perhaps more rooted in the fact that the shooting had destroyed the value of all nearby property in one fell swoop, than that so many had died there. The plummeting house prices had rather efficiently trapped the Alcorns in a negative equity property that they had a snowball's chance in hell of selling – who in their right mind wants to live in a house that looks out onto the murder school?

George had watched as the entire neighborhood went swirling down the latrine in the aftermath of the shooting; those that could afford to leave did so quickly and were replaced by lower income families with loud, disrespectful and unruly kids. And those that couldn't – such as the unfortunate Alcorns – were forced to stay put. And it wasn't just the demographic decline that had George pissed off, for lately there seemed to him to be an unpleasant gray atmosphere emanating from the school, one that drifted over the neighborhood like a faint sickly smog that one couldn't quite see but which sucked the joy right out of even the brightest of days.

George glanced across at the school as they walked by, pleased that Tyson had finally figured out that a quick trot by the place was a much better plan than dawdling, in fact now he fair strained on the leash ahead of his owners. George could make out what appeared to be three nebulous shapes at one of the school's windows – one female and two males. The figures stood silent and unmoving and had sad, blurry faces, their hands pressed – palms out – against the grubby glass. George paid them no mind, it was not the first time he'd seen strange things in one or other of the school's few windows (municipal buildings in the hottest parts of Texas tend not to have too many, to keep air conditioning costs down) and he figured that it was most likely a trick of the jaundiced light from the buzzing street lamps.

Either that or he'd have to accept that the town rumor-mill was correct and the place really was haunted.

Liz felt her husband's shudder as she tightened her grip on his arm and quickened her step. "I do hope they put up a Wal-Mart when they knock the school down," her words puffed out in wisps, "it would be handy to have a Wal-Mart right across the street, wouldn't it dear?"

George agreed with his wife that yes it would be handy to have a Wal-Mart across the street from their house, and with their dumb little dog the Alcorns walked briskly along.

*

"How could they not see us?" Danny smacked his fist on the glass so hard that his knuckles hurt. "We're right – *fucking* – HERE!" his voice was falsetto with panic.

Labeaux watched as the middle-aged couple walked by with their pocket-sized dog and he shook his head. The sad faced old man had looked directly in at them and Labeaux had believed – for a second or so – that he *had* to have seen the three of them banging on the window.

As to why he'd chosen to ignore them – that was anybody's guess.

"Fuck this," Labeaux snapped. With a grunt of exertion, he smacked the windowpane dead center with the rear of his camera. The heavy battery smashed through it like it was cracked ice and jagged shards of glass crashed down into the hallway to shatter at his feet.

"Shit, man!" Danny yelped and he and Carolyn jumped back from the cascade of glass, "you could have warned us."

Labeaux offered not the faintest glimmer of acknowledgment or apology to his companions as he stood and stared through the window he'd just broken.

And out into the black, lightless void beyond.

CHAPTER TWENTY-FOUR

Ashlynn was all but unconscious by the time Labeaux, Danny and Carolyn returned to the Principal's office. She lay motionless on the floor – still clinging on to her eyeballs as if her life depended upon it – and her lips moved as if she was in the midst of some silent but very important conversation. Priestley cradled Ashlynn's head in his arms and held a fresh towel over her face; already her blood was soaked completely through the white material.

Priestley looked up, surprised as the three trooped in. "Hey, guys?"

Priscilla filmed their arrival from the comfort of the Principal's chair, her camera following Labeaux as he carefully placed his camera on the edge of the desk. "Could you close the door behind you please, you're letting the stink in?" she said and wrinkled her nose, somehow actually still managing to look cute in her revulsion.

Labeaux did as asked, although if anything, the putrescent stench was now worse inside the office than it had been out in the hallway.

"Back already?" Priestley stroked Ashlynn's hair, a Bond villain petting his cat.

"Already?" Danny perched on the edge of the spacious desk, unable to hide his annoyance that Priscilla had dared take up residence in *his* chair. "We've been gone three hours, Dave," there was pity for Priestley in his voice, even though he'd tried his best to mask it; it was the self same condescending tone that Danny had heard aimed at himself a thousand times following his diagnosis, and still it never failed to smart.

"I told you they'd not find a way out," Ashlynn stirred, her voice a delirious mumble." "It's not finished with us yet," she cackled like some crazy old witch on a kid's cartoon. "It's all for the best, though," she chuckled, "even if we *did* escape it would only follow us." Then her voice hushed to barely audible, "and there are some things that just don't belong out there." She laughed once more and Priestley smoothed her hair, he looked lost and helpless.

Labeaux, Danny, Carolyn and Priscilla stared at Ashlynn; not one of them knew the right thing to say to her by means of comfort – if indeed there *was* a right thing to say.

"You were only gone a few minutes," Priestley said quietly, "I thought you'd forgotten to take a fresh battery or something, Mo'."

"I can't believe you're still trying to play your games with us, Dave," Labeaux countered. He became acutely aware that the hellish cacophony had gotten louder and he was forced to raise his voice. "Especially after – *this*." He pointed at Ashlynn. "I was wandering around outside in the fucking dark for *three fucking hours*."

Priestley shifted Ashlynn's weight on his lap and squinted at his watch. "It's eleven-fifty-five," his voice was flat. "You were gone three minutes, Maurice. Priscilla barely had time to steal Danny's chair".

Priscilla checked the time on her minicam, for the sake of her own curiosity.

Eleven-fifty-six - close enough.

Labeaux studied his own timepiece, and *it* informed him that the time was three-o-six. "For fuck's sake," he growled, more so from the gut-twisting fear that gnawed at him than with any real anger. He *knew* that he'd been stuck outside the school for an age and that although three hours had gone by according to Danny's watch, it had nonetheless seemed to Danny and Carolyn that he'd only been in the darkness a matter of seconds.

Labeaux's head ached with a loud, dull throb as he tried to make sense of it all. Someone – or *something* – was either messing with their watches, their heads *or* their actual perception of reality and it was starting to freak him the fuck out.

"You *really* need to start telling us the truth, Dave," Labeaux figured he may as well start with what (*who!*) was clearly the source of all of their current problems. "Like how much of this is down to you –" He waved a hand over his head to indicate the noise of the screaming that saturated the room, "– and whatever it is that you think *we've* done." He stepped through the clutter and crouched down next to Priestley and Ashlynn. "It's also time to quit with this fucking make-believe as well," so saying, he yanked the towel from Ashlynn's face.

"What the fuck?!" Priestley exploded.

Ashlynn rolled her head as if to give Labeaux one of her looks and twin clots of jellied blood slopped out from her eye sockets.

"Oh shit. I am *so* sorry, dude," Labeaux deflated. Where he'd expected to see prosthetic make-up covering Ashlynn's eyes, he'd instead found himself staring into the bloody, gaping holes that set back deep into her skull.

Priestley snatched the towel back from Labeaux's hand and laid it gently over Ashlynn's face. She muttered something indiscernible and shifted a little at his touch. Then she lay still.

"This is all your goddamned fault. Dave!" Labeaux rounded on his friend, "you and your goddamned *authenticity this* and *eye for detail that* – you're just a fucking prick!" Labeaux pushed his face towards Priestley's, nose to nose. "I don't know what you think we did here tonight – or just how much of this horseshit is down to you and your motherfucking special effects, but this –" He pointed at Ashlynn, this time with no desire to remove the towel; he never wanted to have to look into those dark, soulless holes again. "– *this* is real, Dave. And all that *dark* is no effect; I know that's fucking *real* too!" Priestley flinched at the raw anger, giving Labeaux little satisfaction; being the bigger and more physical of the two, Labeaux was accustomed to intimidating his friend when necessity arose.

Priestley stared blankly into Labeaux's eyes, as if searching for his own answers.

"And for all we know, your stupid fucking *devil* is real too," Labeaux's voice fell and the anger drained from his face. Voicing *that* possibility out loud spread a chill to the back of his skull that clung to the brain and pricked at it with raw terror.

"That's what I've been trying to tell you all along," Priestley spoke to his friend slowly, as if carefully selecting each word. "When we performed the Mass, we invoked something, Maurice," Priestley paused to let that nugget information sink in. "And now it's trapped us in the school for reasons of its own."

"And why would it do that, Dave?" Danny demanded.

"Are you not listening to me, Danny?" Priestley barked, "how the hell am I supposed to know?"

"Because you're supposed to be the fucking expert!" Carolyn's voice rose high and nervy above the ever-increasing volume of the tormented squall. "You're the one who came fully prepared with baggies of your own shit and piss and fucking come, Dave! So, don't you dare tell us that you didn't know what was going to happen when you went to all the trouble of crapping in a fucking Ziploc!"

"Like I told you all before," Priestley fought to hide his exasperation – and lost spectacularly – at times it was like dealing with first-graders. "It was possible that *something* could happen – there's always a risk attached to fooling around with the black arts – which is precisely why I brought these for protection." He fiddled with the phial that he'd strung around his neck. "But, for Christ's sakes, guys, it was a fucking long shot to say the least."

"Well your dumb-fuck necklaces didn't help Ashlynn much, did they?" Labeaux snarled. "Or Chris, for all we fucking know." Labeaux was disgusted with himself for the low jibe at Ashlynn's expense but he was scared and couldn't help but lash out. Priestley hadn't said much thus far to allay his fears, what with of this talk of otherworldly beings and black magic. Labeaux studied his friend and thought that Priestley looked like a fox with three legs stuck in a trap and wondering which one it should chew off first.

"Really, Maurice?" Danny was incredulous. "You honestly believe that Dave – *we* – summoned a demon?" Danny's forced laugh betrayed him – he was ready to believe just about anything right now, anything but this. "You're as fucking crazy as he is!"

Labeaux sighed and turned to face Danny. "Honestly? I don't know *what* to believe anymore," his voice was calm. "All I have to go on is what I've seen with my own eyes – in here and out – *there*," Labeaux tripped over his tongue as memories of the void and the horrors he'd witnessed raced back afresh through his mind. "Besides," he said, "how in the fuck do you explain that?" Again, Labeaux gestured towards Ashlynn as a nervous Priestley held tight onto the blood-soaked towel.

"It will *make* you look," Ashlynn said. Her body fidgeted against Priestley's as she squirmed in tune with her pain. "It will make you all *see*," she whispered, "and believe you me, there are so many, *many* things that no one should ever have to see." A low, growling crow trickled from Ashlynn's throat and her mouth cracked into a broad grin.

A piercing, banshee yowl filled the room.

Hands pressed tight against his ears, Labeaux stood up and stumbled away from Priestley and Ashlynn. No longer interested in berating his friend, all he wanted right then was to get as far away from the terrible shriek as was possible – even if it meant a return to the blackness outside; at least he knew there was silence in there.

Until electrical-flex woman had started up her screaming of course; but then again, he'd liked *that, hadn't he?*

Priestley grimaced as the noise pressed hard on eardrums. He clamped his palms against his ears and the towel slipped away from Ashlynn's ruined face.

The office lights flickered, teasing them all with fleeting flashes of darkness and the horrors it harboured, whilst the sound of the tormented reached an unbearable crescendo and along with it came the nauseating stink of excrement and dead, decomposing things.

Part of the ceiling fell in.

Shocked, Danny squeaked as plump clumps of damp plaster and crumbled bobbles of Styrofoam ceiling tiles showered down into the office.

Ever composed, Priscilla rocked back in her chair and aimed her camera up at the demon as it dropped down into the room.

Labeaux leapt backwards with a loud grunt to avoid the thing and cracked his hip on the pile of equipment boxes as ceiling fragments scattered from his head in a swirling flurry.

Carolyn screamed, her trill voice entwined with – and echoed by – the deafening, otherworldly screams that cavorted around the room. As she watched, transfixed, the demon straightened up its vile body to its full, five-feet or so in height and crawled towards Ashlynn and Priestley, leaving a glistening wet trail of brownish-gray slime in its wake.

Labeaux skirted around the ATA boxes, limping as he manoeuvered himself away from the approaching creature. Almost absently, he picked up his camera and began to film the uninvited guest, and with a glance over at Priscilla he saw that she had not *stopped* filming, even as she'd slid from her chair to kneel behind the desk until just the top of her fiery hair and her minicam's lens were visible.

Danny crouched down by the side of the desk. He had his eyes closed and was mumbling a prayer to himself. Carolyn stood next to him, rooted to the spot in shock, hands clamped tight to her mouth to hold in the screams that simply ached for release, her eyes wide and intense.

The demon contemplated each one of the people in the room in turn with a blazing curiosity, the dark, ashen skin on its slimy flanks heaving in rhythm as it gulped in the putrid air through its foul maw. The thing's face shifted as it stalked through the office, its flesh detached from the restless, churning bones beneath, providing the demon a fluid, ephemeral countenance. The one constant to those hell-born features were the long, wickedly uneven teeth and the intense blue eyes that were sporadically joined by others – smaller but identical in their sapphire brilliance – which erupted from the displacing skin like angry, staring pustules, only to vanish when their clear, membranous lids blinked.

Priestley looked up at the demon with dread. He was desperate to run but knew that he couldn't leave Ashlynn, her blood caked head was a dead weight in his lap and she was incapable of moving under her own steam. His fingers grasped at the phial that dangled around his neck, seeking its reassurance. Priestley lifted up the holy water for the approaching demon to see and was met with a look of amused malevolence.

"Stay away from us!" Priestley shouted, *"the power of Christ commands you!"*

The demon stared down at Priestley like he was of little consequence and its hideous features twisted into something that resembled an evil, toothsome grin.

"Hey, ugly fucker," Ashlynn greeted the demon. She wriggled out of Priestley's arms and sat up. The bloodied towel fell from her face, flopping onto her lap with a *squelch,* and clotted blood slopped out from her empty sockets.

Ashlynn twisted her head and she faced the demon as if she were *seeing* it. "I know you're there, I can fucking smell you," she growled, "I suppose you're what hell smells like?" A crooked smile split Ashlynn's bloodied face.

Priestley shuffled on his butt to place himself between Ashlynn and the demon that she seemed so intent on taunting. As much as the thought of getting even closer to the repugnant thing terrified him, but stronger still was the need to protect his girl; he owed Ashlynn at least that much.

"I can smell it on you too, Dave," Ashlynn sneered, "your breath stinks like hell."

The demon took another step towards Ashlynn and its thick, muscular arms reached out to her.

"Stay away from her!" Priestley's trembling fingers fiddled to pry the lid off of his phial.

The demon ignored him, of course.

Priestley scrambled to his feet and thrust the phial at the demon, who gave it little more than a nonchalant glance.

Priestley fumbled in his pocket to retrieve the crumpled Post-It. "I revoke thee in the name of God!" his raised voice quivered as he read from the garish pink note, "I revoke thee in the name of Jesus Christ our Lord; I revoke thee in the name of the Holy Ghost! *Be gone denizen of hell!*" Priestley bellowed his finale and took a little encouragement that the demon appeared to have paused at his words. "I command you in the name of all that is holy – return to the abyss of eternal flame and torment!"

The demon covered much of the remaining ground between itself and Priestley with unexpected speed, its bug-legs a blur. In his blind panic, Priestley wrenched the amulet from his neck and hurled the holy water at the demon's face.

The phial chinked impotently on the demon's bared teeth and bounced away to smash against Principal Pruitt's trophy cabinet. Priestley watched his amulet's progress with growing despair and was horrified to see the precious liquid reduced to a splashed, wet stain on the laminated wood.

"I command you to leave this earthly realm!" Priestley read from the Post-It, "leave this domain, leave –"

The words halted the demon. It considered Priestly with serious intent; its ever-shifting features contemplating the words he'd just read to it, as if they actually *meant* something.

Priestley's heart jack-hammered against his ribs and the *swoosh* of blood in his ears all but drowned out the hellish noises around him as he tried to force himself to read more from the note; but his hand trembled too much, his eyes filling with tears of frustration.

Finally, the demon stood toe-to-revolting-toe with Priestley. In the blink of an eye, it had plucked the pink square from Priestley's hand. It crumpled the paper up with long, cruel fingers and let it drop to the floor. The demon raised its hand and mere inches from Priestley's face it unfurled a long, thin index finger from its clenched fist and wagged it as if admonishing a naughty child.

"Please?" if it weren't for his lips moving, Dave Priestley might not have been speaking at all.

A third arm – skeletal, with shreds of unformed flesh clinging to rotted bone – erupted from the demon's back, spraying the room with corpulent gobbets of gore and stinking slime. Flexing its newly formed limb, the demon swatted Priestley out of the way as one would a blood-hungry mosquito.

Priestley flew the full length of the room and crashed into the equipment boxes with a sharp yowl. There he lay, trapped amongst the hefty cases, dazed and with the wind well and truly knocked out of him.

The demon returned its attention to Ashlynn.

"You can't make me look!" Ashlynn's voice was singsong and giggly, like a carefree child reciting a skipping rhyme.

"Leave her alone!" Labeaux stepped in as machismo overruled panic. *"Go away! Shoo!"*

The demon ignored Labeaux and bent over to stroke Ashlynn's hair, a tender lover's caress. It sniffed at her with the ragged hole in its face, drawing her scent deep in to the soft, creased folds of its brain with deep, gasping breaths.

"Please leave us alone," Carolyn broke her own stupor. Her voice was sharp and dripped terror; she wanted to run and never stop but her feet were fixed firmly to the ground, as if glued there. "We are so sorry –"

"I won't look, I *can't* look!" Ashlynn taunted and lifted up her eyes for the demon to see.

The demon grabbed a fistful of Ashlynn's hair and she screamed.

"No!" Labeaux and Carolyn shouted out in unison.

The demon crawled up the wall with all of the ease of a fly on glass. It dragged Ashlynn along behind it by her hair and she cried out and kicked and struggled, slapping her captor's flanks with the eyeballs she still clutched firmly in her hand.

Labeaux lurched forward to grab Ashlynn but his actions were too little, too late and all he could do was look on helplessly as the demon disappeared through the hole in the ceiling a fraction of a second before he got there. Labeaux watched forlornly as Ashlynn's legs scraped upwards through the hole, ripping her hose and leaving shreds of red, gossamer nylon and tatters of bleeding skin on the exposed, jagged joists.

Only Ashlynn's voice remained, it resounded above the hellish screams as she heard her laughing maniacally, taunting the demon with her singsong tone. Ashlynn screamed once more. It was a strident, blood-curdling howl and was followed by a complete and tangible silence.

The screams and wails of the tormented dissipated in that same instant and for the five who remained in the office, the stillness fell thick and heavy about them. Labeaux, Danny, Priscilla and Carolyn stared up at the dark hole in the ceiling, and then at one another in shock; not one of them knowing what to say.

A faint pitter-patter broke the uneasy stillness, like the gentle fall of raindrops in verdant spring woodland. Labeaux was the first to feel the sticky, wet drops splash on his face. "Aww *fuck*," he groaned as he wiped a hand across his cheek and inspected it; it was raining blood from the ceiling.

Priestley struggled to his feet and cringed at the darting pains that shot up the full length of his back. He stared with a heartbreaking sadness in his eyes at the busted ceiling and its morbid precipitation. Carolyn laid a comforting arm around his shoulders whilst Danny dared to venture out from his refuge by the side of the desk to get a better view and Priscilla clambered back into the leather chair, her camera still doing its thing.

A battered shred of white paper fell from the ceiling. It fluttered downwards like a delicate, wounded bird. There was a picture on the paper of what looked to be the school; and through the droplets of blood that spattered the fading crayon lines grinned a red face with yellow eyes and tiny black horns.

With a chill in his marrow, Danny recognized the drawing. He shook his head as if in denial. Then he looked up at Labeaux with a terrified half-smile.

"*Shoo?*"

CHAPTER TWENTY-FIVE

*I*t would keep her alive as it had the others – in the same fashion a spider paralysis its prey in order to keep their bodies fresh, succulent and heinously aware – its venom the blackness it so easily summoned from the pits of its own dominion. It would keep all of them alive for as long as it needed, an eternity if necessary.

Squatting there in the darkness, it paused awhile in contemplation of the twitching, eyeless human and the preparations it had to undergo to make the delicate human body join just so with the others it had reaped so far.

Innate curiosity had led it to manipulate the fragile timepieces with which the humans seemed so obsessed. And thus it had added mischievous elements of confusion and disorientation to the mix – unexpected since it had no practical concept itself of the passage of their time – and the thrill it had experienced at this fresh discovery had been poignant as its education in the strange new environment ever blossomed.

Reflections done, it went about the business of reshaping its newest acquisition; snapping, twisting, splintering the brittle bones, bending the quartet of limbs in impossible contours as the human quietly writhed and whimpered.

Once complete, it would fill the broken body with darkness and drag it away to where the others awaited their fate with grim anticipation, their collective destiny far greater than they could ever even begin to imagine.

*

Everyone was avoiding the corner of the office directly below the hole in the ceiling, even though the gruesome drizzle had ceased almost an hour ago.

It had been Labeaux who'd decided that the best thing they could do short-term was to remain in the Principal's office, although to a man the others had elected to run and keep on running.

Just what would have been the point of that? Labeaux had countered; Priestley's demon (yep, he still considered that ugly sonofabitch to be his friend's sole responsibility) could obviously drop in through the ceiling wherever – and whenever – the fancy took it, so there really was nowhere for them to run *to* for as long as they were unable to leave the school. And whilst the horrendous, impenetrable darkness surrounded the place, there really was to be no getting out.

He'd also argued that in the office they had a smaller space to defend and – pun fully intended – if ever there was a more deserving case for *better the devil you know,* Labeaux had been damned if he'd been able to think of it.

Labeaux fiddled absently with the camera. There was nothing that needed doing to the thing, but all the same the restless fidgeting of his fingers helped keep his mind off of the implausible situation he'd found himself caught up in. Less than twenty-four hours ago, if someone had told him that he'd be more than willing to *believe* that hell and its tormented denizens even existed, Labeaux would have laughed straight in their dumb-ass faces.

But now?

Maurice Labeaux was a man who believed only in what he could see with his own eyes, hence his lifelong and obdurate atheism – he maintained a stance that he'd believe in the Almighty the day He descended from heaven and bought him a beer. But now he'd seen things for himself, *experienced* the manifestations and presence of something so truly and unequivocally sinister; and the comfort of his belief system had been shaken to its core.

No one had had much to say since the vote had been taken to stay put. Priestley had taken up residence in the cushioned Principal's chair and sat with his head in hands – pretty much all cried out. Danny and Carolyn perched on the edge of the desk, lost in their own reverie, their legs dangling absently. As for the inimitable Priscilla, she tiptoed around the room to film the gaunt, drawn-out faces and Labeaux wondered if *anything* ever fazed that girl?

The noise had crept back. Slowly, at first it had been barely perceptible, the cries and guttural ululations had been little more than a harsh whisper, but they had gained volume as time crept on, enough to burrow into everyone's psyche and create the darkest, cruellest of thoughts.

"What are we going to do, Maurice? We can't stay here *forever*," Carolyn's voice was blank, devoid of her typical *joie de vivre,* "otherwise all we're doing is waiting for that *thing* to come get us like it did Ashlynn." She shuddered at the memory of Ashlynn's disappearance into the impenetrable shadows of the ceiling space, along with the especially unpleasant drizzle of blood that had followed.

Priestley lifted his head at the sound of his girlfriend's name but remained silent.

"I have no idea," Labeaux gave his honest answer, "then again; I'm not the one who got us into this fucking mess in the first place. Why don't you ask *him*?" He pointed an accusing finger at Priestley.

"I know this is a bad time an' all, Dave," Carolyn addressed Priestley who stared vacantly at her, "but you *are* the one who started all of this. So, it stands to reason that you *must* know how to get us out of it?" more a statement of fact than a question. Carolyn was met by silence.

"Dave's not in any fit state to do anything right now, Carolyn. Just look at him," there was a thread of sympathy through Labeaux's voice; "God only knows where his head is at right now."

"Look, I don't mean to be unsympathetic or anything," Carolyn's aggressive tone certainly contradicted her words, "I do get that Dave's had a shock – *we all have* – and I understand that he's chewing himself up about Ashlynn," she stood down from the desk and folded her arms neatly beneath her ample breasts, "but *we* are still alive and if we're going to stay that way, Dave is the only one who can help us."

Labeaux shook his head. What he didn't need was yet more confrontation and anger, but he did consider it his duty as Priestley's friend to put a lid on Carolyn's attack, even if it meant putting his own feelings aside. "I hate to be the one to pee on your parade, Carolyn, but I really don't think we should rely on Dave to get us out of this," his voice remained calm. "I think if we to do that, Ashlynn's not going to be the only one that gets dragged through the ceiling."

"Carolyn's right," the sudden, unexpected sound of Priestley's voice startled them all.

"Hey, Davy-boy," Danny said with a smile, "welcome back, buddy."

Priestley rose to his feet and pushed the cushy chair away with the back of his knees. It rolled away from him on squeaking casters and clattered noisily into the wall.

"You're right," he reiterated and looked Carolyn squarely in the eyes. "This *is* all my fault. I got us all into this fucking situation, so it is my responsibility to get us out of it." He set his jaw square and firm, as if trying his very best not to break down and cry again. "And we may still be able to help Ashlynn; she could still be alive up there."

Danny, Labeaux and Carolyn swapped awkward glances as Priscilla filmed them. No one wanted to contradict Priestley's delusion, although they'd all witnessed the blood and heard the gruesome noises that had followed her abduction.

Labeaux spoke up, "Dave, you're in no fit –"

"– I'll be fine, Mo'," Priestley closed his friend down. "If I can focus on what needs to be done instead of –" He glanced up at the gaping hole in the ceiling with an intense expression. "I think I may be able to get us through this." He picked his backpack up off the floor with an inner *thank you* to Chris and Ashlynn for having retrieved it from the gymnasium. He plopped it onto the Principal's desk with a heavy *thump*. Priestley then unzipped the main compartment and delved into the mysterious contents that skulked within.

Labeaux and the others watched on in silence, to a man and woman fearing that Priestley had finally flipped his lid and was about to go postal on them.

"First things first, we *do* need to get rid of the demon," Priestley said as he rummaged around the dark interior of the backpack, "and what we need for that is a simple revocation."

"You tried that already," Danny reminded, "and it laughed in your face – literally."

Carolyn huffed and unfolded her arms. "More hocus-pocus Dave?" she sneered, "if that's the best you've got, we *are* fucking screwed."

Priestley pulled out the book that only Danny had seen before; the ancient, leather-bound, pocket-sized tome. He handled it as if it were the most delicate thing in the world and that might crumble beneath his fingers like cold ash if he were to be anything less than gentle. The book's cover was a plain, light brown and adorned with nothing more ornate than the volume's title in thick, black lettering; '*Containing Daemons & Devils*'. With great care, Priestley placed the book on the desk and then from the backpack he produced a crucifix, a couple of bottles of holy water and a pocket-sized King James Bible.

"*No*, it's not the best I've got," Priestley directed his sarcasm squarely at Carolyn. "I came prepared for even the slimmest possibility that we may invoke some minor demon or other," he explained, "and unless I'm otherwise mistaken, I believe what we are dealing with here is *Tenebrion*." He plucked the antique book from the desk and leafed through it, once more absorbed in his own thoughts.

Labeaux and Danny shared a look, fearing even more for their friend's sanity and their own safety.

"Ah, yes." Priestley's finger came to rest on a crumbling page that nestled close to the book's middle. "*Tenebrion – Demon Spirit of Darkness*," Priestley sounded like a college professor making ready to impart golden, life-changing nuggets of information to eager-beaver students, "*one of the higher orders of Hell's minions; a malevolent beast that commands the night to do its bidding. In common with most demons of its level, Tenebrion possesses the power of hypnosis over mortal man and can thus appear in many forms,*" Priestley moved his finger across the musty page as he read out loud. He lifted up the book and turned it around to show everyone the lithographed picture that adorned the page opposite the cramped, spidery prose.

"That looks nothing like what we saw," Carolyn grunted and leaned closer to squint at the illustration of some tall, satyr-like creature with fur covered legs and large bat wings that erupted from its scaly back. The demon on the picture had the upper body and face of a human, complete with a pair of skinny arms, two legs and a pair of distinctly human eyes; its one anomaly being the huge, sweeping horns that sprouted from its forehead.

Priestley considered Carolyn as if she were stupid; just what part of *hypnosis* and *can thus appear in many forms* had passed her by? "*Tenebrion* can make us see it as anything it chooses, Carolyn – and the same goes for whoever carved the picture in the book. We can't know for certain if *this* is its true form," Priestley wiggled the book to hammer home his point, "or the thing we've seen." He paused. "Or perhaps neither –"

"You said it commands the night?" Danny said. "Would that explain the blackness outside? Is that this *Tenebrion's* doing?"

"I'd say that would be a safe bet," Priestley replied, impressed by Danny's uncharacteristic show of perception.

"To keep us all in here," Carolyn mumbled out loud and Priscilla grabbed a sneaky close up of her grim expression with the minicam.

"If it's using the night to keep us trapped," Labeaux ventured, "then surely all we have to do is sit tight and wait for the morning?"

"It's not that easy, I'm afraid," Priestley read on, "this goes on to say that unless we send *Tenebrion* back to where it came from, daylight will never return. Not for us anyways." He flicked through more of the flimsy pages as if searching for something.

"That's just fucking A-1, Dave," Labeaux's thin veneer of patience was quickly eroding beneath mounting panic.

"Calm down, dude," Priestley soothed, "this book has rituals powerful enough to revoke both mid and *upper*-level demons."

According to the book, it all seemed to be simple enough to Priestley. It was just a case of finding the right incantations to fit your demon, recite them in its face and Bob's your auntie's husband. Pick the wrong one, however and as far as Priestley could tell from the ancient tome, he and his crew could well find themselves facing a whole new shit-storm.

"And you just happened to have the very book in your fucking backpack?" Labeaux's anger seeped through loud and clear. "You *knew* that this was going to happen, Dave! I fucking knew it," his voice boomed in the small office and Danny, Priscilla and Carolyn recoiled from the raw hostility.

Labeaux stepped towards the desk, fists clenched.

"Give him a break, Maurice," Danny attempted to placate, "all Dave did was to try and make our movie as authentic as possible; *none* of this was on purpose," he said. "And I say all credit due to him for coming along prepared for every eventuality."

Labeaux caught the all too familiar sideways look in Priestley's eyes that was a sure sign he was hiding something. He leaned across the desk and looked his friend directly in the face.

"Is that what happened, buddy?" Labeaux growled, "you were only trying to be your good old, authentic self? Well, is it?" He and Priestley glared at each other, a tense staring contest. "If that's the case, then what's with all of this other paraphernalia in your bag?

Labeaux and Priestley simultaneously grabbed for the backpack. Priestley pulled it back towards himself but Labeaux wrestled it from his grasp with a rigorous tug and upended it on the Principal's desk.

The contents of Priestley's backpack spilled out.

There were more crucifixes – a half dozen or so – tiny bottles of holy water, communion wafers, a weather-beaten, gray hoodie (unbranded and with a front pocket for the keeping warm of hands) and a book that was even more antiquated and decrepit than the last one. This olden publication had the resplendent – and most telling – title of *To Catch and Keep a Daemon*. Around the book there was wrapped a leather harness, its thin straps embedded with dozens of miniature silver crosses.

"What's this, Dave?" Labeaux fought hard to remain composed.

Priestley shrugged his shoulders.

"For fuck's sake, Dave, what *is* all this?" Danny picked up the book and turning it over in his hands he found that its covers had the texture of long-dead, papery skin. Danny's fingers snagged on the harness that held the book closed and he pulled a face and plonked the book back down on the desk like it was something abhorrent.

"I should have known that you were up to something when your script and storyline didn't quite add up." Labeaux leaned closer into Priestley's face and saw the fear that resided in his eyes. "This was always about more than making a goddamn movie, wasn't it, Dave?"

Priestley shook his head and attempted a reassuring smile. "They're just props for the film, Mo'," he said, "nothing more." Priestley's eyes darted up and to the left as if the lie was projected on the inside of his skull and he was using it as a cue card.

"That's bullshit." Labeaux pulled back a little to pick up the old book. "*This* is more than props." He waved *To Catch and Keep a Daemon* inches from Priestley's nose. "I know when you're up to something, Dave. Do you want to know what I think?" the question was, of course, rhetorical.

"Enlighten me, Maurice," Priestley postured.

"*I think* that you planned all of this from the beginning, and you've been hiding shit from us from the get-go." Labeaux leaned forwards once more to deliberately invade his friend's personal space. "Only things have gone *too* well and it's all gotten a little out of hand. And now you're as shit-scared as the rest of us and clutching at straws with your old books and fucking artefacts," Labeaux's voiced raced until he was forced to draw a breath. "Am I close enough to the truth for ya', Dave?"

"Look, Maurice – "Priestley started.

"Look *nothing*, Dave," Labeaux spat, his suspicions about Priestley's motives were firmly entrenched and he was fully prepared to bully the truth out of the asshole if he had to. "Let's say you start by explaining this, *buddy*," Labeaux growled as he separated the harness from *To Catch and Keep a Daemon,* in doing so ripping away several finger-nail sized chunks of the book's cover. He placed the book back down on the desk and dangled the harness for Priestley's contemplation.

The harness was not entirely dissimilar to those that pet stores sell to little old ladies for walking their pampered pooches. Only, this was made of soft, brownish leather that had a moist, chamois texture, which made it feel like the thing had been *sweating* in Priestley's backpack. And then there were the miniature silver crosses – dozens of them – each one no bigger than a half inch long; they were sunk into the leather to give the impression that the material had *grown* around them. Sewn onto the dorsal strap of the harness was what appeared to be a dried up, wrinkled strip of hide that reminded Labeaux of Starkiller, the pet Iguana he'd had as a kid – only the texture of the harness was somewhere more akin to that of living skin.

Labeaux wrinkled his nose at that thought and dropped the harness onto the desk as if it had stung him. At that particular moment, it really wouldn't have surprised him any to learn that the thing had been fashioned from human flesh; after all, Priestley had managed to procure a real human skull.

Priestley's eyes followed the harness's descent to the desk and winced as it bounced against the hard wood. He spoke slowly, carefully to Labeaux, "all I had *planned* to do was to make *The Black Mass* as authentic as possible, and that's the God's honest truth." His friend's close proximity and bubbling anger scared him. "You can't honestly believe that I'd thought even for minute that we'd *invoke* something. Why else do you think I had Corinne running around to put the frighteners on everyone?"

"It was the gong," Carolyn, not known for her non-sequiturs, drew puzzled looks.

"What are you talking about, Carolyn?" Danny wasn't sure whether or not to smile at the gal. He decided against it.

"Dave told us that he'd deliberately not brought a gong along to the shoot, even though it's a fundamental part of the ritual."

"And?" Danny asked.

"*And* there was a one at the pub tonight. Melissa had a gong with her," Labeaux spoke slowly, as if he was reluctant to part with the words.

"She always does," Carolyn all but whispered, "and you knew that. Didn't you Dave?"

Priestley gave her nothing save a blank look.

"This book tells you how to catch demons." Gingerly, Danny picked through the pages of the aged book and was thoroughly grossed out by how much the pages had the texture of long-dead, desiccated insect wings. "And *how to keep them*," he said as he looked Priestley dead in the face, "were you planning to acquire a new pet tonight, Dave?"

Priestley stared Danny down and refused to answer the question; Danny didn't intimidate him one little bit, not like Labeaux – Priestley had seen Labeaux lose his temper countless times over the years they'd been friends and it was never pretty.

The problem that Priestley had now was that his inquisitors were skating close to the truth, too damn close.

The medical supply store guy had plucked the harness out from beneath the counter that hid at the rear of his emporium. He'd made a big thing out of donning a pair of thin latex gloves – like the ones surgeons snap on before they delve in to someone's innards – before handling the thing, as if it were contaminated with myriad, unspeakable diseases.

He'd explained to Priestley that the harness was fashioned out of hide torn from living demons and that each one of the shiny crosses had been blessed by a defrocked priest. As for the withered strip of skin, he'd explained to Priestley that it was a sliver of tongue cut from the mouth of one of the highest-ranking devils. In its entirety, the harness had been especially designed to contain demons of lower to middle rank and the proprietor had assured Priestley that it would suit his purpose perfectly.

Why, this harness could contain Braathwaate himself, should the need arise! The guy had laughed and it hadn't been until later and he'd Googled the name that Priestley had gotten the joke that had been very much at his own expense

Of course, Priestley had taken the guy's sales pitch with a healthy pinch of salt; it was glaringly obvious that the man was doing his best to justify the three-thousand-dollar price tag for all of the bits and pieces. Although, to be fair, he could have saved his breath – Priestley was sold the second he'd become party to the secret that such things existed.

"So you *did* do all of this deliberately?" Labeaux accused and Priestley wondered if his friend was somehow reading his thoughts, "you resurrected that thing just so you could *catch* it?"

"It's invoked, Labeaux," Priestley corrected. "We *invoked* it."

"Fucking pedant," Labeaux grumbled. He moved closer and his thighs pressed against the desk as he leaned over to crowd Priestley's space still further. "Whatever the fuck it is that *you* did, you planned to catch that fucking thing and keep it," Labeaux snarled and prodded at the harness as a small child pokes at road kill guts with an inquisitive, pointy stick. "That's what you got this thing for isn't it?"

Priestley stared in to Labeaux's eyes, too scared of the big guy to even begin to make up something placatory; although he could see that there wasn't really much point in lying now. He glanced around at the others for support; Danny remained absorbed by the old book, Carolyn sat quietly on the desk and stared at him with her mouth open and Priscilla simply filmed the unfolding drama as if this was one more scene in their movie.

"Let me explain – "Priestley said.

"Sweet mother of God, Dave," Labeaux groaned, "what have you done?"

"Dude, you don't understand –"

"I understand it all perfectly well, *dude*," Labeaux spat the last word with considerable venom. "By my reckoning, you used *Terrorfest* – you used *us* – to perform your stupid ceremony so you could catch whatever you got to crawl out from hell." He glowered at Priestley who lowered his eyes. "*And* you planned to keep it! What exactly did you think your folks were going to say about that, Dave?" Labeaux leaned across the desk and grabbed Priestley's wrist, gripping it so hard that he felt the muscles slide across the twin bones with a slippery crinkling sensation. "Your HOA won't even let you keep a fucking dog!" And Labeaux couldn't help but laugh at the absurdity of that notion.

"Leave him alone, Maurice," Carolyn interjected. She was scared; this was way too much like when her parents used to fight late at night when they thought she was asleep and she'd pull the covers over her head and pretend she was someplace else. "He's been through a lot tonight and all this crazy talk is not going to get us anywhere."

Like a red rag to a bull, Carolyn's interruption served only to take Labeaux's anger one step closer to complete meltdown. "*He's* been through a lot?!" his voice approached a crescendo above the screams that overflowed the room. "And what about the rest of us, Carolyn? What about Corinne and Ashlynn? And Chris, for all we fucking know! I don't recall seeing *Dave* being dragged through the ceiling with his fucking eyes ripped out!"

"Too soon, Maurice," Danny stepped in. He rested a hand on Labeaux's shoulder only to have it shrugged away.

"Maurice is right," Priestley sighed and everyone stared at him like he'd just beamed down from the mother ship.

"I fucking knew it," Labeaux snarled and let go of Priestley's arm.

"Okay, so maybe I *did* hope that we'd invoke something," Priestley spoke quietly, keeping his eyes focussed on the desk, "there was always that chance, however remote, so that's why I came prepared. But you have to believe me when I say that everything I did was for *our* film."

Labeaux doubted very much that he'd ever believe another word out of Priestley's mouth again. Whilst his bud' certainly sounded conciliatory and was giving the appearance of coming clean, Labeaux just knew in his water that there was a lot more to all of this.

For his part, Priestley sighed and struggled to keep his own temper. He didn't *have* to be told he'd fucked up big time – there was no escaping that harsh chunk of reality – and all because he'd read somewhere that it was possible to invoke and catch a demon and he'd thought it would be an exciting and fun thing to do for the movie contest.

It had worked out that the *Terrorfest* competition had come around at just the right time for Priestley, as it was far easier to pull the team together for a contest (and to get them to work for free – Priestley was nothing if not thrifty). The way he'd had it figured out was that this was definitely an opportunity for two birds, one stone; he would capture himself an otherworldly denizen *and* shoot one doozy of a movie all in the same night. In Priestley's head, in the clear light of day, it had been most decidedly a *win-win*.

In fact, it had made for the perfect plan right up until the point at which people had begun dying.

"Mo', just think how good it *would* look on film if we caught a real-life demon," Priestley said and finally made eye contact with Labeaux, "we'd be able to write our own paychecks when we get to L.A."

"Fuck the paychecks, Dave," Danny stepped in, "you just got three people killed," and immediately he felt disgusted with himself for having written Chris off as one of the deceased, for all they knew the guy was alive and well and on his way home, "and you got the rest of us trapped in this godforsaken stink-hole!" He stormed off to the farthest corner of the office, delivering his parting shot as he stepped over the elongated smear of blood Ashlynn had left in her wake, "good plan, Dave – *fucking* good plan."

Labeaux poked Priestley in the center of his chest – hard – with his finger. "You and your idiot plans have put our lives at risk. This is all down to you, Davy-boy," he said. "You're an *asshole*," Labeaux snarled and punched his friend square in the face.

Priestley staggered backwards and windmilled his arms to keep his balance and prevent himself from sitting back down on the wheeled chair. He stared in dazed disbelief at Labeaux as his own anger and frustration effervesced. He and Labeaux had had uncountable arguments during the course of their long friendship and things had even gotten physical before now, but the last time fists had flown in earnest had been back in high school over some girl whose name they could no longer remember. Priestley felt the warm sticky trickle of fresh blood dribble from his nose and a nebulous red mist swam across his vision.

He lunged at Labeaux.

Despite the six-inch height advantage and the extra twenty pounds or so he had on Priestley, Labeaux was knocked off kilter as his friend launched across the desk like a thing possessed. Labeaux stumbled backwards with Priestley clinging on to his neck and choking him with strong, vicious hands.

The two crashed through the office door in their ferocious embrace and spilled out into the hallway beyond. Danny and Carolyn watched Priestley and Labeaux in astonishment and Priscilla followed them out, filming as she went.

Labeaux and Priestley collapsed in a struggling, rolling heap on the floor, fists vying for undefended targets. Priestley swung wild punches at Labeaux's face as Labeaux held up his hands to parry and catching an opportunity between the flailing fists, Labeaux threw a jarring punch that caught the middle of Priestley's forehead. The connected blow hurt Labeaux's hand like a bastard and he felt the small bones crack – but at least it succeeded in knocking Priestley sideways and off of him.

Priestley's vision danced with startling bright, white pricks of light as he crashed down on to the unyielding hallway floor. His focus swam in and out as he righted himself and struggled to his feet, the walls seeming to swirl and pulse, Labeaux an unfocussed blur looming up out of the gloom to face him with broad, meaty fists raised like some punch-drunk pugilist. Priestley saw that Labeaux's nose was bloodied and dripping red, his bottom lip had split at its middle and streaked dark crimson down his chin. Priestley steadied himself against the wall and faced his friend.

Labeaux grunted and lunged, fists lashing out before he was close enough to connect and thus achieving nothing except to make him look like some lumbering, flailing buffoon. Priestley countered the onslaught with a kick. His foot caught Labeaux square in the belly and knocked the wind out of him with a loud *oooof!* Labeaux staggered back with a bemused look on his face.

"You're fighting like a fucking *girl!*" he taunted and fine droplets of blood sprayed out from his torn lip.

There was a dull splintering noise, followed by a resounding *snap* as the rotted floor gave way beneath Labeaux. It collapsed and he toppled sideways and his right leg plunged lopsided into the ragged hole.

"Mo'!" Priestley cried out.

Labeaux's body continued its downward trajectory under its own momentum, despite the fact that one leg was buried thigh-deep in the floor. There came the inevitable, sickening crack as Labeaux's femur shattered under his body's weight and ripped through the thick meat of his thigh like a spear through ice; jagged shards of broken bone so sharp that they sliced through his jeans and a spreading patch of blood quickly darkened the fashionably faded denim.

Labeaux screamed out loud and pushed at the floor with his hands to extricate himself, but the splintered joists that supported the floor held his leg fast as sure as an expertly set animal trap. And each time Labeaux tried to heave himself up, the splintered bone spiked further through the flesh of his leg and a fresh wash of blood drenched his pants.

At the sound of Labeaux's scream, Danny and Carolyn appeared at the office door and Priscilla lowered her camera.

"*What did you do, Dave!?*" Carolyn screamed.

"I–I didn't do anything," Priestley replied. His chest heaved with the exertion of the brawl, but the fight had drained out of him, "the floor just gave way."

"Get me the fuck out of this!" Labeaux cried out with pain coloring his voice.

"Give me a hand," Danny barked at Priestley as he grabbed Labeaux under one arm.

Priestley gripped Labeaux under the other armpit and braced himself to pull.

On three, they pulled on Labeaux's arms.

"*Fuckfuckfuck*!" Labeaux bellowed as waves of agony shot through his body, "that fucking *hurts*!"

Carolyn made her way over and added her strength to Danny's side of Labeaux and the three pulled once more.

This time, Labeaux's body shifted and his leg eased an inch or so from the hole in the floor. Encouraged, they all heaved again and Labeaux's next scream echoed down the dark hallway and left their ears ringing. They relaxed their pulling and as Labeaux slumped a bright arc of blood squirted high from the tattered rip in his leg.

"Quit moving him!" Priscilla screamed as she filmed the spurts of Labeaux's blood as they spattered the ceiling. "You broke his damned artery." She stripped off her shirt and threw it over to Carolyn. "Put this on the wound," she instructed, "and press down hard."

Carolyn did as she was told, forcing herself to ignore Labeaux's guttural screams as she applied pressure on the ugly, ragged wound and Priscilla's shirt turned bright red in an instant. Labeaux's strong, angry pulse throbbed beneath Carolyn's hand and hot blood gushed out from his leg and into the broken floor like it was feeding the school's foundations.

Priestley was stuck in a blind panic; his thinking brain had disconnected completely and was begging him to flee. "What do we do?" his voice was high-pitched, "what the fuck do we *do*?"

"We stop the bleeding," Danny told him as he pulled Priscilla's sodden shirt away from Labeaux's leg and plunged his fingers into the gaping wound.

Labeaux squealed like the proverbial stuck pig and almost passed out as two of Danny's fingers and a thumb disappeared deep into his leg through the torrent of blood that welled up from the gash.

"Hang in there, buddy, we've got this," Danny said to Labeaux, although he was pretty certain that no, they hadn't got this at all, "try to keep still." *No mean feat that, with someone's hand groping around inside your leg.*

Using the fractured bone as a guide, Danny's probing fingers parted Labeaux's sliced quadriceps and followed the blood flow down to the torn artery that disgorged thick torrents of blood with each of Labeaux's heartbeats. "Stay with me, Maurice," Danny said when Labeaux's eyes rolled back in his head as unconsciousness came calling, and he felt his way down towards the femoral artery that was buried deep in Labeaux's muscular thigh.

And when he located the blood vessel, Danny found to his dismay that it was shredded along its length like a burst truck tyre.

"Shit," he said between his teeth.

"What's going on, Danny-boy?" Labeaux's voice was dreamy and slurred, as if he was tripping on some exceptionally good weed.

"I'm trying to stop the bleeding, Mo'," Danny told him and tried not to look at his own blood soaked arm. Closing his eyes to better visualise the long, raggedy tear in the thick artery, Danny touched along its ruined wall as Labeaux's life pumped out strong and fast between his fingertips. And Danny knew then in his heart that the best he'd be able to do would be to stem the blood flow a little. But for what purpose? Even had it been possible to leave the school, there was no way they'd get Labeaux to a hospital in time to stop him bleeding out; the most Danny's efforts were likely to achieve would be to ensure that Maurice Labeaux bled to death a tad slower.

As Labeaux raced towards unconsciousness with each thrum of his heart, Priestley knelt down and cradled his friend's head. "I am so sorry about all of this, dude," he said, "I never meant for any of it to happen. And when we get out of this, I'm gonna owe you big time."

"Damn right you are." Labeaux looked up at Priestley; his eyes flickered and blinked as he attempted to focus. "I'll have to let you off this bit though – it's my fault for putting my fat ass through the floor." He managed a weak smile. "Although, if you didn't fight like a goddamned little girl –" Labeaux shook his head and glanced down at Priscilla's blood soaked shirt and Danny's hand buried in his leg. "As for the rest of this fucking mess, that is *totally* your fault," he snorted and gave Priestley his very best Clint Eastwood squint. "It looks like you're on your own with that one."

"Quit talking like that," Priestley sniffled as he fought to control his desperation. "We'll get the bleeding under control, patch you up and get the fuck out of here. *Then* you can hand me my ass on a plate." He gave Labeaux a smile that tried to convey *it's all gonna be okay, buddy.* He exchanged glances with Danny, who shook his head. Priestley returned the gesture and Danny slid his fingers from Labeaux's leg with a sickening, *schlurping* sound and a fresh surge of blood followed them out.

Labeaux's eyes closed.

Priestley shook him awake. "I have to say, Mo', this is the whitest I've ever seen you." He gave a light laugh that sounded like a child's. "And to think *you* used to call *me* the white nigger."

Labeaux smiled at that. "You remember in *Hannibal* when Anthony Hopkins shanked that poor sap they sent to get his fingerprints?" Labeaux's voice was weak, *dry,* "and we thought Lecter had stabbed him in the balls?"

Priestley nodded as tears threatened his eyes; he guessed this was Labeaux's way of letting him know that he *knew*. "Yeah, made mine run for cover," he said with a smile.

"But that wily old bastard Hannibal had got him in the femoral." Labeaux's chest rose with a deep breath. "Dead in less than five minutes."

"It's slowing down," Carolyn's voice harboured a tinge of hope. "Oh –" she stalled as she looked at Labeaux's ashen face and her and Danny's blood soaked hands, the realization hitting home that Labeaux's blood flow was slowing simply because the supply was running out.

"We've been friends a long time, Davy-boy," Labeaux croaked, "been through a lot together – hell, I even lost my virginity to your sister."

"You fucked my sister?!" Priestley gave him the rote reply like a seasoned comedian's foil; it was an old, comfortable joke between them.

Labeaux smiled at that. "You've always been there for me Dave, and you know that I love you like a brother," There was a sick, breathy rattle to his words, like a night chorus of raucous bullfrogs. He pulled Priestley closer and whispered into his ear, "but if you ever touch my camera, I'm coming back to fucking haunt you."

And with that, Maurice Labeaux was gone.

Priestley felt his friend's body relax with a long, breathy sigh. Labeaux's bladder and bowels gave up their contents and the acrid stink vied with the school's own stench for attention. He watched the expression fade from Labeaux's slackening face, his eyes already stilled to stare glassy, half-lidded and unseeing at an empty spot on the wall over Carolyn's shoulder.

Priestley held Labeaux's head in his arms and not for the first time in this whole sorry mess, he sobbed out loud.

CHAPTER TWENTY-SIX

The noise was louder now. It rose and fell in both volume and intensity as if undulating beneath some otherworldly, tidal influence; the tortured screams it comprised mocking, yet inherently desperate in their complaints.

Priestley sat on the floor in the Principal's office, away from the others, his face sad and pensive. Labeaux's blood had dried into dark stains on his clothes and stiffened the fabric. He'd donned the hoodie from his backpack; mainly to hide at least some of the blood, in part because it had gotten colder in the office; just how Carolyn in her flimsy dress didn't appear to be feeling it, Priestley couldn't understand, although he had noticed that her nipples were bullet-hard and prominent against the thin material.

With the exception of one of the antiquated books, Priestley had stuffed everything back into the backpack, which he cradled between his knees whilst he studied *Containing Daemons & Devils* in quiet contemplation and with a grim determination. The ancient book was not an easy read as the typeface was rather misaligned and faded and was not entirely written in the Queen's English as he recognized it, but Priestley ploughed on nonetheless. He hoped to high heaven that the answers they all so badly needed would magically leap out and fix the nightmare he'd gotten everyone mixed up in.

Each of those remaining were equally reflective, dealing with the after affects of Labeaux's and Ashlynn's death. Not too mention coming face to face with a demon. (Suggested, simple and shorter)

Danny had reclaimed the Principal's chair and sat wiping his hands on a blood-smeared towel with an obsessive's fervor. He'd managed to clean away most of Labeaux's blood from his skin, but there was nothing to be done where it soaked into his shirtsleeves and the knees of his pants. Carolyn sat on the edge of the desk, her legs limp and dangling, painted toes pointed at the floor. Her dress was spattered with blood, which as it dried served to compliment the garish poppies printed on the light material; in a morbid kind of way it rather enhanced the pattern.

Priscilla had seated herself on one of the larger equipment boxes, her camera busy as she captured the silent, bloodied faces around her. She'd managed to avoid the worst of Labeaux's blood as once she'd donated her shirt she'd hovered on the periphery to film him as he died. She'd dug out an old, plain white T-shirt from the school's *lost and found* box and although it was a little snug around her generous boobs and smelled fusty with age and mould spores, it was comforting to feel less exposed and vulnerable.

"How many more of us, Dave?" Danny split the heavy silence that sat bloated, pregnant between them, his voice all but lost within the tormented cries. He looked up from his red stained fingers and his haunted face twitched as he stared directly at Priestley. Danny was the first one to have said *anything* since they'd forced Priestley to leave Labeaux in the hallway and retreat back into the relative sanctuary of the office.

It had taken Danny, Carolyn *and* Priscilla to persuade Priestley to leave his friend's body behind. At first, he'd steadfastly refused and it wasn't until they'd sensed the foreboding chill that slunk along the hallway that they'd managed to get Priestley to quit cradling Labeaux's lifeless head and go with them.

Odd how they'd been unable to extricate Labeaux's leg from the floor.

Danny had had his hand down there. Labeaux's blood had drained out hot and sticky between his fingers and yet he'd felt nothing beneath the rotted floorboards that should have prevented them from freeing Labeaux's leg – especially once the fear of causing further damage to his femoral artery was no longer an issue. After he'd slipped away, they'd tugged hard at Labeaux's leg, but it was as if the limb was being held on to by something unpleasant and infinitely strong that lurked below.

Either that or Watsonville Elementary just didn't want to let go of its prize.

Eventually, they'd placed a jacket from the *lost & found* over Labeaux to cover his motionless, dead eyes and to afford their friend a modicum of dignity.

"Leave him be, Danny," Carolyn said.

"Come on Dave, say something," Danny persisted. "Surely you can't expect us to just sit here quietly and wait to die," more a statement of fact than anything else.

"Danny!" Carolyn chastised.

"It was an accident," Priestley broke his own silence. He met the others' eyes for the first time since Labeaux's death. "Mo' fell through the goddamned floor. It was an *accident*, nothing more," he iterated, still trying to convince himself.

"We know you didn't mean to hurt Maurice," Danny placated, "tempers flared and things got a little out of hand, is all." He offered an unconvincing smile. "But it *did* happen because of our current situation and you need to take responsibility for that."

"You're not helping, Danny," Priscilla chipped in. She cast a sympathetic glance towards Priestley. "This is hardly the time to be playing the blame game."

"I understand *that*, Priscilla," Danny snapped. He was annoyed that Priscilla was siding with Priestley (in fact, just who the fuck did she think she was, siding with *anybody*?!). "All I'm trying to say is that we have to accept that we're completely out of our depth here," Danny tempered his tone a little – he didn't want to inflame more anger and wind up like Labeaux. "And I'm afraid that we're relying on you to get us out of this, Davy-boy," he said. "You're the only one who knows what can to be done to save our sorry asses," Danny adopted his rational, paternal tone – the one he used to great effect with Addison when she was hesitant to do something she didn't want to.

"He *is* right, Dave." Priscilla lowered her camera, climbed down from her perch and shuffled over to Priestley. She rested her hand on his arm. "We *need* you," she said as she looked into Priestley's preoccupied eyes and couldn't be entirely sure if he'd registered her presence or not. "Tell us what we need to do to get out of here and away from that – that *thing*?"

"Well," Priestley spoke slowly as if uncomfortable with his audience, "according to this book, the only chance we do have is to send it back to hell." He lifted up *Containing Daemons & Devils*. "We just need a stronger revocation."

Priestley's words hung heavy and ponderous in the air.

"That's it?" Panic laced Carolyn's voice, she'd expected some profound and instant revelation that would magically transport them all back out into the street.

"And what happens if we *don't* send it back?" Priscilla asked, ever the pragmatist.

At that point, Priestley didn't know quite *what* to tell them. As far as he'd been able to make out from the book – having ploughed his way through seemingly endless pages of heavy, Olde-English text (every *'s'* was an *'f'*, for Christ's sakes!) – if they failed to revoke the demon then it would hunt them all down, one by one. It wouldn't give up, it would never tire nor grow bored – in fact to even attribute such human attributes to a thing that had *never been* human would be a terrible and fatal mistake; *Tenebrion* simply didn't function in any way the same as they did.

Which came to the *why* part of them being trapped within the darkness to be hunted by the demon. Priestley had happened upon something in the book's leaden prose that had troubled him deep down to his core. It had been all but hidden within an especially verbose chapter close to the end of the book, one he'd not bothered to read before now because this whole venture was supposed to have been straightforward; whilst it wasn't spelled out with glaring clarity, the book alluded to a rationale behind the demon's actions – there was a process at play that was far greater than Priestley dared to even contemplate.

The inferences buried deep within the antiquated text had at the same time terrified Priestley *and* hardened his resolve. Now he knew that he had no choice but to put aside the pain that sat heavy in his heart over Ashlynn and Labeaux – there would be time to mourn later – and do everything he could to revoke the demon and get the rest of them the fuck out of Watsonville Elementary.

"It's imperative that we revoke the demon," he said, "because if we don't, all hell's likely to let loose."

"Are you *fucking* for real?" Danny scoffed. "Stick your clichés up your ass, Dave."

"What else do you propose we do, Danny?" Priestley's face flushed red as fire returned to his belly. "It's not like we can just up and leave is it? You've seen for yourself the darkness outside, and fuck only knows what's lurking in it."

"It couldn't be much worse than what's lurking around *in here*, can it?" Danny chirped as if making a funny.

"I have no fucking idea, Danny," Priestley snapped back, "do you want to go find out?"

Danny recoiled at that, never one to relish being on the receiving end of aggression. "Not particularly," he sounded sullen.

"I thought not."

"Then I guess we have no other choice, ladies," Danny tried to save face in front of Priscilla and Carolyn. Priestley's anger had thrown him off kilter somewhat, having reminded him too much of how his wife had been speaking to him of late.

Danny strained a grin. "So, it's back we go to Dave's fucking bug hunt," he said.

CHAPTER TWENTY-SEVEN

With her typical diligence, Priscilla filmed Priestley as he rifled through the backpack. He pulled out some of the silver crucifixes and fresh phials of holy water and gave them to Danny and Carolyn. He'd relieved them of the phials he'd handed out earlier, since clearly, they hadn't worked and Priestley felt that they were *tainted,* having been in the presence of the demon. All he could do now was to hope for the best with the new batch.

Priscilla took one of each for herself – on Priestley's insistence – although she confessed to holding little regard for hollow symbolism. If they were to face the consummate evil that Priestley had described, she would much prefer to have been armed with something more substantial than quasi-religious trinkets, although exactly what *something more* would comprise, Priscilla really had no idea at all.

"Keep these close to hand," Priestley advised, "they're all we have to keep the demon at bay once we find it." He tucked his own crucifix into the front pocket of his hoodie. "Once we've tracked it down, we can use these to corner it long enough for me to recite the revocation," he held one of the diminutive glass bottles up to the light and jiggled it. The crystal clear liquid sloshed around inside.

Priestley had gone to the trouble of having each of the phials blessed by a real priest. Father Kelley was a friend of the family who was familiar with Priestley's odd activities, although he didn't go out of his way to endorse them and Priestley figured that the old priest had most likely gone along with the blessing simply to humor him. To Priestley, desperate for even the faintest glimmer of hope, the liquid in the phials looked like nothing more than ordinary water.

"And just how exactly do you intend to track your demon down, Dave?" Danny was back to his old cynical self and keen to re-establish himself in what remained of the group's hierarchy. "From what we've seen thus far, *it* seems to be the one that's doing the tracking."

Priestley made the decision not to rise to Danny's bait. Instead, he glared at the man and discovered that he despised the old cunt a little more with each minute that passed. And anyways, who the hell says *thus* in everyday conversation?

"We could always follow the fucking smell," Carolyn griped and crinkled her cute, button nose by means of emphasis. "The stink *really* is making me want to throw up, Dave." She cupped a hand over her nose to block out the stench but still it seeped through. She'd not thought it possible, but the sickly shit, vomit and fuck-only-knew-what reek that filled the school had gotten markedly worse since Labeaux died; it was as if the smell itself was an omen of sorts. From out in the hallway, the metallic tang of Labeaux's blood had compounded the putrescent odour, which had then trailed behind them into the office.

"Hunters or *hunted* – either way, we're going to find that fucking thing, Danny," Priestley's tone carried a hint of menace. "And the way I see it, if the demon is looking for us, and we're looking for *it*, then we're bound to meet somewhere in the middle," he said with a crooked smile that made him look more sinister than reassuring. "The important thing is that we stick the fuck together. Let's not make like one of those dumb horror movies where everybody splits up so the monster can pick them off individually." Once more Priestley attempted a smile. "We. Stay. *Together*," he emphasised each word as if his reluctant companions were slow-witted. "You guys got that?"

Carolyn, Danny and Priscilla nodded that *yes*, they had indeed got that – not that it had really needed to be said though, not one of them had any intention of finding themselves alone in Watsonville Elementary.

Priestley stooped to pick Labeaux's camera up from the desk – *if you touch my camera, I'm coming back to fucking haunt you* – and paused a second or so as he recalled Labeaux's threat. A wry, pained smile played on his lips; if Labeaux were able to make good on his threat, it might just be a bonus to have him along for this particular ride.

"Grab a flashlight each, I'll take this." Priestley hoisted Labeaux's camera up on to his shoulder. At the look of collective consternation, he added, "for the light, it still has most of its battery left."

No one questioned this, there was not even an acerbic comment from Danny, although it was evident what the other three thought of Priestley's motives. Not that it bothered Priestley any; it really wasn't every day that one had the opportunity to film an actual demon. Perhaps something could be salvaged from this clusterfuck after all.

"Will you be bringing this along too?" It was Danny who, somewhat predictably spoke up. He picked up the harness and dangled it at arm's length; betwixt thumb and forefinger for all to see as he accused Priestley. "Didn't you bring it along for this very purpose?"

"I wasn't going to," Priestley lied. "And besides, it's a bit late in the day for that now, don't you think, Danny?"

Danny dropped the harness back on to the desk, relieved to be no longer in physical contact with the objectionable thing – if only he'd known the real truth behind the harness, he'd have most likely run screaming, demon be damned. Danny turned his back on it and selected a flashlight.

And whilst he, Carolyn and Priscilla were distracted by the choosing and checking of the flashlights, Priestley slipped the harness into his front pocket alongside *To Catch and Keep a Daemon*, taking great care to prevent its intricate metal parts from jangling.

With a startling *pop*, the arc lights in the corner blew their bulbs, their harmonized sound like a shotgun blast within the tight confines of the office.

Carolyn's sharp scream pierced the sudden darkness, her panic drowned in a fresh, crashing wave of maddening noise; the shrieks and cries and screams that were filled with infinitely more terror than any human throat could ever create. And rising above the sounds there came protracted, rasping cries that were unbearably recognizable.

"Ashlynn?" Danny mumbled as he clapped his hands over his ears.

Abruptly, the noise ceased.

To be replaced by the sounds of grating sounds of furniture scraped across bare wooden floors, chairs toppling, books fluttering to the cold, damp floor. And then the sickening sounds of rending flesh and the *pit-pat-pitter-patter* of rain that smelled like blood.

Footsteps from somewhere in the office.

Everyone held their breath and played statue in the darkness, as if doing so would render them invisible. Not one of the four dared to click on a flashlight, like scared kids who cower beneath their blankets at witching hour they chose to not see what prowled around them in the darkness.

Priestley heard a ragged snort and felt what his hurtling imagination told him was hot, dank breath against his cheek. The insides of his nose burned with the rancid stink of feculence and putrefaction that brought stinging tears to his eyes. And despite the impenetrable dark that bore down on him, Priestley thought he saw a movement.

Brought to his senses and remembering the camera that nestled heavy in his hands, Priestley fumbled around for the *on* button; as much as he didn't care for the idea of facing what may have been in the room, his instinctive craving for light over-rode his reticence. Priestley's shaky fingers located the button. He pressed it. The camera's tiny LCD screen popped into life and offered some teasing yet welcome illumination for his light-starved eyes. Priestley fancied he saw something nightmarish and wetly bulbous scuttle up the wall to his left.

Priestley jabbed at the screen and the camera's main light burst to life; a stark, blinding glare that banished the darkness and replaced it with tall, lanky shadows. Priestley spun the camera around, swinging it this way and that to scrutinize every corner and dark pool of the office, grateful he was not faced with that evil, light-sucking darkness that lingered for them beyond the school's doors.

Danny blinked and swore as Priestley's light caught his eyes, whilst Carolyn had her hands pressed firmly against hers and hadn't registered that the room was once again illuminated. As the camera's light fell on Priscilla, Priestley realized that she'd been filming him all along — no doubt thanks to the nifty *night vision* mode on her minicam that would pick out practically everything in the dark, albeit in ghostly, glowing green.

"Did you see it?" Priestley asked her.

"See what?" Priscilla looked puzzled.

"Pope Gregory the fucking Third, what do you think?" Priestley's attempt at levity died a woeful death – shaken by his encounter in the dark, his tone too harsh to carry humor.

"There was nothing to see."

"There was, Priscilla. I saw – I *felt* it."

Priscilla shook her head. "I can show you what I shot if you like, but all I saw was you fiddling around with Maurice's camera," this sounded accusatory.

Priestley opened his mouth to further protest but he thought better of it. They all thought he was crazy anyway and there seemed no point adding fuel to that particular fire; but he *knew* that the demon had been standing right there next to him in the dark. Instead he said, "we'd better get on with this – the sooner we get done the better."

Danny and Priscilla flicked on their flashlights and then even the gloomiest of shadows were banished.

"Carolyn?" Danny said softly, "you can open your eyes now."

CHAPTER TWENTY-EIGHT

The hallway immediately beyond the principal's office was cloaked by the same oppressive darkness as that which had filled inside, although even that remained preferable to the absolute blackness they all dreaded. Whatever had caused the power surge that blew the arc lights had done a proficient job on the others Danny had set up around the school, and now Watsonville Elementary stood dark and silent and enshrouded by the intruding night.

It was Priestley who took the first tentative steps from the sanctuary of the office, using the bright white light of his (*Labeaux's!*) camera to stab broad fingers of brightness through the heavy gloom. Behind him, Danny followed closely by Carolyn. Priscilla brought up the rear of the sorry-looking gang to capture every fearful step on her trusty minicam.

Priestley, Danny and Carolyn danced their own lights around the hallway, beams scattering the baleful shadows in their hesitant search for otherworldly quarry. The hellish sound accompanied them on their journey; low and subliminal like a mall's infuriating *muzak*, slowly but surely it nibbled away at their sanity.

In the reeking hallway, Priestley saw that Labeaux's body had gone. All that remained of his friend was part of his ensnared leg; snapped off mid-thigh like a ghoulish drumstick, it had the appearance of *growing* from the splintered floor.

*

It watched them through the dark with keen, inquisitive eyes; after eons in the void, the new domain's night proved no barrier. It delighted in the stink of fear that oozed from their soft, warm bodies – flowing wafts of sour odor so strong as to feel viscous to its sensitive nose. The reek was particularly pungent around the older one, enhanced as it was by the oozing aroma of rot that permeated the sweat-smell; the human was dying from the inside out.

The exertion of moving the dark skinned one had left it exhausted – and also frustrated at having to leave part of its quarry stuck in the floor. There would have to be allowances made for that – but for now it rested.

And waited.

*

"There was an old man called Danny," Danny piped up as they made their way slowly but surely along the hallway. It was all for show, of course, but still it came as a pleasant respite from the tormented wails of the damned.

"Who caught cancer on the inside of his fanny," here Danny paused as humor threatened to fail him. A tremor hitched in his throat.

"The Doc scratched his head. Dude, you ought to be dead. That tumor's the size of Japan-*y*." Danny let out a raucous laugh that echoed through the darkness to be swallowed up by a fresh cacophony of screams.

"You've spent a lot of time on that, haven't you?" Carolyn castigated and pretended to be offended. To counter, she gave him a thin, grateful smile.

"They call it graveyard humor," Priscilla joined in, "I think you're incredibly brave, Danny"

"Thank you, Priscilla. I do try to stay positive," Danny chirped. "Although it can be hard to find the bright side in anything whilst being *replaced*."

"Replaced?" Carolyn's foot slid out from under her as she trod down on a small pile of sodden math workbooks. She slapped a hand against the sweating wall to catch her balance and managed to remain upright, despite teetering precariously on her heels.

"Think about it," Danny went on, "cancer is nothing more than your own cells gone rogue. They short-circuit and multiply unchecked like a bunch of fucking rabbits in a cornfield. Or should that be rabbits *fucking* in a –?"

A scratting noise from above startled them. It sounded like something was scurrying about on the ceiling. In an instant, three flashlights and the camera light focussed on the same stained tiles above Carolyn's head.

Nothing there.

The sound stopped, its perpetrator scared away by the sudden blast of light.

The four continued on.

"And, since one of the major –*universal* – symptoms of the Big C is weight loss –" Danny carried on with his monologue, as if it were his job alone to keep up morale whether the others wanted it or not.

"I don't get it," Carolyn was puzzled. She trained her flashlight on the floor, determined to avoid more rotting workbooks.

"Think about it," Danny said with patience; he was well versed in explaining his *cancer replacement theory* to the uninitiated. "You have cancer cells multiplying willy-nilly whilst at the same time your body is losing weight – ergo, you are being *replaced*!" Danny guffawed at his well-worn observational joke and was pleased to hear both Priscilla and Carolyn chuckle along.

"Oh, for *Chrissakes,* Danny!" Priestley's raised voice hacked through the strained laughter. "Can't you just give it a *fucking rest*?!" he ranted, "ever since you were diagnosed it's been *cancer this, cancer that* and everybody's fucking tired of it!"

"I–I, err–" Danny stammered.

"It's all you've become, Danny," Priestley was on a roll, swept away on his own wave of stress. He twisted around to face Danny, wholly unmoved by the guy's wounded expression. "Can't you see that you're defining yourself by a fucking *disease?!* You sound just like my Mother – '*Oh hi, I'm Lizzie and I'm diabetic.*' What the fuck is wrong with '*I'm a nurse, a mother of three – or even; hey! I'm a fucking Virgo*!" Priestley shone his light into the older man's face and at that moment thought that Danny looked terribly old and frail.

Done, Priestley turned his back on Danny, his anger all but spent. "Just leave it alone for five motherfucking minutes, why can't you?"

Tirade over.

"You're a cold, heartless bastard, Dave," Carolyn draped a comforting arm around Danny's shoulders and hugged him close to her body and he moulded just so into her generous curves.

Danny looked crestfallen yet felt cheered by such close proximity of a woman's body and the gentle nudge of a firm breast in his side. It had been a long time since he'd enjoyed that incomparable warmth.

A muted clattering stopped them dead in their tracks, petty arguments forgotten in an instant. It had come from a classroom seven, maybe eight yards ahead and off to the right. It sounded like someone was gently yet deliberately tipping over the small chairs.

Priestley shone his light towards the classroom and stepped forward. The others followed suit and the half-open door to classroom 3c lit up. "Perhaps we should try in there," Priestley suggested, and the thought was not lost on him that perhaps they were *meant* to go that way. "Let's be careful," he added somewhat unnecessarily.

Leading the way, Priestley approached the rotted, paint-peeling door to 3c. With the camera pressed tight to his belly to banish the shadows that clung to the frame, slowly, carefully, Priestley nudged open the door with his foot and drenched the classroom with light. Danny and Carolyn added their flashlights to the brightness whilst Priscilla captured the dread-laden moment for posterity.

The room looked much the same as those they had seen already; tiny, toppled chairs, faded, damp-sodden pictures half-peeled from the walls, an unfinished lesson neatly printed on the whiteboard. Priestley panned his light about the room and braced himself for whatever it may reveal. He had to remind himself that he *wanted* to find the demon – *needed* to – as his every primal instinct screamed at him to turn on his heels and run.

The room was deathly still, even the dust motes hung in the air as if held in place by tiny, invisible threads.

"There's nothing in here," Danny whispered, "I guess he's just messing with us."

"He?" Priscilla cast a suspicious glance at Priestley.

"Yeah, our *Tenebrion* guy," Danny told her with a grin. "I figured that since we've all gotten to know each other a little better, we can consider ourselves on first name terms." His eyes flicked with desperation from Priscilla to Carolyn to Priestley as his perky brand of humor failed miserably to catch on. "I thought we could call him Danny Junior," he persevered. "Ya know, as in the golden oldie *At the*

Hop?" He was met by three blank faces. "Heathens," Danny said and whistled the tune anyway.

"You really are starting to lose it, Danny," Carolyn's edgy laugh was neither humorous nor convincing; on top of everything else, she didn't relish the thought of being trapped in the school with someone about to go postal.

"It's not in here," Priestley's flat tone quashed once and for all Danny's attempt at levity, "I say we head back towards the gymnasium, since it's the first place we saw the demon." He spun his camera out of the classroom, stepped away from the threshold and left 3c to its dark and dismal memories.

Priscilla saw the demon through the tiny lens of her camera.

It dropped silently down from the ceiling and its slimy, shit-flecked body blocked her shot of Danny as it positioned itself in between them.

Carolyn squealed as her flashlight's beam caught the demon's eyes and its sinister, soulless stare glinted back at her. She tottered backwards until she smacked against the wall at the opposite side of the hallway and loosened plaster showered around her like waterlogged confetti.

Danny turned around at the commotion to find himself face to face with the epitome of evil; its vile features glaring at him with those terrible but sensually blue, unblinking eyes. The demon's ever-gaping mouth oozed putrid saliva that dribbled down its chest to form gray, glistening trails across foul skin that pulsed and throbbed and glistened. Around it, the infernal cacophony rose to a thunderous level as if the wailing voices were taunting the demon. Danny felt warmth as his bladder dropped its acrid load into his pants, and his breath caught fast in his stilled lungs.

Priestley was ten paces or so ahead of the three; he'd maintained a steady stride and assumed they were keeping up with him. He turned around at Carolyn's shriek and his camera lit up the unfolding scene.

Keeping his flashlight trained on the demon, Danny fumbled through his pockets with his free hand. His trembling fingers grasped the crucifix and holy water phial, grateful for the comfort that their touch afforded. With hesitant, jerky movements, Danny pulled out the amulets and thrust them at the demon's face.

"Stay the fuck away from me, you ugly bastard!" Danny yelled.

The demon considered Danny as one would an unusual stain and its malignant eyes burned into his with something akin to amusement.

"I–*err*–I command you, I mean *thee* –" Danny sputtered as the stink that emanated from the demon clawed at his throat; he thought he'd become used to the ambient, excremental stench but this was a whole new level and he couldn't help but gag on the acid bile that crawled up his gullet.

"*Illa quae crescit intus tu te,*" the demon spoke to Danny in a deep, guttural tone that resonated around the decaying walls. Its eyes twitched to the crucifix and holy water that Danny held just inches from its face and a smirk flickered across its iniquitous features. Undeterred by Danny's pious display, the demon reached out for him with a long, skeletal arm, its clawed hand balled into a tight fist.

Danny flinched as he watched that fist rise up before him. He wanted nothing more than to flee but his legs failed him completely and he remained glued to the spot.

The demon unfurled one long, impossibly thin finger – which Danny saw all too clearly boasted an additional pair of joints compared to its human counterparts – and jabbed it at the soft bulge of Danny's belly. There it left a brown smudge of reeking slime on his shirt. The demon then slid its arm around Danny's waist and snaked its hand under the waistband of his pants.

Danny gasped as the icy touch of the demon's claw wormed its way between his butt cheeks and up into his ass and for a fleeting second the entirety of Danny's innards were clutched within the freezing grip of that vicious, grasping hand. Shocked into motion by the intrusion of his body, Danny stumbled out of the demon's grasp. He tripped over his own feet and fell down with little grace, flat on his backside. The crucifix and glass phial jolted from his hand as he put it out to break his fall, along with his flashlight which clicked itself off as it bounced away from him and across the floor.

The demon loomed over Danny, the finger that had been inside of him wriggling over the foul length of its tongue as it savored the taste of his bowel. Closer still and with the heat of the demon's rancid breath on his face, Danny could see every detail of the thing's suppurating skin and smelled the unholy stench that poured out from it. The demon raised its hand to reach for something in the shadows above its head – reached *for* the shadows.

And then Danny George found himself enveloped by a total and utter darkness.

CHAPTER TWENTY-NINE

It took Danny a moment or two to regain his composure and when he did so, he looked up and both the demon and the smothering darkness were gone.

"Well, that was fucking close, then," Danny's faux complacency was given away by the giant piss stain that spread across his crotch and all down his left leg. "Looks like your bullshit paraphernalia actually works Dave," Danny said and forced out a flimsy laugh as Carolyn helped him to his feet; he grunted at the dull ache that had settled in his ass.

"You okay, Danny?" Carolyn turned up her nose at the less than fragrant, brown stain on the front of Danny's shirt. Incredibly, it actually managed to beat the rank smell in the hallway for her nose's attention.

"Yeah, I'm good." Danny struggled for balance on wobbling legs that threatened to dump him right back down on his sore backside. "Man – that thing *really is* one unpleasant motherfucker," his voice cracked at the edges.

"You're lucky you tripped, otherwise –" Priscilla left that one hanging and aimed her camera directly at Danny's pasty face to capture his triumphant return to upright.

"Lucky?" Danny grinned into her camera's eye. "I scared that cocksucker away because I'm a fucking *badass* – luck doesn't even enter into it." What Danny hadn't seen was that upon summoning a slice of darkness with which to surround them, the demon had simply disappeared as an illusionist with a theatrical puff of white smoke. Danny glanced over at Priestley for approval only to be met with an icy stare. "Ruined my favorite T', though," he grumped as he peered down at the reeking stain on his shirt, somewhat dismayed to see that it appeared to have not only soaked through to his skin, but was beginning to spread.

Annoyed by the interruption and in no mood for consoling someone who was so obviously unharmed and milking his 'ordeal' for sympathy, Priestley turned on his heels and continued on down the hallway, taking his light with him.

Finding themselves with just their flashlights and a growing multitude of eerie, substantial shadows creeping up on them, Danny, Carolyn and Priscilla hurried after Priestley like the Pied Piper's rats.

"The trail heads this way," Priestley told them as they caught up, "I was right – it's heading back to the gym."

"Perhaps it just wants to go home," Danny offered with a thin thread of hope in his voice, "just like E.T. – only with shit instead of some fancy-ass spaceship."

There was a large part of Priestley that hoped that Danny's jokey half-assed hypothesis had a ring of plausibility. If that were indeed the case, he may just be saved a shit-load of problems, although he would be disappointed at not having the opportunity to capture the demon. Having said that, after what he'd discovered in the old book, Priestley knew it would be foolish for them to rely on the demon merely being homesick; experience had taught the hard lesson that these things were rarely that fucking easy.

Ulterior motives aside – Priestley *still* harbored some hope that he could capture the thing – to prevent further bloodshed and call a halt to the demon's plans, he knew that he had no option but to keep on with the hunt, even if it was unclear at this juncture just who was hunting whom. "I hope you're right, Danny," Priestley replied and quickened his pace towards the gym, the gentle weight of the harness in his front pocket bumping soft and *reassuring* against his belly. "Meantime, we press on. We're going to have that motherfucker in a corner one way or another before we can all go home."

"I'm sorry, I think I'm gonna have to rest up, Dave," Danny wheezed behind him. "You guys go on ahead. I'll catch up with you later."

Priestley rounded on Danny, riled and set to tear him a new one for being such a pussy. But then he saw Danny's face. Caught in the unforgiving beam of the camera's light, Danny's countenance was an ashen sickly gray, his eyes sunken in sockets bordered by deep, dark circles. Danny really did look horribly sick.

"No, we all need to stick together," Priestley kept the agitated tone from his voice, surprised that he was experiencing something in the vicinity of sympathy for the old man, "we're almost there."

Danny leaned heavily against the wall and shook his head. "I can't," he gasped, "it's the Big C playing up again. Probably all the excitement," he attempted a smile and rubbed hard at his belly, oblivious to the ever expanding stain on his shirt that turned his finger ends brown, "if I could just take five to sit down and rest?"

Carolyn sidled up to Danny and slipped an arm around his waist to support his weight. "Dave's right, Danny, we really can't afford to split up," she encouraged with a tug on Danny's middle to encourage him to lean against her and he pulled away with a groan. "This is no time for your macho pride," she said sternly, "I'm offering to help you here."

"I'm sorry, Carolyn," Danny grunted, "I'm not being proud, I just –" He clutched at his stomach and doubled up. In doing so, he slipped out of Carolyn's grip and slumped to the floor with his back propped against the wall. "Oh Jeez, that fucking hurts," he moaned.

Priestley backtracked and stood over Danny. "You okay, man?" there was genuine concern in his words.

"Yeah, never felt better," Danny grimaced, his face a sickly, waxen sheen. "That *was* sarcasm, by the way," he managed to say with a weak laugh.

Carolyn knelt down next to Danny whilst Priscilla followed suit to best capture Danny's moment on film.

"Do you have any painkillers with you?" Carolyn asked, "you do have painkillers, right?"

Danny nodded through the agony that ripped through his guts and his face contorted in an ugly grimace that made him look oddly primitive. "I just chugged a bunch; they should kick in any minute. Then I'll be as high as a fucking kite for the rest of Dave's fucking bug hunt." Danny bent forward and hugged his belly with both arms. He let out another loud, low moan that sounded uncomfortably like the tormented groaning that filled the hallway.

As if in response, the noise swelled around Danny and his companions, and amidst the all too familiar sounds there rang the faintest hint of laughter.

Carolyn shivered and glanced around nervously. Her sparked imagination showed her multitudes of crawling, writhing shapes that inched their way ever so slowly out from between the murky shadows, their sharp, withered claws reaching for her and tiny, malformed faces etched in silent screams. In desperation, Carolyn grabbed Danny's hand and forced him to straighten up and saw to her disgust that the stain on Danny's shirt had smudged onto her fingers and now they felt dirty and – *violated*.

"Oh my," Priscilla's exclamation sounded Judy Garland cute. She shuffled on her knees away from Danny and Carolyn, dropping the camera down to her lap. "What's happening to him?"

Priestley aimed his light at Danny's torso, lighting up the man's belly as it bulged outwards and the thin material of Danny's ruined T-shirt strained to contain the distended flesh.

Then it split apart.

"What's happening, Danny?" Priestley said.

"I–I don't know," Danny sounded truly scared, "n-never happened before." Then he gagged as his throat filled from the inside with something molten, viscous and rancid. The pain that wracked his body was of a magnitude he'd yet to experience with his disease – it felt to him as if his innards were smouldering on white hot coals; an intense, unfathomable pain that stabbed at Danny's nerves as his cancer multiplied at a preternatural pace, each and every errant cell duplicating over and over to fill and distort his body.

Danny took his hands away from his swelling abdomen – too painful now to bear his touch – and noted with not inconsiderable alarm that he looked to be at *least* nine months pregnant. He screamed out his agony and gripped Carolyn's hand so tight that her bones crackled beneath his fingers and his belly shifted as if something grotesque and very much alive was trapped inside of him. There then came a dull rending noise as the taut skin over Danny's belly split wide open and a gray mess of cancerous flesh spilled out through his torn shirt and *crawled* along his body and legs like oozing, pale molasses.

Carolyn whimpered and attempted with little success to extricate her hand from Danny's; his grip was vise-like and hurt like hell and as his body lolled closer to hers she wanted more than anything to be away from it.

"Help me," Danny groaned and wriggled his legs as if trying to gain footing and stand up. He stared down with a bemused expression at the seeping mess of his stomach. His hands hovered over it, torn between attempting to stem the creeping flow of fetid flesh and an unwillingness to touch the vile, bloodied mush that oozed from his body.

The pain subsided with the release of some of the pressure on his insides, along with some help from his pain meds. "Well, whaddya know?" Danny groaned as he studied the amorphous slop discharging from the yawning hole in his belly. "Seems I was right all along – I *am* being replaced," he said, and his laugh threw up a thick geyser of gray slime in a barking, explosive cough.

And as he stared helplessly down at his disintegrating body, the homogenised slop of Danny's disease flowed out like a slick, living thing, carrying within it the decomposed chucks of viscera; it puddled around his legs in a stinking, spreading halo as Danny George dissolved from the inside out.

Finally, Carolyn wrenched her hand free from Danny's sweat-slicked grip as it loosened. With hopelessly flailing legs, she skittered away from him on her backside as fast as she could propel herself across the floor; her face and chest spackled with fat gobbets of gore that stank of something altogether worse than death.

Throughout the hallway the unholy cacophony had reached its climax, and along with it came the maniacal cackling and the frantic *scritch-scratching* of the hell borne things that were biding their time in the shadows.

Danny looked up at Priestley, eyes bulging with terror and fat tears cascading down his sallow cheeks. "Tell Addison I –" his poignant final words were cut short by the rupturing of flesh and cloth as the seat of his pants tore open and Danny shit out what remained of his body's contents.

Priestley and Priscilla stared with disgust at what remained of Danny; Carolyn hid her face in her hands and wept quietly.

Danny sat there quite still – legs splayed out – in the amorphous slop of his escaped cancer, back pressed against the wall and slumped slightly to the left. A congealing beard of pinkish gray vomit clung to Danny's chin that lolled low on his chest and his stilled eyes continued their staring at his hollowed out belly that showed exposed white ribs and spine and the glistening pink of the twin kidneys embedded in the back muscle.

"Is *that* in your little book?" Carolyn spoke first, so very close to breaking point. She stared up at Priestley from her spot kneeling on the floor, her voice a sneer, "do you have any idea what the fuck just happened to Danny?" She snuffled loudly and wiped away the string of clear snot that dangled from her nose with the hem of her soiled dress. "We're all going to die, aren't we?" she looked into Priestley's eyes as she asked the question and dared him to lie to her. "Why don't we just sit here and wait for the – *your* – fucking demon to come get us and save the cunt some leg work?" Carolyn snickered at that and smoothed out her dress, suddenly self-conscious that she'd eschewed panties upon redressing earlier and now she was flashing her bare pussy. Any other time and being so exposed to Priestley would have gotten her horny as hell, but in the aftermath of Danny it just seemed awkward and inappropriate.

"We can't just give up, Carolyn." Priscilla sat down beside her and draped an arm around her chilled shoulders. "As long as we're still breathing, we have a chance."

"And just how long is *that* going to be for?" Carolyn pointed across at Danny's emptied out, oozing corpse. "It's fucking hopeless."

"C'mon, we at least have to *try*." Priscilla helped Carolyn to her feet

"She's right, babe," Priestley threw in to jolly the girl along, "if we stick together, we can beat this –"

A plump string of brown, clumpy slime interrupted what was about to be Priestley's somewhat misplaced, motivational speech. The slime splattered on his cheek and slid down his jowl, its acrid reek stinging his eyes.

In unison, he, Carolyn and Priscilla cast their eyes upwards.

"Fuck," was all Priestley could manage. "Fuck," he said again.

The demon hung upside down from the ceiling by its legs, feet thrust through the flimsy tiles to cling to the wooden joists that lay beyond. It grinned, grinding its wicked teeth together before twisting its unsightly head a full one-eighty. The demon glowered at Priestley and his companions, and there was the promise of unspeakable torments alight in its eyes.

"Oh dear God," Carolyn panted.

Priestley aimed his camera upwards, shining its light full in the demon's face.

The demon's jaw dropped open and showered Priestley with glistening, malodorous spittle as it conjured up the most unholy of shrieks from the foul depths of its throat. As it did so, the demon made its way down from the ceiling with steady, deliberate movements and crawled along the crumbling wall towards Priestley.

"I think we need to go now," ever the Prince of understatement, Priestley took the demon's action as his cue to turn tail and run. Priscilla and Carolyn needed no more encouragement to do likewise, and in the time it took the demon to reach the floor, all three had forged a formidable head start, their dancing lights picking out twisted, diaphanous shadows that hinted at all manner of sickly, contorted creatures that howled out their tortures for the world to bear witness.

Priscilla dared a glance behind. She pointed her camera at the demon to catch it as it loped along the hallway with an effortless, lupine gait. She saw how it leapt at the wall and dug into the flaking plaster with razor claws to gain purchase and without breaking stride it galloped along as easily as it had on the ground. And not once did it take its gaze away from its quarry.

A scream formed in Priscilla's throat as the demon closed the gap between them in an instant and was no more than a handful of strides lengths away; it was at that moment that Priscilla bitterly regretted slowing her pace to get the shot.

"*Please no!*" she cried and all too late she turned around to try to regain her speed.

Something solid, grasping, grabbed at Priscilla's arm and she screamed as strong fingers dug hard into the supple flesh of her bicep and snatched her off of her feet.

CHAPTER THIRTY

Priscilla's feet slipped out from under her and Priestley braced himself to take her weight. He yanked her into the classroom by one arm and she fell inside and on top of him. Behind them, Carolyn slammed the door shut and leaned her full weight against it.

They heard the demon drop to the floor with a dull, wet *thud*. There then came the rhythmic *click-clack-click* of its clawed feet as it drew near to thump angrily on the door like a petulant child throwing a tantrum.

Carolyn yelped. Her body jerked forward as the demon's pounding reached such intensity the door's wooden frame formed deep, snaking cracks, while the door itself threatened to splinter away from its rusting hinges.

Priestley and Priscilla scrabbled to their feet and joined Carolyn, adding their weight to keep the demon at bay, tormented by the chuntering voices and foul stink that seeped in through the thin gaps around the door.

Abruptly, the incessant pounding stopped and the fetid, earthy reek dwindled to that of the school's pervading smell with which they were now all too familiar. The terrible screams and wails remained though, and somehow, they sounded more pitiful than ever.

Priestley, Carolyn and Priscilla kept their backs pressed against the classroom door, convinced that should they move the demon would recommence its attack on the door with a renewed vigor and this time burst through.

But no, the thing was definitely gone.

They waited a little while longer; listening to the labored wheeze of each other's breath as they peered around the classroom for any signs of life other than their own.

The classroom they found themselves in was eerily reminiscent of 3c. There were the ubiquitous small chairs, the upturned desks, the decaying remnants of schoolwork pinned to the walls – yet this room was markedly *different*. Priestley's light picked out the small, faded chalk outlines that were scattered around the floor, the bullet holes that peppered the walls with neat, dark scars and the light pink remnants of blood spatters that were strewn about the room like macabre graffiti.

By chance they'd happened upon the classroom in which every one of its second graders had been mown down by Rachel Villanueva; the one room within Watsonville Elementary that had witnessed the majority of the indoor killings – only the playground had it beat for sheer numbers.

Priestley studied the ostensibly innocuous black dots that punctuated the walls and floor – they looked to him to be like tunnels gnawed out by industrious creepy-crawlies – and he couldn't help but wish he'd discovered this classroom sooner as it would have made for a great location.

They heard a faint shuffling directly above Priestley's head. Something disturbed the ceiling tiles and Styrofoam beads fluttered down around him like perfectly round snowflakes.

Cautiously, Priestley eased himself away from the door. He cringed at the stabbing pain that danced along his back and the dull throb in his wrist where Priscilla had jarred it when he'd dragged her into the classroom and out of the demon's clutches.

For her part, Priscilla stayed put, still terrified that the demon would return the second the door was no longer guarded.

Carolyn followed Priestley's lead and stepped away from the door. Once extricated, she dashed across the room and threw up in a plastic trash basket that cowered beside the sagging teacher's desk. She collapsed to her knees and expelled what little remained of her taco dinner into the basket as her body shuddered violently with each heave.

Priscilla filmed Carolyn as she threw up, hitting the zoom button on her camera to secure the best shot, an action more out of habit than with any burning desire to capture such a distasteful moment. As her camera whirred, Priscilla screwed up her face in anticipation of the acidic tang of bile that she was sure was on its way, as if the place didn't smell bad enough as it was.

"I am so sorry, guys," Carolyn gasped between heaves, which were unproductive now save for the thick ropes of clear slime wrung from the depths of her pissed-off esophagus. Satisfied that she'd emptied out the last of her stomach contents, and that there was nothing more to throw up, Carolyn pulled back from the basket. "I guess I'm not used to running – and the fucking *smell* in here – I couldn't help it."

Priestley crossed the room and rubbed Carolyn's back with soothing, broad circular motions. She was right, the rotten stench was especially pungent in this particular classroom, and the putrescent odor was making even him gag. There was a plus side, though, Priestley mused; he was unable to discern the smell of Carolyn's vomit, she'd merely enhanced the overall ambience.

"Don't worry about it," Priestley offered what was meant to be a reassuring wink, "if I hadn't thrown up earlier, I think I'd be joining you."

"If *you* hadn't thrown up earlier, we wouldn't be in this motherfucking mess!" Carolyn snarled and shrugged Priestley's hand away from her back.

Now Priestley smelled the fresh puke on her breath. He forced himself to turn away before what little there was left in his own stomach was added to Carolyn's swilling around at the bottom of the waste basket. The last thing Priestley wanted to do was to throw up again, all things considered.

The three stood awhile and listened to the *scratting*, scurrying noises in the ceiling that sounded like those of autumn-fed squirrels in the attic of an elderly house, their tiny footsteps amplified by the ancient joists. Through the filthy rectangle of glass in the classroom door, Priestley, Carolyn and Priscilla could make out the vague, shadowy shapes that shifted and swirled beyond in the hallway and looked to them to be – *impatient*.

"I guess we can safely assume that the tables have been well and truly turned?" Priscilla struggled to keep her voice steady. All thoughts of hunting down the demon now seemed hopeless to her; now that they were only three and the demon appeared to be calling the shots. In fact, she firmly believed that the infernal thing had them exactly where it wanted them.

"Yeah, welcome to the shitty end of the bug hunt," Carolyn chipped in with not inconsiderable venom. She stood up on trembling legs and took several steps away from the waste basket – the sight of her own throw-up always made her want to throw up some more.

Priestley frowned at both women, painfully conscious that they were now totally reliant on him to get them out of this situation, one they were blaming *him* for. He really wasn't sure just how to handle that amount of responsibility, particularly since his own nerves were pretty much shot. Nonetheless, he figured that they still had a chance, providing he could keep his head – and theirs – together. "We *can* make this work," he hoped he sounded assured. "It really doesn't matter who is hunting who."

"Whom," Carolyn corrected. "It's *who is hunting whom,*" she said with a light laugh and shot Priestley a wry smile at the welcome lapse into old banter.

"Whom," Priestley corrected and gave a fake sigh. He tipped Carolyn a wink as he did so. "Thank you, Miss Pedantic."

"That's Miss *Pedant.*"

At that one, they laughed at together – a much needed release – yet it was a sound that was most grotesque amongst the cries of the damned.

"*However* we look at it this way… we have to lure the demon back to the gym, to the – *err* – specific place it came from," as he explained himself, Priestley's guts turned over at the thought of once more facing the stinking pool of his own excrements. "That's the only way we can perform the revocation and send the fucker back the way it came."

Carolyn's fleeting good humor evaporated in an instant. "So, what you're saying, Dave – and do bear in mind just how many people have died tonight before you give us your honest reply – is that we are now *bait*?" she growled, "live bait?" Carolyn paused just long enough to cast a glance at Priscilla and saw that she was equally unsettled by the notion. "For some disgusting creature that you dragged out of hell with your bodily wastes and a few choice words?"

Priestley had little option but to acquiesce. Carolyn had, after all hit the nail squarely on the head. The demon appeared to be manoeuvring them back towards the gymnasium, and since Priestley's plan had been to get it back there in order to revoke *(capture?)* it, there would seem to be a happy synchronicity that both he and the demon were working towards the same goal. Therefore, Priestley postulated, wherever they went, the demon would follow.

"Well, just as long as we know where we stand in all of this, eh, Priscilla?!" Carolyn spat out her sarcasm and sputtered with laughter that made her sound ever so slightly unhinged. "So, why don't you guys just keep right on filming and we'll make ourselves one hell of a movie!"

The ceiling fell in around Carolyn and the manic laughter died in her throat. Startled, she leapt away as clumps of soaked tiles, splinters of wood and the purple fluff of dampened insulation rained down around her. Along with the ceiling detritus, there dripped fat strings of dark slime that stretch down like jellied shit stalactites from the freshly gouged hole above.

The demon's face hovered in the center of the frayed hole. It appeared to be disembodied in the darkness, leering down into the classroom like it was smiling at some depraved and infinitely forbidden secret.

The tormented sounds amplified as if someone – *something* – had twisted the dial all the way up to eleven and Priestley was forced to shout at the top of his lungs so as to make himself heard, "GO!" He pointed at the door.

No further prompting was required. Carolyn grabbed her flashlight and made for the door. She wrenched it open with such ferocity that its hinges tore free from the rotten frame and the splintering door clattered inwards. She bounded over the thing and tore out of the classroom with Priscilla and Priestley close behind her.

*

It lowered itself down from the ceiling and into the classroom that had once borne witness to such terrible things. It paused briefly to sniff at the air and taste the pain and anguish and death that had tormented the room – the dim echoes of which still lingered – and took perverse delight in all that it sensed.

Almost done; it had added one more to the gathering which brought it ever closer to the final objective.

The diseased one had been of particular interest, having provided the experience of pleasure, a curious sensation, new and exciting, and one that piqued its curiosity – one that it was eager to experience again.

Its brethren were growing ever restless, their cacophonous, impatient pleas a constant reminder of the infernal task with which had been trusted; a task it had no choice but to complete – and complete well.

It had yet to gain an understanding of destiny, *but soon – very soon – it would fulfil its own.*

Sated, it followed its prey from the room.

CHAPTER THIRTY-ONE

The light from Priestley's camera danced a merry jig on the gymnasium doors as he ran full pelt towards them. Although he was unable to hear their footsteps above the unholy din that cavorted around him, Priestley knew that Carolyn and Priscilla were close behind, their presence given away by the gleam from their flashlights that flickered maniacally upon the walls around him.

Priestley also didn't have to look behind himself to know that the demon was not far away – he could actually *feel* the thing's presence, as if raw evil radiated from its vile body. And all of Priestley's senses screamed out to him that it was rapidly gaining ground.

*

It galloped along behind its prey with an almost leisurely gait, its slithering black tongue lolling from its gaping jaws. It would have taken only a little effort to have caught up, to have overtaken and overpowered the humans, but that was not part of the plan.

It had them running to precisely where it wanted them, like dumb sheep herded by a well-trained dog.

Only once the three arrived at the double doors that opened out into the gymnasium did it accelerate, impossible legs skittering along the mouldering hallway floor like those of some grotesque insect.

*

Priestley burst into the gymnasium shoulder-first. Both doors slammed open under the force of his momentum and he all but fell into the darkened room. Carolyn and Priscilla ran in after him and all three turned around and pushed their combined weight on the doors to force them to close.

Seeing the demon hurtling towards them along the dark hallway, Carolyn screamed out her frustration and banged her fists on the doors that insisted upon closing at their own slow, steady pace, thanks to the dampeners at their upper corners.

Priestley shone his light through the gradually diminishing gap between the doors and down along the hallway – *did he dare hope that the demon hesitated at the glare?* – and heaved his weight against the door with such force that his shoulder fired an odd, prickling pain down his arm that made his hand tingle and his fingers turn numb.

Finally, the gymnasium doors eased shut.

Back pressed tight to the doors, Priestley reached out with a foot and hooked one of the abandoned boom mics. He slid it within reach of his aching hand and then grasped the cool aluminium pole. With a deft twist, Priestley thrust the pole through both door handles.

They heard the demon as it reached the other side of the doors, and stepped away as it banged and thumped and raged with ear-splitting ululations that spun horrendous images of death, depraved torment and vile creatures deep inside their minds.

And all they could do was hope and pray that Priestley's makeshift lock would hold.

CHAPTER THIRTY-TWO

Thankfully, it did.

After a while, the demon gave up its pounding and with one final shriek it was gone.

If it had occurred to Priestley, Carolyn or Priscilla to question how come an otherworldly being that had crawled up from the pits of Hell, could conjure impenetrable darkness *and* the wailing souls of the damned had appeared to be so confounded by doors, not one of them voiced it; something didn't quite seem to gel.

Sometimes a question simply isn't voiced because one doesn't want to face the answer.

The gymnasium was dark – oppressively so – but mercifully it was the brand of darkness that was easily banished by artificial light; and so the glare afforded by Priestley's camera, along with Carolyn's and Priscilla's flashlights provided adequate illumination of their immediate vicinity. Above them, the night peeked down through the ruined roof – in tantalizing contrast to the darkness that enveloped the school – and hazy, silver moonlight filtered through the sparse clouds that sat like dark bruises against the sky. All too soon even that sparse light would be swallowed by the insidious blackness that was already beginning to creep in around the perimeter of the jagged hole.

The sounds of the tormented were subdued, now little more than a barely audible, if somewhat irritating burble.

Priestley panned the camera around the gym; daring to give light to the horrors that he had convinced himself lay in wait within the darkness. The light proved him wrong, nothing lurked in either the darkness or the shadows and that did manage to provide him a little comfort.

Save the absence of the equipment and cases that Ashlynn and Chris had lugged to the Principal's office, the gymnasium was much the same as Priestley had left it. The fold-out tables stood empty – except for the food table which remained cluttered with brown *Taco Cabana* bags, foil wrappers and soda cans – the film lights stood faithful and erect (but most decidedly *dead*) in their respective corners and the blue tarpaulin that had served as Corinne's shroud remained pressed flat against the ground, glued there by the puddles of congealed blood she'd left behind.

The pentagram Priestley had created still clung to the center of the gym as if it marked out some warped kid's game; the black candles had rolled completely away from the circle and the chalice lay on its side in the uppermost point of the five pronged star with the residue of the Unholy Host and Ashlynn's tampon dried up inside of it.

In the gym's corner sat the oily black puddle that Priestley had thrown up. Refusing to dry, it still glinted wet and sinister in the frosty moonlight, its surface rippling as if stirred by the slightest of breezes.

A movement.

Something small darted away from the prying beam of Priestley's camera. Priestley twisted his body around to follow the shape, but somehow it managed to remain tantalizingly out of sight, as if it were attached to the light's periphery.

Carolyn coughed loudly and Priestley damn near peed himself. "For fuck's sake, Carolyn!" he snapped.

"I'm sorry, Dave, I can't help it," Carolyn apologized as she pinched her nose shut between forefinger and thumb, "this stink is *really* bad." She gagged once more as if to emphasize just *how bad* and her emptied stomach dry-heaved acid fumes into her mouth. By means of distraction, she played her flashlight randomly about the gym and drew some comfort from the fact that all it proved to her was that they appeared to be completely alone in there.

Carolyn's relief was short-lived, however when her light just happened to fall upon the corner in which Priestley had parted company with his dinner.

No longer caressed by slivers of moonlight, Carolyn saw that the corner was enshrouded with corpulent shadows that swallowed up her flashlight's glow, creeping, gluttonous things that *pulled* the beam from her bulb. The familiarity of the suckling blackness chilled Carolyn down to her core and she stifled a cry; more than an absence of light, what she witnessed was the terrifying absence of *everything*. Quickly, Carolyn pointed her flashlight away from the corner – out of sight, out of mind.

Priscilla continued to film as Priestley directed his camera light this way and that about the gym, the features of which appeared so very different without Danny's arc lights which perched lifeless atop the stands that cast long, skeletal shadows over the warped floor. Priestley took one tentative step forward, eager to be away from the doors for just in case the demon renewed its assault on them and the boom mic pole didn't hold. He kept his – *Labeaux's!* – camera switched to *record* as he swept the gym, for despite everything Priestley wanted to be sure he captured those all-important shots.

Something small, its face a yawning, bloodied mask pierced with glittering, pinprick eyes jumped in front of

the light and Priestley almost dropped Labeaux's precious
camera.

CHAPTER THIRTY-THREE

"Did you see that?" Hands shaking, Priscilla prodded at the controls on her camera 'till she hit *rewind*. She then played back the most recent thirty seconds but all it showed was nothing more than a small, dark shape scooting out of shot.

"What's going on, Dave?" Carolyn whispered.

Priestley heard the insurmountable fear that laced Carolyn's voice – she was already pushed beyond her limits, what with Ashlynn, Labeaux and Danny – and now Priestley feared that she could crack any minute. That, he wouldn't be able to handle, and the thought of Carolyn throwing a hysterical fit when they had the demon cornered and he'd need her most filled Priestley with absolute dread.

As it was, his own head was reeling enough for the both of them, and his heart thumped double-time as he scanned the gymnasium for whatever it was they'd just seen, acutely aware that his own hysteria was not all that far away.

"Aren't we supposed to be *doing* something?" Carolyn insisted.

"We're doing it," Priestley offered her a brave facade. He couldn't honestly think of anything else they should be doing at that particular moment; either the demon would show its ugly mug or it wouldn't. Priestley was confident that their nemesis would be somewhere close to the gymnasium – precisely where he *needed* it to be. Although he did understand that it was he, Priscilla and Carolyn who were the cornered ones and the irony of *that* situation hadn't gone unnoticed. "The demon will follow us here sooner or later, and then we'll have it exactly where we want it," he voiced his thoughts.

"Don't you mean that *it* will have *us* where it wants us?" Priscilla scoffed. The red *record* LED on her minicam glowed bright like an accusing eye in the gloom as she rounded on Priestley.

"Not helpful, Priscilla," Carolyn scolded, "do you not think that playing live bait for Dave's monster is bad enough for us without pointing it out?"

Priscilla gave Carolyn a feigned smile by means of an apology. "I'm sorry," she said, "I must have said the thinking bit out loud."

Priestley led the way to the corner of the gym farthest away from Puke Corner and as far as he could get from the pentagram. The three then hunkered down between the edge of the wall bars and the door to the equipment cupboard with their lights fanned out to cover as much ground as was possible. Ever vigilant, Priscilla filmed Carolyn as she looked around the gym and Priestley as he tapped impatiently at his camera's LCD screen with a concerned frown that furrowed his brow.

The camera's battery was running low. That thought – above all others – terrified Priestley. The very idea of the light suddenly snuffing out to leave him alone in the dark gripped his stomach and forced his balls tight to his underside. He thumbed the button to quit recording; he had less than twenty per cent battery life left – which had decreased considerably since he'd last checked – and there was nothing quite like running a camera's light to drain a battery. There were spare, fully charged batteries in the equipment dump – Labeaux always brought plenty along to a shoot – but that was back in the Principal's office and Priestley really didn't relish the thought of having to make a return trip.

"So, I was thinking, Dave," Carolyn split the silence with a harsh whisper, "how come your demon doesn't just walk *through* the walls instead of all of that running around on the ceiling?"

Priestley looked at Carolyn as if she was quite mad. As attractive as he'd always found the girl – *infinitely* fuckable, in his book – he marvelled that he'd never noticed before her propensity for being so fucking dim-witted. Perhaps the two traits had cancelled each other out up until now?

"I dunno," Priestley shrugged, "I think we already ascertained the fact that that I'm not the fucking expert, didn't we?"

"It was just a thought," Carolyn grumped. She seemed offended by Priestley's off-handedness. "And there's no need to be so –"

Priestley felt a twinge of guilt. After everything the poor girl had been through (*what he'd put her through!*), all she wanted was to not have to stand there in silence. "Perhaps it can't," he offered. "It's in our realm now and therefore governed by the laws of our physics – or at the very least, *some* of them."

Priscilla shone her light in Priestley's face and made him squint. "Or perhaps it *can* but chooses not to," she added her own thought. "Could it be that the demon's playing with us – fucking with us before it finishes us off – that all of this is just its own sick idea of fun?"

Priestley glowered at Priscilla, pissed at her taking sides against him. What happened to her being an impartial observer?

"You can't attach human attributes to a demon, Priscilla," he rebuked, "it was, and never will be, human." Priestley *thought* he knew enough about Hell's inhabitants to understand that whatever may be going on in the demon's mind would be as entirely alien to them as – well, an *alien's*. They certainly shouldn't make the mistake of trying to second-guess the thing, especially when they didn't have a clue as to what else it may be capable of.

"Do you think that's how come it's not possessed any of us?" Carolyn said, "ya know, like Linda Blair?"

"Possibly," Priestley said. He really didn't know how to answer that one; there were merits to each train of thought. "I honestly don't – "

Something diminutive and incredibly quick darted across the opposite side of the gym. It was followed almost immediately by a similarly tiny shape; both of them barely discernible amongst the murky shadows.

Another.

Hollow echoes of uncountable, tiny footsteps.

Above Priestley and the others, the demon's darkness went about its ominous work of filling in the gaping hole in the roof, flowing in like viscous, liquid night to obliterate the sprinkling of stars and the moon's shimmering glow to smother the life from the shadows that cavorted around the sides and in the corners of the gymnasium. Beyond the doors, that same stifling blackness crept at a snail's pace through the school's hallways, engulfing them in its evil, inky presence.

Carolyn pointed her flashlight towards the tiny shapes that were hiding from view within the shadows and they scooted away, once more sticking close to the boundary of her inquisitive light. "What are they?" she asked, perplexed as to how she was unable to pinpoint the scurrying forms. "There's another one!" she exclaimed and nudged Priestley who swung his camera around.

"Oh my God," Priscilla whispered. She lowered her minicam and peered at the farthest glimmering border of Priestley's light, her mouth dropping open.

Priestley stammered, "I–it's children."

As they watched, a group of a dozen or so small children walked towards them, slowly across the gymnasium.

"Are you getting this?" Priestley asked Priscilla. He hit *record* and filmed the children as they made their way in the direction of his light as moths to a bare bulb.

"Yeah," Priscilla gasped, at once grateful for her camera's anti-shake that would compensate for the tremble in her hands. "But if they're ghosts, they likely won't show up on film."

Priestley knew that the little kids with their blank, expressionless faces and torn, blood spattered bodies weren't ghosts.

The demon had brought them back.

Ever so slowly, Priestley walked towards the children. He filmed their pale, broken bodies as he did so, and as absorbed as he was, he failed to register that – like them – he was headed towards the center of the gym and the pentagram.

Priscilla followed close behind Priestley and filmed over his shoulder. There was an eerie, unnerving silence to the kids that made her feel anxious, as if their sudden appearance was some deathly, wordless portent; she noted that even the wails of the tormented had quietened to a faint whisper in the presence of the children. Priscilla was also aware of Carolyn stepping closely behind her, so close in fact that she could feel the girl's hot, labored breath on the back of her neck.

"Are those the kids who –?" Carolyn struggled to catch a breath in the chilled air.

"I–I don't know," Priestley was honest; at this juncture he couldn't even be sure if what he was seeing was real or not, although it did appear that the camera was seeing the children too, as they showed up just perfect on the small viewing screen. "I guess they could be." He stopped dead at the perimeter of the pentagram, as if some sixth sense had prevented him from stepping inside its boundaries. "Just try not to panic. The demon's trying to scare us."

And an incredibly good job it was doing, too.

Priestley's wobbly legs and the sick knot in his belly stood testimony to that. In an attempt to counter the anxiety, Priestley consoled himself that this disturbing display meant that the demon had to be close by – he'd already seen how much it relished the terror it instilled, no way would it be able to resist this. And once it did make its appearance, he'd hit it with the revocation and the harness and then they'd get to see exactly who was afraid of whom.

"Dave?" Carolyn skipped forwards and grabbed Priestley's arm so hard that her nails jabbed through his sleeve and broke the soft skin of his forearm.

Priestley jolted and a strangled squeak escaped his throat; he'd been oblivious to the fact that Carolyn had been so close. He followed her shocked gaze across the gymnasium to see yet more children emerging from the blackening shadows and that weaving amongst them were larger, adult shapes.

One was a woman who wore a pretty, floral dress which was ripped and tattered and had heavy, sodden bloodstains where the swell of the woman's breasts should have been, instead the pinky-white of the woman's ribs poked through raw, red flesh. Much of her face was missing too, carved away in thick, bloodied chunks that exposed skull bones and perfect teeth, which shone white and iridescent like she was part of some ghoulish toothpaste commercial. And as she made her way towards the pentagram, Priestley spotted the red stained electrical flex that dangled between her bloodied legs, and how it swung rhythmically to and fro with each of her shuffling steps.

A man walked by the woman's side, holding her hand with fingers entwined as lovers do. His face was frozen in a crazed, horrified expression and fat gobbets of clotted blood flecked with gray and pink stuck to his thin lips. The back of the man's skull was entirely gone; a hollow, brainless bowl surrounded by splintered shards of cranium.

Yet more figures loomed out of the darkness on broken, twisted legs, their arms flopping limp and at impossible angles.

Priscilla gasped and lowered her camera. "Oh no, its –"

"Ashlynn," Carolyn finished off the muted sentence.

Out from the darkness staggered Ashlynn, her face barely recognizable with eyes missing and once beautiful features smeared with clumps of clotted red. She ambled with the slow, deliberate steps of the newly blind, swinging her eyeballs to and fro in her hand.

"It can't be," Priestley's voice was a faint whisper. "She's dead." He had to remind himself that this was all the demon's doing – wasn't *Tenebrion* supposed to be the grand master of hypnosis? – but even as the denial fell from Priestley 's mouth, the thought that he'd left his girlfriend behind and *alive* tormented him.

Chris shuffled along after Ashlynn in an ungainly gait on crooked, broken legs, thick splinters of bone protruding through the shredded skin. His pants were bunched around his ankles and his arms had been snapped and dangled loose by his sides. As Chris drew closer, Priestley made out the ugly, jagged rip in his abdomen through which bulged shiny slivers of viscera, and that his genitals were reduced to a few trailing strings of flesh and empty flaps of gore-slicked skin. Chris's lolling head rocked back and forth in time with the rhythm of his footsteps, his mouth contorted in a soundless wail.

Priestley skirted nimbly around the pentagram to film Ashlynn and Chris as they followed the woman in the floral dress and her consort on their journey towards the dead center of the gym, all four encircled by the bustling throng of noiseless children.

Ashlynn walked up to Priestley and it was as if she could see unerringly where he was standing. She reached out a fractured arm to touch his face and Priestley recoiled; the sight of the shattered fragments of bone sticking out through the skin on her snapped fingers made his stomach heave.

"Why did you leave me, Davy?" The pain of betrayal lay thick and heavy in Ashlynn's voice.

"You're not Ashlynn," Priestley told her, as much for his own sanity as for his dead girlfriend's benefit.

Ashlynn cracked her crooked, toothy smile and the dark, bloody pits of her vacant eye sockets stared blankly at Priestley. Then with the hand she'd meant for him, she dug her fingernails into the soft flesh of her own face.

At this, Priestley staggered backwards and into Priscilla and Carolyn. He screamed out loud, his voice shrill with revulsion.

Undeterred, Ashlynn tore at her skin with rabid fervor to peel away the pale, bloodless flesh of her face and reveal, that of the demon which lurked beneath. She ripped away the fragile bones of her eye sockets and the malicious intensity of the demon's eyes glowered out at Priestley; it then stretched wide its mouth in a broad grin that dislodged Ashlynn's jaw which slid down her chest and clattered to the floor with a soggy *crunch.*

Done, the demon tossed the remains of Ashlynn's face to the floor as one may casually discard an empty candy wrapper. It shrugged away the blood-drenched sweater, shorts and ripped hose and for a moment Ashlynn stood gloriously naked before Priestley in the cold night air. The demon wriggled its body and Ashlynn's skin sloughed away from its slimy, excremental flesh to flop down around its spindle legs. The demon then grinned at Priestley and within that grin lurked the darkest, most malignant promises of hell and all of its torments.

Priscilla and Carolyn added their own distress to Priestley's and the three shuffled backwards to be away from the demon that now paced around them.

They made it only so far before they were surrounded by the crowd of small bodies that jostled them back towards the center of the gym.

With a tsunami's rush, the discordant cacophony once more filled the room; its source the impenetrable darkness that quietly expanded in the far corner of the cavernous room.

Priestley recoiled as the noise assaulted his ears; the tormented screams, agonized cries and pleading wails actually physically *hurt*. Behind him, Priscilla clamped her hands over her ears and grimaced against the pain that shot through her head, whilst Carolyn reeled backwards as if she'd been bitch-slapped full in the face.

Carolyn's foot stumbled over the black duck tape circle and into the pentagram and the heel of her shoe kicked the chalice, which rolled away, rattling its annoyance. As she teetered to regain her balance a small, bony hand erupted from the wooden floor in a spray of soft, rotted splinters. It grabbed Carolyn's ankle and she screamed out loud as she toppled over backwards. The flashlight flew from her grip as she flung out a desperate hand to Priscilla who grabbed for her and their fingertips scraped in mid-air.

Carolyn crashed to the floor and was beset by dozens of wizened, skeletal hands that snatched at her body from beneath the floor. They were petite hands with gray, smooth skin and elongated, bony fingers that seemed all too similar to the demon's and were of something quite unmistakably inhuman.

"No!" Carolyn screamed her protest and thrashed wildly against the grasping hands that held her down, "help me!"

Desperate to help, Priestley and Priscilla struggled against the horde of children that encircled them only to find themselves being manoeuvered further away by the sheer weight of their numbers. Try as they might, they could do nothing more than look on helplessly as Carolyn's struggles were suppressed by the clawing, insistent hands.

Floral dress woman brushed by Priestley and her slight frame knocked him aside as she made her way unhindered through the crowd. Without so much as a glance at him or Priscilla she pulled her lover along behind her by the hand, the gruesome pair followed closely by Chris who stared at Priestley with cold, dead eyes as he pushed by.

"Chris?" Priestley implored, "help us, dude?"

With nary a flicker of recognition, Chris walked past Priestley, his wake filled in with small, bumping bodies.

The children shifted Priestley and Priscilla away from the pentagram, away from Carolyn, across to the side of the gymnasium and uncomfortably close to the pitch black, reeking corner. Priestley fought valiantly against the relentless tide; he even resorted to knocking the children aside with the butt of his camera, but all to no avail. For each child he pushed out of the way, another took its place.

Then the children's small hands took hold of Priestley's camera and pulled it down into their midst. He struggled against the collective and incessant strength of the tiny hands and they tugged and wrenched at the camera, their cold fingers creeping across his hands like moist, slippery tendrils. In desperation, Priestley yanked the camera upwards and its beam flashed across the blackness on the ceiling like an errant searchlight. Yet more tiny hands joined in the throng and their pull became ever more persistent as the panicked sweat from Priestley's hands made his own grip on the camera slick and tenuous.

"Get the fuck off!" Priestley kicked out at the frail bodies and succeeded in knocking some aside and loosening a little of the hold they had on the camera. But then still more children surged forward to grasp at the camera and Priestley felt it slide from his grasp. "No!" he screamed at the kids as it slipped from his hands. "You can't take it!"

But before Priestley could fully register what had happened, the camera was duly wrestled from his hands and disappeared within the multitude, its light dampened by the tiny, jostling bodies until it died altogether.

To Priestley's horror, this left only the glow from Priscilla's flashlight and the wayward beam of Carolyn's that pointed off towards the equipment cupboard.

"Help me! *Please*!" Carolyn's scream rang out in the murk, her voice hysterical and beyond terrified.

"*PLEASE!*"

She writhed against the scrabbling grip of the otherworldly hands that pinned her down to the cold, hard floor but the more she struggled, the more unrelenting the hold they had on her. "*DAVE!*" In the low, jiggling light of Priscilla's flashlight, Carolyn saw that Priestley and Priscilla were nowhere close to her and along with that realization went any hope of salvation.

The demon stalked over to Carolyn with a sinister look of purpose upon its face and a substantial growth that swelled alarmingly between its foremost legs.

Struggling against the impatient pushing and shoving of the children around her, Priscilla fought to keep her flashlight trained on Carolyn; the thin beam picked out the struggling shape and rendered the thin material of her dress all but transparent. Priscilla wanted to give the girl at least the comfort of light, although as the demon approached Carolyn with obvious evil intent, Priscilla wondered if in fact total darkness would have been preferable.

The hands that held Carolyn down jutted up from beneath the floor like devilish stalagmites, each with elongated digits that dug deep into her flesh and drew blood with their cruel, twisted nails. Accompanying those hands came a fervent chattering; the sound of excitement and eager anticipation which grew ever more intense as the demon approached Carolyn's helpless body.

"Recite the revocation!" Priestley yelled at Carolyn against the deafening noise, *"for Christ's sakes, Carolyn!"* But Carolyn appeared entranced by the demon and he doubted if she'd heard the instruction at all.

"Stay the fuck away from me!" Carolyn screamed and kicked out at the demon. In doing so she dislodged the hands that held her feet and her shoes slipped off in their clutches. Carolyn lashed out again and this time a bare foot connected with the demon and slapped against its repulsive skin with wet *smack*. The demon recoiled ever so slightly and Carolyn's foot bounced off of its bloated body smeared with strings of foul slime that slithered from her skin.

The woman in the floral dress stared down at Carolyn, her half-face fixed in grim disapproval. She positioned herself by Carolyn's left leg, her partner by the right and in unison they both knelt and grabbed one each of Carolyn's flailing legs. As they did so, the demonic hands they'd made redundant retreated beneath the floor, their accompanying groan one of sour disappointment.

"Motherfuckers!" Carolyn tried to kick away the couple's hands but they held her legs fast with a vise-like grip. *"Get the fuck off of me!"* They stared blankly down at her and blood dripped from their raw wounds to decorate her skin.

Chris joined the couple and kneeled with a leg against each of Carolyn's shoulders. He took a firm hold of her wrists and pulled her arms up over her head.

Suddenly, the arc lights snapped on and the gymnasium was flooded with cold, white light. Priestley and Priscilla screwed their eyes closed against the glare; which no sooner as it appeared, had began to dim as it was devoured by the ravenous darkness. When they squinted open their eyes, they found that although the children had vanished like a mirage on a cloudy day, they could still feel their small hands and unrelenting, warm bodies pressing them against the wall; and still they remained powerless to help Carolyn.

Carolyn screamed and cussed and yelled 'till her throat was raw as she struggled valiantly against her captors – but all to no avail. The garish arc lights – deliberately aimed at the pentagram – lit up the demon's repugnant form in all of its distasteful glory as the hell-spawned thing crept ever closer, its despicable intentions all too terrifyingly clear.

She stared up at the demon with wide, frightened eyes that were blurred by tears. She wrenched her wrists and ankles against the unrelenting grip of her captors but Carolyn felt not the slightest give and all she could manage was to twist her torso side to side and buck her pelvis in a peculiar kind of horizontal dance.

With no warning, the woman and her lover yanked Carolyn's legs apart; so wide and with such force that her poppy dress tore open and her hip joints displaced with a loud *pop*.

Carolyn wailed as unspeakable agony coursed through her entire body, a white hot, searing agony that washed through her in powerful, gushing waves. She slumped limp and moaning against the cold floor as her consciousness faded to black around the edges yet failed to provide the *coup de grace* of merciful oblivion.

The demon reached down with a crooked, curled claw and lifted Carolyn's ripped dress up to her throat, exposing her untethered breasts and gaping, bloodied sex to the damp air. The demon's face shifted and undulated as it fought valiantly to outline something akin to a smile.

The swollen growth between the demon's legs pulsed and throbbed and expanded until the taut skin that contained it ran with a glaze of gossamer cracks. Promptly, those cracks ran together, grew longer and thicker until they split into raw, oozing sores. The demon howled as the grotesque bulge split apart with a gush of stinking, shit-brown slime and out from it jutted a monstrous penis. Easily as long as Carolyn's arm, the demon's phallus unfurled as a butterfly's proboscis in the presence of a nectar-filled flower and pointed its wicked intention towards its victim.

Again, Carolyn screamed and her voice seemed impossibly strident, yet her pitiful cries were soaked up by the dispassionate, encroaching blackness.

*

Its penis was a vibrant purple that proved a vivid contrast to the deathly gray pallor of its body, the shape an approximation drawn from what limited knowledge it had of such organs; this was its own interpretation. The long, fat thing twitched as if with a life of its own and oozed vile fluids from its seeping pores as it engorged to its full and magnificent length.

Of course, it knew what it must do – what had *to be done – but whilst this experience offered little expectation of physical pleasure, the assimilation of knowledge was pleasing in itself. It had experienced the penetration of its own body by the young man it deceived, and with that the sensation of having part of another living, breathing thing inside itself and that, it had found to be of some interest.*

And now, now there was to be this…

*

"No!" Carolyn begged as her body wracked with sobs. "Please no!" She twisted her head to the side in the vain hope of salvation, only to see that Priestley and Priscilla remained huddled by the wall at the far side of the gym and Carolyn couldn't understand why they weren't helping her. *"Help me you fuckers!"* she screamed and she saw with incredulity that Priscilla was filming with that ridiculously tiny camera of hers – the mercenary *bitch*.

Carolyn's attention snapped back to the demon which now stood between her displaced thighs with its impossible dick dangling long, hard and glistening with its bulbous tip pointed directly at her yawning vagina. "Please, no," she cried. "why are you doing this to me?"

"Quoniam i'm diabolus," the demon growled as it readied itself over Carolyn's vulnerable body.

In anticipation of her fate, Carolyn thrashed and twisted against the hands that held her tight, but the violent motions served only to aggravate her dislocated hips and push the ugly knobs of displaced bone upwards to stretch the skin at the top of her thighs. The pain that rode along with that was beyond excruciating, it blazed through Carolyn's body and screamed through her brain until her whole being was nothing more than all consuming pain.

The demon positioned itself over Carolyn, supporting its upper body weight on its arms like a considerate lover, its face close to hers. Carolyn sobbed and jerked her head to be away from the stinking breath that crammed into her nose and the rank saliva that slithered down on to her face.

With great care the demon aimed its gargantuan phallus between Carolyn's splayed legs and entered her vagina with an expert's precision, appearing to take an inquisitive delight at the squeal that its action solicited.

The unnatural girth of the demon's penis stretched the walls of Carolyn's vagina way beyond their limits and the thing felt so horrendously and bitterly cold. To Carolyn it felt as if the demon's prick was freezing her insides as it invaded, that her delicate inner tissues were sticking to its chill flesh as a child's tongue to a cold metal pole.

Carolyn wept as the icy coldness spread out from her sex and out through her body. She shivered and trembled as ferocious spasms wracked her body and chattered her teeth with such violence that they chipped and split and dusted the back of her throat with gritty, scraping enamel.

Indifferent to – or perhaps *encouraged by* – Carolyn's suffering, the demon thrust ever deeper until a full third of its extensive protuberance dwelled inside her body

On the cusp of senselessness, Carolyn groaned with the repugnant combination of unwelcome pleasure and unbearable pain as her insides began to split apart to accommodate the demon's frigid dick and her blood oozed out to soak the demon with steaming, sticky crimson.

The demon uttered a resonant, rumbling sound from deep within its throat and with a forceful thrust into Carolyn the phallus buried itself up to the hilt in her wrecked body. The final violation jolted Carolyn from her flirtations with unconsciousness and she let out a hideous, banshee wail as the demon's penis tore clean through her body and burst out through her screaming mouth, and in that instant it silenced her forever.

Carolyn struggled no more; she lay flaccid and ruined and bleeding beneath the demon, her lips stretched wide and thin around the bloodied head of its penis in a gruesome parody of fellatio.

There came one final spasm and Carolyn coughed up a glob of blood that sprayed out through her nose and into the demon's face and the thing's disgusting penis reciprocated with thick, brown ejaculate.

"No!" Priestley yelled as tears flooded his eyes. He pulled out *Containing Daemons & Devils* from one pocket and his phial of holy water from another. *"I confess sin and seek God's forgiveness for all my occult involvement!"* he shouted the book's incantation above the deafening cacophony that buffeted him from over in the darkened corner.

Struggling to position herself against the tide of unseen hands that pressed her firmly against the wall, Priscilla pointed the minicam towards the gruesome scene within the pentagram and tried not to look directly at the blood-spattered mess that was Carolyn's lifeless body.

The demon flinched at Priestley's words, which seemed enough to distract from its post-coital contemplation of Carolyn. As it withdrew from her, its phallus snagged inside on the splintered edges of Carolyn's shattered ribs and the fat, bulbous head tore and thick, black liquid oozed from the wound and dribbled over Carolyn's breasts.

Chris and his cohorts released their hold on Carolyn's arms and legs and allowed them to flop lifelessly to the floor. Faces blank, unfeeling and uncaring, the complicit three clambered to their feet and stood by Carolyn's body. There, they stared across to the darkest corner of the gymnasium as if it had called to them.

"I confess having sought from Satan that which should only come from God," Priestley read from the book. He'd taken encouragement from the reaction the first line of the revocation had elicited in the demon and raised his voice to better make himself heard. He shook his phial towards the demon as he spoke and whilst the holy water fell woefully short, Priestley was sure he'd seen some hesitation as the demon stared at the clear splashes on the floor with something akin to disdain.

"And I beg forgiveness for my actions and that God put right that which I have undone!"

The demon's eyes met Priestley's and for a heartbeat, human and *inhuman* contemplated one another with mutual understanding. It grabbed Carolyn's ravaged body by one ankle and lifted her up until she dangled loosely with her head resting on the ground, her arms and disjointed leg flopping like a broken puppet's. With little effort, the demon swung the body around and hurled it high and across the gym towards the lightless corner.

Priestley and Priscilla ducked as Carolyn sailed over their heads and they cringed at the warm blood and icy, sticky fluids that rained down on them. Carolyn's body hit the ink-black corner and slid down into the crawling darkness that brooded within.

There was no sound of Carolyn's body hitting the floor.

The pressure of innumerable hands abandoned Priestley and although they remained unseen, he had a *sense* of them being drawn towards that corner and its ever expanding gloom. Chris, the woman in the floral dress and her lover followed suit, all pulled like errant stars that had the misfortune to stray too close to a black hole. Mindlessly, they staggered as if their feet were not their own and were quickly, greedily embraced by the blackness. Chris and the couple vanished into the *nothing* and the hellish sounds soared high as their screams were added to the hubbub.

And then Watsonville Elementary's gymnasium was devoid of life save Priestley, Priscilla, and the demon.

Priestley faced his nemesis.

Priscilla filmed.

The demon returned Priestley's stare and as its unnaturally blue eyes burnt into his, its mouth split wide open with a savage grin.

Slowly, and with great deliberation the demon stepped out of the blood soaked pentagram and towards Priestley.

CHAPTER THIRTY-FOUR

"*I renounce all occult activity!*" Priestley read once more from his book, in as loud a voice as he could muster; calling on every exorcism movie he'd ever seen to draw the gravitas he thought the words deserved. He splashed the holy water towards the demon and fought against every instinct to force himself to walk slowly backwards towards the dark corner in the hope that the demon would follow. "*I renounce Satan and all his works, I renounce evil in all of its sinister permutations – and I renounce* you!"

At this, the demon paused to grimace at Priestley and to judge by the thing's expression, Priestley thought it looked *offended* – as absurd an idea as that was.

Priestley took another step backwards. Then another. The stinking odor of his own vomit reached out for him through the permeating stench that clogged the air, exuding from the corner in a foul, hellish exhalation, and it seemed to Priestley as if the blackness itself were alive and breathing.

The demon continued on towards Priestley, matching each one of his steps with two of its own to close the gap between them – soon it would be upon him.

Priscilla skirted away from the inevitable altercation. Unlike Priestley, she had no desire to be anywhere near the cloying shadows and sickening reek, nor the demon that stalked him like some twisted, persistent predator. Ever in motion, Priscilla alternated her camera's gaze between Priestley, the demon and the oozing darkness and before very long, the demon was close enough to Priestley for them both to fit neatly in frame.

"Get thee to hell!" Priestley screamed till his chest ached and the delicate tissues of his throat tore. He flicked his phial at the demon and now that it stood no more than six or seven strides away, the holy water found its mark. *"The power of Christ compels you! The power of Christ compels you!"*

The arc lights dimmed, the blackness grew ever denser, darker and it reached out groping, stifling fingers to suck at the light.

The demon recoiled at the splash of the water. It lifted up its face and let rip an unholy scream – the sound of uncountable agonies and unspeakable suffering.

A powerful, pulsing energy charged the air and thrummed through the gymnasium's crumbling walls with a low, resounding growl. The walls in turn groaned their displeasure and crumbled, showers of debris cascading from the ruined ceiling as the entire school shook on its foundations, buffeted by violent tremors that bubbled up from deep within the earth's bowels.

Priestley took his final step back on increasingly unsteady legs, all the while gagging at the stench that clawed at the back of his throat. His foot slid from under him as he trod in the mess he'd created earlier, his memory awash with vivid clarity of the coagulated cocktail of his own wastes he'd so readily chugged. Priestley flailed his arms, struggling to maintain balance, and almost tumbled backwards into the darkened corner that stank of excrement, death and putrefaction – and of *him*.

The demon howled once more and its otherworldly voice brought forth a reply of hellacious voices that roared out from within the darkness; a roar so intense that Priestley felt an eardrum rupture and a chill rush of cold air that invaded his head. Reeling from the sharp jab of pain, Priestley spun on his heels to face the source of the fresh dissonance and watched as the darkness in the corner receded, creeping away like a timid, beaten animal.

"Oh fuck," Priestley mouthed.

As the fluid blackness drew in on itself – sucked inwards the same way in which it absorbed light – it revealed a yawning hole twice as wide as Priestley was tall in the corner where he'd thrown up his profane concoction.

Priestley stared into the gaping fissure and it reminded him of a huge, gaping mouth, its lips comprised of the writhing, broken – though still very much alive – naked bodies of his friends, the lady in the floral dress and her lover. The grotesque throat of the cavernous hole was constructed from the lifeless bodies of innumerable children and it plunged deep into the lightless abyss from which wailed the lament of untold tormented souls.

Labeaux stared up at Priestley from his place within the circle around the infernal gash, his bloodless eyes pleading and filled with unbearable pain. His remaining leg had been broken in a half-dozen places and had been coiled around Chris's snapped arms. Chris in turn lay tightly squeezed against the lady in the floral dress, the raw, ragged flesh of his groin pressed into her ruined face, his shattered legs entwined with her twisted arms. The bloodied electrical flex coiled out from the woman's charred vagina and dangled down into the thick blackness that prowled below.

Priestley saw Danny's face smiling out from between the woman's thighs, his disjointed, twisted arms wrapped around her slender legs. His own legs – bent forwards at an impossible angle at the knees – were entwined with the woman's lover's arms so tight that the protruding ends of both men's broken bones had fused together. Danny's torso was hollowed out sternum to pubic bone, with the pink-gray bone of his spinal column and the nubs of his pelvic girdle protruding through what little remained of the dissolved flesh.

Danny's grotesque bedfellow had his legs plaited around Corinne's, who was the next one along in the nefarious group. Stripped of her catsuit – and so much of her skin that her innards spilled out and draped down amongst the small bodies below – her spine was snapped in several places and her head twisted all the way around and she was staring at Priestley over her own shoulder. Corinne's crooked arms were in turn interwoven with Carolyn's and Ashlynn's raw-scraped legs that had been smashed and inserted into Carolyn's devastated vagina.

Ashlynn rolled her unseeing head from side to side, her mouth wide open as if in a scream that just wouldn't form. In her hand, she still clasped her eyeballs in broken fingers, with which she reached out in vain for Labeaux who lay across the only gap in the circle.

That break in the fissure was infinitely more terrifying to Priestley than even the twisted, mutilated bodies of the people that were kept alive by the demon and its foul, unearthly forces. The gap – by its very nature an *absence* – screamed volumes in declaring its vile promise.

It was exactly and perfectly the size of one person.

The school renewed its determined effort to shake itself apart, the walls bulging inwards as if pressed from the outside and the floors undulating, cracking, splintering. The arc lights flickered on and off and the snatches of dark grew longer as their light weakened – soon it would all be completely consumed and darkness would stake its claim.

The demon strode towards Priestley. As it walked it flexed its fiendish claws and its dripping maw chomped open and closed as if the demon were trying to converse with Priestley above the cacophonous din. It ducked low to avoid the plump clods of rotted roof that rained down around it to thump on the ground and disintegrate in plumes of saturated wood and plaster.

"Dave!" Priscilla cried out as she hurried over to him, minicam flopping loosely in her hand.

"Keep filming!" Priestley yelled and although he was sure she'd be unable to hear him, she got the gist and pointed the camera just as the demon caught up with him.

Priscilla lifted her camera to capture the moment and caught her first sight of the fissure in the corner and its gruesome construction; all she'd been able to discern until that moment had been the encroaching blackness that guzzled the light. She froze at the sight that greeted her, the camera aimed squarely at the naked, squirming people who looked so hideously pitiful and in so much pain.

The demon advanced until its claws were half an arm's length from his face.

"*I loose myself from* him, *and from you,*" as Priestley read his voice was swallowed by the dissonance. All he could do was to hope to dear, sweet Mother Mary that it was the words themselves and not whether they were heard that would have the desired effect on the demon. "*And I take back all the ground I ever gave to* him, *and to you, foul creature of Hell's darkest pits.*" Priestley tossed a tad more holy water at the demon, all too painfully aware that his phial was almost empty.

Wondrously, the demon shrieked with pain as the water hit home. It held its arms aloft to shield its face and as if in response, the school convulsed with a fierce heave and hefty chunks of debris tumbled down from the walls amidst a shower of mildewed dust. The gymnasium floor cracked at its center, dismembering Priestley's pentagram and spewing up greasy, black dirt that crawled with all manner of minuscule, jostling creatures.

Encouraged by the demon's reaction, Priestley flicked over to the next page in the antiquated book and continued, *"that which I invoked, I now revoke; in the name of God our Father –"* He threw the final few droplets of holy water at the demon in synch with his words.

The demon wailed and clawed at its face where the water made contact. Its razor claws scrabbled and scraped away clods of vile gray skin to expose raw flesh the bruised colors of decay as it staggered towards Priestley, growling its rage. As it neared the corner, the demon's feet slipped in the sickly brown ooze that seeped and rippled around the bodies that encircled the fissure.

Priestley managed – just – to sidestep the demon as all five of its legs slid from under it. With a yowl of indignation, the thing fell with a wet thump on top of Ashlynn and Carolyn, its bare flesh slapping wetly against theirs.

"The power of Christ compels you!" Priestley shouted at the demon and waved the phial in its direction, although the amulet was now completely empty.

The demon struggled to gain purchase amongst the broken bodies that were slick with reeking slime, blood and the sour sweat of pain. Its frantic actions served only to slide it yet further into the fissure and there it clutched at the frail bodies, tearing apart the exposed skin with its frenzied hands. Sprays of blood and clumps of disembodied flesh flew out of the fissure and the naked people around its rim squirmed and wailed their protests.

"Be gone thou inhuman beast!*"* Priestley bellowed, *"dwell forever in the fiery torments where thou belongeth!"* Myriad tiny hands reached out for the demon from amongst the small bodies that formed the descending tunnel of the hellish hole; they burrowed their bony fingers into the demon's rippling flesh and drew it ever deeper into their midst.

The demon glowered at Priestley with eyes ablaze as it kicked and fought against the tide of grasping hands. Oblivious to the tiny fingers that tore miniscule lumps of slimy flesh from its body, the demon dug its claws into Carolyn's shapely buttocks and heaved itself up, crooked fingers slipping into the crack between the twin mounds of firm flesh.

Priestley looked on with a sinking heart and watched as the demon hauled itself out of the fissure, its delicate feet seeking purchase amongst the creases, crevasses and rends in the violated bodies. Standing with its feet rooted in the meat of Danny's body cavity, the demon fixed its eyes firmly on Priestley and as it reached for him with terrible, spindle fingers he felt beaten; he'd done everything the book had instructed, and that hadn't been enough.

He didn't even have it in him to run.

"Fuck you!" Priscilla screamed so loud at the demon that Priestley heard her even above the cacophony. She hurled a shower of holy water from her phial in the demon's direction. The water caught the artificial light and glinted a cruel, ice blue as it caught the demon full in the face and the innocuous liquid looked *divine*.

The demon let out an eagle's shriek of pain. Its claws slipped out from the naked flesh of the perversely woven circle and it plunged down into the fissure with its bloodied hands flailing.

A brutal tremor tore through the school as if the building itself was trying to shake off the evil that festered within its walls. The arc lights were felled beneath thick chunks of the ceiling that crashed down to blind them once and for all. Dark, steaming splits snaked up along the walls, clouds of dust billowed out into the darkness and viscous darkness oozed out like congealing blood through every crack.

Priestley was knocked clean off of his feet by the juddering floor and he fell face first towards the slick pool of stinking slime. He slid forwards on his belly towards the contorted mess of interlaced bodies, arms outstretched like a clumsy kid on a sled.

Behind him, Priscilla tottered backwards and lost her balance as the ground groaned and shifted beneath her feet. She was dumped unceremoniously on her shapely ass with a jolt that clattered her teeth together and knocked the camera, flashlight and phial from her hands.

Priestley grabbed at Carolyn's bare foot to halt his forward momentum, it was stuck out in a crazy angle between Ashlynn's flaccid thighs and Priestley could feel the splintered bones grinding against each other as his body jarred to an abrupt stop.

He heard – *felt* – an ugly snarl to his left and twisted his head and strained his eyes to see in the sparse light that barely managed to reach him from Priscilla's flashlight. To his horror, Priestley found himself once again face to face with the demon.

With a desperate burst of strength, the demon buried its fingers into the pliant flesh of Ashlynn's belly to gain purchase and Ashlynn's scream rose loudly above the cacophony and sounded something akin to an orgasm. The demon's face grimaced with strain as it drove its claws deep down to hold on to Ashlynn's spine and heaved itself up from the fissure's hungry throat.

Priestley attempted to push himself away, but the combination of slime-slicked floor, quivering ground and his own mounting panic prevented him from finding the grip he needed and his legs skittered a crazy dance as the demon scrambled towards him.

The demon struggled valiantly against the tide of tiny hands that grabbed at the thin flesh of its legs, the scrawny muscles in its arms bulging with taut knots with the effort. Hands stuffed deep inside Ashlynn's squirming body, it gripped the knobbed vertebrae – so hard that the bones splintered and crumbled between its fingers – and with a foul grunt the demon dragged itself the final inches to the edge of the fissure.

Under the weight of the demon, the grotesque circle began to give way at the gap between Ashlynn and Labeaux and the whole thing collapsed inward. Desperate to keep the fissure open, Priestley's friend and girlfriend reached out for each other's hands like star-crossed lovers, but their fingertips merely brushed as they plunged down into the blackness.

The demon yanked its arms out of Ashlynn's body a moment too late and as the unholy circle fell apart it was dragged back into the fissure with her.

Acting on instinct, Priestley let go of Carolyn's foot and pushed himself backwards with both hands. But to his horror, Carolyn's leg looped itself around his wrist, its fractured bones forming ugly bulges beneath the bruised skin. Priestley cried out as he was pulled towards the tangle of bodies as they tumbled into the fissure.

The demon thrashed and fought against the implosion but with the circle of bodies broken, the fissure contracted fast and it was sucked down to the awaiting darkness. The demon let out one final, angry shriek as the portal it had so carefully constructed closed in around it like some repulsive, puckering sphincter.

Priestley watched as the demon was dragged deep into the fissure, along with the twisted and naked bodies of his friends that writhed and grinded together as in a gruesome orgy. They resembled the teeth of that vast hadean mouth, as if there were *chewing*. (Suggested)

And then the demon was gone.

The fissure closed in around Priestley's arm and his limb disappeared into the floor to just above the elbow. Despite the pain that seared his shoulder, Priestley tugged to break free, but he was still entwined with Carolyn's clinging leg beneath the gymnasium floor; her warm, clammy flesh clung tight to his arm and sucked him down inch-by-inch into the ground. Priestley imagined all too clearly Carolyn's ravaged body dangling the other side of the hole with the entire weight of her body suspended from his arm and panic swept through him.

The horror of joining his friends, all so cruelly broken and infernally *alive* in the stinking blackness infused in Priestley a strength he never knew he had. He gave another concerted push against the floor with his free hand, willing and prepared even to wrench his trapped arm out of its damned socket if necessary. But alas, his fingers slipped and slid with impotence in the putrid mess that seeped around him.

The school groaned and shuddered again and the gymnasium's walls bowed inwards to shed their damp plaster in thick, decaying clots. There came low, muffled thuds as beyond the gym as Watsonville Elementary's neglect-weakened walls collapsed, the sound accompanied by the melodic tinkle of shattering windows.

Priestley fought for breath as an overwhelming dread pressed the air from his chest. His arm was now buried up to the shoulder in the floor, his face pressed tight against the cold wood and he was couldn't help but imagine the host of diabolical creatures that likely contemplated the delicious temptation of his fingers from below.

Something grabbed his other arm and Priestley cried out in surprise. He twisted his head to see, braced himself to meet the demon's wicked grin. Instead there was Priscilla, standing over him in a most unladylike pose – legs braced wide apart, hunched over and tugging on his free arm.

"A little help?" she grimaced.

Priestley shifted his body weight the best he could and felt the bones in his shoulder grind together with dull pain and the fissure's grip eased up just a little on his trapped arm.

A dull, reverberating rumble came from beneath the ground and Carolyn's grasping leg loosened its grip on Priestley's arm – as if she'd been forcibly *pulled* downwards – and he slid free of the shrunken fissure. Caught unawares by Priestley's sudden release, Priscilla was carried by her own momentum and she staggered backwards, wrenching him out of and up from the floor.

The two landed in one untidy heap as what little remained of the infernal fissure squeezed itself closed with an audible *pop*.

CHAPTER THIRTY-FIVE

ilence.

The wailing of the tormented, the darkness, and whatever had shaken Watsonville Elementary to its core were all gone in the same instant the fissure and its gruesome supporting structure had vanished. Priestley's regurgitation remained in the corner and it still looked fresh and warm, although, mercifully, the unholy stench that wafted from it was a fraction of what it had been before.

Priestley and Priscilla stayed where they'd fallen – his legs draped heavily across her waist – more concerned with getting their breath back and gathering their frayed wits than with extricating themselves from one another. They lay back on the hard, damp floor together and stared up at the welcome spectacle of the night sky; the inside of gymnasium glowing bright as the moon's pearlescent light shone boldly through what little remained of the ceiling

Finally, wordlessly, Priscilla wriggled out from under Priestley. She pulled a face at the bruised muscles that twinged in her butt and at the covering of brown ooze that was smeared all over her jeans and across the swell of her breasts. She made her way over to where she'd dropped her camera, flashlight and phial. She picked them up.

"We did it," she said.

"I guess we did," Priestley sighed as he sat up.

"For a moment there I was thinking that all your hocus pocus was nothing more than hot air and hope."

"Truth?" Priestley's smile was a weak one. "So did I."

Priscilla turned the minicam over in her hands, checking for damage. She flipped out the LCD screen and jabbed at it with a trembling finger.

"Did you film all of that?" Priestley asked.

"Most of it – I think," Priscilla replied, "it's going to be a little shaky though."

"Don't you worry about that, it'll add atmosphere," Priestley told her through a forced smile and together they shared a nervous, relieved laugh. He picked himself up off of the floor, taking great pains not to step in the greasy stain. Although subdued, the gut-churning stink still drifted from the soiled corner and was making him feel quite ill. Happily, he found that if he turned his head away, the air was fresh, albeit tinged with the fusty, damp aroma of a rotting building.

"So, it looks like you opened a gateway to Hell then?" Priscilla finished up the examination of her camera and as far as she could see, it was all in working order.

"I don't like the term *gateway*," Priestley understated – he *hated* the word, it simply *screamed* cliché. From what he had observed in horrific close-up, he considered the fissure a *tear* in whatever flimsy fabric lay between this existence and which ever one the demon had crawled out of – *wound* may have been better word. "Gateway implies something that can be closed."

"And isn't that what we did just now?"

"Possibly," Priestley said quietly. He was contemplative and beginning to have serious doubts about that; somehow it had all seemed far too – *straightforward.*

"Any thoughts as to how you're going to explain all of this?" Priscilla stepped over the debris and made her way back towards him.

Priestley shook his head, even gave his aching shoulders a shrug for good measure. Short of getting the fuck out of Watsonville Elementary school alive, he really hadn't given too much thought to anything else. "I have been kind of preoccupied, you know," he attempted levity, "but I'm sure as hell gonna need your help when we get out of here," he said. "Explaining what happened, I mean. I guess there's going to be some trouble." Priestley gave a thought to his dead friends as he stared at the half-demolished gym and the pentagram awash with Carolyn's drying blood and figured he'd just made the understatement of the motherfucking year.

"You think?" Priscilla looked at Priestley as if he were quite insane. "It's hard to imagine just where they'll start throwing the book at you, Dave," she said and gave him that smile again, "let alone *which* book they're going to throw."

At this, Priestley crumbled. Tears welled in his eyes, which made Priscilla and the gym all blurry about the edges and all at once he felt like a frightened little kid who'd lost his Mom in the grocery store.

Ignoring the repugnant slime that covered Priestley's front – easy to do since she was fair covered in the stuff herself – Priscilla took him in her arms and pressed her body close to his.

"I'm not sure I fully understand what I've seen tonight, but I can promise I'll back you up. As long as we stick to the truth – no matter how bizarre we think that actually is – I'm sure everything will work out alright," she whispered her words of comfort into Priestley's heaving chest.

Priestley allowed himself to relax into Priscilla's arms; the warmth of her body, the *closeness* of another human being was infinitely reassuring. He nuzzled down into the soft skin of her neck, seeking solace in her nearness and of her warm breath on his ear.

Behind them, the fissure opened up once more; the broad, yawning mouth again spewing out the diabolical noise and infernal stench. The naked, mutilated bodies that formed its perimeter shrieked and howled out loud with their torments as the expanding gash stretched their broken bodies beyond all human limits. The blackness gushed out from the darkest depths, crawling over and amongst the tiny bodies that lined the fissure and as impossible as it seemed, the grisly hole appeared more insidious, thicker – *darker* than before.

The demon bounded up from the fissure and rose up behind Priscilla before she even had time to react to the suddenness of the fresh activity; its body glistened fresh, slick and was devoid of the wounds previously inflicted upon it.

Priestley stepped back and pulled Priscilla with him. He felt her body tense in hesitation, and she pulled away from him.

"No." Priestley grabbed for Priscilla's hand and urged her with widened eyes to take a look over her shoulder.

"Don't worry, I *do* know it's there," she said with a smile, her face serene. "Don't try saving me, Dave." Priscilla kicked off her shoes and stepped barefoot into the rancid slime, backwards towards the demon.

"What the fuck, Priscilla?" Priestley tried to get his feet to move to go after her, but his body simply refused to budge.

Priscilla allowed her camera, flashlight and holy water to drop from her hands and all three fell with a wet *plop* into the sickly brown gloop that suckled at her naked toes. She pulled her T-shirt up and over her head, then unhooked her bra. "There's no need to be concerned," she purred above the fresh cacophony as she discarded her clothes, "this is how things were meant to be."

"It's controlling you," Priestley stammered. He stared over Priscilla's bare shoulder at the demon's grinning face, "you have to fight it."

Priscilla's laugh was a gentle one. "There's nothing to fight, Dave. There never was." She unbuttoned her jeans. "Why do you think that you only arranged *five* for your ritual?" She hooked her thumbs under the waistband of her jeans and thong panties. "When you knew that you'd need six?" She tugged her jeans and panties down, stepped out of them and stood between Priestley and the demon so achingly naked and vulnerable. "You *knew*, Dave. It was always going to be me." Priscilla tossed her head and flame red hair tumbled over the smooth, flawless skin of her shoulders. "I'm the final piece of the – "

Priscilla gasped as the demon pulled her into its deadly embrace, its tenacious grasp forcing the breath from her lungs as the icy chill of its claws tore into the tender flesh of her back and she soared far beyond mere pain.

The demon ripped away the flesh of Priscilla's lower back and cold air caressed her exposed spine and ruined viscera slopped out of her body in glistening pink and gray coils which slopped wet and steaming at her feet. The demon reached its gnarled hands around Priscilla's chest to cup each breast as if it were a playful lover and the tips of its claws gouged into the heaving mounds to create thin rivulets of blood that meandered downwards to her deep navel.

Then the demon manoeuvered Priscilla towards the fissure; her body was limp and compliant in its arms and her escaping guts slithered along behind as if trying to catch up.

Priestley stood rooted to the spot with absolute terror and desire for self-preservation. He found himself once more unable to help or run, and incapable of looking away.

Priscilla found her voice as the demon plunged her into the monstrous mouth of the fissure, screaming as more of her innards slipped out from the splits along her flanks as the demon positioned her into the ghoulish circle between Labeaux and where Ashlynn lay broken and bleeding.

Willingly and with a smile through the pain, Priscilla offered the demon her left arm. The demon took a firm hold of it and snapped the bones just above and just below the elbow. Priscilla howled and her legs spasmed, her feet slapping uncontrollably against the demon and the bare human flesh that crowded her. Undeterred, the demon repeated the action with Priscilla's other offered arm and finished off by wrenching both of Priscilla's shoulder joints from their sockets in one skilful movement.

The demon forced Priscilla's squirming legs together and leaned its weight on her knees. A nauseating *crack-crack* resounded as the limbs buckled in the wrong direction and the joints gave way and once more Priscilla screamed. The demon then snapped Priscilla's legs at the femur and midway along the smaller bones below her knees – the left leg with such vigor that the splintered tibia jutted out through her shin and showered them both with a thin spray of scarlet – followed by a nimble twist of the ankles to shatter those bones too, and this time Priscilla screamed so hard and so loud that her voice dampened those that cried and wailed from deep within the demon's pit.

Stirred into movement, Priestley simply couldn't help himself.

Ever so slowly he knelt down to pick up Priscilla's minicam and half-empty holy water phial. Wiping away the slime on the leg of his jeans, he pocketed the phial and switched on the camera, aimed it at the shattered, entwined bodies that remained so horrendously alive and with hopeless desperation in their eyes. Priestley filmed the demon as it went about its gruesome work with Priscilla's acquiescent body like some grotesque, oversized bug repairing a breach to its hive.

Taking hold of one of Priscilla's crooked legs and twisting it around Ashlynn's arm, the demon wove the broken limbs tightly together until it became difficult for Priestley to distinguish the two. Repeating the procedure with Priscilla's other leg, the demon thus entwined the two women in a grim embrace. Ashlynn moaned her protests at the further violation of her ravaged body, but was unable to cry out as Priscilla's gaping crotch was pressed firm against her mouth in a squalid, sapphic pastiche.

Priscilla's cries grew weaker as the demon went about the business of braiding her snapped arms with Labeaux's until her face rested against his chest as if in the glow of a post-coital embrace; she moaned softly into Labeaux's skin whilst he cried.

With determined finality, the demon placed one of its scraggy hands on Priscilla's neck and one at the base of her exposed spine and folded her body backwards; the crackling, kindling stick sound as it fractured reverberated throughout the gymnasium.

The camera shook in Priestley's hand as he zoomed in on Priscilla's eyes that were squeezed tight, her mouth stretched so wide in a scream that its corners split and wept blood as her torment joined those from deep inside the fissure beneath her.

As the demon folded Priscilla's body in two, the living perimeter of its fissure pulled tight on itself, no longer rendered weak by a missing body. Complete, it now resembled something hideously *vaginal*; now a vast, gaping vulva with fleshy labia created from the bodies that the demon had collected so diligently and broken, the vagina proper comprised of the small, lifeless bodies that plunged deep down into the lightless abyss from which came the lament of innumerable souls that grew ever louder, *closer*.

As Priestley filmed, the demon stepped back to examine its handiwork, its legs gaining purchase on the intertwined bodies that twitched and undulated, squirming now as if in eager anticipation of something imminent.

And on the demon's face, a smile.

*

With the final piece of the puzzle in place, its work was complete. It stalked the edge of the opening between this new, exciting existence and the one it had always known, its steps unsteady amongst the slippery, shifting bodies of those it had so meticulously assembled for the unholy recipe;

The slaughtered innocents.

Tormented lovers.

Flayed.

Self-castrated.

Blind.

Exsanguinated.

Diseased.

Violated.

And– most important of all – the Willing Sacrifice.

The gateway that was not a true gateway had been opened, and soon the brethren and kin with whom it had once shared the dark, cold void would also find freedom – its work was indeed done.

CHAPTER THIRTY-SIX

Priestley dared himself a smile back as he watched the demon – *his* demon – clamber out from the fissure and make its way over to him with steady, deliberate steps; every gaping pore on the thing's glinting, slippery body oozing malevolence, its eyes smouldering with evil intent.

Priestley pressed back against the clammy gymnasium wall and the cold, mildewed water seeped through his clothes and chilled his flesh. He trained Priscilla's minicam on the demon as it came to a halt a stride or so in front of him and figured that the shot would most likely turn out a little too shaky for his liking, but given the circumstances, that was somewhat unavoidable.

"I had a feeling you'd be back," Priestley tried his best to sound valiant, although he *was* dangerously close to soiling himself. He fumbled around in his pocket, then pulled out the harness and held it up for the demon to see.

The demon closed in on Priestley and its unblinking, cobalt eyes burned deep into his soul.

"Everybody's gonna shit when they see you –"

The demon's mouth split wide in a sinister grin, its teeth dripping long, stinking strings of drool that puddled on the floor. With little ado, it snatched the harness from Priestley's hand and examined it with a look of amusement, repeatedly turning the straps over and over again between its fingers to caress the soft leather. The demon scratched at the harness with a probing claw, interested to discover what lay beneath the surface of the vile material and the tiny silver crosses that tinkled so harmoniously. Lifting the harness up to the heart shaped hollow in its face, the demon sniffed deeply at the shrivelled shred of dried flesh attached to it. With a violent snort, the demon blew a fine spray of putrid snot into Priestley's face and dropped the harness to the floor, as it had no more interest in what it held. (Suggested) The demon leaned in close; now it was Priestley's turn to be scrutinized.

Now Priestley was terrified. He'd clung on to the belief that the harness would do its job and offer him the opportunity to control the demon, or at the very least to hold the thing at bay long enough to afford him an escape.

But that last grain of hope had evaporated.

"Be gone, foul denizen of Hell!" Priestley shouted in the demon's face as he pulled Priscilla's phial from his pocket. He snapped off the cork stopper with his thumb and hurled holy water in the demon's face. *"The power of Christ compels you!"*

The demon let out a long, pained shriek and tottered backwards, hands clutched to its face.

Priestley made ready to seize his chance to run but his eyes struggled to find his bearings and locate the exit within the encroaching darkness. Disoriented, Priestley stepped away from the wall and turned towards where he *thought* he remembered the gymnasium doors to be.

The demon lowered its hands from its face and stepped towards Priestley. Its mouth twisted into the sinister veneer of a grin and in its eyes, Priestley saw what was unmistakably a mischievous twinkle. A peculiar rumbling sound bubbled up from the demon's throat that could easily have been a *chuckle* as it wiped its face dry and made a show of licking the holy water from its palm with long, languid strokes of its tongue.

"Please, no," Priestley sobbed as he realized that the thing was mocking him, the holy water was impotent against the demon, and had been all along. "I–I'm sorry," Priestley blubbed and lowered the minicam, "I didn't mean to –"

The demon slammed Priestley back against the wall and held him there with one hand so hard against his chest that he could barely catch his breath. It brought up its other hand and wagged a gaunt finger in front of Priestley's terrified face, as if chastising an errant child.

In that heartbeat, as he gazed into the demon's sapphire eyes, Priestley felt the final threads of connection between himself and the demon slip into place.

And he *understood*.

That he and the demon – *Tenebrion* – were kindred spirits entangled within one malignant destiny, as inexorably entwined as those the demon had used to wrench open the infernal fissure between their dominions.

The demon had manipulated him from the beginning, with the same ruthless efficiency it had used to manipulate Rachel Villanueva, Gregory Harris, Priscilla and those countless others in order to achieve its nefarious goals. The books Priestley had acquired, the objects and effluents he had gathered – all had been nothing more than garish adornments – even the words he'd so meticulously selected to recite for the ritual of the Black Mass had been little more than background noise; it had been the alignment of the people and their terrible fates that had burst open that diabolical gateway.

Gateway implies something that can be closed.

Priestley also understood that he had served the demon well as its unsuspecting puppet and that he had one more function to fulfil before his own destiny could finally be realized.

The demon wrestled the minicam from Priestley's limp fingers and lifted it up to film his face.

Priestley stared blankly into the tiny glass lens of Priscilla's camera, at the miniature red light that told him he was being recorded and he was surprised to discover that he was crying uncontrollably – swollen globes of tears streamed down his cheeks and thick green snot strung down from his nose. Priestley experienced an unexpected, uncomfortable heat around his cringing balls as his bladder had let go when the demon had taken the camera and its vile skin had inadvertently brushed his fingers.

The demon panned the camera around the gymnasium, as if taking great pride in the carnage it had created and was keen to preserve the memory.

"I'll do anything you want," Priestley pleaded and even he thought he sounded pathetic, "please, I don't want to die."

The demon swung back around to better capture Priestley's misery, manoeuvring the camera closer still to fill the frame with Priestley's distressed face.

"I'm sorry, I am *so* sorry," Priestley's snivelling was most unbecoming; "it was just a movie." Behind the demon, Priestley saw movements around the fissure's rim. Multitudes of dark, slithering, creeping things crawled over and around the writhing, interlaced bodies of his friends. "It was just a *fucking* movie!" he screamed.

In one swift, fluid movement the demon let go of Priestley's chest, grabbed hold of his face and pushed his head so hard against the wall that it dented the plaster.

Priestley's scream was dampened against the shifting slime of the demon's palm; the flesh was so unbearably hot yet at the same time painfully frigid, it scorched the delicate skin of Priestley's face. Struggling, panicking, Priestley thumped his hands against the demon's hand, and kicked at its legs, letting rip another muffled scream as the demon's razor claws sliced through the flesh of his face and scraped harshly against the skull bones beneath.

The demon held the minicam steady to keep Priestley's head framed squarely in shot as it flexed its fingers. Thin, wiry sinews strained against taut, leathery skin as the demon's fingers pierced Priestley's skull and burrowed inwards towards his brain.

Priestley bellowed out his agony and tugged in vain with both hands and every ounce of his strength at the demon, desperate to be rid of the pain.

In response, the demon yanked its arm back and with a fleet twist and a jerk it peeled away the front of Priestley's head.

Priestley's final scream jammed in his throat as the bones surrounding his face splintered and crackled and he felt the sick, *pulling* sensation as his face tore away from his skull.

Blood gushed out from the gaping hole and Priestley choked on his own fluids that poured down his throat. His lower jaw remained in place and the fat worm of his tongue lolled over the side like a panting dog's, drooling saliva and thick, crimson blood down his shirt. Priestley's eyes – trapped by their severed sockets – were drawn away along with his face and as the optic nerves tugged on his exposed brain it slopped out of its ruined skull like half-set Jell-O and hung down Priestley's neck like an obscene, portly tie.

Priestley slumped to the floor where his body twitched and jerked and skirted around the grim release of death – but there was to be no escape from the latter, for the demon he'd conjured had plans for David Priestley; and already he felt the darkness seeping into his body, its pitiless fingers probing, exploring, becoming a part of him, bringing him life.

The demon filmed its subject's descent as he hit the gymnasium floor with so little grace, the closing shot complete.

It then turned the minicam about to commit to film the liberation of its brethren.

The fissure was now spread wide and vulgar like the slick, glistening sex of a diseased whore; a grotesque, gaping gash that pulsed and contracted as it squirted out Hell's denizens in a stinking, unholy parturition.

In their hundreds they poured out from the nefarious blackness like stinking, living liquid; clambering, crawling, slithering their way up from the sinister passageway and across the naked, broken bodies of the humans that effected their escape, they filled the darkness with their haunting laments. Amongst the myriad occupants from the farthest, darkest reaches of Hell, there came *Incubus, Yan-gant-y-tan, Djinn, Imps, Kappa, the Marching Hordes, Poltergeists, Nightmares, Rokurokubi, Gomory, Succubus, Ghouls, Sabbat, Drudes* and *Familiars* of every description; after innumerable eons banished to the darkness they were all prepared to write their own history.

Where before they had peered out with envious eyes and slithered and squeezed through the narrowest chinks between the worlds like worms burrowing within a corpse's putrid flesh, now they spewed forth in an unrelenting torrent, free from their torments and eager to explore their new and exciting dominion.

Satisfied with this, the demon switched off the camera.

EPILOGUE

**Prince William Pub, Watsonville, TX
Sunday night.**

The Prince William pub was once more filled with movie people, the difference being this time they were to a man, woman and child thoroughly exhausted; a full weekend of intensive film-making and very little sleep had physically and mentally drained each and every one of them. Still, there remained the excited – if somewhat subdued – buzz amongst the crowd, accompanied by an unmistakable air of achievement.

Melissa Bracken sat at her fold-down table, all but obscured by the unruly mountain of large brown envelopes that threatened to topple at any moment. She eyed the pile with disdain, dreading the upcoming weeks of late nights she would be spending ploughing through the plethora of short movies – potentially seven hours' worth of unrelenting bilge – whilst Phil insisted on critiquing each and every one as if it were *Spotlight* or something. And speaking of which, just where the fuck *was* Phil?

Somewhat predictably, he'd not yet made it beyond the bar.

Melissa sighed and reached for the tiny wooden mallet that lay beside the envelope pile. She banged its head on her little gong a half dozen times and shouted above the hubbub "Last call for hand-in!" she called out. Her voice was croaky, worn hoarse by an evening of re-explaining the contest's rules to the less intelligent elements of the crowd; *yes, you had to have* all *the forms filled out; no, MP4 file format* wasn't *acceptable; no, you won't qualify if you're* only *ten minutes late because you got delayed by a train* - and so it had been going on since before six that evening. "It's ten minutes to midnight, people!" she reminded the weary throng at the top of her voice.

A fresh handful of filmmakers burst in through the door and brought along with them the refreshing cool of the night's air. They chattered excitedly amongst themselves and they all appeared unnaturally bright-eyed and bushy-tailed for such a late hour in the competition. This was something to be expected from Jesus Longoria and his merry crew – rumor had it they boosted their stamina with generous helpings of various Category A substances.

Longoria gave Melissa his trademarked, shit-eating grin and dropped his bulging envelope on to her desk. "Ta-da! The winning movie!" he declared and high-fived each of his team in turn.

Behind Longoria's crew walked a solitary figure in dirty jeans and a gray hooded top that obscured his face. He skirted around Longoria and his sycophants to place a grubby brown envelope on the edge of Melissa's desk. Without a word he turned to leave.

"Jeez, Priestley!" Longoria spotted the guy and wafted a hand in front of his nose with an exaggerated flourish. "Ya not showered *all* goddamn weekend?!" he blustered.

The guy didn't acknowledge Longoria – or any of the others who wrinkled their noses at him – as he made his way out through the pub's door and disappeared outside.

In the dark anonymity of the night, the demon pulled down the hood and reached up to its face with a gloved hand. It slid Dave Priestley's face off of its own, tucked it carefully into the hoodie's front pocket and stalked off into the darkness.

END

ABOUT THE AUTHOR

James H. longmore hails originally from Doncaster, a mining town in the south of Yorkshire, Northern England; he relocated with his family to Houston, Texas in 2010. James boasts an honors degree in Zoology and a former career background in sales, marketing, and business. He is an accomplished, published author (and publisher), and ghostwriter of popular fiction - he writes across a wide range of genres and subjects: novels, shorts, and screenplays. He has written and directed award-winning short movies, is an affiliate member of the Horror Writer's Association, and has run/hosted the popular podcast/radio show *The New Panic Room* since early 2016,

In addition, James is the founder and owner of the indie publisher, *HellBound Books Publishing LLC* (est. 2016), which publishes horror, bizarro, and a whole manner of dark fiction.

http://www.panicroomradio.com

http://www.hellboundbookspublishing.com/authorpage_longmore.html

BUDS

Wildus Guidry, amateur scientist extraordinaire, invents time travel. To his bitter disappointment, he discovers his device only transports him mere fractions of a second into the past. Inhabiting the new, alternate world of that fractional past is a variation of *Homo sapiens* that reproduce asexually by budding and uses sex as a recreational pastime and as a means of feeding.

Disappointed by his discovery, Guidry and his entrepreneurial girlfriend decide to bring back some of the Buds and open the world's most bizarre and exclusive brothel - the Buds' unique appearance as grotesquely erotic conjoined twins, triplets, quadruplets (and more!) prove to be incredibly popular amongst the brothel's elite clientele. Of course, all goes terribly wrong as the Buds turn out to be not as benign as first thought, and chaos and the end of the world ensues.

Buds is a unique, sexy take on the popular time travel trope, and a must for all lovers of conjoined twin tales. An erotic, at times brutal and disturbing, story told with lashings of dark humor.

Following a drunken, hedonistic night out in New Orleans, highly successful businesswoman and sexual deviant, Claire Jepson, accidentally soils herself in her car. The resulting excrement comes to life as a sardonic fecal spirit, and not only dishes out a gruesome death to Claire's unfaithful, gold-digging fiancé, but also thwarts a kidnap/murder plot by her employees. It then introduces Claire to a world of depraved pleasures beyond her imagination.

A year later, the errant spirit has spiraled wildly out of control - its insatiable appetite for perverted sex and human flesh and has destroyed Claire's life. Then, to her horror, Claire discovers the fecal spirit must consume her unborn child to attain immortality; she must return to the seedy underbelly of the Big Easy in a heart-pounding race against time to confront the spirit's creator - a high priest of an ancient, deadly order, who is the only one who can put a stop to the spirit's murderous intentions. A wicked, fast-paced story laced with tongue-in-cheek, dark humor, which is at the same time incredibly erotic and stomach churning. Most definitely not one to be read whilst eating!

PEDE:

An affectionate homage to the creature feature! The once luxurious Mountainview Spa Hotel in the heart of California's Coachella valley lies decaying, abandoned and heavily boarded up - the site of a radioactive, "dirty" bomb explosion five years' previously. Zoology Professor, Jane Lucas, harbors a lifelong phobia of *Scolopendra gigantea,* the Giant Centipede, despite being the world's leading authority on the creature. Following the savage deaths of two teenagers who broke into the hotel to cavort in the natural underground spa and the discovery of centipede remains almost three times natural size, the professor teams up with four of her students to investigate.

Their expedition soon becomes a fight for survival when they're trapped inside the hotel with a gang of violent thugs and a voracious swarm of oversized centipedes that infest the place - and then discover another creature even more terrifying is hunting in the Mountainview's deserted hallways: a centipede of impossibly monstrous proportions… ravenous and desperate to feed.

FLANAGAN

"The Devil's Rejects meets Fifty Shades – heart-pounding, gut-wrenching, sexy as all hell, and with a twist you'll never see coming!"

Meet the Sewells, an all-American couple; happily married for ten years, respected high school teachers, still crazy about one another, and with a mutually-shared dark side.

During their annual Spring Break vacation to recharge batteries and reconnect, the Sewells are waylaid by a perverse gang of misfits in the one-horse, North Texas town of Flanagan.

Taken hostage to be the focus of the gang's twisted games, the Sewells are brutalized into performing vicious physical, sexual, and emotional acts upon one another, until events take an unexpected turn, triggered by an unintentional death.

As their circumstances descend into the worse nightmare imaginable, the Sewells find themselves involved in an altogether different situation...

THE EROTIC ODYSSEY OF COLTON FORSHAY

Colton Forshay dreams himself into a bizarre sexual dystopia - a world in which nothing is as it should be, it alternately rains semen and menstrual blood, sickening sex acts and sexual violence are the norm, and the currency is deviant sexual acts.

In this dream world, Colton inexplicably finds he has gotten his dog pregnant and his wife is brutally murdered as a contestant on a popular TV show.

At first disturbed, then intrigued - and shamefully aroused - by his dreams of the other world, Colton is drawn in deeper and begins to spend more time there with the help of sleeping pills. His real-world wife forces Colton to see a psychiatrist, who encourages him to explore the dream world. And thus, our hero embarks on an odyssey with his dog/son, Eric, to discover the disturbing truth behind his dream world.

There, Colton gets caught up with the resistance, who believe the government - lead by a mysterious, telepathic ocelot - controls the people by means of dreams of another realm, which sounds uncannily like his actual world.

The storyline alternates between Colton's real and fantasy dream worlds, and the two become inexorably blurred until Colton unearths a disturbing truth not entirely against the perverse tastes he's developed.

This is fantastical tale populated by a whole host of bizarre characters, set in an incredibly peculiar world. Chock-full of startling, sexy imagery and told with incredibly dark humor, Colton Forshay is a bizarro tale both engaging and disturbing.

BLOOD AND KISSES

*"Think of what late greats James Herbert and Richard
Laymon may have given birth to had they ever
collaborated"* - Richard Chizmar

The definitive short story collection from James H
Longmore - an eclectic mix of dark horror, bizarro and
Twilight Zone style tales of the downright disturbing.
Welcome to the long-awaited collection from the writer of
horror novels *'Pede* and *Tenebrion*; a foreword by Richard
Chizmar (co-author of *Gwendy's Button Box* with Stephen
King), 18 short stories, 5 flash fiction, and a poem - all
skin-crawling, soul-shredding tales of the darkest things
that skulk among the night's inky shadows and of the
everyday gone horribly awry.

Discover the implication of technology becoming
self-aware, enjoy the acquaintance of a charismatic new
pastor promising his flock a brand new place to worship
his God, spend a little time in the company of a nice young
man who is inexorably caught up in his home town's
terrible secret.

Then, there's Cupid's revelation he's never experienced
love, we discover that very emotion alive and not so well
among the ruins of a post-zombie apocalyptic world, and
bear witness to childhood innocence forever destroyed in a
distant, war-torn city.

Observe, too any unsavory individual's obsession with the
ever-elusive snuff movie, and join an elderly bunch of
forgetful sleuths out to solve the mystery of brutal deaths
that occur with alarming regularity at their memory care
facility.

Now, have you ever considered what may happen should
you have the misfortune to bump into your family's
doppelgangers on a long, tedious road trip? And, can you
even begin to imagine being the doting father who finally
realizes the apple of his eye's true identity, or the parents

who spend what is left of their crumbling lives waiting by a silent telephone for news of their addict son?

There is more, Dear Reader, much, much more; for within the pages we have devils, demons and ghosts, lycanthropes, and demi-gods, all rubbing nefarious shoulders with the most vile of Hell's offspring, who have slithered up from the netherworld to doff their caps and wish us all the sweetest of dreams…

FEEDER

A deliciously bizarro, darkly disturbing peek into the world of gainers and feeders: grotesquely obese individuals and those people who facilitate their growth for the lascivious pleasure of both parties. The heroine of the piece, Novella, Embarks upon a journey into the dreadful netherworld that dwells within the obese, fleshy folds of a woman especially engorged for the perverted delights of her Internet audience. Aided and abetted by a former feeder, she fights to escape before the grim portal closes and she's trapped forever in the ghastly realm of fat, flesh, and death most gruesome.

I AM JOE'S UNWANTED PENIS

A darkly comedic tribute to the much-loved Reader's Digest series *'I am Joe's…(insert body part here)'* and a bizarre parody of the Bruce Jenner story, *I Am Joe's Unwanted Penis* is told from the point of view of a penis discarded as a man is surgically transformed into a woman.
Upon learning if his high-profile previous owner's regret at having made the transformation, the penis embarks upon a perilous journey for them to be reunited - aided and abetted by a motley, wonderfully personable and, engaging selection of other discarded body parts.
In parts grotesque, laugh-out-loud funny, and undeniably poignant, in others, *I Am Joe's Unwanted Penis* is a buddy-story absolutely like no other!

**A HellBound Books LLC
Publication 2021**

www.hellboundbookspublishing.com